"Sandy McCutcheon's latest novel *Through The Peacock Gate* is the kind of book those of us who live between Occident and Orient have waited an entire lifetime to read. The interweaving layers, the quality of the prose and, most of all, the raw bedrock of cultural knowledge on which it is founded, makes this an invaluable handbook to the mysteries and complexities of Eastern lore. Its pages conjure the mesmerizing, magical heart of secret Morocco."

TAHIR SHAH, author of *The Caliph's House*

For the people of the Fez Medina and for Zaki and Malika

Please note: There is a glossary of Moroccan Arabic words
at the end of the novel

Through The Peacock Gate

First published in the UK by Beacon Books and Media Ltd
Innospace, Chester Street, Manchester M1 5GD, UK.

First paperback edition published 2018
Printed in the UK
www.beaconbooks.net

Cataloging-in-Publication record for this book is available from the
British Library

ISBN 978-1-912356-14-0

Cover design by Bipin Mistry
Cover graphics and concept by Bryan Dawe
Front cover photo by Seb on Unsplash

Through The Peacock Gate

Sandy McCutcheon

Acknowledgements

Special thanks are due to anthropologist and musician Frédéric Calmès from the Ecole des Hautes Etudes en Sciences Sociales (EHESS), Paris and the Hamadcha Sufi brotherhood in Fez, led by the muqaddim Abderrahim Amrani Marrakchi, without whom the research for this book would not have been possible.

Thanks also to the folk-rock band, The Mammals from Woodstock, NY for introducing me to the 1952 Vincent Black Lightning motorbike and British singer/songwriter, Richard Thompson, for composing the song about it, Eric for approaching me in Casablanca with the gift of himself as a character, Carrie Hauxwell for all the butterflies and Erich Groat in Fez for checking the Darija and Arabic.

Thanks also to Jamil and his crew at Beacon Books. And finally, to three women without whom this book would never have been completed; Suzanna Clarke for constant encouragement, Sue Bail who believed in the book from the beginning and provided feedback as it developed and Rachida El Jokh for insights into the lives of Moroccan women.

CONTENTS

THROUGH THE PEACOCK GATE

Thanks to Allah and Sidi Ali
you will eat bread that is not
prepared by the hands of men
—but by the hands of angels.

A'isha:

The Moroccan boy looks delicious, but he is not my prey tonight. Richard, however, is another story. While I have rarely been interested in foreign men, there is something about him that attracts me. It has done from the beginning, almost two years ago. There is a tension buried deep beneath the slightly bumbling exterior—that and an air of death I find almost irresistible. There are many deaths inside him and the attraction is too great. I, who usually do the drawing, am drawn—drawn by death and my craving for water. Inside, in the waters of the fountain, I will be in my element. It is night now. It is my time.

Richard? Is he so different from the others? Did I, who am without pity, feel something back at the beginning, something that held me back? It is a dangerous course he steers and yet he is unknowing and it is this unknowing that stays my hand. For I am used to being feared and loved in equal measure and yet here is a man who does neither. True, he senses me, but in a way that I have never experienced. Inside him there is an unease—a dis-ease—and death, many deaths... is that to be our bond?

We inhabit the same world, opposite sides of the same world. In the hours of darkness, the world is mine. From the cities to the villages in the countryside, from the plains to the mountains, I am everywhere. During their day I rest, sinking deep into the water, in the pools and rivers, in the pits and grottos, in the drains beneath the floors of their houses—in all of them—simultaneously. During their day I rest, except for the part of me that speaks to my lovers. Two voices. The little voice that keeps them safe and the strong voice that keeps them obedient. In return they love me. Without question.

Book One

A'isha: Bismillah r-rahman r-rahim

Who is this man who disturbs my dwelling place, this stumbling human with his noise and his strange smell of death? Who is he? And why does he intrude into my realm? He descends the stairs from the street, his feet scuffing over the tiles.

Richard: al-Maghreb al-Aqsa

My feelings of impatience are such that I won't linger over descriptions of my journey from Australia—via Singapore (an hour of squeaky-clean boredom) and Dubai (a theme park dedicated to consumerism, risen from the sand into which it will one day, hopefully, return)—and move as fast as possible to Casablanca and a bleary jet lag fog through which I finally managed to find my way to Casa Voyageurs Station and the train to Fez.

Morocco begins with sound. The old carriage clatters over the tracks, the metal work shrieking its protests, the hydraulics hissing concern. Despite the apparently new tracks, I shudder along in my shabby first-class compartment and suppressing the memories of my last trip on a train to Fez, tiredness or fatalism beguiles me into purchasing a stale cheese roll, which I manage to consume without any deleterious effects.

Arriving back in Fez, I caught a *petit taxi* from the train station and sat back as the driver threaded his way through the Ville Nouvelle and then, above Batha, swung down the twisting road to R'cif. On the first corner, another taxi swung too wide and nearly collided with us. I refused to react, after all this was Fez and such things were

3

expected and the outcomes beyond anyone's control. In the hands of *Allah*, I thought, enjoying the fatalism. The taxi driver, less sanguine, cursed and honked his horn and increased his speed, tearing down the road to the old hump-backed bridge where *Allah* decreed he should wait for yet another taxi and two cars.

It was an early spring evening and with the window of the taxi down, the breeze bathed me in the melange of odours—spicy smoke and cooking smells—the all-pervasive incense that marked the proximity of the Medina. Along the roadside above the gully carved by the river, students escaping from the overcrowded confines of their homes, studied under street lamps. One per lamp, solitary scholars seeking degrees that would give them the single thing they all sought; a way out of the Medina.

'*Hmuk bezzef!*' the driver spat, swerving to avoid a child chasing a soccer ball across the street.

Nine at night, and although my café was closing—I thought of it as *my* café, despite the fact at that time I had not learned its name—the street was crowded with people, strolling in an unseasonably warm evening. Men in *djellabas*, hand in hand, stood in the street, oblivious to the traffic. Opposite the café, the steps that lead to the Andalusian quarter were lined with women, gossiping while waiting for their men. Children threaded their way through the crowds, chasing, hitting and laughing. A teenager, fresh from the *hammam*, squatted beside the curb, his head wrapped in a lime green towel, while he smoked a last cigarette before heading home.

'*Ici Monsieur?*' The driver asked, nodding in the direction of the cinema.

'Yes, here.'

The meter said twenty-three dirhams. I forked the coins from my pocket and gave him twenty-five. The tiredness and jet lag that had been building up in my head, was beginning to take its toll and it was with some relief that I got out to find the driver already fetching my bags from atop the taxi.

A concern that there would be none of the men or boys with trolleys to cart my luggage proved unfounded and I was not even half way to the pavement when an old man materialised at my side.

'*Carossa?*'

His baggy cream trousers were ripped, his once blue shirt sweat stained and, like the man, similarly worn. He looked too old to be pushing luggage trolleys through the steep alleys of the Medina.

'*Carossa?*' he repeated, tugging at my sleeve with one hand and pointing to his trolley with the other.

'If that means *trolley,* the answer is yes.'

'*Ashrin dirham.*'

'How much is that?'

Aside from Greek and Latin at school and a smattering of Spanish, which I learned before I knew better, I am not a linguist, and over the years have developed an active aversion to the superficial study of another language. Not for me the tapes or CDs with accompanying book that promises to have you learning several hundred useful phrases in just one week. Once, I thumbed through a friend's phrase book and decided that it would drive me crazy.

'I listen to the tapes while I am asleep,' he reported.

'Is it working?'

'It will. First it has to penetrate deep into my subconscious...'

Drivel. Mind you, I never did enquire how he went. Finnish, I think that was it; very useful.

There is a much more primal reason for not learning a language and that is the preservation of the pure pleasure of being exposed to the unknown. Words and phrases don't exist in the world of the untutored ear. It is just sound, raw and foreign, excluding no possibilities and containing whatever you want it to. It is a music undiluted by understanding. Time of course mitigates this pleasure and soon your mind connects a word to an action or an object. *Tea* or *coffee* becomes recognisable. *Thank you* becomes a reflexive vocal response and before you know it the pleasures of Babel are reduced to mutterings and frustration. No, for me the innocence of the foreigner, while fleeting, is a delight. On my first trip to Morocco, I took pleasure in ensconcing myself in my unnamed café, surrounded by a sound-scape of language as dense as any wall.

'Ashrin dirham.'

For a moment the swirl of sound and haze of jet lag fazed me; a misted stream flowing, taking me away... and then the man's voice demanded my attention.

'Ashrin dirham.'

The man was opening and closing his fingers, indicating twenty, so I signalled in reply.

'Ten. I will give you ten.'

The man looked at me as if I was crazy, then pointed to the cases and held up four fingers. *'Reb'a?'*

'Yes four.'

By this stage, a small crowd had gathered, the men staring openly at me, a couple of younger women glancing shyly. *I've become entertainment.*

'Fifteen dirhams is all I'll pay. No more.'

'Quinze,' someone translated.

The *carossa* man's look of non-comprehension was accompanied by a shrug.

'Khamstash,' translated a teenager.

My four bags were hoisted into the *carossa.*

'Wakha.'

Okay.

The situation resolved, the entertainment over, the crowd stepped aside to let me through and I followed in the man's wake, wondering why he had set off before knowing where he was going. Hurrying to catch up, I tapped him on the shoulder.

'Excuse me.' My lofty, jet lag induced theories about the wondrous Tower of Babel in ruins, I mumbled, *'Aqabt el-Firane.'* I hoped that by saying the name of the street very fast I avoided the pitfalls of incorrect pronunciation. *I should have purchased a house in a street I could get my tongue around...*

'*Wakha.*'

Up to this point the man hadn't paused in his forward progress through the crowd, but here the pavement was teeming with people hemmed in between the road and the wall above the souk. Any space not occupied by the strolling pedestrians was taken over by vendors squatting on the ground, their wares spread in front of them. Second hand shoes, kettles, clocks, radios, a range of gaudy plastic *hammam* buckets and stools and a row of smoking, charcoal fires where fresh chestnuts were cooking, all competed for space. Then there were the beggars, the blind and the crippled, whose misery is as much part of this city as is its beauty. I had read accounts of trips to Morocco that never mention the subject of poverty but I could not, in all honesty, describe this country without mentioning the beggars huddled on doorsteps, the widows squatting in the shadows, their hands permanently extended in the hope of embracing some small coin. Could I shut my eyes to the blind, who bring coins to their lips to taste the value of your generosity? I could not do so on my first visit and I swore than that I should not do so now.

Although tired, I would have liked nothing better than to prop myself up on the wall and drink it all in. The slow, swirling mass of people had a hypnotic effect and I found myself mesmerised, stopped in my tracks, letting the people flow around me. Gaunt elderly *Fassis* in faded *djellabas* and white skull-caps, younger women in designer jeans and tops, boys in chest-hugging shirts, open necked, sleeves rolled almost to the shoulders and old women in headscarves or, occasionally, a black face mask, pulled unflatteringly tight beneath the nostrils.

In a moment of mild panic, I looked around, aware that I had lost sight of my luggage—my remaining worldly possessions. Then I heard the man's voice rise above the burbling river of chatter. '*Balek! Balek!*' he chanted, warning those in his path to make way.

Hurrying, I caught up with him just as he was forced to slow down by the steps at the entrance to Derb Oued Chorfa. This was the only area of Fez that I knew well, having traversed it countless times on my previous visit. To my right, where Derb Jamaa Zellij led through to Boustouniya and Bab R'cif, the souk was closing down, with only a few hole-in-the-wall food stalls still operating. Their owners, unnaturally pallid troglodytes, wreathed in smoke, bathed in dusty neon, crouched behind sizzling grills awaiting the last customers and a few more dirhams. The thought crossed my mind that I should buy bread for the morning, but the *carossa* man was already down the steps and pushing up the incline to Oued Chorfa Square.

Here, at the entrance to the Medina, the lights had failed and yet it was at this moment that my excitement returned and the adrenalin kicked in, overpowering the jet lag. I was home. This was Fez. This was what I had come for. A huge unknowing lay ahead—weeks and months of it, with every day offering new possibilities to get lost in the streets and alleys, to explore and discover and then return to the perfect peace of my little haven of tranquillity. Bliss.

Beneath my feet I felt the sudden softness of what I instinctively knew were donkey droppings. Slowing down, I reached out and steadied myself against the wall. The sweet smell of *kif* drifting on the night air reached my nostrils. I became aware of someone in the shadows, crouched on a doorstep.

'*Msalkhir*,' a man whispered.

A single spot of red glowed in the dark as he drew on his *kif* pipe.

I grunted "hello" and kept walking. Ahead, in the Chorfa Square, a light was flickering and from the silence, away from the crowds in R'cif, came the sound of the small fountain tinkling. A sudden gust of wind shifted damp air down the street bringing with it an unexpected chill. Maybe a spring storm was coming, brewing in the Middle Atlas, waiting to descend between the neighbouring mountains, Djebel Zalagh and Djebel Tghrat.

Impatient to get to my house, I increased my pace, striding across the square and catching up with the *carossa* as my porter switched from pushing to pulling the trolley up the first steps of Ras Jnane. Falling in behind, I put my weight behind the *carossa*, easing it up the steps and was rewarded by a toothless smile.

'*Shukran Sidi.*'

Caught between tiredness and expectation, my brain was becoming erratic and a phrase that I hadn't uttered since the nightmare that was my school French class slipped out, unexpectedly. '*Pas de problème.*'

Once over the steps, the man was away from me again, speeding along Zenqat Chedda and vanishing around the corner into the short stretch of Gzam Ben Amar. There seemed no point in calling for him to wait as he was obviously going at the speed he knew best, with little heed for the owner of the bags. If I had been a tourist it might have been different, but the old man had sensed I knew the area and was unlikely to get lost. Or he may have known who I was from my previous visit. Strangers in this part of the Medina are a rarity and it is not unreasonable to surmise that my comings and goings had been remarked on.

How many times had he been up and down these streets? Probably hundreds of times and yet I felt I knew them just as well. Not from years of back breaking labour but from concentrated observation. In my notebooks, I had set about capturing and containing the sprawling chaos of my neighbourhood on paper. Looking back over that particular book I have to admit that I was an obsessive note taker. Every sign, every distinguishing feature, I had committed not only to memory, but jotted down in my "blue book"; so much like the mapping of the cloud forest but here it was not trees, vines or a stream. Copied down instead were descriptions of the mosque on the left of Derb Chorfa, the scaffolding in Zenqat Chedda, erected by the city engineers after several buildings had collapsed with fatal consequences and details of every one of the *hanuts*—the tiny shops in Gzam Ben Amar. During quiet moments in my local café I would sit and study my notes, often drawing small maps, testing my memory by attempting to write in the name of every street and alley. At this, I am pleased to say, I was reasonably successful. A solid pass if not a high distinction.

Despite the evidence to the contrary provided by my years of motorcycle restoration, I do not consider myself obsessive; fastidious maybe or simply just thorough. Yes, "thorough" feels right.

On the corner of Aqabt el Firane the *carossa* man was stopped, waiting for me.

'*Fin?*' He shrugged, awaiting instructions.

'A little further,' I replied and, squeezing past the *carossa*, I now went ahead up the hill. To my surprise, given the time of night, I heard a familiar tapping coming from the next corner. The workers in the tiny factory that manufactured Fez hats were still labouring away, the smell of the glue wafting from the open doorway. As I passed, I caught a glimpse of five or six young men lined up at a bench, hard at work. They were smiling, but it may well have been the effect of the fumes they were breathing.

Turning the corner, I stopped, aware that something was dreadfully wrong. My stomach lurched. The door was not there. The beautiful cedar door, with huge iron hinges and two large brass knockers, was gone. In its place was a metal door. And it was not locked. My mind flailed around seeking an explanation, any explanation. Anything other than what I could see. I thought that maybe the contractor had people working overtime in preparation for my arrival and had taken the door to be stripped of its paint. But, even as I thought it, I knew I was wrong.

Behind me the *carossa* man coughed.

'*Khamstash.*'

Feeling the first shivers of shock ripple through me, I nodded, fished a crumpled twenty dirham note from my pocket and handed it to the man. Then I turned and pushing the door open, stepped over the threshold and I found myself in a sea of mud and rubble.

Worse awaited me down the stairs; even in the darkness I could not miss the fact that the two enormous salon doors had gone, as had the window frames, the plumbing fixtures, and the lights. The wall-fountain in the courtyard was minus its beautiful brass tap, the water running, God knows where. Large beams had been removed and part of the second-floor salon had collapsed into the ground floor salon. Somewhere was another source of running water. Following the sound, I stepped into what was to have been a functioning, re-plastered kitchen, and found myself sloshing deeper into a muddy flood.

That instant, standing looking at the wreckage, was a moment I wish I could eradicate from my memory banks. Selective amnesia is preferable and at that, although I am well practised, I am not always successful. There are times when the past slips past the guards I have posted, times when I see a *Leptophobia subargentea* and smell the South American cloud forest and the overwhelming stench of guilt. As a young man I had thought it fanciful when people talked of "haunting" images—after Peru I knew what they meant.

Having dragged the luggage inside, I fumbled with the door until I located a bolt. This, at least, appeared to be in working order. However, having secured the door, light—or rather lack of it—became a real problem. Above me I could see nothing but the framed sky, only marginally lighter than the blackness within. Ironically, if the atrium cover had not been stolen there would have been even less light and I would have been unable to see anything at all.

Large spots of rain fell on my upturned face and somewhere, far away, I fancied I heard the rumble of thunder in the Middle Atlas. It was closer than I thought. The square of sky above me was suddenly ripped by lightning; the churning clouds revelled for a moment then folded back into darkness. The crash of thunder overhead was deafening. My eardrums hurt and so I stopped until I had recovered.

It seemed odd that the thieves had not stolen the beams around the atrium. Maybe they had been too heavy or simply too difficult to remove, although it could hardly have been beyond them to climb to the terrace and pry them free from above.

Strangely, I wasn't angry at this point, but numb and confused. Part of me refused to believe that I was in *my* house, and for a ludicrous moment, I wondered if I had instead stumbled into another, and mine was further along the street, intact and waiting for me.

I had to know the full extent of my loss. Feeling my way around the courtyard, I located the entrance to the small bathroom and kneeling down, ran my fingers across the floor. At least the *zellij* was intact. Better still, it was dry. Groping along the wall, my fingers searched for the small niche where on my previous visit I had stashed soap, razor and toothbrush. Amazingly they were still there, either too insignificant to steal or simply overlooked in the rush to loot valuable doors and wood. Also in the niche, pushed to the back, was the candle stub and Moroccan cigarette lighter.

With one hand grasping the spluttering candle, I tiptoed around the ruins of my house, feeling foolishly like Wee Willie Winkie. Even moving about was no easy task, as it was difficult, nigh on impossible, to distinguish shadows from beams, dislodged rocks from holes. All the while, my mind kept veering off into flippancy, skating across the surface of the pain that threatened to overwhelm me. For one peculiarly Gothic moment I found myself standing stock still, with the ridiculous thought that I had stumbled into an old Hammer Films Studio and that at any moment Peter Cushing or Christopher Lee would materialise.

It occurred to me that the sensible thing to do would be to decamp to the Hotel Batha and take a room, but that would be a defeat, a retreat. I had not come all the way to Fez simply to be driven out of my house on the first night.

With the candle guttering and threatening to go out, I returned to my luggage and unpacked a blanket. Having spread it on the floor of the bathroom, I added a couple of towels and sweaters and my fleece jacket for a pillow. I blew out the candle and lay shivering, listening to the tinkle of water from the courtyard wall-fountain and the distant grumbling thunder.

Richard: Terra nullius

Here is where Australia ends. It is not where I once might have expected; not across the Jardine River at the steamy tip of Cape York, with the thunderheads of the monsoon massing over turquoise waters as I hunt the elusive *Hasora celaenus* or the ghostly *Appias albina*. Nor is it at the extreme eastern point, at Cape Byron with its white lighthouse and sheets of rain lashing the scrub as I searched for that illusive butterfly, the Richmond Birdwing, *Ornithoptera richmondia*. It is not in the southernmost reaches of Tasmania, although the cold feeling is the same.

No, the end of Australia is not found in geography. The end of Australia is a tipping point where, on one side of the fulcrum lies frustration and on the other, emptiness.

Let me start with the emptiness, as over the last twenty years or so, I have become somewhat of an expert in the subject. A collector, you might say. Not by design but by default. I am not straying into the metaphysical, in a Zen way. No, simple emptiness—it was there and now it is not. Like that.

'It's gone,' Eric had said. He hadn't believed me when I phoned him with the news, insisting that he come over and see for himself.

'There is nothing to see,' I had told him.

'There must be something.'

Eric is like that—literal but not literate. Practical but not practised. If someone suggested to Eric that I was his best friend, he would be perplexed by the notion. Somewhere in his head the thoughts would become jumbled. *Best* implies that there were others and Eric had no other friends. For a while, one could observe his face—a perfect vacancy—and his most likely response would be to pick up the bolt or sprocket he was cleaning and to start gently polishing it. If I needed something polished, there is no better man than Eric.

'You didn't move it.'

'No.'

'Jesus.'

It is the only time I have ever heard him swear and I was so stunned that I hardly registered when he picked up something from the corner of the garage.

'You won't be needing this then.'

It was the spare speedometer; Smiths, yellow face, part number PR33/4.

I suppose the amount of time I spent restoring the motorbike could be seen as an indication of obsession. Ten years of part-time restoration is a sizable chunk of anyone's life. Yet, it is only with hindsight that I think of it like that. Day by day, month-by-month and year-by-year I was concentrated in the moment. Sourcing parts was a full-time job in itself. There were fakes and copies of course and there are those who would have simply had parts manufactured. For me, however, authenticity was important. No, that's not quite correct. The bike came to me by an accident of death, so to speak, and in the beginning I couldn't have cared one way or the other about its authenticity. At first it was simply the perfect deflection; an escape from the images of Peru and the pursuit of the *Leptophobia subargentea*. It was only much later that I became involved to the point where my scientific training kicked in, demanding that, if I was going to spend so much time on the restoration, then everything had to be correct—right down to the last nut and bolt.

My uncle Eddy was one of the reasons I chose Australia. He was my only living relative, and, with no interests in the world other than raising budgies, I knew he wouldn't be concerned or informed about the reasons I had fled Dublin or why I had changed my name. He certainly knew nothing about butterflies. We liked each other and yet I never told him about my nightmares. I told no one. When Uncle Eddy died, it fell to me to clean out his shed and had I been alone—if Eric had not insisted on accompanying me to Adelaide—I have no doubt that the engine, frame and collection of parts would have ended up at the tip.

In Adelaide, the work moved slowly. It was the third day of sorting through the detritus of Uncle Eddy's life when we came upon the crate and Eric, who knew a thing or two about motorbikes, pulled out a torn black seat.

'It's a Black Lightning.'

'A what?'

'A motorbike.'

'The seat?'

'Genuine Feridax,' he grunted.

'And?'

'They made them. It's a special.'

'Is it important?'

He looked at me as if I was stupid. 'Better than the Norton, Richard.'

Back in the early nineties Eric had restored a couple of bikes, which because he had never managed to pass a driving test still sat in the hallway of his mother's house. I had never been into bikes and didn't have a licence but I liked to have a beer and help out while Eric fiddled.

'You do remember the Norton, don't you?'

'A 1951 Norton Big 4 with dusting sidecar. The plunger rear end model,' I responded dutifully.

'Better than that.'

There was more like this, but eventually I managed to extract enough information to understand that what we had in the crate were the mortal remains of engine number F10AB/1C/9470 with frame number RC11370. Then we had a breakthrough. We found a notebook where Uncle Eddy had recorded the details. The bike was, as Eric had recognised, a Vincent Black Lightning, one of only thirty or so ever manufactured and had been imported into Singapore on the twenty-sixth of June 1952 by a company called Eastern Auto. At some stage the bike travelled to Adelaide and ended up with a dealer, Sven Kallin, who subsequently sold it.

Several owners later, Uncle Eddy had purchased the frame, engine and spare parts for five thousand pounds. According to Eric, if we could restore it the machine would be worth a great deal more and he added that he would be happy to work on it with me. It suited me fine as I had the workshop space and Rachel would probably be happy to get me out of the living room a little more.

It amuses me that up to this point I have avoided mentioning Rachel. My tendency not to do so is well ingrained. But since she has popped into my mind, let me dispose of her. Rachel is my wife. Well, ex-wife, if I am to be pedantic. Rachel and I were married shortly after I arrived in Australia to take up a position at Latrobe University. She came with two children from her previous marriage—Toby, currently working in a refugee camp in Jordan and Peter, who according to the most recent email, is doing something vaguely socialist in Nicaragua. I blame modern education for that.

The downside was that I didn't bring much into the marriage other than a desire to build a new life in a new land. Rachel, while aware that I suffered from nightmares, knew nothing of what haunted me and never enquired. She had seen me as a safe bet and a safe haven for her and the children. However, although Toby, Peter and I became good friends, they soon left home and subsequently Rachel and I discovered that we had little in common and didn't really like each other much.

At around the time the boys left, I had something of a windfall when two books of mine that I had written since changing my name, did the unthinkable and became accepted as set texts for university courses in several countries. So I not only had a regular income, but was also in demand as a speaker at conferences. Back then my speciality was the taxonomy of Lepidoptera and all of my early publications are suggestions for a new taxonomic approach that does not rely on the currently trendy notion that the superfamilies of Lepidoptera can be classified into natural groups. It is simply not an option, as I point out, because in all the suggested models, one of the two groups is not monophyletic, that is, does not share a common ancestry.

However, these were not the only books that raised my new profile and produced a profit. My other great love being literature, I had penned a couple of unashamedly populist offerings on Lepidoptera in literature—*Moths to a Flame* and *The Muse has Wings*. Hence, I found myself addressing both literary audiences and those consisting of lepidopterists with a literary bent. My worst fear—that someone from my old life would recognise me—never eventuated. I attribute that to the fact that my life has been a rather solitary one and my circle of friends very small. I confess to having enjoyed my five minutes of limited fame. All good fun, except that, to Rachel's dismay, I gave up my position at the university and began spending more time at home. It occurs to me now that she was espousing a position diametrically opposed to that which my lover Aisling had voiced so loudly in Ireland back in the late nineteen eighties. Aisling is Irish for "vision" and unfortunately her vision was one of having me around all the time, Rachel not so. Sadly (and maybe predictably), the results were exactly the same.

As a birthday present to herself on the occasion of turning forty-five, Rachel decamped with an indecently young African yoga teacher, and by email demanded custody of nothing less than the bank account and half the house, which it was my duty to now sell. It was a painful and acrimonious divorce. When I questioned who was to look after Puddles, our Old English sheepdog, Rachel shrugged and two days later announced that she didn't care if I had him put down. Fortunately a neighbour wanted him. Then, a month before the divorce came through, the Vincent motorbike was stolen; twelve years of marriage and ten years of restoration—gone.

As I say, I do emptiness very well.

The other side of the tipping point is frustration and this was almost totally political. In the previous few years I had grown increasingly despondent at the direction Australia was heading. The government's attitude to the less well off, the poor, the homeless, the disabled and, in particular refugees, had become hard-hearted. I was not alone in thinking that our Prime Minister was bereft of a moral compass. As an antidote, I took to reminding myself that I wasn't actually Australian. In fact, I would describe myself as an Irish citizen who found himself living in the colonies; a lepidopterist who loves books more than butterflies and, most of all a romantic. Eric, in an uncharacteristic moment of insight, once told me I had been born in the wrong era and moreover if I thought myself romantic (he screwed up his face as he said the word), then I was fooling myself. When questioned about which era would have suited me he simply glared and said, 'Not this one.'

It was about this time that I came across the dancer who can spin both ways. It was on the Internet, an email attachment that most people probably saw as a silly distraction but that I found fascinating. It is the silhouette of a ballet dancer and she is spinning; a *fouetté rond de jambe en tournant*, I was once told by Rachel who fancied she knew a thing or two about ballet. Now the trick is (so they claim, without offering scientific proof) that if you are left-brained she spins anticlockwise, if you are right-brained, clockwise. However, when I look at the illustration I can decide which way she spins and change her direction at will. I have done so a dozen times. Of course I can't prove it because Eric, who was watching her spin anticlockwise, couldn't see the difference when I switched her, even when I told him I had done so. In this respect I like to think that I am special. Looking back at my notebook entry I see that I attempted to draw the ballerina but something was wrong with my technique and she failed to spin in any direction.

All of my life I have kept notebooks, usually blue, but occasionally black ones, with my name written on the cover in exactly the same way I have done since my Blackrock College days back in Dublin. The only difference now is that my name has changed. When I begin a new notebook I still have to concentrate to write Richard Duane. Changing my name by deed poll was a simple process compared to the difficulty of living with a new name. Identity is not a coat that you can shed before slipping into a new one and I still find it difficult, even though until recently I have not uttered or written my real name for the longest time. The temptation to do so, just to prove I can, is strong but I resist it.

Over the years some have described me as stubborn, but I prefer the word "tenacious". It is a trait the Holy Ghost brothers at Blackrock drummed into us and for which I have to thank Father Shanahan in particular. When I was struggling with the wooden approach to Latin and quipped that I would prefer to learn Greek, he took me aside and said that while Greek was not on the official syllabus, if I could convince at least five other boys to take part he would find us a Greek tutor each Saturday morning. Dropping Latin was not part of the deal, but I convinced six boys to join me and Father Shanahan, true to his word, employed a young graduate, Thomas Semple, who was a revelation. No rote learning and only one text; the *Alcestis* of Euripides.

Saturdays, the SGS (Secret Greek Society) would meet and, taking parts, read the lines first in Greek and then in English from the Browning translation. This went on for four years and from pretty scratchy beginnings we became more than proficient, to the point where we would act it out, with Thomas as Alcestis never failing to enthral us with her dying speech. It is strange—I haven't thought of Thomas Semple or Father Shanahan for years—but looking back now, I do so with a huge amount of affection. I fancy that if they were confronted with the ballerina they would both have the ability to make her spin in whatever direction they chose.

Ever since I can remember I have never been good at confession. Even on paper. Reading back through my early notebooks I see the word "confession" appears many times but invariably it has a line through it. Self-image is a confusing thing to nail down. How do I see myself? Or, to invert it, how do I not see myself? Here goes...

I don't like to think of myself of as a mass murderer. It occurs to me that there is probably a definition of "mass" in the context of murder. When do a few become many? When does a pile of bodies become a mass? And so far, I haven't even considered the ripple effect. I killed only twelve people (is that a mass?) and yet, if you take the normal breeding equation of 2.5 children per person, reasonably those twelve would have produced thirty offspring and they in their turn gone on to have seventy-five more and so on, exponentially. Now the question is where does my culpability stop? Seventy-five children don't exist because of my actions. Have I reached a mass yet?

There is no suggestion or admission to myself of anything heinous here. It is not as if I were a serial killer, or a sex murderer. Reviewing my case I always remind myself that the sex of the victims was 8:4—eight women, four men. It is not, in itself, important, but nevertheless, it remains a fact. Most times I try not to think of them; at this I often fail spectacularly. It is not, however, without a lighter side.

While I'm in the realm of quasi-science such as the spinning dancers, let me raise the issue of the "butterfly effect". Most people know the theory. A butterfly in the Amazon jungle flaps its wings and because of Chaos Theory the effect ripples out and ends up causing a rainstorm in Dublin. My reaction has always been to ask why the ripple has to grow and why it does not simply fade away decently and give the fine folk of Joyce's city a fair-weather break. God knows they need it. Yet, to use the "C" word, I must confess that what haunts me started with the flapping of a butterfly's wings; to be geographically accurate, not in the Amazon but in the cloud forests of Peru.

Since I am in an introspective mood, another thing I have noticed and that fascinates is the propensity of my brain (both sides) to think that all change is progress. It is like when someone leaves—they go and I move on. Just like on the trains. Sitting in a train at a railway station when another train moves off in the opposite direction produces the undeniably real sensation of moving forward. It has never occurred to me to try but it is possible that I could command my brain to make it feel as if I was going backwards. Anyway, in order to start, let me get a few things from the past to leave.

Back around the time Aisling left me I told myself it was not a loss but a release, a move forward. It occurs to me that I avoided dwelling on Aisling in much the same way as I always skirt around thinking of Rachel. They are very different, for unlike most of the ghosts from my past, Aisling is not so much terrifying as infuriating and it is unlikely she will keep herself out of my story completely. She was a strange one, but beautiful; freckles, gorgeous long black hair and a fury in her that you could temper steel with; a furnace, a volcanic demon. Her habit of demanding attention was always dramatic and the transformation from sex-goddess to gargoyle (is there a feminine for "gargoyle"?) often took less than a minute. Something (usually me) would set her off and the lava would flow, searing everything within range. Grown men backed out of pubs when she erupted. A tongue like a flame-thrower. I've seen it happen in tough pubs; IRA pubs—and in those days that meant thugs, not patriots. Aisling hated butterflies. She said that I thought them more important than her; that they came between us.

When I left Dublin, and moved to Australia and then later when I departed Australia, each time it felt as though I was moving forward.

So, having thus prepared the groundwork, I come to the point—the departure from Australia. It was not a snap decision, but a long term, well-planned exercise that I had been covertly scheming for some time. Deciding to leave Australia was not the difficult part. Finding where to go was. There was no way I could return to Eire and one or two public speaking engagements in England had cured me of any thought of moving there. Not that I have some deep-seated republican hatred of the English; in fact I rather enjoy the grunting Anglo Saxon tongue, or what remains of it. I will also own to having a soft spot for the English pre-Raphaelites, to the point where, if I could find a link between William Morris and butterflies, I would be tempted to write another book. No, England was not the temptress I needed to uproot me. The cold, the damp and the taxes put paid to that.

A couple of years earlier, at the stage when Rachel and I were still married but living together in well-constructed silences, I happened to be a guest at a lepidopterists' convention in Spain and after an enjoyable conference and a successful expedition into the northern mountains to hunt the beautiful but difficult to find *zygaena contaminei peñalabrica*, I decided to venture into Africa. Maybe, I thought to myself, I am recovering from my encounter with the *Leptophobia subargentea* in Peru and if I test myself out in Spain then perhaps I could return to... But at that point my mind veered off in another direction. What cowards we are when the past threatens to rise from the depths to which we have consigned it. No, Peru no longer existed, but Morocco, on the other hand, was possible.

As an undergraduate my main fieldwork had been two trips to Sumatra in search of the *Curetis saronis sumatrana* and so it was not until after graduation in Dublin and at a time when my career at University College was still a reality, that I added Africa to my list of destinations to visit. The Central African Republic was important, naturally, but also South Africa. The latter was high on the agenda because of the Brenton Blue, *Orachrysops niobe*. What a remarkable story that was.

After being first described by Roland Trimen in 1868 it had been recorded along the Cape Garden Route south east of Cape Town on a few occasions in 1975 but then it vanished and was thought to be extinct. What a splendid feather to add to one's cap, I had mused, to find a Brenton Blue. Of course, events in Peru put a stop to any notion of pursuing this dream and the following year, 1991, it was re-discovered by the lepidopterist, Ernest Pringle, near Knysna. If I had gone to South Africa my other target species was the ant-dependant Roodepoort Copper *Aloeides dentatis dentatis.* Despite my familiarity with the ant-lepidoptera symbiosis, I found it fascinating that in the case of the Roodepoort Copper the species was in reality held hostage by the finite number of ant (*Lepisiota capensis*) nests. Of course, I am daydreaming. It could never have happened; not after Peru. No, I chose Morocco, simply because it was close to Spain. Jump on a boat, cross the Med and you were in Africa. Simple.

Though romantic sounding, in reality a tedious ferry ride, followed by squalid accommodation in Tangier and a bout of a gastric disorder that was as eruptive and colourful as it was unpleasant. I spent the entire train journey from Tangier to Fez in a toilet with the train tracks visible and humming between my legs. It is not necessary that I divulge more than that.

The long and the short of it was, that for me, Fez was an epiphany, a release, a paradise for the senses. If ever there was a moment where I could have proven to Eric that I had a romantic side, this was it; my rational left brain went on vacation and in my right brain the dancer was celebrating her elevation to prima-ballerina with a blistering series of *fouettés.* Like a drunkard experiencing a rare moment of lucidity, I realised that another life was possible and that here was a place that would never allow my past to intrude.

Far from being disconcerted by the alien nature of the culture in the walled city, the Medina, I was suddenly plunged into a world of new discoveries. Sometimes, after recovering from an illness, I have discovered that I get a real zest for life, and so it was in Morocco.

Walking the Fez Medina, my senses were on overload, assaulted by the scent of spices, the auditory arabesque of the intertwined calls to prayer from a hundred mosques, the sounds interwoven as intricately as the beautiful carpets being thrust at me on every side or freshly washed and draped from windows or terrace walls like so many flags, and all this under a sky so bright that the blue was washed out. Pressed into the flow of the people in the souks—I felt as if I had come home.

To clear my head, I walked out of the Medina and up a hill beside an ancient and abandoned graveyard. The sensation of belonging that I experienced in the streets of Fez seemed so inappropriate, so out of character with my usual existence—that is, if you could call spending days crouching over the parts of a motorbike "existence"— that I was obviously not thinking clearly. Yet, even as I mused on my confusion, something rose from the graveyard—a portent, a sign, a messenger. It was a member of the *Satyridae* family. The mottled stone and lichen patterns and the characteristic white band across the forewing left me in no doubt that this was my first *Chazara briseis*. Transfixed, I squatted down amongst the dried broom and thistles as the silvery specimen alighted on a nearby rock. It was a perfect moment.

What happened next was a complete abandonment of my normal analytical approach to situations. I would not have you think that spontaneity had not featured in my life, but where it had occurred it had been of the muted variety. Back at UCD in the late sixties I was part of what came to be called the 'gentle revolution', when even the staidest students set out on a collision course with the University. Yes, I abandoned the dress codes and I took part in the demonstrations that eventually led to the move from Earlsfort Terrace to Belfield. The idea that my actions might jeopardise my academic future never occurred to me because, frankly, I was too busy having a good time to think much past the next pint or drag on whatever was being passed around. There were girls too, all of them distracting, a good number of them that I fancied but sadly few that were interested in butterflies. All of which may explain why I ended up with a PhD (Hons) a couple of years before my more sexually successful contemporaries. But, to get to the point, I do have a spontaneous side and that day in Fez it surfaced—on steroids.

Of course, portents and omens are fine, but like dreams, are of little use unless you can interpret them. Fortunately, I was suddenly struck with the gift. The common name of the *Chazara briseis* is the Hermit. Simple, no? Well, it was to me. The butterfly was telling me to land on something firm. A rock. It was so obvious. Some would call me crazy (and they would not be the first) but it was in that moment that I did something so impetuous that, even now when I think of it, I am amazed at myself; in awe, truly. I decided to buy a house.

There were plenty to choose from—*dars* and *riads*, in the local language. A *dar*, it was explained to me, was small and humble, not grand like a *riad*. No trees or central fountain as in an expansive and airy *riad* courtyard. That was not my style. I soon learned that there are *dar* people and *riad* people. I was a *dar* person. Not because of budget, but rather that I loved the style. For the incredibly low price of thirty thousand Australian dollars, I became the owner of a beautiful house containing an enormous cedar door, with massive iron hinges and two large brass knockers, a shabby entrance hall and a wall-fountain in a tiny courtyard that was open to the sky. Three floors towered above me, and on all sides, and on every level, little rooms that cried out to be restored to what I imagined must have been a glorious past.

The courtyard, little more than six paces wide, was tiled in small, ancient ceramic squares called *zellij* in Arabic. They were formed and fired in the furnaces up on the hill overlooking the city and when I took the opportunity to visit the pottery where the tiles were created, I was amazed at the labour involved. Each tiny tile was hand cut from larger tiles, fired in old brick furnaces, fuelled with dried and crushed olive-pits, the oily-black smoke from the furnaces belching up into a bleached-denim sky. The thought struck me that the famous blue of the Fez *zellij* had been stolen from the sky and imprisoned in the glaze.

My multi-coloured *zellij* was much older than the simple blue and white of the more modern *dars*. Not that I was averse to the cobalt-blue; the stairs to my terrace were set in it, paired with pearly white. Blue and white also graced the two pillars that stood so solid and tall outside the ground floor salon, the *zellij* extending above head height, capped by delicate carved plaster that flowed in floral motifs—relief from the linear geometry of the *zellij*. As I say, a simple house.

Looking back on it, I realise I should have stopped to ponder the giddy excitement I was experiencing. But at the time the siren was in full voice and I, to steal one of my stepson Toby's expressions, just "went for it". I had found my "era" even, if the house was any indication, I had missed living in it by at least three centuries. Had I paused, I might have considered the difficulties that lay ahead, but instead I made contact with some of the expatriates in the Medina and organised for the renovation work to begin while I returned to Australia to plan my exit.

My first mentor was Sandra Masters whom I met in what was to become my local café. Sandra ran a chic little *maison-d'hôte* called *Riad Menara*. It was really only a large *dar*; a *dar* with *riad* pretensions, as far as I could see. Originally from California, Sandra had been in Fez for eight years and considered herself an authority on everything, including men who might turn out to be pleasant distractions. It would be flattering to think that she saw me as such, but I quickly discovered her interests centred on boys half her age. However, she did take great care in imparting detailed instructions regarding the restoration of old buildings and with her considerable knowledge she was generous. At some time in her forty or so years she had studied Islamic architecture and now, I suspect, rather enjoyed the role of renovation guru.

'Richard, your salon doors are worth a fortune,' Sandra said, 'but the rest of the house needs a complete makeover.' It sounded alarmingly like a reality TV concept. Seeing my dubious expression, she patted my arm and assured me that at least it was worth saving, unlike many she had seen. Looking back, I realise that even from the start I didn't much like her but she was instrumental in what followed, as she was the person who introduced me to Abdellatif.

Abdellatif, I was told, was a traditional builder. Abdellatif would lovingly restore my *dar* to its former glory. Nothing would be damaged. Old wood would be preserved, the ancient *zellij* cleaned and only in a couple of spots, where it was truly necessary, repaired. The beautiful cedar beams around the atrium would be gently stripped of the offensive green paint, the ceiling of what he referred to as the *massreiya*, the ornate apartment opposite the second-floor salon, would be saved from further damage by removing the floor of the roof-top terrace, repairing the beams and replacing the terrace, not with a slab of concrete, but with soft-brown terracotta tiles set off by small blue *zellij* diamonds. Abdellatif would do it all.

It was not that I wasn't cautious, or so I tell myself now. The ornate detail I loved as much as I had loved the simple lines of the Vincent but I couldn't abide the idea that anything would be damaged. My father had died two years earlier and the proceeds from the sale of his house in Rathfarnham were sitting in an Irish bank account, so money was not an issue. A clear plan was what was needed and so I filled an entire blue notebook with sketches and calculations, double checked everything, as well as consulting with the circle of ex-pats who had bought houses and been through the renovation process.

While all reluctantly acknowledged that Sandra did know a fair bit, I sensed some resentment from others and I soon found myself being bombarded with information and offers of assistance. A young and overly earnest German couple, who had recently reno-vated a house, wanted to charge me exorbitant sums to run what they termed "your project", others simply proposed that I share their workers. Irish Fiona, originally a prod from Belfast, kindly offered me her plumber, Rashid. Fiona's partner, a silent French woman named Isabelle, found me an electrician. South African, Hansie de Villiers, warned me about a carpenter called one-eyed Hafid; sev-enty years old and no good on structural stuff, was the verdict. Ca-nadian Matt knew a plasterer who he swore was the best in the Medina, cheap too. Matt had gutted his house—stripped it back to the walls, pulled out all the old *zellij*, knocked down the plasterwork and started from scratch. I didn't like Matt's *dar* at all. It looked like something new in an old shell; the history carted away as rubble.

Eventually, Sandra, who, to my bemusement had started address-ing me as "Irish Richard", to differentiate me from an Englishman—English Richard—helped me secure a *roqsa*. This was the permission necessary for restoration and without it nothing happened. I also employed an overseer, recommended by Sandra, who in turn or-ganised Abdellatif and his team of three labourers to undertake the work. Satisfied that everything had been set in train, I flew back to Australia, to bushfires and drought, to mendacious politicians, to Rachel's manicured silences and, looming over the horizon, the inevitable divorce. It was all fine with me. I could face anything be-cause deep inside I had faith that "Irish Richard" would return to Fez.

Through the long, drawn-out process that is divorce, I kept de-pression at bay by working on the Vincent with Eric and dreaming of my house in Morocco. Once or twice I tried to describe it to him, but he didn't seem to understand why I needed to move so far away.

'Because it's beautiful,' I told him.

'Beauty is subjective.'

It should be mentioned that whenever Eric used the words 'sub-jective' or 'objective', he did so with a huge amount of pride and satisfaction. A few years earlier he told me the story of the time when, in his mid-twenties, he first heard the words and was concerned by the inability of his brain to grasp the concepts behind them.

'I do things with my hands. I make things. Words are not easy for me.'

'But you understand the terms now?' I said, hopefully.

He nodded; put down the spark plug he was cleaning and looked at me with his big sad eyes. 'It took me two years. But I finally worked it out.'

Probably it is a condition. Eric has only read one book, ever. It was Ian Fleming's *Casino Royale*.

'I was in the bath at my mother's house and the book was on a chair. The water was very cold by the time I finished it.'

'You read it all?'

'I think so. I certainly got to the end. But I couldn't tell you what it was about.'

'He was a bit of an ornithologist.'

'What?'

'A birdwatcher.'

'Who?'

'Ian Fleming.'

'Who is that?'

'The man who wrote the book.'

Eric looked at me blankly for a moment and then nodded. 'Oh.'

Conversations with Eric were like that.

'Beauty is subjective,' he repeated.

'So is distance; for people it may seem small, but for a butterfly? Monarch butterflies fly from the Great Lakes to the Gulf of Mexico, a distance of about two thousand miles, and return to the north again in the spring. Think of that. Four thousand miles on butterfly wings.'

He looked at me long and hard, squinting with concentration. 'How fast do they fly?'

'On average? I would say around ten miles an hour, although they have been recorded at twice that. Mind you, at altitudes of up to ten thousand feet, they can get some tricky wind conditions...' Too much information, I realised as he replaced the spark plug and started polishing the already gleaming front forks.

We worked in a comfortable silence for a while and then he wiped his hands on a rag, drew a long breath and said, 'Ten miles an hour. That's not very fast.'

That's why I love Eric. His silences are constructive.

It is probable that Eric didn't really understand that my going away was final. Even after the motorbike was stolen, Eric still came around every morning. As punctual as a Swiss clock, he knocked on the door at ten and would spend the day assisting with my packing. The house was on the market and, apart from the notebooks, which I had decided I would take to Morocco; my half of the marital possessions was going into storage. In retrospect, it seems an odd thing to have done because I had no intention of returning and certainly didn't intend that they should be handed on to Toby or Peter. I couldn't imagine that either of them would want the complete set of *Old Bike Mart* or the boxes of assorted classic bike magazines. In what I considered a burst of inspiration I offered them to Eric. The perfect recipient—except for two things—he didn't like to read and, as he reminded me, 'I gave them to you in the first place'. For a second I wondered if Eric's condition was catching.

Maybe I should have buried the remains of the marriage in the back yard, where some future archaeologist could eventually dig it up and spend happy years analysing what sort of people we were in the year 2017. No, that would be too cruel. So, half a world away, a little piece of my history is in storage. Each month a couple of hundred dollars leaves my bank account in order that my belongings can hibernate in peace and calm and I don't need to worry about them.

To tell the truth, apart from the motorcycle magazines, I don't remember what is in those boxes, yet it still gives me pleasure to think that one day someone, other than me, will have to deal with them.

At last it was over. Rachel and I signed off on the settlement, paid our lawyers and with an awkward handshake I became single again. Afterward, I returned one last time to the empty house to find Eric contemplating the "For Sale" sign marked with a sticker announcing that the property was "Sold".

'Happy birthday,' he said.

Eric remembered things like that. He handed me a small parcel and waited while I opened it. It was a model motorbike with detachable salt and pepper shakers in the shape of sidecars.

'It's an Ariel Square Four.'

'Thank you,' I said, feeling suddenly tired and emotional. He wasn't one for hugs, but I gave him one anyway. 'I'm off tomorrow. I'll take this with me.' I suspect his quizzical look was because he didn't understand that I was actually leaving.

'I worked it out.'

I knew better than to enquire.

'Sixteen point six days.'

Seeing the perplexed look on my face, Eric smiled kindly.

'That's both ways, of course—' He stopped abruptly.

'What is it?'

'Do they stop on the way?'

'What? Who?'

'Those butterflies.'

Then I got it.

'Sure to.'

He thought about it for a moment then heaved a sigh. 'Then I don't know how long it takes them.'

At the moment the plane lifted off, it struck me that I was actually leaving Australian soil, possibly forever. It sounds embarrassing when I write it now, but at that moment every regret I ever had about anything welled up in me. I regretted hurting Rachel; I regretted not spending more time with her boys, with the dog. I regretted wasting my life on the Vincent, even though I would probably never have ridden it. I regretted abandoning Aisling after I returned from Peru. I regretted kicking Molly Connor at primary school and calling Tommy Sheehan a "bogger". The thought of all those Australian butterflies... For a second my mind betrayed me and flitted with an image from the cloud forest in Peru. A flash of light, the silent wings of the butterfly whose movement, deadlier than the cliché, had turned my world around and plunged me into the nightmare that persisted years and continents away. *Damn it, where is my detachment? Why can't I remain numb?* I wondered about all sorts of things.

A'isha: Thami—a café diversion

'Bismil'lah,' I whispered in Thami's head. Even he, whose head is full of voices, knew that it was not his. Sometimes it was his voice, sometimes mine or when things were really bad, the afarit. There were others too and he fooled himself with the thought that he dismissed the others, but part of him knew that it was delusion.

Thami is not handsome, but he is mine and it amuses me to watch the way his mind fights so hard to understand the world. A world where sounds and objects glow with colours his fellow humans cannot see—even simple things. Listen to him. Watch, as he takes the Coca Cola from the waiter...

Coke. Cold. Bluish, maybe purple. Outside hot. Sunshine and bus full of people coming, going and nowhere I know. Thami. My name. It glows colour of copper. Sometimes in Seffarine. I know my name. Bismil'lah, for the Coke. A shadow crosses the table. Hand snatches my bottle of Coke. Not the qahouaji's hand. He is always friendly. He finds me a seat at the café even when it is full. 'Thami hmuk.' The voice is from outside my head. It is a sneer the colour of the sludge when the drains overflow.

Poor Thami, he is a half and half. A nus-nus; half in his world, half in mine. See! He wants the Coke and begs me to intercede but I abandon him and watch as he tries to speak. Instead, because the words will not emerge when he is angry, he wags his finger and screws his eyes tight, almost closed, shutting out the sludge, reducing the human who is a shadow, to a black dot. He thinks all he needs to do is blink and the man who had stolen his Coke will vanish.

'Kill him,' says the afarit from deep inside. Thami twitches as he always does when the strongest of the spirits talks to him. Harsh, green and

35

shimmering, that is the colour of the afarit. Not like me, the djinniya who loves him. He sees me as young and soft and golden.

'Can't,' he tells the afarit. 'Can't kill anyone.'

Thami's twitch turns into a shiver as the afarit dismisses him.

'Here, half-wit,' the black dot says.

Thami opens his eyes to find the bottle of Coke back on the table. The man has drunk some.

Bad man. Sludge man. Should not have come today, Thami is thinking. Storm last night so the demons had energy to burn. Storm demons from the mountains are circling the medina, flinging their curses down on the humans; brightest white, searing electric curses.

Thami knows that he is immune, protected by the demons that had lived with him since birth.

He shakes his finger and whispers 'Allah, Allah...' This time the words emerge sweet as Coke, but warm. Around him the other patrons of the Café Bnihya are following his familiar shakes and quivers with shrugs.

Crazy Thami, that's what they call me. As long as I keep the djnun inside they won't be harmed.

He shakes his head and rolls his eyes as the men like him to and is rewarded with smiles of encouragement. The qahouaji, Si Mohammed, pauses in serving coffee and smiles.

Soft pink. Drink Coke before another sludge takes it. What? A movement from the underworld. A golden face emerges from the tunnel beneath the Medina wall. A djinn? No, a gawri, a stranger, a Nazarene, a tourist?

Thami sees the man at the same time I do. That man—the man who stinks of death. Thami senses something too and slides his fingers tighter around the Coke, feeling the sweet, blue chill.

'What do you see Thami? It is only a tourist.'

But although the world may think him crazy, Thami is not stupid.

'No camera. No backpack,' he hisses, knowing that wherever I am I will hear.

Thami shakes his finger at the stranger.

'Danger,' I whisper, 'Don't look at him.'

Because he knows I love him, he nods and closes his eyes, screwing them tight. But he cannot shut out their world. Noises. Chairs scraping. Qahoua-ji shaking dirhams onto his tray. A silver waterfall, coruscating. Coffee smells and cigarettes. 'As-salaamu 'aleikum,' says a voice so close to his ear that for a moment he thinks it is the afarit. A hand touches his and he feels a cigarette slide between his fingers.

Shukran, Sidi, he tries to say but the words dissolve and dribble from the corner of his mouth. There is silence in Thami's head and then he opens his eyes and sees the bearded face of Yazami, standing in front of him. Behind him, sitting at the next table, is the Nazarene. The foreigner no longer looks golden, his colour faded to grey behind the slender stream of Thami's cigarette smoke.

'Danger,' whispers my beautiful voice in his head.

Yazami: Café pour deux

Outside the damp house a soft breeze herded gusts of warm air from beyond the Medina, carrying with it all the spicy smells of the souk that it had picked up along the way. It was only just after nine but the streets were busy. Young boys, trays on their heads, were skilfully weaving their way through the press of early shoppers in the narrow lanes, delivering bread and cakes from the bakeries to the already open shops. A gaggle of school children giggled at me, the bravest girl venturing a shy "*bonjour*". In a side alley, a green-uniformed rubbish collector was paused, packing his load deeper into the wicker panniers with a large piece of wood, while his donkey, blocking my way, explored the contents of a plastic bag full of scraps. I nodded, squeezed past and headed for the café that now had a name—Café Bnihya.

'There is a power cut.'

'What?' I had been jotting down some notes on the condition of my house and had to squint as the man had the sun over his shoulder.

'A power cut.'

'Ah...'

'Which explains the absence of coffee.'

'That would be it.'

'You like Moroccan coffee?'

The man who moved around and pulled up a chair bore a remarkable likeness to Fidel Castro or was it a young Saddam Hussein? Now, facing the light he blinked, a black-eyed mole freshly emerged from beneath the earth; Saddam pulled from his subterranean hiding place. The beard was Castro, the hair was Saddam. The bandana around the neck was confusing the image and for a second I saw a forty or forty-five-year-old Fidel on a horse... a *gaucho*.

'Of course...'

'With milk?'

'No. Is it important if there is no power?'

'Ah *Sidi*! This is Fez and so it follows that the power is only off on this side of the street.'

I shrugged and turned my attention back to my notebook, unwilling to be engaged in a conversation—a seemingly pointless one at that—with someone who was probably going to either want money or cigarettes, or had some other scam in mind. Even as I thought it, I felt unworthy. However, before I could engage him again in an exchange of pleasantries, he was gone, weaving his way like a skilled dancer through the throng of people in front of the café and vanishing down the street. Taking up my ballpoint I wrote down "Saddam Castro", then crossed it out and wrote "Fidel Hussein". This too I crossed out.

It was more than a week since my arrival back in Fez and I was still seething with anger at what had happened to my house. The destruction, the devastation had been so complete that I felt unable to face it, let alone do anything to repair the damage. My initial response had been to clear a space to sleep and a small dry area in which to set up my gas stove, but apart from that—nothing. The shock and the sickness in my stomach, while not abating, had at least become focused. Not, as you might expect on the actual perpetrators, trusty

Abdellatif and the overseer (both of whom were now allegedly living in Spain), but those who had let it happen, my so-called friends in the ex-pat community who had sworn by these people, insisting that they could do the perfect job. At times, I had even sensed a competitive edge—"Use my man, he is far more skilled." "Don't use that carpenter, you should see what he did to Gabriel's house."

The image of the *Satyridae*, my first *Chazara briseis*, came back to me, along with its revelation at the time. Its common name, *the hermit*, was even more portentous than I had imagined on that first visit to Fez. At the time, I had thought of it in relationship to my life in Australia but now I saw it was more than that. The small graceful butterfly had been far-seeing. Better to be self-sufficient. The foreign community in Fez was not the reason I had come here, indeed, they were a barrier between me and the city, a distraction from getting to know the "locals"—the people that made the Medina so vibrant. It was a mistake, I told myself, to try and get to know the city as bricks and mortar, as *zellij* and cedar. It was more than that. Without the people, it was a decaying mausoleum, an anachronism, a museum perhaps—a breeding ground for orientalist fantasies. No, this was a living city whose heartbeat and rhythms I could get to know.

Yet, despite these mental games I was playing with myself to quell the anger, the images of my house percolated up, invading the sunlight and surroundings, filling me with a sense of dread. Were those who Abdellatif and his collaborators had employed to destroy my house, in the café? Were they sitting next to me, watching? Gloating? Was I really intending to cut myself off from the expatriate community and throw in my lot with the thieves who had robbed me?

The recording of my recollections of that horrible night was interrupted by the sight of a young man stumbling and tripping on the gutter in front of the café. Instinctively I sprang to my feet and, taking him by the elbow, helped him up. For a second or so he teetered, his attention not on me but on the offending gutter as if checking that it was not about to trip him again. It occurred to me that he was drunk or stoned, but then he lifted his face and stared into my eyes and I realised I had seen him before, but only never like this.

How to describe what I saw in that moment? It was a face full of pain and grievance, yet at the same time resignation. From behind the mask of confusion I sensed a burst of hate so powerful that it made me shiver. His eyes were not the brown I expected, but vivid blue. More startling was the power with which he held my gaze. His face was at the same time vacant and yet inhabited and in an unnerving moment I thought that they were not his eyes, but rather they belonged to someone else.

On my first visit to Fez and my frequent trips to the café I would often see him and indeed, on those days when he did not appear, I felt cheated as if something was missing from the scene around me; some vital ingredient. His twitching, his mumbling and other odd behaviours became so much part of the texture of the place that its absence—his absence—left an unsatisfactory hole. During those first encounters, I thought him older as he walked with a slight stoop that made him appear so. He was, as I later found out, only twenty-seven years of age. Thin, barrel-chested, he was short—not more than five-five—thick necked and his very round head sparsely covered with straight black hair. He was cinnamon-skinned, his face wrinkled, studded by hooded eyes, the vacant droop of his lower lip giving him what my father would have described as a "gormless" look. His lack of dental care was evident; his upper front teeth large and yellow while several of his lower teeth were missing. However, his clothes, while unusually neat and pressed, were oddly coloured—red and black—always red and black, as though it was a uniform. To be truthful, when I first saw him I made a concerted effort to avoid staring at him, as when I did, it was as though I was indulging in some guilty pleasure or intruding—an unwelcome voyeur—intrigued by the man's peculiar mannerisms.

Now he brought his face close to my ear and in a faint voice whispered, '*Shukran bezzef.*' Then, taking my hand from his arm, he brushed it away as if it were an annoying insect. I returned to my seat and watched as he shuffled around the tables looking for an empty chair.

'They call him Crazy Thami,' said a voice beside me. It was Fidel. He slipped a glass of coffee onto the table and pulled up a chair. 'It is because they don't understand that the spirits, the *djnun,* speak to him.'

I pointed to the coffee. 'How did you...?'

The man waved in the general direction of the street. 'Over there. The power is on.'

'Thank you.' Embarrassed by his generosity I fumbled for some coins but he shook his head.

'*La shukra 'la wazhib.* Not necessary,' he said, as he tipped his chair back and stretched out his legs. In front of us a team of donkeys threaded their way through a tangle of traffic. Taxis hooted, a bus began a three-point turn and a group of heavily laden Berber women, fresh from the country, seized the moment to surge across the road with their baskets of produce.

Everything came to a halt when one of the donkeys lost its load of empty plastic bottles, causing the bus to brake suddenly. There was a crescendo of shouts and honking and then, just as quickly as it had begun, the commotion died away. The bus completed its manoeuvre and exited the scene, the donkeys clip-clopped off down the road towards Bab R'cif and the Berber women, their backs bent under their loads, heads down, eyes on the cobbles, walked down the steps and merged into the crowded souk.

'Chaos,' Fidel muttered, then shot me a quizzical look. 'Of course, they don't see it. But you do.'

He didn't wait for me to catch up, but waved at the crowd flowing along the pavement. 'They live it—on the inside. Whereas, you and I, we see.'

'Sorry?'

'The outsider's eye; it's a gift; a very precious one. We should hon-our it.' He pointed to where the man I had assisted was sitting. 'He sees it too. But differently I think.'

'Really?' I didn't have a clue what he was on about.

'I am the writer, Yazami.' He shot out his hand and grasped mine, shook it vigorously, released it to touch his heart, then took it again. 'It is a pleasure to meet you. You came before and then went away but I knew you would be back and that we would be friends.' He didn't let go of my hand and I experienced the western male's dis-comfort at the Moroccan habit of men holding hands. I forced my-self to relax.

'How did you know I would return?' It came out too stiffly.

'You looked relaxed here. You didn't carry a camera.'

I removed my hand and opted for the safety of picking up the coffee. I dropped in a sugar cube and ground at it with my spoon. 'Is that important? Not carrying a camera, I mean.'

Yazami laughed dryly and tugged at his beard. 'Two eyes reduced to one? Have you seen them, the tourists, getting off the buses with their smart phones or video cameras? Two eyes are better. For them it is not possible to see what is really here, only what is on their little screen. It is a safety barrier between them and the exotic zoo. For them that is what is real. Not for you or me.'

'The exotic zoo?'

'This fantasy Morocco they are capturing to take back to their safe little lives. A trophy they can display. "See! I went to Morocco and survived!" Like that.'

His mock American accent grated, as I am certain he intended, but despite my earlier reservations, I found myself warming to him. I placed the glass down carefully and extended my hand. 'Richard. My name is Richard.'

He shook my hand and laughed to himself, his face a picture of contentment as I mimicked his earlier gesture and touched my heart.

'Ah, my friend, I knew that already. You are *Sidi* Richard, you have bought a house up the hill in La'ayoune and you like writing in your little blue book. We are both writers. Do you know the *Darija* word, *khoya*? It means "brother". You and I are brothers, *khoya*.'

'*Khoya*,' I mumbled. Right, now I was getting *Darija* lessons. I jotted it down.

A muffled cheer came from inside the Café Bnihya.

'Ah! Electricity has arrived, *humdullilah*!' Yazami spun in his chair and signalled to the nearest waiter. 'Si Mohammed! *Qhawa, afuk. Zhuzh. Cafe pour deux!*'

'That man, Thami, you said?' I pointed to where the man had taken a seat and was talking to himself and fumbling with a cigarette lighter. Yazami didn't appear to think his behaviour strange.

'His name is Thami, yes.'

'Why do they do that to him?'

Yazami snorted. 'They are afraid.' He smiled then leaned close to my head and whispered. 'And so they should be.'

Over on the other side of the café one of the boys had just snatched Thami's cigarette away and was taunting him with it.

'But not everyone treats him like that, do they?'

'No. There are those who think that madness brings him closer to *Allah*. Thami has *baraka*, so to respect him is important.'

'*Baraka*?'

'Blessing; spiritual power, maybe. Some believe that.'

As I wrote the word down, the coffee arrived and then, in what seemed like a kind gesture, Yazami ordered a bottle of Coke to be delivered to Thami.

'*Bismil'lah!* ' he exclaimed, and then, slurping his coffee, sucking it in between his teeth, beamed at me. 'You are not a Muslim, so maybe you think this *baraka* is simple superstition. Some of them,' he waved in the general direction of the street, '... they may say they don't believe anymore, but deep down they do. Certainly, many have stopped going to the mosque five times a day, others have stopped praying altogether. The young ones say they don't believe in anything but cell phones, text messaging and the Internet. They are a new generation. But some things they can't shrug off. *Baraka* is one, *djnun* are another. Modern but with the old traditions still attached. Who knows, *khoya*, maybe they text message *Allah* with their prayers.'

I waited for him to continue, but instead he raised his hand and waved to someone in the crowd around the bus stop to our right. An old man, with a face like creased papyrus, nodded, shuffled between the tables and tapped out a cigarette from a crumpled packet. Yazami handed him a couple of dirhams and then leaned forward and waited while the man struggled to get the cigarette lighter to work. It was not the lighter, I realised, but his fingers. They were bent and crippled with arthritis. Eventually, he simply handed the lighter to Yazami.

For several minutes we sat in silence as he smoked and I continued to jot down some observations about the passing parade of people. I found the extraordinary diversity wonderful. It was the faces, the races and body shapes: the clothing too, varied in colour and style. Old women, in black from head to foot, even their hands gloved. Like ravens or crows I noted. There was something odd about the angle of their heads; stiff and very upright. Then I realised it was so they could see, because their vision was restricted to a narrow slit across their eyes. The image was something I could have imagined belonged in the Middle Ages and yet they walked in front of me, hand in hand with their daughters or younger friends wearing designer jeans and t-shirts. There were men in business suits strolling beside those in *djellabas*, cloaks and occasionally pantaloons and loose-fitting tunic tops. Young men whose style guide appeared to be American homeboys or rappers, in stylish sunglasses, caps backwards, heavy-metal t-shirts hanging almost to their knees, roared past on scooters or stood in groups eyeing up the girls. I wondered how far I would have to travel the world before I saw two policemen in smart blue uniforms, holding hands as they chatted in the middle of the road.

'Our revels now are ended and I must go.' Yazami was on his feet. 'I will visit you in your house, *inshallah*.' He had tossed a ten-dirham coin on the table and turned away.

'Thank you...' I began. But he had gone before I could compliment him on his unexpected appropriation from Shakespeare.

Over in the shadows Thami was sipping his Coke, lost in himself and the demons around him. I had meant to ask Yazami about the *djnun*, the spirits, but it would have to wait.

One thing I have come to understand about myself is that, while I suppress many things, I don't usually lie. It is not even that I have some deeply held belief in truth, for in our time truth has become simply another product to be bought and sold, used and abused, spun, nuanced, bent or distorted. My not lying is more about not needing to. In all but one part of my life I have nothing to hide. That I lied to the investigators about what happened in Peru I can't forgive myself for but I... *No, don't go there; leave it alone.* In the ten minutes that followed Yazami's departure I was to lie three times. In retrospect, I'm glad I did and would do so again.

The moment I saw the two of them get out of the taxi I knew I was going to lie. There was no decision to be made one way or the other, no balancing up of moral arguments, no internal discussion. Perhaps it was the effects of the caffeine. Maybe it was delayed shock. The images of the destruction in my house had not been laid aside. There was anger too. Undirected, until the moment I saw them— Canadian Matt and Sandra Masters. Matt in grubby jeans and a once expensive but now frayed black overcoat wrapped tight against the chill. His hair, lank, more grey than I remembered and longer too, looked as if it had been cut by a Moroccan barber.

The description I wrote down is pretty accurate: *a gaunt face, aged and lined by too much sun and cigarettes, pinched and squinting as he looks across the road.* A weasel, worried, or maybe annoyed by the bustle around him; by the donkeys carrying huge panniers of rubbish, a motor scooter, two more *petits taxis* pulling up. He eyed them all as if they were threats and I remembered how he once told me he didn't actually like Moroccans. For a moment, I wondered why Matt had moved here in the first place. He glanced at Sandra who was paying the taxi driver, then up again and saw me. A nod of recognition and, not waiting for her, he stepped around the rear of the taxi and strode across the road.

'Welcome back.'

'Thanks.'

He looked me up and down.

'You look like shit,' he said and flopped down into a chair.

Thanks Matt, I thought but didn't say anything.

'When did you get back?'

'A couple of weeks ago.'

Sandra materialised behind him. They are not a couple, was the thought that went through my head. It would have been an odd pairing, given her rumoured predilection for young boys. Mind you, I had the feeling that anything was possible here. Her boots were bright blue, calf length with spots of mud on them. The ankle length woollen skirt was red and her thick wrap looked like wool and cashmere. It was the colour of her boots but flecked with gold, stylish. Her complexion could not be more different to Matt's. Maybe it was the comparison but she did look extremely healthy. The round face glowing, her ruddy cheeks free of makeup and the naturally blonde hair bobbed and held in place by an amber clasp. Her blue eyes were sparkling.

'*As-salaamu 'aleikum,*' she said and offered me her cheek.

'Hi, Sandra.'

'Just back?'

'Yes.'

'Fantastic.' She looked around and signalled to a waiter, then, spotting my glass. 'You want another?'

I shut my notebook and slipped the pen into my top pocket. 'No, I was just going.' That was the first lie, as I would happily have sat for another hour or so watching the ever-changing life on the street.

'Sure.'

'Tea for me,' Matt grunted, took out his cigarettes and turned to me. 'How's the house?'

Lie number two came out without hesitation.

'Great.' To my credit, I also kept the anger out of my voice.

Sandra pulled up a chair. 'I can't wait to have a look.'

'A bit of decorating to do first, then—'

'Then a house warming,' Matt said and fished his lighter from his coat pocket. 'Angela is having a party as well. She'll be thrilled you're back. You're a bit of a party animal, Richard, I can tell. It's always you silent types.'

'Something like that.' I got to my feet nodded a farewell and started to thread my way through the chairs towards the steps into the medina. One pace in front of my anger, hurrying, I stumbled against the leg of a chair. Pausing, I mumbled and apology. The man, thirty or so years of age I guessed, scowled at me.

'*Gawri*,' he hissed.

'Sorry,' I repeated and pressed on.

'You have my number?' Sandra called after me.

'Yes.'

That was lie number three.

Not ready to face the chaos of my house, I changed direction, turned right and followed the road around to the vegetable souk. *A house warming, a party animal*, had Matt really said that? For a split second, I contemplated inviting all the expatriates who had "helped" me to see the result of their recommendations. That would be some house warming. Of course I would never do it, but the very notion caused me to smile. If I were to have friends in Fez they would be Moroccan with only two definitely off my list. I made a mental note to try and find out if the rumour about Abdellatif having fled to

Spain was really true. And then there was the so-called supervisor that Sandra had recommended. It could wait until later. Right now I needed supplies.

The press of people in the souk was strangely comforting; a sea of people and noise; smells too. *Nobody knows me.* The city has so much past that mine is swallowed up and rendered irrelevant. There is a joy in being the alien; the white face in a mass of brown and black; Berbers and Arabs. I am in Africa, yet it feels like elsewhere—somewhere. Not the Middle East, but somewhere in between. *Mo-rocc-o,* the three syllables tripping forward on the palate tasted so sweet. This sense of displacement was a thrill that cut through the jangling effects of the coffee and I found myself relaxing and letting the natural rhythm of the souk move me along.

The lack of electricity at my house was a real pain and so my first purchase was a dozen thin candles and a plastic bag full of tea-lights that looked as if they had been in the shop for a decade; they were yellowed and cracked and despite the plastic, covered in dust.

'*Andek! Andek!*'

Friendly hands tugged at my sleeve and pulled me out of the path of a *carossa* piled high with trays of brown eggs. There was no danger of being run over as it was making very slow progress through the crowd, pushed by a young boy who didn't look more than six or seven. He grinned up at me.

'*Bonjour.*'

I smiled back.

Sensing a sale, the boy halted and with practiced dexterity juggled a couple of eggs and then with a flourish held them up for me to inspect. Another boy squeezed through the throng and, positioning himself right in front of me, began a rapid-fire sales pitch in *Darija.* Suddenly I was the centre of attention; entertainment for the other shoppers, who instead of being annoyed by the traffic jam building around me, paused to watch the strange foreigner who had started shopping in their souk.

Eggs had not been on my mental shopping list, but now that I had brought this part of the souk to a standstill I felt obliged to buy some. 'How much for half a dozen?'

'*Français?*' asked someone.

'American?' chimed in another.

My vehement head shaking needed no translation and elicited some laughter. What should I say? English? Irish? No.

'Australia.'

'Ah, *Australie.*'

The looks on the faces around me indicated that I might as well have said Jupiter.

The boy beside me grabbed my hand and pushed a black plastic bag into it, indicating I should select the number of eggs I wanted so I took six and pulled a note from my pocket. To my surprise the boy frowned and pushed the note away. There was a murmur from the bystanders and I realised that my proffered note, one hundred dirhams, was big money—twice what most of them could expect to make in a day. Embarrassed, I stuffed it back in my pocket.

'*Sidi...*' The boy with the eggs produced a coin and showed it to me '...'ashra.'

A ten-dirham coin, it seemed a reasonable price. But as I fished in my pocket for the change I had been given at the café, a voice called out from the other side of the narrow alley.

'*Hshuma, khoya! Khamsa.* Five dirhams, sir, only five dirhams.'

The boy, suitably admonished, shrugged and held up five fingers. '*Khamsa.*'

Five dirhams. Despite myself I was learning the language.

Having paid the boy, I waited for a break in the slow-moving throng and went over to thank my benefactor who turned out to be the proprietor of a hole-in-the-wall spice shop. He was a man in his late thirties or early forties, round faced, a full head of black hair and a remarkably perfect set of teeth, which he displayed with a permanent smile.

'*Shukran Sidi,*' I said, road testing my limited *Darija*.

'*La shukra 'la wazhib.* I am only performing my duty. He was try-ing to extract an unreasonable sum from you. Such action is not in the spirit of Islam and he is shamed. *Hshuma* or shame is not taken lightly in Fez. But now the *hshuma* is mine, I have failed to introduce myself. My name is Yusuf and I am extremely glad to meet you.'

His accent-less English was delivered with ponderous and old-fashioned precision.

'Richard,' I said, shaking the proffered hand. This time touching my heart almost came naturally.

'Of course, I have heard of you.'

'You have?'

'Indeed, sir. Your patronage of our local café is appreciated. You shop in the souk and not the supermarkets in the new town... and, naturally, your purchase of a fine house did not go unnoticed—'

'I was robbed,' I blurted out, suddenly desiring to share my burden with a complete stranger. 'I mean my house was robbed.'

'Sadly, only *Allah* is perfect, *Sidi* Richard.'

'Doors, beams... even the plumbing all gone. The place is an ab-solute disaster.'

Yusuf tugged at his chin and nodded. 'This too is known. Those responsible will be judged, *inshallah*.'

'*Inshallah,*' I echoed, unsure that I was ready to accept that as an excuse. Was this what it felt like to be raped? Did rape victims sim-ply console themselves with the notion that the act had been God's will? I think not. While it was true as I have said before, that I do emptiness well, there are limits and the destruction of my house was way over any imagined boundary. My house had been, well, *my* house and, for all its defects it was now all I had left. A simple theft I could have dealt with but the fact that the internal structure of the house was compromised and might even be beyond repair, was too worrying to dismiss with platitudes. Yusuf, not having suffered the injustice was, however, far more philosophical.

'Comfort yourself with the thought that it might have been worse,' he said with a hint of a smile.

My scepticism must have shown for he hurried to explain.

'Believe me, those bandits would have done much worse if it had not been for the spirits.'

'Spirits? What spirits?'

He paused, smiled shyly then gestured for me to lean forward so he could whisper. 'Listen, *Sidi* Richard, your house is known to have powerful guardians, spirits who will protect you if you gain their favour.'

Sure, I thought, and the Christmas Fairy and a couple of elves might help. 'And how exactly does one do that?'

'Many methods are known,' he confided. 'It depends on what you can afford. Here...' He took a red plastic scoop and dug a small quantity of greenish-coloured powder from a sack. 'Please accept a humble gift as a welcome to the Medina.' He poured the powder onto a square of newspaper and sealed it with a deft twist at both ends. 'Put a little of this in the corners of your rooms. A quantity of milk in a saucer is also advantageous. She likes that. And please never spill salt or pour boiling water down your drains; on no account.'

And don't mention the Scottish play, was the thought that flitted through my mind. 'Your English...' I began, needing to change the subject before I let my scepticism rise further.

'It is clumsy, I am afraid. Like a tool that is not in constant use, it develops rust. Thankfully your arrival will afford me many opportunities to polish the imperfections, yes?'

'Far from it, your English is superb.'

'But a barren field from which I gain no profit.' He shrugged. 'I desired to teach literature, but alas a combination of economic factors and an elderly mother in much need of caring proscribed a different fate. In a word, I could not afford the bribe necessary to avail myself of a post.'

'You have a degree?' I asked, relieved that we had moved from the realm of spirits to that of learning.

'I gained a doctorate in English literature with my speciality being the works of the masterful Joyce.'

'James Joyce?' I felt an unhealthy shiver run through me. Joyce was a subject of discussion I had avoided for years. Joyce, who was inextricably linked in my brain to the nightmare that now, even in broad daylight, I suddenly struggled to suppress.

'The very same. I studied in the same years as your friend Mohammed Yazami, although his doctorate was on Master Shakespeare. Do you remember what Joyce had to say about him?'

'Who? Shakespeare?'

He nodded. 'Shakespeare is the happy hunting ground of all minds that have lost their balance.' He paused, ran his fingers through his hair and let a smile filter across his face. 'Ah, yes, we know everything that goes on in the Medina. Your coffee companion Yazami is a little crazy, but the possessor of the most perfect English due to foreign acquaintances of an intimate female kind. He is however, a man to be careful of.'

'Really?'

'There are those who say he is too close up to the *djnun* or may even have some of their blood in his veins. Not that it is of my business, but I would heed with him carefully.'

Not the construction I would have chosen, but I understood the sentiment of his sentence. 'Well... Look, I must go.'

'Of course.' He smiled and held out the gift he had wrapped. 'Do not forget the henna.'

'Henna?'

'For the *djinniya*.'

A'isha: The sweetness of blood

At times he is nervous, even in his own company. Stiff, as though bound with ropes of reeds. This Nasrani—this foreigner—is in my space and so easily I could strike him down or drive him mad and yet I stay my hand. I, who do not fear, fear this hesitation in myself. What right has this Nazarene to disturb my realm? My fascination with him will not last for he is but one among hundreds; only a man and in the end I will destroy him utterly—but not until I have drained every last drop of pleasure from him.

At other times he walks the streets alone and yet, not like those around him. His eyes are not on the cobbles but on the sky. Neck craned, he scans the narrow space above the walls but what he sees I do not know. The stars? The moon? Maybe he is hemmed in by the ramparts and craves the space that sane men fear. His heritage is not that of the sands, of the endless dunes. His blood does not understand the tyranny of the sky, for if it did he would scuttle like the other fools, back to his rat hole and hide. He would delineate the acceptable space with walls and tiles, knowing the length and breadth of sanctuary, the geometry of safety. This may be his weakness and if so I shall exploit it.

Sometimes late at night he remains indoors, scrabbling in the dirt and ruins of his house; all the while talking to himself. This he moves, that he discards. Like some restless, driven being he cleans the smallest things while all around is destruction. One small tile at a time; sorted by colour, size and shape. All this he does, not during the time of his people—the day—but during my time, the night. In the last weeks he has cleared a space in which to sleep and a place to cook and in doing so has stopped the water that flowed so sweetly over the floors; water that I craved. It was inevitable that I should punish him.

As he bent to remove some fallen rubble I let him glimpse me. Not in my fury, neither in my beauty but as a ghulat—a ghoul. The effect was immediate. He started and caught his head on the ragged edges of a broken pipe that protruded from the wall. The gash was perfect and the blood flowed sweet and thick like warm honey. My body shivered with the ecstasy and it was only my resolve to tease my body that kept me from making him mine at that moment. My restraint was richly rewarded as even without my guidance he stumbled across the floor to wash his face in the water of the wall fountain. Such subtle colour in the water. For a long while I allowed the ripples of pleasure to wash over me as I merged with the wet nectar. His blood is sweet and I will have more. But for now, I enjoy the reversal of roles. It is I who anticipate our congress. I, who am stimulated by the smell and taste of his blood to the point where I feel my hunger growing. Later—soon—his desire for my body will drive him insane... but not yet... not yet.

He has taken to coming out at dusk—just as I do. The two of us are evening moths. Maybe he thinks this way about himself. The romantic in him would like the notion of moths following the last scent of the sun perhaps or the first fragrance of the moon. He did not used to be this way.

He has developed the nervous habit of glancing over his shoulder as if he was aware of being followed. Now, for the first time, he does it when he leaves the house; looking back, down the stairs to the tiny courtyard, as if something or someone is there. He shuts the door, double locking the top lock. For a second I wonder if he is locking something in or something out.

Fumbling with the key ring, heavy with keys and insecurity, he locates the square key for the lower lock. Three clicks this time. Then, nodding to himself, confirming he has done it right, he slips the keys into his trouser pocket; changes his mind and drops them into his jacket pocket. He cannot see me.

Walking along the alleyway beside Riad Mokri his feet send up puffs of dust, small clouds around his shoes. He pauses to catch his breath and once again checks over his shoulder. It has been so dry these last few months. Not my kind of weather. For me? Rain, damp, mist anything with water—even dew, if that is all that is on offer. With water I am... but this is not about me.

54

Turning right, he pauses to listen to the call to prayer before continuing the long slow climb up the hill towards Derb Skalia. A mule stumbles as it comes down the hill and again he pauses, pressed against the wall. The men wandering down towards the souk and the cafés cannot see me, although one old man, shuffling on the cobbles, grips his walking stick, halts, the gnarled fingers and wood becoming one tight knot as he senses me.

'Allahou akbar,' he mumbles and resumes his slow progress down the hill.

A little further on he turns into a narrow passage, stops beside an ornate door and searches for the bell. Finding none he grasps the Hand of Fatima, hesitates a second and then knocks. In the silence that follows I can hear the sound from behind the thick walls of a courtyard fountain tinkling and my spirits lift. At the same time his demeanour changes and he turns, tightening, regretting perhaps that he has come. He steps back, turns—but too late. The door opens and a young Moroccan boy greets him.

'Salaam aleikum, Mister Richard...'

'W'aleikum salaam,' Richard mumbles and turns back to the door.

As he is about to step forward the boy is pushed aside by a woman in a shimmering white gown, her hair cut short like a boy's; an image at odds with the full cleavage that the plunging neckline reveals. She is probably in her late thirties. When she speaks the accent is American.

'Ah darling!' the woman beams, flashing teeth too perfect and too white. 'James was just betting that you wouldn't come.'

'Angela... I didn't realise that I should have dressed up—'

'Nonsense! You need a break from...' she hesitates and pulling him towards her, kisses the air beside each cheek. Holding him by the shoulders, she looks into his face at the cut on his forehead and shaking her head as though confronting a naughty child that deserved forgiveness. 'A break from whatever it is you do all week. What on earth have you done to your face?' With that she takes his arm and propels him inside, pausing only to call over her shoulder to the Moroccan boy left marooned on the step.

'Angus and Heather are on their way, so wait and show them in will you?'

Richard: Down among the barbarians

Ironically it was Eric back in Australia who had said that socially I was an ill-fitting sprocket. However, I never really understood what he meant, at least not until recently. Back then I avoided parties and shunned public events, other than those necessitated by my speaking tours. In those instances, I at least had the podium between me and the chattering, sleeve-tugging cocktail class. Using the excuse that I needed to prepare myself before a speech was greeted with disappointment but understanding, but my rapid exit after an event on the grounds of jet lag or a headache was usually received with less cordial sentiments.

Eric? I had not thought of him in weeks until, in what must have been an uncharacteristic moment, he wrote me a letter. That he did so was extraordinary enough but that it was delivered was a miracle. It was not that he couldn't write, but rather that in all the years I knew him I never saw him with a pen in hand unless it was to circle spare parts in a motorbike magazine. The letter was addressed to me *"c/- of the Medina of Fez, Morocco, Africa."*

When I complimented the postman on his sleuthing skills and diligence he responded with a shrug.

'Everyone knows about you, *Sidi.*'

He also delivered an invitation to "drinkies and nibbles", from Angela and James, her *homme du jour*. To be fair, James had been on the scene for a while but Angela was renowned for her dedication to serial monogamy—with the occasional "side salad"—as she put it.

I tossed the invitation to one side, picked up Eric's letter and was rewarded with a profound sense of pleasure. He had plastered the envelope with stamps depicting butterflies, a joyful shimmer—a riotous fluttering—if you will; far more than required by the crass demands of postage. How he had found them I have no idea but there were a couple of two dollar stamps showing a scene from the Daintree rainforest complete with a beautiful brilliant metallic blue and velvety black *Papilio ulysses* and the red *Cethosia cydippe*. A Nymphalidae, the *Hypolimns alimena* graced a ten-cent stamp and two fifty-cent Papilionoidea, *Graphium agamemnon* completed the collection. It was such a sweet gesture.

Eric's letter contained a list of towns with the number of inhabitants noted in parentheses beside each name. None of this made sense until I came to a paragraph tacked on at the end. Eric had sold his mother's house, bought a small motor home with a "pop-out extension", and after getting a driver's licence, hit the road. He was, he assured me, keeping an eye out for my stolen Black Lightning. For the life of me I couldn't imagine Eric camping but decided he would be an asset among the grey nomads circumnavigating the continent, filling in time between heart attacks and hip replacements. Each evening, as they circled their wagons around the campfire for "happy hour", Eric would be on hand to give them advice about things mechanical. God help them. Under this paragraph was a scrawled signature "your friend Eric" followed by: *ps. I hope the Ariel is well.* The Ariel? Then I remembered his gift—the salt and pepper shaker—still packed away in my bag. With a grin on my face I dug through my suitcase, retrieved it and placed it carefully on the side of the wall fountain and slipped his carefully considered envelope behind it; a little bit of Eric in Morocco.

A couple of evenings later, feeling restless and uneasy, I decided I had to get out. My old nightmares had returned with a vengeance and I had been sleeping unwillingly, fitfully, all the time haunted by images from the cloud forest. Faces from the past, dead faces that I had thought obliterated by time and distance, loomed large in my dreams and left me distressed and shaking.

In the weeks that followed my return from Peru all those years ago I had been offered counselling and with hindsight it was an offer I should have accepted. However, at the time I could think of nothing other than escaping from the endless round of questions about my actions; questions that I had to answer with lies. Meeting with the relatives of those who had died were some of the worst moments of my life. Not one of them accused me to my face, but in their eyes I could see they knew where the blame lay. Afterwards I remember rushing to a toilet and vomiting.

Just as terrifying was the knowledge that total strangers had seen the television footage of my return, or would recognise my face from the newspaper coverage. Guilt plays havoc with the imagination and in the street, I was convinced people looked at me accusingly. *You are the one who survived, you are the one who abandoned your colleagues, you are the coward.*

It is true; I was a coward. I ran.

That my past should have caught up with me here in Morocco, after the passage of so much time, I found deeply disturbing. So, I did what I always do; I walked away. Driven by the need for distraction, I set out with no clear destination. Remembering the invitation and, with a vague idea about the date, I made my way through the alleyways towards Batha where Angela lived. Her *riad* (she is definitely a *riad* person) is set back off a narrow passage at the top end of Derb Skalia so I threaded my way up Oued Souafine. I took my time and, having left my fears back in the house, found myself enjoying the walk, the scent of the evening air and the fading light on the uppermost facades of the buildings. From faraway the call to prayer rippled over the rooftops, passing from mosque to mosque, getting rapidly closer until it rang out from a minaret almost directly above me.

Turning left into Aqbet Sba', I paused to catch my breath and watch the bats flitting in the dusk; darting silhouettes against a sky turned sullen apricot. A storm was coming, I thought, as I began the slow trudge up the first set of steps towards where, thankfully, the street levelled off and became, for no apparent reason, Derb Skalia.

My normal level of fitness appeared to have deserted me and so I used the excuse of an approaching mule to pause; propped against an already chill wall. The mule, laden with gas cylinders, was finding the steep downhill section difficult, its steps tentative as the weight on its back caused its feet to slide precariously on the cobbles. Thoughtfully the owner was coaxing the reluctant beast into tacking back and forth and taking my breathless halt for consideration, he grinned and touched his heart.

At the junction of Derb Skalia and El Hamiya some boys were kicking a soccer ball, ricocheting it off the walls then trapping it with extraordinary skill and dexterity. It crossed my mind that with such young talent Morocco should be a major football nation. It was foolish of course because the scene in front of me was being played out in countries across the world. Morocco didn't have a monopoly on skilled eight year olds.

'*Barça! Barça!*' one of the boys called to me as he flipped the ball up and headed it to his friends.

'Ronaldinho,' I replied. It hadn't taken me long to learn that to support any other team than Barcelona was tantamount to heresy. Indeed, the FBC graffiti was one of the few things I could read on the medina walls. My response was rewarded with broad smiles and a thumbs-up from the youngest boy. Deciding to capitalise on the moment he ran over and shook my hand.

'*As-salaamu 'aleikum.*'

'*W'aleikum salaam,*' I responded.

'Dirham?' the boy asked, dropping the smile and adopting a well-practised forlorn face that was almost cute enough to have me reaching in my pocket for a coin. However, I have a rule about beggars that excludes children. The trembling palms of the very old and the liquid shine of the eyes of the blind will always extract a few dirhams from me, but to encourage children seems irresponsible.

'Bugger off,' I said gently.

Angela has what some people describe as chiselled features; chiselled from alabaster. Yet, though she was beautiful in a conventional way, so much of her personality was locked away beneath the stone facade that I never had the faintest notion as to what she really felt about anything. Her lips would move, a smile form and then vanish as though it had been called up by an autocue machine and then just as quickly cancelled; to be replaced with the next appropriate expression. Somewhere, deep inside there must have been someone programming her, but they were never revealed. My reading of her, in the instant between her first air-kiss, accompanied by "darling!" and her turn to her Moroccan houseboy to take another glass of champagne, must have been transparent because James sidled up to me and muttered, "Cold bitch."

'And how are things in your *chez?*' He asked, passing me a glass.

'Pretty bloody, actually,' I responded, then cursed myself for having said so. Thankfully, James's interest was small talk, and if he registered my reply he gave no indication. A banker or investment advisor, I forget which, James hailed from London and took a perverse pleasure in dressing as though he could only afford to frequent second hand shops. Being taller than most and favouring trousers that expose his sockless ankles added to the effect; dressing down, he calls it. A shaven head gives him the appearance of a Buddhist monk or at times like this, in the fading light, a cancer sufferer after chemo.

James nodded in the direction of the small group of people sitting on banquettes on the far side of the fountain. 'Usual suspects, usual topics. Lena's house is finished. Bridie has a new Moroccan boyfriend. Matt seems to have hooked up with Sandra; won't last of course. Mad Mario's gone native and Pascal is having a fight with the bureaucracy over his building permission, something about having used modern bricks. All pretty ho-hum, eh?'

The only two I knew were Matt and Sandra, though Mario was easy enough to spot. He had to be the only westerner wearing a *djellaba*. His beard would need a few more days to be convincing.

There were a couple of Moroccans present but apart from one snappily dressed man with a proprietorial arm around an elderly woman, they were carrying trays of savoury snacks.

'Come on, into the fray,' James grunted and shepherded me forward. 'Bridie, do you know Richard, he's from your neck of the woods.'

'Know of, but never met,' the woman chirped. 'You're Irish Richard then. I'm from Dublin and this is Si Mohammed from Marrakech.'

'Hi,' Si Mohammed said. He took his arm from around Bridie and shook my hand.

No heart touching in these circles, I noted. 'I'm pleased to meet you.' A pleasant looking fellow, young enough to have been her son, but I guess desire for immigration papers makes for odd bedfellows. No, that was uncharitable of me. It may well be love, what the hell would I know?

'Don't you just adore what Angela has done with the house,' Bridie said. 'She is so clever.'

'It is certainly beautiful,' I agreed, wondering just how much Angela had actually done herself. 'You have a house?'

'Off Derb el Hora. Not on this scale of course but I have an architect who thinks he can create five bedrooms with *en suites* and he has wonderful ideas for the terrace. Of course, we are having the usual battles with builders and plumbers.'

My sympathetic nod was well received and to my astonishment she winked as though we were somehow co-conspirators. She then began what was obviously a well-rehearsed litany of her woes.

'It all depends on how you treat them. Silly me, I was far too soft in the beginning and so they tried to take me for a ride. I explained very clearly that I was not a walking cash machine but they simply got slower and slower. The plumber was the worst; an absolute thief. Can you believe that they think we are so stupid that we don't know the price of things? And why order ten metres of pipe when a job needs only two? Because they are going to sell it or use it on another house, I wouldn't be surprised. What is it with plumbers, anyway? Anyway, to make things worse, Malcolm came around and pointed out that the builder was using second grade cedar when I had specifically ordered and paid for first quality. You know Malcolm, of course?'

I nodded. Everyone knew Malcolm. He was an American who had been living in the Medina for years, long before it became trendy. As *the* expert on Islamic architecture he was much in demand as an advisor and his sage advice was treated with respect; the gospel according to Malcolm. Even Sandra Masters, while also being an acknowledged expert, always deferred to Malcolm, although I suspect there was a trace of jealousy present when she did so. In one respect Malcolm and I were kindred spirits in that he detested social functions and so his not being amongst the "usual suspects" was normal.

'Well, Malcolm also suggested I needed an overseer whom I trusted and so *voila* Si Mohammed, my knight in shining armour!'

Si Mohammed looked at the ground between his feet. Either he was remarkably shy or, more probably, he sensed that I knew where he intended his knighthood to take him.

James leaned forward to join the conversation. 'And what do you do, Mohammed, other than rescue maidens in distress?'

Si Mohammed either didn't register the icy tone or chose to ignore the jibe. 'My brother has a shop in Bordeaux. I find merchandise for him and arrange all the freight and customs details.'

'That's interesting. A regular treasure trove in Marrakech, an Aladdin's cave eh?'

'Not anymore. All the best stuff is gone. The French have recolonised the city and bought everything there is; at least everything of any value. That's why I'm in Fez.'

'What kind of things?' I asked. I had visions of my beautiful doors ending up in a shipping container headed for France.

'Antiques mainly, but some pottery, oh and carpets of course.'

'Of course,' James nodded, clearly bored. 'Carpets; there are certainly plenty of those in Fez.'

'But not the best place to buy...' Si Mohammed said and launched into a description of the Berber villages that he favoured and where, so he claimed, he had entire families weaving away all winter just to fulfil his orders. The wisdom of the local is a powerful magnet and soon most of the group had gathered around Mohammed, keen to glean the best tips, right from the horse's mouth. The stink of cultural plunder was in the air and so I slipped out of the admirers' circle and perched on the edge of the fountain, letting the tinkling sound of the water wash over me. Darkness had fallen and high above me the clouds that I had seen massing appeared to have vanished, for the stars were out—bright and unusually sharp.

Sitting there, trailing my fingers in the cool water, I felt for a moment totally at peace for the first time since being back in Fez. Even though the party was at the shrill laughter and guffawing stage and the smell of *kif* was drifting across the courtyard, I was content. Like a storm when the wind drops, or a single shaft of sunlight on an otherwise rainy day, it wasn't to last.

'You're an odd one.'

Sandra sat down beside me, a glass in one hand, bottle of champagne in the other.

'I am?'

'You haven't been round.'

'I've been busy...' I shrugged. 'A house is a tough mistress.'

Sandra laughed and leaning across me filled my glass, brushing my chest with her arm. 'And you would know about those, I suppose?'

Her perfume was part floral, part chemical and disturbing. 'Not my area of expertise, I'm afraid.'

As she straightened up she pierced me with her eyes. 'And what *is* your area of expertise Richard, exactly?'

'Butterflies,' I said and immediately regretted it. However, instead of the snide remark that I anticipated, she looked at me long and hard then raised her glass to me.

'You're serious, aren't you?'

'Serious? I was, a long time ago.' I sipped the drink, giving myself time to extricate myself from the downward path into self-revelation. 'I studied Lepidoptera, but I've really left that part of my life behind.'

'Ah, a refugee from butterflies!'

I allowed myself a smile at the accuracy of her remark. Flippant, but unwittingly accurate, I thought. From over the courtyard walls wafted the sound of the local muezzin calling the faithful.

'The call to gin and tonic, huh?' she quipped and seeing my frown, distanced herself. 'Sorry, Matt's joke.'

'Oh, Matt—'

'Not what they think, by the way.'

'What? You've lost me.'

'We are not—what's the phrase—an item?'

'Oh really? I thought that...'

'You know this place, my darling, rumours built on rumours, just to justify their petty little existence. Matt has an investment in people believing that we are... you know.'

No, I didn't know and had no interest in whatever game was being played. 'Whatever, Sandra, I'm not one for judging.'

'Trust me.' She leaned against me and sighed. 'There is nothing to judge. If I was interested in any man here it wouldn't be Matt.' Then she straightened up and flashed me a smile. 'However, I do like butterflies.'

Time to make an exit, I thought, as my contentment switched to depression, but couldn't see a way of doing it gracefully. Thankfully, just at that moment a rather drunken Matt lurched over to us.

'Few more weeks and it will be warm enough to skinny dip in the fountain!' He sat down next to Sandra and flung his arm around her.

'Now, that would be the way to spice up a boring party. Of course the bloody locals wouldn't approve.'

'Excuse me,' I said and made my escape.

Instead of going home, I did a quick check of the sky. It was changing rapidly; the stars of a few minutes ago were now being given a curtain call by clouds that threatened a storm before morning. Still time, I decided and headed up the hill, past the Tazi Palace to Place Batha.

A beer in the Hotel Batha felt like the right thing to do, but after climbing the stairs to the rectangular courtyard beside the pool, I was dismayed to see every table occupied by German and Spanish tourists. From the pool came the squeals and splashes of children. It sounded as if it was long past their bedtime. Why couldn't their parents control them, or (better still) have chosen the Canary Islands or Cape Verde? Executing an about turn, I made my way down the stairs, figuring on getting a late-night glass of mint tea at the Café Firdaous, an idea that lasted until I exited the hotel and saw that across the road in the café the chairs were already being stacked and carted inside for the night. Frustrated and with a growing weariness I plunged back into the Medina.

'The Medina is closed, Monsieur,' said a voice from the shadows.

'I live here,' I responded automatically, and then laughed, because, despite my depression, my tiredness and the state of the house to which I was heading—it was true. I lived here and the bittersweet taste of it was the most tangible thing I knew. This sprawling, chaotic city was my home and my tenuous grip on it was not about to be pried away by expats, tourist or voices from the shadows.

'You are going the wrong way,' the voice called after me.

'Hopefully,' I replied

This is not a city for everyone. The claustrophobia it can induce in some is suddenly palpable to me in this moment. Around me the windowless walls, broken only by an occasional spear of light through a mesh of rusted latticework, rose to merge into a darkness that is unbroken by moon or starlight. A cat—a streak of fur and sinew—speeds past me. From behind me I hear the sound of a door closing, the click of a lock and the thud of a bolt being slammed into place. Further on I am startled by a muffled cry from behind a wall. I pause, but the sound is not repeated.

Moving on, I turn an unfamiliar corner and find myself going down a narrowing and increasingly steep street. The cobbled surface is broken every few paces by broad stone steps, worn smooth and slippery over the years. Unwilling to risk a broken ankle, I slow down and make my way cautiously towards the next corner, where mercifully there is a lamp set high in the wall. The street signs are in indecipherable Arabic and so I choose the middle path.

Oddly, my anxiety dissipates as the first heavy drops of rain reach me. From the distance comes the oddly Celtic sound of a low-whistle. I stop and listen to long notes soughing like the wind. It has the air of a tune stolen from a Saharan zephyr, strained through the teeth of the mountains and momentarily enthralled in the man's whistle. Then the music is released back into the ether to continue its journey, subtly altered and enriched; as I was. The night was no longer unfriendly but embracing.

This is *the* adventure, I mused as I plunged deeper and deeper down dark alleys and around unexpected corners, some lit, but most not. Trailing my fingers along the walls beside me I could feel the textures change from stone to stucco to plaster and back again; an architectural Braille that I took pleasure in reading.

From somewhere there was a drumming, which at first, I was convinced was the blood in my temples, but it grew louder until it resolved itself into the rhythmic beating of a craftsperson working late into the night. As the rain increased, the cobbles under my feet became slippery and I slowed down, even more aware that within the last few minutes I had been sailing close to the outer limits of contentment. The diagnosis doctor? *You are totally lost.* I found myself laughing in a faceless unlit street that, at least for that moment, I shared with no one.

But I was wrong.

The laughter that echoed back was not my own. It was a moment of what the Greeks would call *parakrousis*—a slightly discordant note in an otherwise pleasant harmony. Yet it was a welcome discord for the laughter was that of a man in the shadows, who, when he slipped back the hood of his *djellaba*, turned out to be Fidel. It was Yazami.

'*As-salaamu 'aleikum! Labas?*'

'And you too, Yazami. Yes, I am very *labas*.'

'*Al-Humdullilah*. I had a feeling you would come this way.'

'Why?'

'Because all lost people take this path.'

'Ah! Smart.'

'Indeed,' Yazami grinned.

'I think you are far cleverer than you pretend to be.'

Yazami looked at me slyly. 'That, Mr Richard, is because my mother was mixed; half *djinn* half human and I am a somewhat lesser a fraction of either. Which is why I keep the company of strangers, poets and Irishmen.' He gestured down an alley to our right. 'We go this way.'

He took my hand and I allowed it. For a few minutes we walked in silence and eventually arrived at my door.

There was another man there, standing, waiting. Beneath the man's black hood I caught the flash of his smile.

'See! Hell is empty and all the devils are here! Well, at least one devil in particular,' Yazami grinned. 'This is Mernisi. He is a hard man to find, more difficult to catch and impossible to pin down. I have hunted a long time to find him.'

It sounded like a pursuit of a rare butterfly.

A'isha: Sinking in contentment

He is here with me but he has company. There are other men here now, none of whom interest me and I must wait. This Richard however, his man-flesh smell excites me, so for the moment I am content.

Does he know that I will have him? It is of little import, for I always get my way and the pleasure is in the fine detail of how I will seduce him, how I will destroy him—utterly. He will imagine he is eating from the hand of an angel.

I will sink beneath the waters and bide my time. Time is something I have plenty of. Waiting builds my appetite.

Richard: The onset of deconstruction

Mernisi entered the house, tossed back his hood and stood peering into the blackness.

'Sorry,' I mumbled and brushed past him to the edge of the wall fountain where I kept my stash of candles and tea-lights. 'I don't have electricity...' I located my box of matches and, as the darkness divided itself into light and shadows, turned to Yazami, propped up at the courtyard entrance, watching both of us with equal amusement. 'Does he speak English?'

'No. He hardly speaks anything.'

'Then what's the point of bringing him?'

Yazami shrugged and taking one of my candles, used it to light several more, which he placed around the corners of the courtyard. With the illumination improved, Mernisi produced a small hammer from beneath his *djellaba* and began to move around the space, knocking on the walls, listening to the sound as if expecting some reply. Without hesitation or even asking my permission he reversed the hammer and using the small blade began to attack one of the walls, chipping away larger and larger sections of plaster until he had revealed the stone and brick work beneath. Then he stopped, picked up a candle and began to climb the broken stairs. He was a big man and yet he moved with surprising grace, bending beneath one broken beam and then, after testing a foothold, kicking some loose rubble away and continuing upwards until the light had sealed itself behind him. All that could be seen were occasional huge shadows against the walls on the second level. By the noise and the showers of dust and the odd lump of debris I could tell that there too he was removing more plaster.

'His family comes from the Rif.' Yazami had taken up position, squatting on the floor, his back against the side of the wall fountain. 'But he has lived in Fez for most of his life.'

'What does he do?' I asked, 'Other than damage people's walls?'

'He mends broken houses.'

'You mean he's a builder?'

Yazami snorted. 'Calling him that would not be wise.'

'Right, so what should I call him?'

'Mernisi.'

It was clear that Yazami had been smoking a bit too much *kif* and I decided I was going to get little sense out of him. So, I sat on the edge of the fountain and waited as Mernisi from the Rif descended the stairs—his black robe in a halo of candlelight and dust—architecture's avenging angel.

'*Enta hmuk bezzef,*' Mernisi grinned.

'He says I'm crazy,' Yazami interpreted with relish.

'Because?'

Yazami just laughed as if I had said something hysterically funny. Then, suddenly sober, he looked me in the eye. 'He will cost you a thousand dirhams each week.'

'And for that I get... what?'

'You get your house unbroken, *inshallah*... and you get me.'

'You?'

Yazami looked down at the *zellij* tiles. 'I am only asking ten per cent.'

'Is that normal?'

Now he looked up. 'Of course not, there is nothing normal about employing Mernisi.'

'I meant about employing you. What exactly is it you do?'

'I make sure that Mernisi turns up.'

'And that's all?'

'My friend, that is a lot.'

I had many more questions, but Mernisi, who had wandered off, reappeared from the kitchen and began a heated exchange with Yazami who eventually turned to me with a rather sheepish expression.

'Have you any henna?'

It was my turn to laugh. 'Naturally. Does he need it to keep the *djnun* at bay?'

For an instant Yazami looked as if I had slapped him, then he hissed at me. 'You mustn't joke about such things, especially in front of Mernisi. What he is asking...'

Something in my expression must have alerted him because he stopped and squinted into my face.

'You really do have henna?'

'For the *djinniya*,' I said, mimicking Yusuf down in the souk.

That seemed to floor him. For what felt like the longest time he stared at me, his face a picture of incredulity. Finally, I shattered the moment by admitting that I had no idea of what to do with the henna.

On the other hand, Mernisi did not seem at all surprised that I should have a supply of henna. I didn't understand a word he said but the tone, as he sifted the small quantity through his fingers, was crystal clear; he was complimenting me on the quality. What happened next was as close to the truly bizarre as I think I have ever experienced—at least until that moment.

During the subsequent half hour, my house transformed from a poor ruin to something that belonged not in the realm of architecture but in fantasy; a location for occult practices. With the candles in each corner and the two *djellaba*-robed figures floating across the tiles, I would not have been astonished if one of them had produced a chicken, sacrificed it and drawn a pentangle on the floor with its blood. Had I been a cultural anthropologist I may well have found it utterly fascinating, but this was a long way from any reference point available to me. The sight and sound of grown men muttering incantations and placing small amounts of henna in each of the corners, was absolutely arcane, the stuff of fantasy. An Anne Rice moment, I thought, or, lapsing into Eric's realm—a Buffy moment.

All the while, my rational brain vacillated between the notion that I was witnessing some ancient ritual that would have had even a seasoned ethno-anthropologist salivating and the conviction that this was a hoodoo-voodoo confidence trick that only the gullible would fall for. Had I agreed to pay this "Mernisi from the Rif" a thousand dirhams a week? For how many weeks? And the henna? Was that so some previously blonde genie could emerge from a lamp with Titian tresses? Yet, either because it was so late at night and I was too exhausted to object, or that it was genuinely interesting, I refrained from comment. At one point Mernisi vanished out of the house and Yazami remained, ignoring me, his attention on his *sebsi*, his *kif* pipe, which he packed and without even a glance at me, smoked. Having tapped it out, Yazami repacked the *sebsi* and handed it to me with a muttered "*Bismillah*".

By the time Mernisi materialised again (and it was *materialised* as he simply reappeared and carried on as if he had never left), I was *kiffed* to the eyeballs and happy to see him. He had returned with a bound bunch of twigs, a plastic bag full of milk and several ghastly pink plastic bowls; the kind of thing one might use to feed a moggie with no aesthetic sensibilities. The twigs, it transpired, were a broom and after having swept the floor, he filled the bowls with milk. Expecting a lot of cats, I nearly asked out loud, but managed to control myself.

A rush of happiness flooded through me as I looked at the relatively clean tiles. Here, in the small arc of candlelight was the beginning of a home. The blue was so deep you could drown in it—the white, the pearly opalescence of mother-of-pearl; radiant and coruscating with each flicker from the candles. It seemed to me that there was also a perfume, incense perhaps, but if there was I was incapable of finding its source. Thinking back, I seem to recall feeling that the air was heavy with the scent of damp mushrooms and that the weather had changed from soft to loud. Yet, I could be mistaken. In any case, it would not be an exaggeration to say that in that moment I began to like my house again. No, more than before—truly loved it. And Mernisi, whose smile appeared to encompass every muscle in his face, was indeed an angel. Fidel, too, Yazami, if you will; he was my brother.

Somehow, I must have excused myself and gone to lie down or maybe they eventually completed their work and left, for my next conscious memory is of the muezzin's early morning call to prayer and the admonition from the nearby minaret that it was far "better to pray than sleep". In reality sleep would have been preferable to waking and finding (as I once did as a child) that the jigsaw, so beautifully completed the evening before, was in pieces again. The previous night's beauty had vanished, the *zellij*, no longer translucent, but chipped and dirty, the entire floor covered in plaster dust and grit. Something had even disturbed the small bowls of henna and milk; their contents now contributed to the ungodly mess. It had rained in the night and the mixture of henna and milk was like a child's smudged attempt at a henna tattoo and not a colour I would recommend for your hair.

Wandering to the middle of my little courtyard I looked up into a gunmetal grey sky. No consolation there, I pouted. Don't be so negative, I replied. The conversation with myself then degenerated into a childish, am/not/am cycle until a positive thought interjected. At least it kept the *djnun* away. What was the hoary old joke? Rub this blue powder on the floor and it will keep your home free of elephants. Something like that. The proof being that... well, can you see any elephants? I appear to have regressed during the night or else I was enjoying the lingering effects of the excellent *kif*.

Around eight o'clock I was preparing to venture out to the café for breakfast when someone pounding on my door startled me. I opened it to find a beaming Mernisi accompanied by three scruffy individuals carrying sacks on their backs.

'*As-salaamu 'aleikum,*' Mernisi said, shaking my hand and then touching his heart.

'*W'aleikum salaam,*' I replied.

'Mustapha!' Mernisi snapped and the oldest of his three companions, a man in his early seventies, dutifully stepped forward. His face looked as if it had been sculpted from leather and old leather at that. He was short, hardly up to my shoulders and yet his grip belied both his size and age. As Mustapha pumped my hand he nearly crushed my fingers.

His mumbled greeting was accompanied by an attempt at a smile, an action rendered grotesque by a lack of teeth. The man's astonishingly blue eyes held mine and after touching his heart he fished a set of dentures from the pocket of his grubby shirt and popped them in his mouth. There was a moment of chewing and then, once his grin was fixed in place, he bowed his head. '*Bonjour Patron.*'

Mernisi then pushed the next man forward. He was a tall skinny individual of about thirty (though he could have been younger) and slightly stooped, which may well have been an unconscious compensation for his height. Getting through a lot of the extremely low doors in Fez must have been a problem. However old he was, he looked to have packed a lot of hard living in those years. His sun-baked face was hard and lined like crazed terracotta.

'Ahmed Ali,' Mernisi announced.

There was more hand shaking and heart touching but the man didn't utter a word and kept his gaze fixed on the ground at his feet.

The first two men stepped aside and I saw that the last member of Mernisi's gang was just a boy of eight or maybe ten.

'Si Mohamed,' Mernisi said and cuffed the boy on the ear.

'Simo,' the boy protested, shooting a glance at Mernisi as he took and held my hand.

'*Wakha*, Simo,' Mernisi responded.

'*As-salaamu 'aleikum, ya sidi, wa barakallahu fik, bezzef, Sidi,*' the boy recited as if he had been tutored and was nervous about getting it wrong. He glanced at Mernisi for approval and was rewarded with a curt nod of approval.

'*Bravo, khoya,*' Mustapha said.

Then, without another word to me, Mernisi pushed the door wide and lead the way inside.

Entering the courtyard, the men and the boy placed their bags down and turned to look at Mernisi. If you are looking for inscrutable, then forget Moroccans. The look on all three faces needed little translation. It was obvious that Mernisi had downplayed the state of the house and, confronted with it for the first time, the men were wondering what they had signed up to. Mernisi ignored them, feigning indifference. In a slow but theatrical gesture, he held his hands out, palms upward in supplication and intoned, '*Bismillah er Rahman er Rahim.*' That seemed to satisfy the others, for they relaxed, moved forward and started unpacking. It was not what I had expected. No, that is not correct, for I had been expecting nothing. Indeed, my intention had been to collar Yazami and call the whole thing off. The notion that I, unasked, was going to pay Mernisi a thousand dirhams a week was ludicrous. Not that it was in my terms a huge amount of money, but rather that I was unsure that this was how I wanted to proceed. Yet, there was something about the quiet confidence of Mernisi that caused me to postpone the decision until I had discussed it with Mister Ten Per Cent—Fidel Yazami.

Within minutes Mernisi had the two older men cleaning up rubble and Simo dispatched to fetch something. Then he gestured to me that I should move away from the wall fountain. Its continually running water was a real worry and so I decided that if he could restore it then I would be satisfied and Mernisi dispensed with while I pondered my future. However, repairing the plumbing was not on Mernisi's agenda. To my surprise, he removed his socks and shoes and, squatting beside the fountain, proceeded to wash his feet, followed by his face and hands. Next came the prayer mat, which I assumed was unrolled towards Mecca. For some reason, I felt in equal measure intrigued and embarrassed, unsure of the protocol, as it was the first time I had been in the presence of a Muslim at prayer and not sure if I should avert my eyes. For his part Mernisi was oblivious to my discomfort and the other men carried on their chatting. This is normal, I told myself. This is what happens here, so get used to it. So, I sat and watched as he alternated between standing and kneeling—many times. He prayed in silence, his hands repeating a number of gestures that clearly indicated supplication and submission. It looked a lot more complicated than a few Hail Marys.

When he was done, he rolled up the mat, put on his footwear and sat himself next to me on the edge of the wall fountain. He seemed in no hurry to commence work. I thought that maybe he had sent Simo to get some tools, but when the boy returned it was with a small gas burner, a pot, packets of sugar and tea and a large bunch of fresh mint.

Mernisi inspected the mint and, satisfied, called out, 'Mustapha! Aji! Atei!'

Mustapha washed his hands in the fountain again, picked up the packet of tea and with a chuckle thrust it at me while pointing to the trademark, a small violin. '*Voila! Grand Patron! Le petite viol! C'est le premier!*'

'Great,' I said with what little enthusiasm I could muster. 'Grand'.

'Mustapha is the *Malam* of tea. The tea master,' said a voice from the doorway.

It was Yazami, who looked as if he hadn't slept, or if he had it had been in the streets amongst the stray cats.

'I'm glad you've turned up...' I began but he was already passed me, greeting the men with handshakes, cheek kissing and a shower of *salaams, labases, kulchi bekhirs* and *humdullilahs.*

Having done, he turned to me and put out his hand. 'Simo will need twenty-six dirhams.'

'Look, hang on. We need to discuss all this and besides I haven't even had breakfast yet,' I was doing my best to keep control of my rising unease.

'*M'kench mushkil!* No problem. Give him thirty and he can get some *mlawi* or *b'ghrir.*'

The first sounded like a country in Africa and the second a communicable disease—not at all what I wanted. 'No, I need coffee.'

Yazami looked crestfallen. 'But you can have Mustapha's tea.'

'Listen, I don't want tea, I don't want people in my house and most of all I don't want to pay a thousand dirhams a fucking week to have people drink tea and pray.'

If I expected my outburst to set him back I had sadly underestimated my powers. All it evoked in Yazami was a quizzical glance and then a rapid-fire conversation with Mustapha, who nodded and stopped his tea preparation to go and collect one of the ridiculous little plastic cat bowls. The two men conferred over it and then turned to me with nods of satisfaction. 'Problem solved!' Yazami said.

'It is? Well, that's news to me.'

'Only one thing can explain it. This.' He held the bowl out for me to examine.

'It's a bowl,' I snapped.

'Yes, but the henna is gone, spilt all over the floor. She has rejected our offering. So naturally you will not feel very happy. But we will make stronger offerings, ones she can't resist and then she will make you happy, *inshallah*.'

There were a lot of things I could have said, maybe should have said, but all of them contained words I am at pains to normally avoid, so I glared at him for a second then turned on my heel and went out for coffee and something that would hopefully resemble a French croissant.

With hindsight, I would have been better to stay. It would have saved the life of two chickens and kept a lot of blood off my tiles.

A'isha: A difference of blood

I smelt it. From deep down in the dampness where I slept came the sweet scent of blood. Not the purest essence that is that of the humans, but an offering nevertheless and I rose up to bathe in it. The blood was everywhere and I moved upwards in the dusk through the sweet perfumed stickiness with the pleasure coursing through me like a river of tingling desire, drawn by the offering, for such it was. The slaughter had been carried out by another, I am certain, for a Nazarene would not have chosen fowl of different colours, one black, one red? How could he know how to draw signs that I alone could read? No matter. If it had been his work then how did this Nasrani know what to do? It was a mystery but not one I cared to ponder at that moment. The courtyard was damp with fresh blood; the bodies of the birds tossed aside for me to inspect.

Inside this house the Nazarene sleeps and I will reward him—but not yet. Tonight I will enjoy the blood, allowing its nourishment to feed me, to pleasure me, while I ponder how to take this man and wring him dry. First he will love me and then he will serve me. He will call my name again and again as he cuts himself for me. Oh yes, he will bleed. From his scalp the red rivers will run and he will offer me his face to lick and kiss. I can almost taste the offering on my face, on my mouth, lips... tongue. The thought is exquisite and for a moment I clasp my breasts to still the trembling pulse of desire. He, however, will tremble with fear even as he begs me to accept his blood and lead him through the cities of the restless dead.

Richard: Dismemberment and acquittal

There is no exact moment that I can pinpoint when the decision was made to go ahead with the restoration and repair. The capitulation to Yazami and his plans was more of an evolution. The man's enthusiasm was infectious and yet it was not this that influenced me; it was his unswerving belief in our friendship. Born out of nothing, he simply abided in its possibility until it became a reality. In the end we had no discussion about restoring the house—we just began it.

I suspect that there was a deep loneliness in Yazami that found some solace with me. With the exception of Mernisi and Mustapha, Yazami's relationship with his fellow countrymen was cordial, almost business-like, but not once did I see anything much deeper.

The one time I asked him about his other friendships he appeared to drift off into an internal conversation, nodding as he did, then turned his face to me, his fingers twirling the end of his beard.

'Have you walked through the streets at night and heard the city breathing? It does, you know, and beneath the breathing is a heartbeat that has not ceased in more than a thousand years. That is what I live for, a conversation that has gone on for centuries and which I am trying to translate because I am no longer sure what language it speaks.' His face tilted as he checked to see if I was following. Then he gestured towards the street in front of the café. 'All the chatter is a distraction. It is fear. The old families have left the city for Rabat and Casablanca, and those who have moved in from the countryside are too busy surviving to listen to what the city is trying to say to them. If I ever discover what it is I will tell them, but until then I just walk and listen.'

His words struck me as indescribably sad and yet I wanted more.

'Fear, you said people have fear?'

'Deep down, yes, because they see only the street in front of them and that leads to another and another, but always around and never out. They struggle and end up where they began, huddled in their windowless houses in the blue glow of the television. And what is it the satellite beams down to them? Not a dream they can emulate, but a cruel display of a world that is beyond them.' Yazami straightened his back, his eyes suddenly burning. 'You know the cruellest irony? For a majority of these people to find themselves in Paris or London would be a nightmare. My people are not the educated who can slip into polite society. A man I grew up with married an English woman and went to Manchester. It was not a happy experience. Here, he had his brothers, sisters and cousins. There he had nothing. His wife worked all day and did not cook, the sun never shone and each night after his wife came home he would go out in a van to large office blocks and spend the night with a vacuum cleaner and cleaning cloth.'

'What happened to him?'

A frown washed over his face and he sounded perplexed. 'I don't know. He couldn't write and so the news was second hand. The world is a difficult place...' he shrugged, '... I suppose he died.'

For the next few weeks, as the summer rolled towards us, I adopted a strategy to protect myself from dust, noise and the general insanity that swirled around inside my house. As soon as I had let Mernisi and his band of wreckers in to begin the day's mayhem I escaped to my café on the edge of the Medina for a long slow breakfast. After breakfast, I would sometimes catch a taxi up to Batha and have a mint tea at the Café Firdaous or wander the Tala'a Kebira before going to lunch at a little hole-in-the-wall restaurant around the corner from the Bab Bou Jeloud, up the top of the Tala'a Sghira. An engaging fellow by the name of Tuhami ran it and although not understanding a word of English, always kissed my cheek and called me *khoya*—brother. Then it was home for a sleep.

Yazami, having observed the fact that I was far more reasonable after food than before it, also adapted and never once arrived with the workers but timed his appearances to coincide with my purchase of a second glass of coffee at the café in R'cif. There was something comforting in our inexplicable but deepening friendship and I began to believe that my conscious move away from the expatriates in

81

favour of attempting to build friendships with the Moroccans was a good thing.

Together we would sit in silence, watching the passers-by and then after about an hour would meander back into the Medina.

'Shall we check progress back at Aqabt el-Firane?'

It soon became clear that my interpretation of the word "progress" differed from his. The higher the amount of rubble, the thicker the clouds of dust, the happier he was. For my part I longed for it to be all over and for any sort of calm to descend. There seemed no imminent prospect of that occurring, so I bit my tongue and simply nodded with feigned satisfaction at each new assault on the ancient structure.

The latest attack had come in the form of a Moroccan Tom and Jerry act—Ahmed and Driss; apparently electricians, although to date they had done nothing but gouge a spider web of tracks over every surface. The elderly Mustapha appeared convinced they were top artisans, referring to both of them (in French) as "the professors of sparks". For his part Mernisi just laughed and, using Yazami as a translator, informed me that everything would be fine and that *Allah* existed inside electricity.

Operating on a less metaphysical level, Ahmed and Driss ordered a huge number of rolls of orange conduit and continued their high-level attacks on my walls.

'The wires will live inside and Ahmed will pull them through while Driss coats them with soap,' Yazami explained when I asked him about the conduit that snaked around the courtyard before vanishing up the now repaired stairs.

'Live wires?' I had already pointed out that there appeared to be no power cables leading into the house.

Yazami didn't pick my tone or meaning. 'Of course,' he replied. 'You must have electricity.'

'Why?' I was becoming quite attached to my candles, tea lights and most recent purchase, an antique silver oil lamp from Syria (or so the salesman had sworn). 'Why do I have to have electricity?'

'Because the ancient Medina in your head does not exist; in the real world we have electricity. How can you offer me a cool drink in summer if you have no refrigerator?'

'Will it be ready by summer?'

'*Inshallah.*'

Inshallah? From my perspective it appeared that summer had been knocking on the door for several weeks.

Late one evening I was sweeping a piece of floor on which to lay a newly acquired single mattress when there was a knock at the door. For a moment I considered ignoring it. Most times my visitors were neighbours with improbable stories.

'My mother is ill and needs money for medicine.'

'What is her problem?'

'Illness.'

'I have some medicine for stomachs and headaches. Will that do?' This would always elicit a crestfallen face. 'No, she needs money.'

Or some urchin would wipe away a miraculously manifested tear to tell me that his family could not cook food because they had no gas.

At first I gave in but soon realised that I was responsible for an exponential increase in the Medina's quotient of sickly mothers and gasless households, so I stopped altogether. Over time the begging had decreased to an acceptable level. On this occasion I did answer the door. It was Yazami.

We exchanged greetings and then he stepped aside to reveal his companion. It was the crazy young man, Thami, with his peculiar mannerisms and scissored gait. A palsy of some description, I guessed as I dredged back through my limited supply of knowledge about it. Cerebral palsy caused by bacterial meningitis or viral encephalitis. Yes, that could be it—or a knock on the head. Did it make you dribble? There were cuts on his head as if he had walked through a glass door.

'We have come to pay you a visit,' Yazami smiled. 'Thami has never been to your house and I told him you would be very happy to see him.'

'What happened to him?'

'His face?'

'Yes, Yazami, his face.'

'Ah, an accident.'

They followed me down the stairs and into the courtyard where Driss and Ahmed had installed a single bulb, until such time as the wires were in the conduit piping that snaked around my walls and I officially had electricity. In the light of the naked bulb I saw that despite the "accident" Thami was as neatly dressed as ever, neat but not exactly stylish. The red trousers only needed flares to make them suitable for an Abba revival and the black tunic top was pure Bollywood. There was something different about him, something that had changed since I had last seen him in the café. Then, as Thami shuffled towards the wall fountain I realised that it was his hair. God knows there had been little enough of it, but now it was completely gone, shaved right down to the skull and badly so, if the scratches and scars were anything to go by.

Yazami smiled at me. 'A hair cut too. Quite smart, no?'

No, Yazami, "smart" was not the word I would have used. But I didn't say anything. The sooner I got the rituals out of the way the sooner they would be gone.

'Thami, atei?'

'Iyeh! Atei benna'na,' Thami replied and grinned dopily at me. I am not sure what I was most surprised at; Thami speaking so clearly or my understanding. For all my enjoyment of being in a linguistic no-man's-land, I was picking up a word or two. Despite my protestations, Mustapha had taken to calling out the name in *Darija* of every object he came across as well as the essential words connected with making tea.

'You want mint tea as well?' I asked Yazami, but he was already heading to what passed for my kitchen to retrieve the gas burner and kettle. Without consulting me he took the broom, the bound together twigs I had been sweeping with and cleaned a space for us to sit. Or more exactly, he swept a pile of dust from the floor into the air and invited me to sit in its midst.

Once the kettle was filled and heating, Yazami lead Thami over to a pile of old *zellij* tiles and set him to polishing them with a damp cloth. This appeared to make him very happy for he smiled and chuckled to himself as he went about his work.

'He seems to be getting on okay,' I observed as we squatted around the small stove.

Yazami poked two fingers deep into his *djellaba* and extracted his *sebsi*. 'He has had an acquittal.'

'A what?'

'An acquittal. He has repaid the Lady.'

'Who?'

'I can't say.'

Frowning he turned his attention to rolling the *kif* between his fingers and then packing the pipe. 'But yes, he is much better.'

'What is an acquittal?'

'A treatment.'

Uncharacteristically his lapse back into silence annoyed me and for once I regretted having invited them in. But then I remembered that I had in fact not done so, they had simply come in once the door was open.

'Let me tell you a story that I am working on for a play. It is about acquittal.'

'A play?'

The pipe was now in his mouth, so he nodded, pulled a stalk from the broom and poked it into the gas flame until it caught. Then having lit the pipe, he inhaled deeply. 'I have the pleasure and pain of being drawn by *Allah* to write for the theatre like my beloved friend, Shakespeare. Such a curse is not to be wished on a dog, for there is no producer of theatre in Fez who will accept my plays. I am seen as a little crazy.'

'You write Arabic drama?'

'*La.* No, my wonderful Nazarene, I write in *Darija*.'

'I thought it wasn't a written language.'

'Humph! Tell that to the young pups with mobile phones. They manage very well, even those who know little of the language of the Holy Qur'an. No, they text in *Darija* and I write it for the theatre in my mind.' He prepared the pipe again while I fetched my supply of fresh mint that I had rescued from Mustapha earlier in the day.

'Let me tell you about Sanhaji, my hero. Sidi Ali Sanhaji was a *dacoit*, a bandit, who was much feared as he had killed ninety-nine people. Now at the same time... This was many years ago, *fhemti?* Understand?'

I nodded and took the pipe.

'At the same time, there was a man in the hills below Djebel Zerhoun, a shepherd named Ighud, who was chasing after a young girl called Bouchra who was incredibly beautiful, but who was virtuous and had wisely refused him saying that he stank of goats. This incensed Ighud who swore by the *shayatin*—the devils—that he would possess her—dead or alive. The poor virgin was taken ill and shortly after she died and was buried on the hillside above her village.'

As the water had come to the boil, Yazami gestured for me to fetch the sugar while he tossed in some gunpowdertea, pulled the mint to pieces and fed it into the pot. Once I had tossed in the required seven large blocks of sugar and had it heating again he continued.

'By the grace of *Allah* it happened that on that very night Ali Sanhaji was walking in the hills and saw Ighud go to the girl's tomb. Ali Sanhaji hid himself behind a lone olive tree and watched. To his horror, he saw the man digging the soil off the grave and then taking the poor dead virgin from her resting place and laying her on the grass. Worse was to follow. The man ripped the shroud from her body leaving her naked beneath the stars. He then released his own clothing and prepared himself to penetrate her.'

This was not the moment to start fussing with tea and glasses, so I leaned over and turned the gas off. While he had been talking, Yazami had repacked the pipe and once again handed it to me. Although uncertain I wanted to be too stoned with the images of the grave robber in my brain, I took it. Suppressing my paranoia, I took a tentative puff and handed it back to Yazami who rolled his eyes in mock derision at my timidity before finishing the pipe and continuing his story.

'At that moment a miracle occurred. As Ighud lowered himself down onto Bouchra's body the dead girl raised her arm and placed it across her breasts. Ighud, frightened and angry, leaped back, grabbed his sword and with one mighty blow sliced off the dead girl's arm. Again he tried to enter her but her remaining arm again protected her and this too he cut from her body. Satisfied that Bouchra could no longer resist him, he dropped the sword and prepared to enter her. However, as he fell on her Bouchra's legs crossed and closed as tight as a shellfish at low tide. The way was blocked. This threw Ighud into a rage and swearing loudly he proceeded to hack the poor girl's bloodless limbs from her body.'

'Jaysus!' I reached for the pipe and inhaled deeply as Yazami, his gaze fixed on the floor, continued.

'The sight of the man cutting the defenceless girl's legs from her torso so offended Sidi Ali Sanhaji that he cried out to *Allah*, exclaiming that he would now kill his one hundredth victim. He swore it would be his last and begged the Most Merciful that this "righteous" death would atone for the other ninety-nine. As he reached for his sword he heard a voice saying to him. "So be it, Ali Sanhaji, acquit yourself and become the Father of Acquittals." So, Ali leaped from his hiding place and with a huge blow removed the man's head, which he then kicked far down the hillside. Tugging and pulling Ighud's body he dragged him to the hill's edge and threw it into a deep ravine for the beasts and ghouls to feed on. Having done, he carefully placed the dead girl's limbs back in the correct places and wrapped her securely in her shroud. After burying her and repairing the grave he took a twig from the olive tree and pushed it into the soft soil at the head of the tomb. As he did, he prayed out loud. "*Allah, Allah,* show me that you accept my vow that I will never kill again by making this small twig spring to life." With that he fell asleep beside the grave and when he awoke at the time of the first call to prayer he found the twig was now a small and healthy olive tree.'

Yazami paused and glanced at me to judge my reaction. Horrified and entranced, I nodded at him to continue.

'Little remains to tell, except that from that day on Ali Sanhaji has been known as the Father of Acquittals and spent the rest of his life wandering from village to village spreading the message of the glorious Holy Qur'an.'

It was an amazing story but as a play I felt that the dismemberment of a naked actress on stage might pose a few theatrical problems. 'And you have written this already?'

'*Iyeh.* Several times, but I can't find anyone crazy enough to stage it.'

There was nothing I could say, no advice, no solace, so after fetching the glasses I poured the tea in the manner that Mustapha had shown me; first filling a glass and then returning it to the kettle before raising the kettle high above the glasses and pouring all three in one fluid movement. Fluid was the appropriate word as the transition from one glass to the next splashed sweet tea all over the tiles.

'Careful!' Yazami snapped, 'She doesn't like hot water.'

'She?'

'*Her*,' he said, dropping his voice to a hoarse whisper and nodding in the direction of the wall-fountain. 'It's not wise to say her name aloud. People get scared.'

Getting rather unsteadily to my feet I took a glass of tea to Thami, who was still applying himself single-mindedly to the task of tile polishing.

'*Shukran bezzef, Sidi*,' he mumbled taking the glass and slurping noisily.

Returning to sit beside Yazami I found he had kicked off his old yellow slippers and was lying back, staring up through the small opening to the sky. After a time, he started to speak, but his voice was faint and I realised he was praying. Then, propping himself up on his elbow he raised his half-empty tea glass and squinted through it examining me for a moment, his eye a clouded golden orb. He's very stoned, I thought, and held my glass to my eye in the same manner.

'Cyclops,' Yazami laughed and drained his glass. 'You know, *Sidi Nazrani*, I may have reached the peak of my career as a playwright. Maybe I should consider retiring?'

'The peak?' How many plays have you written?'

'Twelve, eight in prose and the remainder in verse.'

'And produced? How many have been performed?'

He laughed dryly. 'All of them... in the theatre of my skull.'

'Your head,' I interjected.

'In my mind. None on any stage built by man and yet this is no failure.'

'It's not?'

Yazami placed his glass carefully on the tiles and sat up, clasping his knees and resting his chin on them. 'This is no failure because my love for theatre is the love of the...' His face screwed in concentration, '...what is that magnificent English word?'

'What word?' I laughed suddenly feeling more than a little light headed.

'Ephemer...aaal.'

His elongated final syllable was wrong, but I knew what he meant.

'Theatre is ephemer...aal. That is what I love. The theatre is dark and dirty then the company moves in and for a few brief nights the space comes to life, transformed by magic. Each evening the alchemy of the performance is different and then one night it is gone. Once again the theatre is just an empty shell, gutted of life, noise, lights and culture.' He uncurled, stretched out his legs and lay back again. 'What I have done is cut out the middlemen. My plays never undergo the torture of rehearsal or dismemberment by the critics. They lie, undisturbed...'

'Like Bouchra,' I offered.

'*La!* No! She was a virgin. My plays are whores that I share around on nights like this.'

'I am honoured.'

'Don't be! I share them only with the worthless. My audience are the poor and the hungry who have nothing to chew on but my tales. Not for me our elite French-speaking bourgeoisie who crowd to the gallery openings and festivals simply to be seen, to be photographed on each other's cell-phones and who come away untouched and unaware of the art that was laid before them.' He spat and reached for the soiled yellow *babouche* that he had kicked off. 'My limousine is made of leather and now I must board it.'

After Yazami and Thami departed I wandered around the courtyard with a jug and splashed some fresh water on the *zellij* in order to get rid of the stickiness left by my inexpert tea pouring. I used cold water. It was all nonsense of course but at that moment it seemed best not to offend "her". Then I slept, but not peacefully.

All night I was haunted by the images of Ighud with his sword hacking at limbs, but not those of the hapless Bouchra. Neither was it the dry gullies of Djebel Zerhoun with its olive trees, but the treacherous, steep, muddy slopes of the cloud forest. My old nightmares had returned and for a terrifyingly long time I stood in a sea of blood surrounded by the body parts of those whose deaths had haunted me since that last trip to Peru. Twelve corpses; a number to match Yazami's plays and yet unlike his story I saw no possibility of acquittal, redemption or even simple release. Rachel used to swear that I screamed in my sleep and I suspect she was right, for something woke me well before dawn and it was not the call to prayer.

A'isha: A question of identity

This Richard is changing. But the change is superficial. He is not who he says he is. His blood is tainted. Yet he begins to play my game. He calls me "her" as he does not know my name. He plays with henna and water like a child.

What should he call me? My name? Many names I have consumed. And who truly knows me, but my victims? An evil spirit? A cannibal water djinniya? A sister of Astarte? Some say I am the Sidi Shamharush's daughter. But the king of the djnun is no father to me. Some say my mother was human and my father Ighud, the shepherd of the winds and storms. Such nonsense. I am She and I am everywhere. I am in the mountains, in the lakes. I stalk the towns, the banks of the Sebu river, the trickling Oued Serrafine and the smallest fountains. And I never leave.

Richard: Going to the mountain

Indolence is seductive. The road to indolence, I discovered is paved with *kif*. This was no bad thing, as with the onset of summer the heat was sapping and life far more pleasurable stretched out on a banquette in the cool of a small salon. It was Mustapha who decided that I needed at least one room free of workman and Mernisi who decided that workmen needed to be free of the constant supervision of the *"grand patron"*. Thus motivated, the work moved apace and in a remarkably short time the small ground floor salon opposite the wall fountain was wired, plastered and (at huge expense) two ancient cedar doors were purchased and installed. The doors were even more impressive than my memory of the original ones that had been stolen; three metres high with each encompassing a smaller keyhole door that could be opened independently. It occurred to me that my new doors may well have been stolen from some other house, but I banished the thought as soon as it surfaced.

The credit for the interior decoration of the salon must go to Yazami, who, also convinced of the need to quarantine me, organised two banquettes, a riot of cushions, a very low round Berber table he called a *taifor* and an electric fan that proved a real boon, especially when I took to sleeping through the long hot afternoons. Yazami also suggested that together we purchased several old carpets.

A carpet buying expedition would have necessitated a trip outside of Fez; something I hadn't done since arriving. When Yazami first proposed it I was reluctant, preferring to stay in the shade of my one near perfect room. However, Yazami was nothing if not persuasive.

'You will meet the Beni M'Gid.'

'Is that a good thing?'

'They are the Imazighen, the Berbers who founded Azrou.'

'Which is where?'

'It is where we are going.'

I pushed myself up from the banquette and opened one of the small keyhole doors and peered out. Hearing the door or sensing my presence Mustapha and Mernisi turned, greeted me with a wave and resumed their task of cleaning the fountain. They were immensely proud of the retiling work all of which was done with the old *zellij* that Thami, over a number of weeks, had cleaned so meticulously. Now the fountain sported a new spout, recycled the water from its basin and best of all, tinkled delightfully in the still of the night. My concerns that it splashed a fair amount of water onto the area of tiles around the front of the fountain had been dismissed because "*She* likes the water". I couldn't argue with that, so every couple of days I dutifully topped up the water level and ignored the slippery *zellij* at my feet.

Stepping through the door I threaded my way through the piles of timber, around the bags of lime and sand to the centre of the courtyard and squinted up. *Allah* had turned on the light at full beam and the heat hit my skin like a splash of acid.

'Too hot,' I told Yazami as I scuttled back to the shelter of the salon.

'We are not going today. We go on Tuesday.'

'Ah... and that would be, why?'

Yazami paused in packing his *sebsi*, rolled his eyes and examined me with an expression that rested between amusement and resignation. 'You really have to get out more. The Tuesday Souk is on Tuesday and so we shall go then. You will enjoy.' Seeing my lack of enthusiasm, he handed me the pipe. 'And we shall investigate the joys of *majoun*.'

'Which is?'

'*Majoun* is the sweetest hashish in the world.'

I grinned and filled my lungs with the *kif*. 'Yazami, I think I am probably smoking more than enough already.'

'Then you shall try it in coffee.'

There was probably a rebuttal I could have made but it hardly seemed worth the effort so I lay back and asked when Tuesday was.

'Tomorrow, but this afternoon we will make a smaller excursion.'

'Fine then, we will make an excursion.'

'To a mountain.'

'Ah, now you are being annoyingly mysterious,' I laughed.

'My brother, all will be revealed later, *inshallah*.'

'*Inshallah*,' I mumbled. 'But right now, I think I will sleep for a while.'

When I was roused by the afternoon call to prayer I emerged to find all the workers except Thami had knocked off in order to go home or to the mosque. Thami was still hard at work on his latest task, sifting sand in preparation for the soft-golden coloured plaster that was to soon (hopefully) grace the walls of the courtyard. The plasterer, a highly-strung and rather testy perfectionist with passable English, had lectured me on the necessity of taking the walls back to their ancient colour. 'Not white,' he insisted. 'That is too modern.' His method was to stir the sand into buckets of water so that the finest particles remained in colloidal suspension and imparted their colour to the plaster mix. 'It is the colour of Fez,' he announced as he showed me a small section of wall he had rendered in order to demonstrate the colour. It was splendid so I gave him the go ahead. 'You will need to get a lot of sand sieved,' he warned. Thami, having completed his work cleaning *zellij,* was happy to comply

There was something appealing about Thami's innocent enjoyment that was captivating. Despite the heat he had covered his immaculate red and black outfit with a loosely fitting chartreuse green *djellaba* and was perched on a pile of sand bags while he sifted the course sand through a circular sieve. Although he hardly spoke—and when he did it was usually an incomprehensible mumble—I enjoyed his company and I sensed the feeling was mutual. Whatever his mental problems they didn't include a lack of concentration. As the fine-as-flour pile of sand in front of him grew he would simply add another bag to his seat until he was in danger of unbalancing.

I walked over to where he was sitting, squatted beside him and watched the conical sand mountain with its tiny avalanches trickling down its side with each new sieve full. The bottom half of a giant hourglass, I thought and one that has failed to indicate that it was time to stop.

'Enough, Thami,' I said. Of course he didn't understand. There was a word somewhere in my head but for the moment it wouldn't come to me. I tried "*Shukran*", but the thank you only encouraged him to greater efforts. He began to mumble. I didn't understand the words but there was intensity to them and I could discern a repetition. Whatever it was he was saying it over and over like a mantra. The growing ferocity of his chanting transmitted itself to his sieving as he dipped and sieved, dipped and sieved, casting the remaining larger grains and small pebbles into the pile behind him, the tailings mountain which would be used for mixing the rougher mortar for the still unprepared walls in the second-floor rooms.

It was then that something extraordinary happened. His voice changed from the slurred upper-register, the almost boyish quality—to which I had become accustomed—and dropped to a masculine rumble that arose from deep inside him. I could make out what he was saying; not the meaning, but the words.

Hahiya jat! Hahiya jat! Hahiya jat! Lalla 'A'isha. Hahiya jat! Hahiya jat! Hahiya jat! Lalla 'A'isha.

Each syllable was spat out with equal doses of clarity and ferocity that became a crescendo. At the height of the chant he began to hit his head with the edge of the wooden sieve with such force that the blood flowed down his face. Alarmed, I got to my feet and reached forward to intercede but at that moment the bags on which he sat toppled forward, propelling him face up into the mountain of sand. If it had been anyone else the moment would have been less disturbing; even comical. But I wasn't laughing.

The man who struggled free of the pile of sand looked like a crazed, unfinished sculpture. The sand on his bald head and adhering in streaks to his face where the blood had flowed seconds before, gave the appearance of a stone ghost. He still chanted but now the deep masculine voice was gone and again replaced by his boyish whisper.

'Hahiya jat Hahiya jat Hahiya jat Lalla 'A'isha.'

He stopped and looked up at me with the wide, startled eyes of a child. *'Sidi* Richard?' It was the first time I had heard him utter my name. The tears started to flow, eroding the sand and blood; the tiny rivulets trickling down his face. I took him by the hand and lead him to the kitchen where I fetched a cloth and dabbed the sand from his face. All this I did one-handed as he wouldn't release me. At one point I tried to push him back slightly so I could inspect his wounds, but he grabbed my shirt and clung to me like a child with his mother. *'Safi,'* I said remembering the *Darija* word I had been unable to recall previously. '*Safi*. Enough. Come, I will walk you back to your home.' He couldn't have comprehended my words, but as I helped him out of his stained *djellaba* and brushed down his black shirt and red pants, he appeared to understand, taking my hand and leading me to the door.

Outside, it became clear that my hand was not going to be relinquished and as I had no idea where he lived, I found myself in the peculiar situation of being tugged through the streets in the wake of a man the locals all deemed totally *hmuk*.

The speed with which he walked surprised me until I figured out that it was probably his best defence against being picked on by those Fassis who didn't consider him the holder of vast stores of *baraka*.

He headed unerringly down the quickest route to the R'cif souk where we turned left beside the *hanut* that sold milk and sweet cakes, past the vegetable stalls, piled high with figs, preserved lemons and rose petals. Then it was on by the small mosque and the blood-stained cobbles of the meat stores with the live chickens, camel heads and the carcasses of sheep and cattle, until we came to the fork where the fishmongers had just tidied away the last of their produce, much to the disappointment of dozens of bedraggled cats.

Without breaking his stride or slowing down for the late afternoon crowds, Thami took the right fork crossing the Steps of a Thousand Thieves to the Alley of the Knife Sharpeners and on to Place Seffarine. Here he slowed, staying close, the grip of his hand tightening around mine. He doesn't like this place, I thought, wondering what had happened to him here. Again, we turned right and I was plunged into the unknown. The narrow alley was new to me though I made a point of noting the copper and tin workers with their displays of knick-knacks and rolls of bright copper. Then it was left through a short dark tunnel where a house spanned the alley. In the shadows, a huddle of men were arguing over sheep and goat hides; skin traders who, lacking a shop, conducted their business squatting in the streets. One of them recognised Thami and grunted a greeting but Thami did not respond, continuing on, eyes down, dodging the donkey droppings and pulling me out of the way of an overloaded mule, piled high with copper sheets. Then, just as the smell in the air gave me an indication of where we were—nearing the tanneries, which I had read about but never visited—Thami stopped, released my hand and without a word of farewell, turned right and descended a narrow flight of steps. Having come this far I decided I wanted to know where he lived and so after letting him get twenty or so paces ahead, I followed. The steps twisted once left and then the alley narrowed further, but thankfully levelled out. As I rounded the corner I thought I had lost Thami, but then I saw him only a few feet away. Fortunately, there was another alley leading off to the right and I slipped into the shadows and watched. The door he knocked on would once have been a traditional wooden one with the five fingered metal hinges in the form of a "Hand of Fatima" but at some time in the last few years the family had probably needed the money and the door had been sold and replaced with an ugly, grey painted, iron one.

Several seconds passed before the door was swung inwards. In the shadows I could see a woman in a loose shift, her long hair was un-braided and uncovered, red slippers on her feet. She obviously had no intention of showing herself on the street as the flimsy yellow skirt was hitched up, held by a sash at her waist. But then she saw the state of Thami's face and her hand flew to her mouth.

'*Ay ay ay!*' she wailed and bounding up the steps and out the door, wrapped him in her arms. For a fleeting moment her head nestled next to Thami's face, her chin on his shoulder as she whispered to him. In that moment, as she held him, I had a clear view of her. There is no language I can employ to adequately describe either her face or its impact on me. She was indescribably beautiful. In the soft light of late afternoon, her cinnamon skin glowed like burnished gold. Her hair was the colour of night. Then she sensed my presence and held my gaze, her eyes narrowing. In a slow, dignified movement she straightened up and placing her arm around Thami's shoulder, shepherded him inside and closed the door without a backward glance.

For a long time I stood there; stunned. Beauty is not supposed to be an assault, but I felt as though I had been slammed in the chest. Desperately trying to stem the rising wave of panic, I put my hand out and steadied myself against the alley wall. She was much taller than Thami. I noticed that. Black hair and eyes of deepest amber, like... Christ! I had only seen her for a few seconds. Eyes so sad... and then it came to me; Prosperine. A Moroccan Prosperine, straight from a Dante Gabriel Rossetti canvas. A shiver went down my spine. I was fantasising of course but the woman's face, the shadowed eyes, ringed poppy-purple, the point of the nose and chin, the long dark hair, they were pure pre-Raphaelite. How old was she, thirty-five, thirty-eight? *Oh for fuck's sake get a grip!* Apart from her age, she was off limits on all counts. Muslim, Moroccan and married. Prosperine had something in her hand, didn't she? In the painting, a fruit, open, inviting... It was a pomegranate. My mind spun off at a tangent as I visualised the pomegranate with its pink carnality, slit open, the seeds exposed. Then a dusty memory of my father explaining that the French word for pomegranate was the *grenade* in hand-grenade. Grenade; seeds the colour of blood. Shrapnel tearing flesh. I pushed off from the wall and climbed the steps and walked as fast and as far away as I could. *Keep ahead of it. Do not stop. None of this is real anyway. Keep going up the hill. Don't look back because there is nothing there.*

The mind is a strange organ. In all the confusion I knew that I could switch the dancer. She was no longer a spinning ballerina but a dervish whirling around in my right brain. All I needed to do was slow her, stop her and then spin her in the other direction; anticlockwise. Think rational thoughts. Think scientific. The heart is an organ. Blood is in my veins. The soul does not exist, despite what the Holy Ghost fathers taught me. The butterflies of the cloud forest... No, that is the wrong direction. Let her spin. Just walk. And so I did. I walked, breathing, recovering from the shrapnel, or so I thought until I realised you can't outrun a hand grenade.

I was sitting. Somehow, I had found a seat.

'*Mahia, khoya,*' said a voice, as a mug was placed in my hand.

The voice was that of Tuhami and *mahia,* firewater made from figs, distilled by Moroccan Jews; *eau de vie,* an antidote to shrapnel.

It was there, at Tuhami's street-food stall that Yazami found me. In front of me the plate of *kefta* had only been picked at but the chipped mug was empty.

'What have you done to yourself,' Yazami asked as he greeted Tuhami and slipped into the seat beside me.

'First I was hit by a pomegranate,' I snorted, 'then by a fuck of a lot of *mahia.*'

The expression on his face left me in no doubt that I was a mess.

'Coffee,' he said and catching Tuhami's eye mimed the act of drinking. The communication went wildly astray, as the next thing that arrived at the table was a second chipped mug of *mahia* for Yazami frowned, muttered *bismillah* and drained it in one hit.

Finally, a coffee arrived from the café on the opposite corner and we sat watching the constant stream of people, four or five deep, flowing up and down the Tala'a. Donkeys, *carossas,* porters stooped under bundles and carts or trays of delicacies weaved their way in and out creating little eddies that changed the flow. Every now and then boys would peel off from the mainstream and present us with their merchandise; oranges, coconuts and slices of seed cake or leather belts, shirts and even underwear. Tuhami called one boy over, handed him some coins and presented Yazami and I with *gazelle*; crescent shaped pastries filled with sweet almond-meal. They were delicious.

When two old men with a cartload of fruit with familiar, blotched-red birthmarks, rounded the corner, I decided it was time to leave. Seeing the direction of my gaze, Tuhami asked if he should buy some for me.

'No pomegranates,' I said and handed him a fifty-dirham note to pay for the food and coffee. To my surprise, I received thirty dirhams change.

'*Safi khoya*,' he grinned and whipped the mugs off the table and out of sight.

Beside me, Yazami, an evil smile on face, scrambled to his feet and tugged me after him.

'Why are we going this way?' I asked as we joined the crowds going in the direction of the Bab Bou Jeloud. Normally I would have gone down the Tala'a or across to Batha and caught a taxi outside the post office.

'You need a break from the Medina. It will be light for a few hours, but the weather is changing. It will rain, inshallah. It's time for our trip into the wild.'

Outside the Bab Bou Jeloud there was a heated argument going on between the people waiting for *petits taxis*. An older woman had ensconced herself in the back seat and was refusing to budge despite the fact the crowd were blocking her husband and daughter from joining her. The driver was out of his car and yelling at the crowd to back off. We decided to walk on and twenty or so paces later flagged down a taxi whose solitary passenger was happy to have us join him.

The journey from the gate into the Medina to the Ville Nouvelle only took ten minutes, but the transition from the mediaeval to the modern felt like a leap of several hundred years. Time travel in a *petit taxi*, I marvelled, was a trip in a Tardis from *djellabas* and donkeys to Paris fashions and Peugeots.

Checking that the driver and the front seat passenger were involved in their conversation Yazami found my hand, slipped something into it and whispered 'Its *majoun*, eat it slowly.'

Being only slightly but happily drunk, I followed his instructions, popping what felt like a small wad of chewing gum into my mouth. *Alice in Moroccoland*, I mused, one pill makes you larger... A hookah-smoking caterpillar... The nutty taste was somehow familiar; a melange of flavours, ginger, nutmeg, honey and possibly anise. I chewed slowly, making it last.

Finally, we stopped at a bus station, where Yazami bundled me aboard a decrepit looking vehicle. He gave me no indication of what he had planned, but rather, just sat grinning at me.

'Where?' I asked.

'There is a place in the mountains I want to show you,' was all he said.

We waited as the bus slowly filled up with passengers, while, outside, the weather had suddenly changed. A cold wind buffeted the bus and then, to my surprise, as Yazami had predicted, it started to rain and, for the first time in weeks, I started to feel cold.

I must have fallen asleep, for when I awoke we were stopped in a small town. Cold and shivering, we huddled over a lukewarm coffee in a mud-floored café. Then, exiting through a back door, Yazami hired a donkey.

For two hours we struggled up steep muddy paths, climbing higher and higher into the mountains, while around us as the light began to fail, the weather deteriorated, the mist descended and the snow and sleet began.

Then, suddenly, I was struck by a bout of fever that had me feeling weak and delirious.

'Shelter here for a moment,' Yazami said, pointing to a small stone building beside the track. I ducked under the low door and sat on the giant grinding wheel of an old olive press.

'I am going back down,' Yazami said.

'Where?' I asked.

'To the village. You need medicine. When you get your strength back,' Yazami continued, 'go up the hill to the ridge. My family house is there.'

He clambered onto the donkey and vanished into the mist.

After a time, I struggled out into the wind, rain and sleet.

How long it took to climb the hill, I had no idea, but eventually I saw a low-set mud-brick house perched on a barren ridge. I managed to get to the shelter of the house and knocked on a rough wooden door, but nobody answered.

Opening the door, I fell inside and collapsed onto a cold stone floor.

I must have passed out, for I had no idea of how long I lay there, before I felt a hand on my shoulder.

'Get up and come beside the fire.' The woman's voice was soft and soothing.

Although uncertain if she was a product of my delirium, I nodded and struggling to my feet, followed her to a room that was warm and welcoming. The floor was covered in carpets and in one corner a small fireplace, glowing and sparking, provided enough light for me to see the woman properly for the first time. She was middle-aged, a big woman, with a face creased by years of exposure to the elements yet blessed with a smile as warm as the fire.

'My name is Malika. Come, eat and drink,' she said, and dipping a spoon into a bowl she began feeding me as if I was a child.

After I had eaten she fetched a blanket and wrapping me in it, pulled me to her, nestling my head against her large breasts. It was comforting and soon I was lost in the warmth and sweet musty smell of her body.

For a while we just nestled there and then I realised Malika was talking to me, her voice not heard but felt. And this is what she said:

When Malika was born, there was a problem. Her mother died and the woman assisting in the birth ran from the room, leaving the window open. It was at that moment that the djnun entered and swapped the human baby for a child who was *nus-nus*—half *djinniya*, half human. It was the beginning of Malika's tragedy.

Growing up with her father and her older brother, Jilalli, Malika was a strange child who, in an attempt to fit in supressed the part of her that was not human. But, though she was always smiling, her father noticed that no cat would come near her and her brother complained that when she milked the goats, the taste was sour.

Later, when she was 12 years old, her father was struck by lightning and died. Her brother Jilalli was now in charge, but unhappy in a house that was cursed with so much sadness. When a local man came, asking for his sister as a bride, he refused. 'She is still too young,' he said.

One autumn, when the crops failed and their goats sickened, Jilalli decided they should leave the mountain, cross the sands and go to the coast, hoping that the bad luck would not follow.

In a coastal village, he found work on a small fishing boat, and for three years it seemed that he and Malika's fortune had changed. The fish were in good supply and he had no problem providing for himself and his sister.

One day he told Malika that, as she was now 15 years old, it was time she was married. But she was obstinate when the suitors came, sitting in an icy silence that was message enough to those who visited her.

Then one day Jilalli did not come home. Neither the boat, nor his companions were ever found.

The following month, the weather was fine and warm. Malika decided it was time to go back to the mountains, though she did not know the way. Packing a few provisions and a blanket, she set off.

For a week she walked, until she came to the sands. There the going was far harder and as she trudged on, she knew that unless the sands ended soon she would perish from lack of food and water.

One night, weak and thirsty, she came to a small oasis and lay on her blanket looking at the stars. In the dark, she heard the cough of a camel. Alarmed, she sat up and waited, hoping that it was a wild camel and not some savage man from beyond the dunes.

'The peace of God, be with you,' said a voice.

'And with you,' Malika mumbled, and watched as a tall man emerged from the darkness, leading a beautiful white camel. He was swathed in a black djellaba, his head wrapped in a blue turban. He held out a goatskin. 'Drink sister, I wish you no harm.'

'Thanks be to God,' she said and drank.

The man stood watching but made no move to sit or make camp for the night. Reaching into one of the bags on the camel he produced a small packet made from woven palm fronds. 'You have a long journey, sister. Here are five dates. They are very special dates. Eat only one each day and you will survive. And keep the goatskin. The water will be enough for you, God willing.'

'May God bless you,' Malika said. But the man said no more and turning, led his camel away into the sands.

The dates were indeed special and for the next couple of days she walked steadily, with neither hunger nor thirst. Then, on the third day, she saw the faint outline of the mountains rising up from the haze on the horizon.

The following day the mountains were clearly visible and as she passed the last of the dunes she found herself in a green oasis, where there was shade and the tinkling sound of a stream running over some rocks into a clear pool. There was no sign of houses or human activity in any direction, so she took off her clothes and bathed. Then, under a full moon, Malika laid her blanket down for the night and thanked God and the stranger who had helped her survive the sands. Feeling certain of her deliverance she ignored the stranger's advice and celebrated by eating the two remaining dates.

In the middle of the night Malika awoke to find a *djinn* crouching beside her. His dark eyes flashed and he was so close she could smell the aroma of cinnamon and jasmine on his skin. He reached out a hand, touched her face and then withdrew his hand abruptly.

'You are of the *djnun?*'

Malika shook her head. 'I am nobody. Please go and leave me in peace.'

'Little sister, all I want is a date to eat.'

'I have no dates,' she whispered.

'Then you will suffice,' said the *djinn* and began to stroke her.

Malika opened her mouth to scream, but no sound came out. She tried to struggle, but instead found herself relaxing into the *djinn's* increasingly fervent embrace. The *djinn*, in the form of a handsome young man, made love to her without uttering a word. Then, he rolled away and vanished up into the air.

For a long time Malika lay, until the first rays of dawn were painting the sky apricot. Then, after dressing, she rolled up her blanket and continued her journey. The faint fragrance of cinnamon and jasmine on her skin were proof enough that her night visitor had not been a dream. She also knew, without a trace of doubt, that she was pregnant. Under other circumstances she would have felt shame but her only thought was that God was great and that this was her fate.

When she passed through the nearest village to her home, she found only one old woman alive. Everyone else, the woman told her, had died from the smiling sickness some years before—all dead with smiles on their faces. Malika wished the woman long life and continued the steep climb up the mountain to the lonely house on the ridge.

When she arrived at the house, she found a man in his thirties living there. 'This is my house,' she told him. He didn't seem perturbed, but simply nodded and pointed to the small garden. 'Then you had better pick some carrots while I attend to the goats.' He then pointed to himself. 'I am called Hassan.'

For the next two months. Malika and Hassan lived together, each in a separate room. Then one night, he touched her stomach. 'We had best get married before the child arrives.' Malika nodded and the next day Hassan went to another village and found an Imam who, for two hundred dirhams, agreed to read the Qur'an over them.

Life went on as before, until Yazami was born and, for the very first time, this humble house was blessed with happiness.

The old woman's voice faded away and she spoke no more. For a few moments, I dozed and then fell deeply asleep.

At dawn, I awoke on a cold stone floor. Sometime in the night a woollen blanket had been laid over me and a rough pillow placed beneath my head. Yazami was lying snoring beside me. He was so close I could not only smell alcohol on his breath, but also a vague aroma of cinnamon and jasmine.

My fever had passed in the night and, feeling wide-awake and surprisingly refreshed, I shook Yazami until he woke.

'I'm sorry,' he mumbled, 'but I too was ill in the night and drank all the medicine.' He pointed to the empty vodka bottle on the floor.

'I met your mother, Malika,' I said. 'She was wonderful.'

Yazami shook his head. 'No, that is not possible, my mother died of the smiling sickness, twenty years ago. There is no one living here now.'

A'isha: Balancing accounts

The moment he stumbled in I could smell the cinnamon and jasmine of his infidelity. He had been entranced by another woman, some half djinniya; some abomination. There is no incense that can blot this out, no offering great enough to make me forgive his actions. This kafir has stumbled against the inevitable, the immovable stonewalls of eventuality; he has betrayed me.

The time for his torment is at hand for I will not share him.

The light from the candles guttering around the fountain scatters glittering golden sparkles onto the liquid surface. I will change that. Rose and saffron will be the scales on the water as the blood drops form underwater smoke rings. As his blood flows into the water, the richer the colour will become and the paler he will grow until he is as white as the snow on Ras Kharzouza and just as cold, inshallah.

Richard: The price of amber

After the short cool change, the full force of summer returned and baked the Medina. Then, as the Holy month of Ramadan arrived, the tempo of life changed. The tourist season tapered off but the long conga lines of funny hats, wide eyes and video cameras were still a regular sight. Consequently, the stallholders, hawkers and shopkeepers were in action later in the mornings and after closing for several hours in the heat of the day, open again after breaking their fast and remaining open, often until midnight.

'They will not buy from me,' Yusuf grumbled, pointing down the souk to where the regular flow had come to a halt to make way for a tour group trailing along behind a woman carrying what looked like a golf flag above her head.

'They don't know what they are missing out on,' I commiserated.

Since discovering that the Joyce scholar and spice vendor ground wonderful coffee, I had taken to visiting him on a regular basis. For just twenty-five dirhams he would sell me half a kilo of Arabica beans which he ground in an ancient machine held together with twisted wire coat hangers and packing tape. What made his coffee so different from the perfectly fine coffee in my café was the addition of spices. While the coffee was grinding, he would toss in sesame seeds, cinnamon bark, black peppercorns, a couple of ingredients that I didn't recognise and he couldn't tell me the English name for and then, finally, he would take a hammer and break up a nutmeg to add to the mix. The quantities were haphazard and so each week the flavour was delightfully different. Usually half a kilo would have lasted me a fair while, but such was Yusuf's local fame that at least once a day I would be required to make coffee for Mernisi, Mustapha and whoever else I was apparently employing. Often this would include the donkey driver who delivered the sand and lime and took away the bags of rubble and day labourers who came and went according to no schedule I could determine. Thankfully, Ramadan meant that no one was drinking anything; at least not during the day.

'Smile,' Yusuf mouthed at me.

Turning I found myself confronted by a semicircle of Japanese, some of whom had the lower part of their faces covered by white masks, the upper part by cameras.

'This happens a lot?'

Yusuf nodded and held up a small plastic bag. 'Couscous.'

'Cous-cous' came a chorused response from the tour party.

'See, I am training them,' he laughed. 'But they never buy. One day, *inshallah*.'

'*Inshallah*.'

We watched the group snake up the souk towards where I knew that the next photo-opportunity would be a camel's head hanging above the camel butcher's stall. One morning I had seen him preparing it for display and wondered if the Japanese would notice that the poor beast's eyes were made of glass.

'Why do they wear masks? They are like doctors on television.'

'Bird flu.' Then, seeing his squint of incomprehension I added, 'It's a disease. But I read somewhere that wearing a mask was an act of supreme courtesy. They are trying to protect you from their germs.'

'Ah, very noble.'

'Do you mind being gawked at?'

'Gawk-ed?'

'Stared at... and photographed.'

For a moment he paused, his face losing the smile as he sought something. 'Ah, now I remember. Joyce wrote, "my mouth is full of decayed teeth and my soul of decayed ambitions". My grandfather and my father both worked in the tanneries. All their lives they worked, freezing in winter, suffering the heat in summer. Compared to them I am in paradise. To be looked at is not such a hardship.' Then he laughed. 'It is looking at them that is the hardship.'

'Looking at the Japanese?'

'Not so much. The French trouble me more. I do not like the way they dress without respect, men and women, with naked arms and wearing underwear only.'

'You mean wearing shorts?'

'Such things we only see in the *hammam*.'

'The elderly Americans as well...' I started, thinking of the innumerable tedious variations on the basic beige safari suit I had seen. Maybe nobody had told them that the last lion in Morocco had been dead for almost a hundred years.

Yusuf shook his head. 'No, they are ignorant and do not understand but the French were here before and should know such things.'

He tapped the coffee grinder to make sure I had my full half-kilo. 'Oh, before I forget, my mother sends you her warm greeting.'

'She is well?'

'*Humdullilah.*'

'And her legs, any improvement?' Yusuf's mother was a tiny woman who, despite old age and crippling arthritis, still came down to the souk at least once a day in order to check on her "little boy" as she called Yusuf. On the occasions we had met she had always greeted me and although we couldn't communicate very well, I sensed she liked having me for a neighbour.

'Sadly, I must say no. But we are saving for medication. My mother's relatives in Bhalil gave her one of the carpets they made last winter and she wonders if you would be interested in it. Of course, it would not be at the tourist price.'

'Of course. Tell her I will be happy to look at it.'

Yusuf beamed. 'I will bring it around for you to inspect. The carpets of Bhalil are very traditional.'

We chatted for a couple more minutes before I bade him farewell and returned home. A carpet from Bhalil sounded good. I made a mental note to ask Yazami where the village was.

When I arrived home, I told Yazami about my encounter with Yusuf and his failed attempt to sell couscous to the Japanese tourists. He paused in packing his pipe and laughed.

'Maybe the Japanese know more than you think.'

'Meaning?'

'Couscous can be dangerous stuff.'

'Sure...'

'I'm not joking. It is very popular for poisonings.'

'Poisonings plural?' He made it sound like a national sport.

'Yes, a lot of Moroccan men are poisoned by their wives.'

'Why?'

'Usually they do it to get their hands on their husband's money or because they suspect him of being unfaithful. Sometimes he is poisoned by her relatives because his wife doesn't get pregnant. There are many reasons.'

Recently a tourist guide, so he said, had married a woman from the mountains and a year after the wedding he went to visit his in-laws and they were angry that their daughter was not yet pregnant. The grandmother-in-law had decided he was evil and impotent. She started poisoning him and when he tried to go back to Marrakech for treatment the family locked him up. It was only a text message from his mobile phone that eventually saved him. Then there was the story of Hadda the *'aguza*.

'An *'aguza* is an old woman, a witch, whom the *Imazighen* call "*haha*" women,' he explained. 'And Hadda's speciality was dead-hand couscous.'

'I've never seen that on a menu.' The look on Yazami's face killed off my smile.

'*Skout!* It is not something to laugh at.'

'Sorry.'

'Hadda was famous for her special couscous. Of course, she is not the only one who does it but her technique is unique. When a woman comes to her because her husband is sleeping with too many other women, Hadda swears the woman to secrecy and then late at night the two of them go to a graveyard and uncover a body in a fresh grave. Any other *'aguza* would scrape at the grave with the dead person's hand and take some dirt to mix with couscous, but Hadda knows a deeper magic. She cuts off the hands and, placing them one at a time between her legs, she circles the grave. Once that is done, she takes the woman home and helps her prepare couscous but with one important difference; it must only be tossed with the dead hands. Then, once it's cooked, it's presented to the husband on a silver platter.'

I had stopped laughing. 'What happens when he eats it?'

'He is cursed. He will never be happy and often he goes very yellow and loses weight. The couscous can also be given as a gift on Fridays to anyone you wish to curse. Their luck and health will desert them.'

Twice since I had been in my house neighbours had brought me couscous. Both times had been Fridays, but I had suffered no ill effects.

Yazami saw the look of consternation on my face and rolled his eyes as he lit his pipe. 'Do you know how the camel goes into the couscous?' he asked.

I shook my head.

'*Shwiya b' shwiya*, little by little!' Then he laughed so hard he nearly choked.

The carpet hunting expedition to Azrou had not taken place on the day after Yazami and I had visited his family home in the mountains, or indeed in the weeks that followed. Summer continued with a vengeance and while I still made my daily trek up the hill to the top of the Tala'a Sghira to Tuhami's for my evening meal, more and more I spent the best part of the day inside. Although a functioning kitchen now joined my one completed salon, I could not get it together to shop and cook. Most probably my lethargy was as a result of the heat but there were other factors at play such as the constant supply of pharmaceutical distractions; all the essential food groups—*kif, majoun* and *mahia*. Normally I am not given to over indulgence but normality no longer seemed part of the equation. For example, I have never been a big drinker but the soothing effects of the *kif*, the tasty dreaminess of the *majoun* simply cried out for the occasional rush of stimulation that came with the fiery liquor from the mountains. The variation in the quality of the *mahia* was extraordinary and I soon became expert enough to know when it had been made from figs or dates and when it was of more dubious provenance.

When I arrived back at the house I discovered that my new ceramic topped circular table and four chairs had been delivered. I was delighted, as I had ordered it from a man at Aïn-Zleten so long ago that I had given up hope of ever seeing it. However, as I stopped to admire it I was taken by the hand (literally) and lead up the stairs to the second floor where the entire work crew were standing outside the salon door.

'*Aji Sidi!*' Mernisi beckoned me forward and nudged me through the doors.

It was not only completed, but superbly so; the green *zellij* repaired and extended in a skirt around the walls to protect the plaster from over enthusiastic use of water whenever it was washed. Over the windows the new carved plaster, in great recessed scallops, looked as if it been there for centuries and above my head the cedar beams were stripped and glowing from a coat of linseed oil.

'*Safi?*' Mustapha asked.

I clapped him on the back. 'More than *safi*—more than enough. *Mezian bezzef!*'

'*Humdullilah.*'

There was another surprise awaiting me, but I was not to see it until after I emerged from my afternoon siesta. Thrilled with the progress on the house, I went to my salon, gave silent thanks to the electricians as I switched on the fan and lay down. Sleep came quickly and if I dreamt I have no recall of it.

A soft tapping on one of the keyhole doors woke me and I rolled over, groped for my watch and forcing my bleary eyes to focus, checked the time. It was half past three. '*Esbaa*, wait!' I had taken to sleeping nude and in my befuddled state I struggled into a t-shirt and pulled on my trousers.

'Sorry, Richard, take your time.' It was Yazami.

The moment I unlatched the door and pushed it open I knew he was up to something. He was dressed in traditional clothes—white *djellaba*, yellow *babouche,* his head wrapped in a golden turban—and had a grin like a mad mullah. 'You've been smoking too much,' I said.

'*La, Ya Sidi!* Not today, at least not yet. You are coming with me.'

'Where?'

'Please get a towel. We are going to the *hammam*.'

'The bath house?'

'Of course. We have time before.'

'Before what?'

'You and I have been invited to a *lila*.'

I yawned and rubbed my eyes. 'Good and when I wake up you can explain what that is and why I have to go to a bloody *hammam*.' My lack of enthusiasm appeared to be beyond his comprehension so I explained that only minutes before I had been deeply asleep and that before I committed to anything I needed coffee.

'*La!* You will have tea. *Aji khoya!*'

Knowing that it was useless to argue with Yazami and truly not wanting to disappoint him, I let his enthusiasm push me along. 'Okay, tea first, then you explain.'

Out in the courtyard I sat at my new table. It was, I had to admit, worth waiting for. The top was a mosaic of soft green *zellij* at the centre of which shone a sunflower-yellow star. I ran my hand over it, enjoying the texture, and the craftsmanship.

'Very fine,' Yazami said as he took a seat opposite. 'Tea is coming.'

'Ah, Mustapha the *malam* of tea is working his magic—'

'Mustapha and the others I sent home.'

'Oh really, why was that?'

'He is going to a wedding this evening and I didn't think you would want the others working without him.'

'But Mernisi...'

'Mernisi is in Tétouan, his brother is dead.'

'I am sorry.'

'There is no need. He died six years ago.'

It occurred to me that I was still asleep or maybe dozy. I was certainly missing something. 'Then why does Mernisi need to suddenly fly off to Tétouan?'

'A family matter. He must decide things for his mother and sister.'

'Then,' I said, leaning across my beautiful table, 'who is making the tea?'

'Mira.'

'Mira, right,' I said cautiously. 'And who exactly...' But before I could enquire further a woman carrying a silver tray with the teapot and glasses rose up the steps from my kitchen. At first I thought my mind had completely lost the plot. A woman in red slippers, a woman in a pale duck-egg blue *djellaba*, the hood thrown back, her long black hair exposed. She avoided my stare, keeping her eyes firmly down. It made no difference. I knew the colour of her eyes; deepest amber; my Moroccan pre-Raphaelite.

I think Yazami was introducing us. Her lips moved. I saw the tray being placed on the table. Her fingers, pale, long... I was drowning, fighting for breath. The tea was poured, the froth rising on the amber liquid. The teapot was back on the tray, her hand moved and like a blue shadow she slipped away, merging into the shadows of the house. It could not be real.

'Yazami?'

'Her name is Mira.'

'But why on earth? I mean how on earth?' I gripped the table in an attempt to stop the universe from spinning out of control.

'Richard, *Amira saqati!* It is only five hundred dirhams a week! You can afford her.'

I could do nothing to hide my shock. 'You employed her?'

He nodded, his face showing that he was now concerned that he had done something wrong, something he didn't understand.

'How did you find her?'

'Richard, listen. If you don't like her, then we can get someone else. She will clean the *dar* and wash your clothes. She will even cook if you like. And, of course she will keep an eye on Thami. She worries about him.'

Taking a deep breath, I tried to stop my mind spinning. 'Yazami listen, I saw her with him.'

'Naturally, Thami is her brother. She has looked after him all her life.'

'You know her well?' I asked.

'Of course I do.' Then he laughed. 'Oh *Allah! Allah!* I thought you knew. Brother, I swear I thought you knew.'

'Knew what? Oh, stop it Yazami, I'm sick of the riddles.'

'Thami is my younger brother—'

'Your brother? You and Thami...' I shook my head, trying to make sense of a world that was spinning out of control. 'And this woman...'

'Mira is my sister.'

'That's not possible...' I began, but of course it was.

'When my mother died, it was my duty to work. Times were even harder back then and I was very young. Mira was only eight but she knew the path *Allah* had laid out for her and she set her feet on it and never once in all these years has she complained.'

'She never married?'

'Richard, it was not possible. Everyone knew she would never give up caring for Thami and no man would take on that burden. When he was a child he was very troubled, not able to walk or talk at first. Slowly, over a very long time, Mira has worked with him, refusing to believe that she could not make him better. He will never be like you or I, but you see the miracle she has worked. Now he walks and talks and though he does very simple work, it is something, *humdullilah.*'

'Do you live with them?'

Yazami shook his head and slurped noisily on his tea. 'Our family house is small and I am paid to look after a house for a foreigner.'

He went on to explain that he had been close to some German woman who bought the house but never returned. Married now, I think he said, but my mind was off on another tangent, trying to imagine Mira giving up everything to look after her younger brother. Now I understood how it was that Thami was so neatly dressed each day, why his hair was always cut, his hands so clean. What sort of life was that, alone all day in the house, cooking and cleaning for the two of them? Surely, she had friends at least, other women who visited and kept her company? It seemed so cruel. A life with no expectation other than death and so little in each day to sustain her would be a recipe for depression and bitterness. Haunted by an empty future, was that better than being chased by demons from the past, I wondered?

'We should go,' Yazami said as the call to prayer from the nearest mosque reverberated around the courtyard. 'Oh, tonight is music. Okay?'

'Sure, but what should I do about... the woman?' I didn't feel right saying her name.

'I can send her away—'

'No!' I said a little too forcefully. 'I mean, of course she can work here if she wants.'

He laid his hand on mine. 'Thank you. Five hundred dirhams will make such a difference to her.'

But I was not concerned with the money but about the prospect of having this woman in my house. I was shaking; splinters of beauty, or nightmares, of longing, cut me, shredding my grip on reality.

'I have given her my key,' Yazami said, 'until I get another cut.'

'What I meant to say was how does she feel about being in the house with a man and a foreigner at that?'

'It is a job, Richard, simply a job. There is no shame in that.'

'If you are sure...'

'I am sure. Now...' he fished out a brown paper parcel from under the table. 'This is for you. Please put them on and then we must go.'

Inside the parcel were a simple cream *djellaba* and a pair of yellow Moroccan slippers.

'I'm going native?' I laughed.

'Slowly, I think. But for tonight it is necessary that you become *shahbi*.'

'*Shahbi?*'

'One of the people.'

One of whose people, I thought, his... hers? The universe refused to settle beneath me. Through the floor, up from the depths I imagined I could hear the grinding of the tectonic plates, shifting, protesting, and moving.

It was dusk as we strolled down the hill, Yazami humming happily away to himself while I tried to juggle competing thoughts; part of me trying to hide the self-consciousness I felt at being dressed in a *djellaba* and *babouche*, the other part of me wanting to return home and simply stand in the kitchen and... It was idiocy, of course. Now that I knew the woman's name and that she was Yazami and Thami's sister, I felt somehow guilty for having harboured such craving. I kicked myself for not recognising the bond between Yazami and Thami. Still, the complexities of Moroccan family bonds were far beyond my comprehension and so I excused myself. I had never questioned why Thami had turned up at my house with Yazami and yet in the café Yazami had always been protective towards Thami.

Yet, all this chatter in my mind was camouflage. What troubled me was none of these things. Her beauty devastated me. Seeing her again had been as disturbing—no that is too light a word—as destructive of my reason as that first encounter. To have her in my house, always there... it was impossible. And yet, and yet... I could not summon the strength or courage to say no. This woman, this creature, would be invited in. An assassin, a killer, she, who would wreck my stability, my peace of mind, I would open the door for her. I would invite her inside and put the knife in her hand. *Here, take it, destroy me.*

My mind took evasive action. It flipped back to the way I was attired. The notion that I might run into other expats was terrifying and I imagined the derision that Sandra, Matt or most of the others would express; not directly of course, but behind my back. Why do I care, I thought, but knew I was fooling myself.

Our first stop was at the R'cif souk where I became the owner of a yellow plastic bucket and scoop as well as a scrubbing-mitt and a single serving sachet of shampoo. Then it was across the road and into the steep winding alleys of the Andalusian Quarter. Although this was unfamiliar territory I relaxed in the knowledge that it was also far away from the areas where a majority of the expats lived. The extraordinary thing about being dressed as a Moroccan was that absolutely nobody took any notice of me and far from being an obvious outsider (the way I felt), I had become invisible. It was liberating and I happily followed Yazami's hooded figure as he took us deeper and deeper into the maze.

The smell of cedar smoke announced our destination—a wood-fired *hammam*—long before we turned the final corner. Local knowledge was imperative because like so many of the *hammams* that had been pointed out to me, this one had no sign outside the narrow door and I would have walked straight by had Yazami not stopped me with a hand on my arm and guided me down the steps.

After stripping to our underwear Yazami handed our clothes and a few coins to an elderly attendant who grunted and indicated we could proceed. As we entered the next room the heat hit me, but it was the atmosphere and architecture that commanded my attention, transporting me back through the centuries. Lit only with oil lamps, the room glowed like a moist grotto, each flickering light surrounded by a small halo of steam. Towering some four metres above us in the gloom the arched roof of rough plaster, blackened with age, had three circular openings to allow ventilation. Surrounding us the walls were tiled to head height with green *zellij*, much of it in need of repair. The floor was bare concrete, shiny and wet.

Only three other men were present and after glancing at us they called out a greeting and resumed their quiet conversation. Stripped of the anonymity the *djellaba* had afforded me in the street, I was acutely aware of the colour of my skin, yet the fact that I was white and obviously foreign didn't even rate a raised eyebrow.

'Come. Give me your bucket. I'll get the water, while you bring us two stools,' Yazami said and handing me the scoops, scrubbing gloves and shampoo, took the buckets and ducking under the wooden lintel of a low doorway, vanished into the dark. Five or six stools were stacked in a small niche and I fetched two and placing one beneath me, lowered myself down. It was a long way. The hand-made wooden stools were extremely small, awkwardly so, and I felt decidedly exposed, sitting, inches from the floor; a shag on a rock, had been my father's expression.

Yazami returned and placing the buckets to one side, positioned his stool directly behind me and donning one of the gloves, wet my back and producing a packet of a dark brown substance that looked like industrial waste or axel-grease, proceeded to smear it all over me.

'*Sabon beldi,*' he explained before I had time to ask, 'it's a soap made from olives. It is very good for your skin.'

I had to take his word for it. Then he scrubbed me. Or, to be more precise, began to remove layers of my skin that peeled off in the most horrid-looking little black rolls. At first it was as though he was taking out some deep frustration on me, and instead of re-laxation I felt agitated and alarmed at his force, but gradually the atmosphere and heat did its work and I relaxed.

But just as I succumbed to the scrubbing, Yazami laughed quietly, tossed the rough mitt to one side and said something to the other men. There was a grunted response and a tall muscular chap came over and with no word of warning pushed me to the floor where he began to massage me—if massage is the correct word. Between bouts of pummelling he manipulated my limbs, pulling and twisting my arms and legs into no shape intended by anyone's God.

Through it all, Yazami squatted beside me and told me that the man, Abdulla, was considered one of the best in Fez.

'You should be honoured. This he is doing as a gift because he understands where you are going tonight. It will help you enjoy the music.'

'If I get out alive,' I gasped, 'there's a United Nation's convention against this kind of thing,'

Despite the yawning gap between my idea of a massage and what substituted for it here, when we departed forty minutes later I had the weirdest sensation of floating; my body totally relaxed. Dressed again in the *djellaba*, I was now ready for anything, or so I thought as I draped my towel over my wet hair and followed Yazami back along the streets towards R'cif.

Over the years I have had the ability to be totally wrong about my preparedness for any eventuality. My track record in that regard was not, I discovered later, in danger of being broken.

After crossing the road at R'cif we looped back to my house and left our *hammam* paraphernalia inside the door. Then we were off again. Yazami's unerring instinct for direction was uncanny and not once did I see him glance up, around or check a landmark. In a matter of minutes we were beyond the lanes and alleys I knew and weaving our way upwards. Emerging into a vaguely familiar street I had a feeling that maybe we were in Qettanine near the Dar Aqiba guest house but then we turned hard left through a tunnel towards Guerniz. At this point I gave up trying to locate myself on my mental map and followed Yazami.

Five minutes later Yazami came to an abrupt halt, rapped on a door and then stepped back and turned to me. 'You are ready for this?'

We were in the narrowest alley, hardly wider than my shoulders. On either side the walls leaned in dangerously. A portent of future collapses, I thought. Obviously nobody of any clout in the community lived here, for it must have been decades since any work had been done in the area. Beneath my feet the cobbles were broken, uneven and at times loose. It was too dark to see but I guessed that the soft bits were donkey droppings, although in such a confined space it must have been a particularly skinny donkey.

'I have no idea what *this* is,' I replied as I steadied myself against the rough stone wall, catching my breath.

'Good, then keep it that way. You are very lucky to be invited.'

Invited to what, by whom? I wondered. But I said nothing.

'Here, this will help.' Yazami handed me a small lump of *majoun*. 'The people you will meet are members of a Hamadcha brotherhood.'

'I don't understand what that is.'

'The Hamadcha are an ancient Sufi brotherhood and play very special music; a ceremony not a performance. You are not to talk to your foreign friends about what is going to happen. Can you remember that?'

'I am hardly likely to do...' I began, but before I had a chance to protest that I considered few of the expat community as "friends", the opening of a door opening interrupted me and a small boy leaned out and beckoned us to come inside.

After traversing a low and very narrow passage, we emerged into a large courtyard and I was struck, not for the first time, by the wondrous mysteries that lie behind the anonymous doors of Fez. Little or no ostentation is displayed outside and so the interior is always a surprise. You can be greeted with everything ranging from extravagant opulence to abject poverty and squalor, from cramped and overcrowded chaos, to splendid cool spacious gardens with fountains and huge citrus trees.

The *riad*—you could have fitted my *dar* into the courtyard with room to spare—had four large trees and a central fountain, but little display of wealth beyond its sheer size. At one end of the courtyard a group of twenty or so Moroccan men and women were seated on carpets, sipping tea and chatting quietly. Beyond the fountain, which was not only working but lit from under the water, several more carpets were laid out and on the farthest one a group of musicians were sitting, smoking and preparing their instruments.

Seeing our arrival, a corpulent individual at the centre of the group lowered his instrument—a lute of some kind I guessed—hauled himself to his feet and strode over to greet us. He was relatively short but built like an ox. His round face, set with sparkling brown eyes, sported a neatly trimmed moustache, the downturn of which gave him a vaguely lugubrious look. After a rapid fire exchange of pleasantries, ritual kissing, handshaking and heart touching, Yazami turned to me.

'Richard this is the Hamadcha *muqaddim*, Abderrahim.'

Before I had a chance to respond the man grasped my hand and pumped it hard and addressed me in English. His voice, French accent and broad smile swept over me, a tsunami of enthusiastic welcome that had me wondering what he wanted from me.

'It is a pleasure, Mister Richard, I have heard much about you.'

'Thank—'

'Tonight, you are my special guest and we...' His broad gesture appeared to encompass the entire courtyard and possibly beyond, 'We are honoured, very honoured. All of us have been anticipating your arrival with prayers that it would happen. And, *humdullilah* here you are! *Humdullilah!*'

'*Humdullilah*,' I echoed.

'Of course my dear and wise brother Yazami has explained our small Hamadcha ritual to you, but should you want more informations, please do not hesitate to ask and if it is within my limited knowledge to assist, then *inshallah*, I shall.' He checked himself and flashed a glance at Yazami before turning back to me. 'How rude of me that I did not enquire after your house restoration; forgive me. We are all grateful that you have chosen to save our heritage in such a magnificent way—'

Although I had grown accustomed to the floral embroidery of phrase that accompanied so much of everyday conversation in Morocco, the combination, of "heritage" and "magnificent" in reference to my house was too much even for me.

'It is a humble little *dar*,' I interjected, 'nothing like this.'

To my surprise, Abderrahim chortled. His eyes narrowed in amusement as he brought his hand to my shoulder and tugging my face close to his, he whispered. 'Every house is of value and some more than others. Your undertaking is brave and worthwhile but you should always remember the words my grandfather taught me, "no man can climb a hill of mice". True, don't you think? Certainly, not without skilled and powerful allies and in this you are blessed for in your house dwell such beings as others can only dream of.' He winked and nodded obviously pleased with this precious confidence.

'I do?'

'*She* has favoured that dwelling for as long as memory permits. My father talked of it when I was a boy and no doubt his father too. Yet few men have lasted long in the house because they feared her but with you I sense it will be different, *inshallah*. Good, we understand each other.' Then he leaned close and whispered, 'Thanks to *Allah* and Sidi Ali tonight you will receive bread that is not prepared by the hands of men—but by the hands of angels.' With that he thumped me on the back and dragged Yazami away to talk with the other musicians.

Yazami who had explained everything to me? Not in any conversation we had had, and what was that about climbing a hill of mice, or rather the inability to do so? The image was bizarre; feet scrambling up a mountain of rodents, soft, squishy and constantly moving. I sent the thought off to the back of my head, it wasn't the sort of thing I wanted around when the *majoun* I had been chewing kicked in. Then I laughed because Abderrahim's conspiratorial confidences and the images they evoked could well have come directly from *majoun* central. You have to love the creativity of synapses on the rampage and the wonderfully anarchic and random associations that the brain can toss up. A teenage game came to mind; the one where you insert an obscene word into a film or book title, so for several minutes I played with idiotic combinations such as *The Blair*

Majoun Project, Pulp Majoun and *Phantom of the Majoun*. When I found myself giggling inanely at the notion of *Carry on Majouning*, I decided that while the hashish confection worked delightfully, I had better grow up.

Thankfully, the boy who had opened the door for us located me loitering in the shadows of one of the big orange trees. He pressed a glass of very sweet mint tea into my hands and for the next fifteen minutes I switched my attention back and forth between the crowd and musicians. It was as if there was an invisible barrier erected in the middle of the courtyard beyond which the audience did not move, whereas from time to time one of the musicians would cross the frontier in search of tea or a cigarette.

While the musicians were all in simple red *djellabas* with white scarves wrapped around their *tarbouche*—soft felt hats—the audience had dressed in their traditional finest. All the men and women, ranging in age from early twenties through to three or four elderly men and women of indeterminable age, were wearing beautifully embroidered *djellabas* and with only a couple of exceptions, brand new *babouche*; the men's uniformly yellow, the women's every colour of the rainbow. Slowly I scanned the crowd looking for someone I knew but this was not my district and not one face was familiar.

Eventually I tired of standing and finding a spot on the carpet, nodded to my neighbours and took a seat. In a typically friendly Moroccan fashion, several of the men around me leaned across and shook my hand, the women nodded and smiled. There was some movement the other side of the courtyard as two musicians with drums warmed them over a small charcoal brazier and Abderrahim added some chips of bark or wood to a very large silver incense burner. Within a minute a sweet fragrance flowed across the courtyard with an unexpected effect—the audience fell silent. Then, as Yazami squeezed in beside me, two more musicians carrying what looked like stunted but slightly overweight oboes, entered from a door at the side of the courtyard. Both were older men and with a nod to Abderrahim they raised the wooden instruments to their lips. The sound they produced was a wild braying wail that sounded harsh to my ears. Music it may have been, but not as I knew it.

'*Ghiyyata–ghita* players,' Yazami hissed in my ear.

'So, what is this all about?' My question went unanswered for Yazami and every other member of the audience were wrapped up in the proceedings and I saw it was pointless to ask anything at that moment.

How to describe what took place? It is possible that I can recall the mechanics, the structure, but the effect on me was outside of my experience and almost beyond my powers of description.

For the first while there were prayers and chanting that to my untutored ear were discordant; lyrics in search of a song, notes in search of a key. My eyes locked onto the smoke rising from the incense burner and the strange way it rose just so high and then formed a thin transparent layer of blue across the courtyard to where it intersected with the dance of air around the fountain. Watching a fountain, as I did for a considerable time is, I discovered, as soothing and seductive as watching the fire-fairies fishtail their way up from a fire, or the sparkling rings of soot magically spreading out inside a fireplace. The difference was that here there was no crackle and spark, but a gentle tinkling only heard in the spaces in the musicians' performance. The water from the fountain rose, not powerfully, but in an almost lazy upwelling from which large globules of liquid silver emerged to trace an arc up and out before surrendering; curving gracefully under the force of gravity and descending into the drop-dappled surface where they lingered as bubbles waiting to be reborn and once again enjoy the thrill of their circuitous journey.

The chanting grew in intensity and then, suddenly it was raining. No, not rain but beautifully fragrant orange-flower water. Two women were moving through the audience sprinkling everyone's heads from slender silver dispensers. Behind them came four young boys carrying trays of dates and small glasses of milk.

'This is the traditional welcome to the *lila*,' Yazami whispered.

'What's a *lila*?'

'Shh...' he admonished.

Then it was music. Having a total lack of understanding of Moroccan music meant that I missed the subtle nuances (I am relatively sure there were nuances) which appeared to be captivating the locals; missed them by a country mile. The atonal wailing of the *ghiyyata*, the drumming of the *gwal* players, their small drums nestled into their necks, and the plucking of the lute, all seemed in competition with the singing. For these musicians the idea of a short catchy four or five minute tune, or even a set of tunes, was totally alien. Yet, to my amazement, not only were the audience entranced but about an hour into this performance, a group of men got to their feet, kicked off their *babouches* and crossed the frontier onto the carpets in front of the musicians.

The Hamadcha formed a line and Abderrahim laid his instrument down then moved to stand in front of them and, like a choir master at college, began a chant and response session, complete with hand movements and gestures. It appeared pretty chaotic at first but slowly the men synchronised their swaying dance; heads first to one side then the other. The music grew louder

'The beginning of the *hadra*,' Yazami yelled into my ear, '...the ecstatic dance.' He had the look of a man intoxicated, his eyes gleaming wildly.

Ecstatic hardly seemed the word for what I was experiencing, unless the word had become a synonym for boring. My hitherto only vaguely conceived goal of getting to know and hopefully understand individual Moroccans was difficult but probably not impossible. The music was another matter. It was like their religion; only comprehensible at the level of intellectual investigation. No skill of mine could penetrate the depth to which it was inculcated in the fabric of their lives, an unknowable tapestry—the foreign symbols interwoven by generations of Arabs, Berbers and Africans. It was little wonder that the expatriates huddled together behind their barrier of unknowing. Were they genuinely disinterested, or did they think their own culture superior?

Worse was to come. With the glazed expression of a man in the thrall of some deep rapture, Yazami explained that the next couple of hours would be even more thrilling. Actually, the word he used was "entrancing" but it was the throwaway inclusion of "hours" that perturbed me.

'Hours, how long does it go on?'

'Until dawn.'

Resigned to my fate, I drifted off into the realm of the visual. Here at least there was colour and movement and, as I watched, the beat of the drums resolved itself into a tempo I could follow. Either it or I had changed, for I found myself nodding as I watched. The carpeted area in front of the fountain was now crowded, mostly with men, but a couple of the older women were now on their feet swaying, eyes shut, to the insistent rhythm.

The tempo changed, picking up speed and volume. More incense was burning, emerging as a stream of pale blue smoke. When it met the air currents caused by the dancers, it swirled and dissipated leaving only a sweet perfume on the night air.

Again the music changed and this time I was swept up into it, the rhythms and patterns no longer foreign, but intriguing and seductive arabesques; a musical calligraphy as intricate as carved plaster. And I could read it now because the waves of music were in me at my core, the music of my genes, the sound of my heart. Yet it was not a revelation that came like lightning from the sky, but rather by osmosis, the understanding seeping into me, coming up from the depths of the ground beneath me.

That was the moment I became aware of the impossible; a woman who had not been there but was now, smiling, side on to me, leaning languidly against the *riad* wall. Like a *naiad*, a phantom, raised from the spray of the fountain, misted, wreathed in the blue smoke of incense, was Mira, amber eyes smouldering, looking directly at me. Like a pale rainbow, she seemed and for a moment I thought her no more than a trick of the light, a reflection maybe, a mirage conjured by the heady mix of *majoun* and longing.

Dance for me.

Her mouth had not moved. Yet, despite the distance between us, I heard her with crystal clarity. For a moment I could not move, transfixed by the vision, afraid to break the moment or lose the link that sparkled so brightly between us. Surely, I was embarrassing her, staring, mouth open, and feverish. Surely others could see or sense the energy flowing. I risked a look around but I was alone on the carpet. Somewhere the other guests were swaying, chanting and moving, oblivious to the drama behind them; a drama in an aqua *djellaba*, filmy and transparent, glistening with sequins, the hood tossed back revealing her dark hair, the black-brown of burnt wood, cascading down her back.

Perform the hadra for me now.

With an almost imperceptible movement of her head she indicated I should dance alone on the carpet. There are few things as embarrassing as a foreigner attempting to join in a traditional dance, even more so if it is a sacred ritual. Dancing is something I have avoided all my life, claiming incompetence to mask the fact I abhor making a spectacle of myself. Yet Mira was commanding me and I was powerless to resist.

I danced the *hadra*.

Untutored, I knew the steps. Though ignorant, I knew the gestures.

Through the cascade of feelings and the tumult inside, I danced around a core of bliss that held me, a satellite in its orbit. This was true chaos. A place where the atoms danced with me, where colour was at my command, where light and sound blended, solid and liquid were not different and everything could be created in a flux of passion that was outside of time.

I danced.

Watch carefully, my beloved.

Mira was directly in front of me now, her scent—orange-flower and rose—around her like a halo. She held a small knife in her hand and fixing her eyes on mine, binding me to her, she raised it above her head and then brought it down so it sliced her scalp, not once or twice, but five times. There was no horror, just blood, flowing so sweetly down, matting her hair. It was an offering, as was the knife, handle towards my hand. She had no need to speak again as I had always known how this was done. Five times I cut and was rewarded by her hands either side of my face, cupping me. And her lips and tongue on my brow, savouring what I had so willingly offered.

Dance for me.

And so I danced, until there was no more. No more blood, no more night and no more Mira. A lingering scent of turpentine maybe, and hands, I remember hands, lifting me from where I had collapsed. Not her hands, of course, and a face, Yazami, his look one of bemused concern.

'Did you see her?' I asked.

'See who?'

Book Two

Richard: A stone from the hand

'*Humdullilah*,' Yazami said and belched as he pushed himself back from the small table. He glanced over to where Thami was sorting a pile of new *zellij* into their separate colours, meticulously polishing each individual tile as he did. Contented the boy was happy, Yazami squinted across the table, shielding his eyes from the candles so that he could see me clearly. 'You must eat.'

'I have eaten.'

We had been through this several times in the weeks since the Hamadcha *lila*. It was not as if I was eating nothing, it was just that I was eating less.

'When did you eat?'

'Before.'

'Before, when?'

'Fuck it, Yazami, I don't know; yesterday, last week, does it matter?'

'It matters. Self-love, my liege, is not so vile a sin, as self-neglecting.'

Bloody Yazami, despite his quotes from the bard, could be very irritating like that. For some bizarre reason, he felt I was not looking after myself; that I was getting sick. It was nonsense of course and mollycoddling was not what I needed. Yet, to please him I took a piece of bread and dipped it in the *besara*. It was already past eight but I was content for them both to stay a while as long as Yazami dropped the lecturing. 'There, are you satisfied?'

He looked at me for a long time then sighed. 'I am not a good friend, Richard. I should be harsh with you, but I cannot.'

'So, don't be. I am perfectly okay. All my vital signs are function-ing. Just make me another pipe, will you?' I was already rather stoned but it was a state I felt more comfortable in than any other on offer.

'Listen, I will make a deal. I will tell you a story and then I think it is your turn to tell me one. We all need stories.'

'Fat lot of good they have done you so far Yazami.'

'*Skout!*' he hissed in mock outrage. 'They are bombs waiting to go off; my little acts of terrorism.'

'Sure, I can see the authorities quaking, frightened of one of your plays exploding!'

'Don't fool yourself they will not, one day brother, one day.' He spread his hands. 'Boom! Like so, but for now, we swap our stories.'

'Whatever. Will this be another one of your plays?' A story I could cope with, even enjoy, anything but his concern. Summer was just over its peak and the long warm evenings were perfect for sitting talking.

'As it happens, no.' Almost absentmindedly he rolled a ball of *kif* in his fingers, packed the pipe and handed it to me. 'Let me tell you the story about the importance of bread.'

'Not a lecture!'

'I swear it. It is an old story, history if you prefer, concerning a man called Sidi Ahmed in Fez. Sidi Ahmed Dghughi was a very learned man. Some say a saint. We are talking a long time ago, the year 1130 in our calendar.'

'Which was when?' It sounded like a very long time in the past.

'It would probably be 1717 or somewhere round there.'

'Sorry, go on.'

'Sidi Ahmed was studying in our famous university...'

'The Qarawiyne?' Realising I had interrupted again I raised my palms towards him. 'Sorry, last time.'

'Yes Al-Qarawiyne. The scholars were jealous, suspicious of him, and tried to trap him. They asked him what the basic necessities for prayer were. While they had expected a long and complex answer,

Sidi Ahmed replied simply, "Two silos; one of wheat and one of barley." The scholars laughed at him and called him a fool. Instead of being shamed, Sidi Ali invited them to his house and before they knew what was happening he locked them in without meat, bread or vegetables. For three days the scholars prayed, conversed and slept but on the fourth day they called out for food. "Keep discussing the necessities for prayer!" Sidi Ahmed responded. The following day the men were so hungry they couldn't think, let alone pray. It was at that point that Sidi Ahmed taught them that without bread there is no prayer and no devotion. This time they believed him and honoured his wisdom.'

'Clever,' I acknowledged, 'but if you are trying to teach me something with this fable, forget it. I don't want to pray, Yazami. I just want to understand, that's all.'

'I am truly your brother,' Yazami said, reaching across the table and grasping my hand. 'But I have so little to give.' He tossed back his head and laughed. 'My father always said that a stone from the hand of a friend is an apple, but I caution you against eating it.'

The two of us had spent hours discussing what had happened on the night of the *lila* and, on every occasion we ended up with an argument; Yazami telling me it was quite usual that participants went into a trance, and my trying to convince him that what I had experienced had been real. It didn't dawn on me for a long time—weeks in fact—that he drew no distinction between what I considered to be contradictory positions. All Moroccans, he explained, believed that the two worlds—ours, and that which was entered through the doorway of trance—were obverse sides of the same sphere. To say I found this a difficult concept would be an understatement, for despite my epiphany on arrival in Fez, my mind still veered towards the path that science had mapped out for me.

There are many roads that do not lead to the heart and over the decades I have travelled them. The frontiers of feelings, of intuition, have always been a no-man's-land whose borders are mined with deception, and protected by lies. I do not cross those frontiers will-ingly because to do so would be to admit that all these years I have been wrong. According to Yazami the Moroccans have a saying; "an old cat will not learn to dance". They may well be right, but if I am to succeed in understanding I need to analyse what happened and therein lays my problem, for though I know nothing of meta-physics, my heart keeps telling my mind that what happened was real and that the only problem is one of interpretation. My head has become a scrambled Rubik's cube but one with no discernible design to re-configure.

'So, *khoya*, tell me a story about your butterflies.'

Although Yazami's voice was soft I saw Thami turn with a smile on his face. Maybe he had learned the English word "story" or maybe he was responding to Yazami's tone, but whatever it was, he pushed a pile of tiles closer and moved his candle next to them. He looked at me; his wide eyes a picture of expectation. *A story about butterflies?* Under normal circumstances the mention of butterflies would have set alarm bells ringing, but for some reason the guards had aban-doned their posts. It may well have been the effects of the *kif*, or simply my tiredness, in any case I not only found myself responding, but, to my surprise I began to tell them about my experience in the cloud forest of Peru; not in the language of the nightmares that have haunted me since 1990, but in a casual way, as though recounting some normal event.

As is the way with *kif*, the story took over and it felt to me as though I was back there, seeing it for the first time.

'Butterflies are so small,' Yazami murmured, refilling the pipe. 'It's a wonder you can see them in a forest.'

Thami kept cleaning the pieces of *zellij*, but I knew he was paying attention.

At times, I told them, it is only a silver flash in the dark wetness—a single spot of light and then nothing—a shadow in the shadows. Again, a tantalizing glimpse as it moves in and out of a spear of light, like a drunken actor who can't find his spot. Butterflies are silent. However, although there is no noise from the wings, there are other sounds—the ever-present buzzing of the insects I have no time for. Other people's insects, I liked to think. On this particular evening, I had been following one specimen in an area free of the perpetual mist that cloaks the cloud forest. Here the late sun was able to break through and visibility far better than was usual in the region.

'How do you do that?' Yazami peered at me. 'How do you follow a butterfly when it flies in the air and a man is on foot?'

Before I could stop it, I was back there. The smell, the light... 'Listen,' I said.

With the location of the last sighting firmly fixed, I slowly inch forward, avoiding the sucking pools of deep yellow mud, stepping carefully over the vines that hang like abandoned abseilers' ropes from the canopy and, on reaching the jungle floor, trailed sinuously across the moss-covered rocks to tie themselves in knots whose only botanical purpose, it appears, is to trip me up and cause me to lose sight of my prey.

In a blink, it was gone and for a long time I stood stock still forcing my eyes to pan across each level of the understorey; left to right. Using the trunk of a giant strangler fig as my guide I elevated my gaze to the next level and pan again; left to right, methodically. Nothing. Craning my neck, I searched the region above fifteen metres. Given the colour I had observed it should logically be there, in the blue zone, as the altitude between fifteen and thirty metres is called. Yet, I reminded myself, it had landed at a much lower height when I had first seen it and that didn't make sense.

The initial sighting had been electrifying. My greatest joy would have been to have seen a dirty grey butterfly...

'I thought they were all beautiful,' Yazami interjected.

'No, not at all, some are so plain, insignificant looking, but nevertheless valuable to study. If I could have found any butterfly in the world at that moment I would have wanted to see a *Styx infernalis.*

In butterfly terms, it was considered the missing link that might have given us a clue to the relationship between riodinids, lycaenids and nymphalids...'

Yazami rolled his eyes. 'And it's dirty grey?'

'The wings are, and transparent but the body is distinctive; narrow and black. Oh, and with short antennae.'

'And that makes it easy to see?'

'Not at all. In any case even though I was above 1000 metres and in the right area of the forest, it was too late in the day. According to everything I had read they were known to fly around midday.'

Yazami nodded and went back to rolling a tiny ball of *kif* for his pipe.

While it is true that the fabled *Styx infernalis* was always on my mind, in the forest I had actually been observing a white butterfly fluttering around in the crepuscular gloom in the lowest level of the rainforest. A *Pieridae*, I assumed, possibly a *Leptophobia subargentea*. For a moment, my concentration was disturbed by the swift flight of a Purple-throated Cotinga shooting through the trees. It was as I turned back that I noticed an unusual splash of colour on a leaf above a red and yellow *heliconia*. At first, I thought it was simply the effect of the Cotinga's passing, a disturbing of the foliage allowing a tiny shaft of late afternoon sunlight to penetrate the mist and shine for an instant on a drop of water. But it was too iridescent for that; too vibrant. Moving cautiously forward I peered through the shadows and then, just as I was about to give up and return to my pursuit of the *Leptophobia*, I saw it.

The butterfly, poised on the broad dark green leaf appeared to be a perfect specimen. There was no obvious loss of wing-scale, a problem that plagued so many of the Lepidoptera in that environment. The creature's wings were closed and so I had no idea of the upper surface colours, but the underneath was a sublime work of art; a deep electric cobalt-blue, splashed with silver and what looked like tiny shimmering flakes of gold leaf. The mottling of the colours reminded me of colours swirling in molten glass. The antennae graduated from dark blue nearest the head to milky white at the tips and... But then the butterfly had taken flight.

'Beautiful,' Yazami sighed. 'Shimmering flakes of gold leaf. Just like Shakespeare.'

'Shakespeare?'

'So we'll live, and pray, and sing, and tell old tales, and laugh at gilded butterflies.' He handed me the glowing pipe and nodded for me to continue.

Back then, although just forty years of age, I already felt as though I had spent half my life in the Peruvian cloud forest. At home in Dublin, my lover at the time, the peevish Aisling, swore it was longer. It had, in fact been only seven trips, but in that time I had seen nothing that came close to the brilliant butterfly that was now eluding me. Instinct told me that unless I continued my search now, I was unlikely to come across it again. I hesitated, common sense dictating that I begin the long journey back to camp. It was getting late in the day and I had strayed further afield than I had intended. Yet, what if I had discovered something new? It was probably nothing of the kind. Sometimes the light, mist and humidity played tricks with the colours and at the end of the day I might put myself at risk only to discover that it was a common species or more likely would never see it again.

Perhaps it was a *Dione glycera*? Not new, but certainly worthwhile observing. However, at what risk? The words from one of the Latin poet Horace's odes came to mind.

I'm inflamed by Glycera's glow,
Far outshining the blaze that Parian marble casts;
I'm inflamed by provocative impudence,
And a face hazardous just to see.

To hell with the hazard, I thought as I saw a fluttering movement high in the foliage ahead.

Yazami, let me tell you, when a man is moving deeper and deeper into the jungle lured on by a sense that he is about to make a wonderful discovery, his gaze is fixed firmly upwards.

'This is truly amazing; such a landscape.' Yazami's eyes were glowing.

A man does not see the army of leaf-cutting ants beneath his feet. Neither does he notice the three-toed sloth observing him with mild interest from a branch, safe in its moss-green camouflage. At rare moments like those a man's gaze is so sharply focused that it excludes all else and, while this may be of inestimable value in the pursuit of elusive Lepidoptera, it has its drawbacks. For example, for all my keen intellect and fine eyesight, I did not see the man standing in the shadows behind a tangle of liana vines. The first I knew of the man was when he stepped around the liana and blocked my path.

For a moment the two of us looked at each other. He with the languid curiosity afforded to those who are sure of their place in the world, and me with stark amazement that another human being should be here in the jungle.

'You are a long way from home, comrade,' the man said softly, extending his hand. 'My name is Lucho.'

The man's Spanish was educated, unaccented. In his forties, I guessed, short, thickset and barrel-chested, with a complexion that a police report would have described as "swarthy". The slightly puffy face was pleasantly rounded under short black hair, the chin swathed in dark stubble. The eyes were arresting—dark glowing orbs with a tinge of yellow –sharp and alert. The eyes of a jaguar, was the thought that flitted through my mind.

Taking a step forward, I took the man's hand.

'Marcus Brennan.'

I paused, wondering how much of this Thami was following. Sensing my hesitation, Yazami glanced at Thami and nodded for me to continue.

'Not your name,' Thami mumbled. His speech may have been indistinct but there was a brightness in his eyes and he nodded at me to continue.

'It was my name back then.'

'Fuck you,' Thami grinned. 'Your name Richard.'

Yazami laughed. 'Your English is improving.'

'Marcus Brennan,' Lucho echoed softly, as though tasting the foreignness of it on his tongue. He took a short knife from his belt and looked at the blade as though pondering what it could be used for.

'You startled me,' I said, eyeing the knife with some concern.

'There are many dangers in the trees and under them, no?' He reached out and with a swift action cut a short length of Liana and, tilting his head back, sucked the water from it. Satisfied, he wiped his mouth and grinned. 'Somehow, I don't think you are one of them, eh?' He cut another length of vine and passed it to me. 'So, what brings you to this part of the forest? Are you lost?'

I accepted the vine and sucked gently on it. I had been feeling thirsty for some time and although I knew about the water in the Liana but before leaving my camp and first seeing the butterfly, I had unbuckled my knife. I had not intended to go far, but here I was, deep in the cloud forest without a knife. If it had been one of my students I would have read the riot act. 'Butterflies. I study butterflies.'

The man thought about that for a moment and then nodded slowly. 'Butt-er-flies.' He said the word slowly, breaking up the syllables as though hearing it for the first time in his life. A smile spread across his face. 'Lepidoptera.'

'Precisely.'

'And what *exactly* about Lepidoptera do you study?'

'In layman's terms? My main interest is taxonomy, but on this trip I'm leading a party of post-graduate students studying the relationship of colouring to operational altitude; from the forest floor that it is, not above sea level.'

'And you are solving this puzzle?'

There was something in the man's tone that made me wonder just how truly interested he was. His face seemed engaged, the eyes, locked on mine, and in addition he had known what Lepidoptera meant. He was probably a timber worker, I thought, a boss most likely. The man's hands didn't appear to be those of a manual labourer.

'To a certain extent. It is difficult to work in an area bereft of absolutes.'

'I feel for those bereft of absolutes.'

'You do?'

'Naturally. Without them how do we chart our progress? Even if our absolutes are personal they just as essential as the certainties we all rely on. The sun rising, the rainfall coming...' He stopped and looked up into the canopy, judging the shifting angle of the sun, reading the sunlight and shadows like a clock. 'You are camped near here?'

'El Paraiso. We've a small party of students doing a range of research. Twelve of them.'

'El Paraiso, the abandoned logging camp beside the river?'

'We've spent some time making it habitable.'

'I know the place well. Indeed, a beautiful spot, and one I have been intending to visit again soon.' He paused and looked at the small backpack slung over my shoulder. 'If you don't mind my saying, it isn't advisable to wander around in the jungle by yourself. You have a radio to keep in contact?'

'Yes, but the damn thing is useless once you cross over a ridge.'

'The limitations of technology, eh?'

'Precisely.' I squinted at my watch. 'In fact, I had better be setting out...' I stopped as Lucho put a hand on my arm.

'You are English, no?'

'Irish.'

'Ah, but I can most surely still practice my English,' Lucho grinned, scratched at the stubble on his chin and switched languages. 'You think you can understand my accent?'

'It is surprisingly good.'

'Why are you surprised? Do you think a man who works in the forest has no education?'

I remained silent, aware that I had offended the man in some way, although it had not been my intention to do so.

'I like the Irish, they have had a long hard struggle,' Lucho said and, his brow furrowed with concentration, recited slowly; 'One by one they were all becoming shades. Better pass boldly into that other world, in the full glory of some passion, than fade and wither dismally with age.'

'Joyce?'

'History is a nightmare from which I am trying to awake.'

'Stephen Dedalus. I am truly impressed.'

Lucho's face relaxed and he shrugged in a good-natured manner. 'In this part of the world I owe much to the shortwave service of the BBC and the odd book left behind by travellers.'

To say I was intrigued would be an understatement. 'What is it you do?'

Lucho frowned. 'You are a professor of butterflies. I am a professor of nothing. But I have the honour to lead a small group of...' he hesitated as if searching for the correct English word. 'Students.'

'And they are studying, what?'

Lucho gave a throaty chuckle. 'Life.'

'A big field.'

'Political life, economic life...'

'In the cloud forest?' I allowed my scepticism to show.

'It is a mistake to assume that all learning must be done in the cities. While the intellectual elites maintain their focus on the major centres they are like a bird with one wing. There is much that can be learned from the rural areas and as a society we ignore the voices of the *campesinos* to our peril. And the rainforest is also important. It has been the mother of our culture, the lungs of the planet and our source of sustenance. Here, under the canopy, we can learn much.'

To me it sounded suspiciously like the rhetoric of the far fringe of the environmental movement. However, I nodded and checked my watch again. Time was becoming critical. 'I really must go.' I put out my hand to shake his; to say goodbye, but Lucho had turned away and was peering into the tangled understorey.

'*Oye choche*, what do you make of this?' He stepped back so that I could see what he had found.

On a leafless twig sat what at first glance appeared to be a caterpillar with a swept back Mohawk of flaming orange hair.

'Wonderful isn't it, but not a rarity.' I explained. 'It's the larval stage of the megalpygid.'

'*No es un peinado punk?*'

'No, it's not a punk hairdo,' I laughed, 'S*ino la peluda larva de una polella megalopigida.* It's the furry larva of the megalpygid moth.'

'So it won't turn into a beautiful butterfly,' Lucho said. 'But it is something, no?'

'Sadly it is nothing special. A Flannel Moth. I have seen larval specimens from Arizona. *Megalopyge lapena* and *Megalopyge bissesa.* In their final larval stage they look more like a slightly teased-up orange cotton ball. The *Megalopygidae* are a small family of some two hundred and twenty species mostly in South America and Africa. Like the *Limacodidae*, the larvae possess urticating hairs which can cause extreme allergic reactions on human skin.'

'Urticating.' Lucho said. 'Now I have discovered a new word.'

'From the Latin for nettle. *Urtica.*'

Lucho peered at the larva again. 'You mean this little punk can sting me?'

'No, but its hair can. It would produce a burning sensation and it would probably be very itchy for a while.'

'That is amazing. Such a little thing. I think I like this creature.' He turned back to me. 'And I like this word. What was it again?'

'Urticating.'

'Urticating,' Lucho repeated with obvious relish. 'This is a good word.'

'In university we made a poem to remember it. If the plant is urticaceous the rash will burn most hurticaceous.'

'Hurticaceous?'

'It's a made-up word. A joke,' I explained, feeling suddenly foolish.

'It is a good joke,' said Lucho generously. 'And I must repay you for the new word.'

'Repay me?'

'Of course. I am already thinking that this word will prove very valuable to me students. So I will show you something special Professor *Mariposa*.'

'Doctor—'

'Doctor then. Doctor Butterfly. This is also a good name.'

I knew I was losing valuable time and also, so it seemed, the thread of the conversation. I held up my hand. 'I must go.'

'No. Believe me, I know this area well and there is not enough time for you to return to your camp. So, I have a suggestion. You will come and spend the night with us. It is only a short distance and I am sure we can find food and a comfortable place to sleep.'

Glancing up through the rapidly darkening canopy, I knew the man was right. Night came quickly in the mountains; fingers of darkness reaching out through the mists. Pools of blackness rising from the valley floor like a flood would engulf me before I made it even as far as the next ridge. My students would be concerned and maybe even put themselves at risk by coming looking for me. No, I dismissed the thought, I had stressed time and again that if one of us was separated at nightfall that they find a safe place to spend the night and a search would commence at first light; common sense. I hoped they would remember.

'That's very kind. If you are sure...?'

Lucho laughed. 'More than sure, I insist. Come!'

I paused to accept the pipe that Yazami was offering.

'Go on,' he said. 'There is much of the storyteller in you.'

'Some stories tell themselves.' But he was right and at this moment my fear of releasing this story from where it had lain so long and so deep, had vanished.

It was quickly obvious that the man knew this area of the forest extremely well. Not once did he break his stride as he led me unerringly through the trees and undergrowth until we came to a narrow path that traversed the side of the hill in a long slow climb. The man had been right, I conceded, as I saw how fast the light had faded, I would not have even made it halfway back to El Paraiso. Even now I was having trouble seeing the path beneath my feet.

'You must pause a moment.' Lucho had stopped at what looked like an impenetrable thicket. 'Our camp is nearby and I am concerned they may think we are a marauding jaguar. A bullet hole is not the way to welcome a visitor. So I will warn them we are coming. Wait a moment.' Not waiting for a reply, Lucho vanished into the dark cover of the dense foliage.

The rustle of leaves faded. A faint snap of a twig. Above me I could hear the sigh of soft wind in the canopy and on the far edge of hearing, the call of a nightjar, faint as a memory.

I strained my ears but all I could hear were the familiar sound of the first night creatures; the chittering of bats, the chatter of the frogs from the creek somewhere below in the dark and far away to my right, the call of a distant Screech Owl. I wished that Lucho had not mentioned the jaguar. My imagination took over. Around me the forest was breathing, a soughing, both elongated and melancholy, and to that soundscape, I conjured up the low rattling growl of the mountain lion, the soft padding feet of a predator moving inexorably towards me; a crackling sound in the nearby undergrowth. Tense now, holding my breath. Had it been daylight I knew I would have turned to see a Glaucous Cracker, the *Hamadryas glauconome*, the species of butterfly that used the sound as a form of communication. But not now. Not in the dark.

'*Oye choche*, it is safe.' Lucho materialised by my side, his teeth exposed by his smile, a white flash in the darkness.

'I was hearing things,' I admitted.

'It is when the jungle becomes totally silent that one should be concerned.' He moved off and still feeling a tinge of apprehension, I stayed close behind.

A few minutes later we emerged from the forest into a small clearing beside a stream. At the centre of the clearing, on a jutting shelf of land, was a low shack, its old timber slabs bleached silver by the elements. From the open doorway and the pair of windows came the soft welcoming orange glow of kerosene lamps.

Instead of going directly inside, Lucho led me to the edge of the land and pointed to a second clearing some hundred metres away below. From the low glow of lanterns and a cooking fire I could make out two wooden huts and a series of long tents. A few people were around the fire, their faces barely discernible points of light. Fireflies—moths around a flame. Away from the firelight the figures moving between the tents were barely visible shadows. I felt Lucho studying me and turned.

'My comrades' accommodation is not as grand as mine,' he said. 'But come. You must be hungry and I am impatient to show you my collection.' He stroked my arm with his finger. 'Can I say that? Is "impatient" the right word?'

The touch of the man's fingers on my arm was disturbing and I flushed, thinking for a moment of Aisling back in Ireland. Thinking of the way she touched me. *Manhandled*, Aisling liked to say.

'Impatient? Yes, or "keen". I would probably use keen.'

'Keen,' Lucho repeated with obvious satisfaction. 'Yes, that is better. I am keen.'

There was no door. In its place, as with the glassless windows, was mosquito netting hung in double folds, the lower edges brown and mud encrusted. Neither was there a wooden floor, but earth, its deep ochre surface worn smooth by constant use. There were no internal divides and very few furnishings. Underneath the window nearest to the door was a stone fire box with a mass of glowing coals. The window obviously served a dual purpose for the room was remarkably free of smoke despite the absence of a chimney. At one end of the room were table, chairs and a makeshift sink, at the other; three hammocks were slung from the rough-hewn bush poles that served as rafters. A small family of fat cuy scuttled about beneath the kitchen bench, playing chasing around an old kerosene drum that appeared to be used for water storage. I had kept guinea pigs as a kid and found it hard to accept their usual fate in Peru.

Lucho's fingers on my arm again; gently tugging me to pay attention. 'There,' Lucho said and nudged me forward. In the centre of the room, against the rear wall, was a large bookcase, its shelves, fashioned out of planks bowed under the weight of hundreds of books. There was no doubt that this was Lucho's "collection".

'From Akhmatova to Zola. Alphabetic,' Lucho explained, his voice a whisper as if he did not want to intrude on my appreciation.

I ran my finger along the spines of the books. 'Truly remarkable, the last place on earth I would have expected to see such a library. You have read them all?'

'Every one. Some I have read several times. When the rain comes here it lodges for many days and there is little else to occupy the mind. Without my friends, I sometimes think I would be lonely.' Lucho clapped his hands together. 'First we eat and then we talk.' He bent under the sink and took out two bottles of beer and, holding the caps against the edge of the bench, gave each a sharp tap that removed the top.

For a few minutes we worked in silence, Lucho, washing potatoes, rolling them to me and indicating the knife with which to peel them. After placing two pots of water on the coals he took a head of garlic and with an expert twist, separated the individual cloves.

'Cut the potatoes into pieces,' he instructed, 'and crush a couple of cloves of garlic.' He paused and looked me in the eye. 'Do you mind?'

Embarrassed by the directness of the visual contact, I sipped my beer. It was warm and sweet in my throat. 'Not at all, no, I'm enjoying it.'

'What else do you enjoy? What books? What writers?'

'Mainly the classics but a smattering of contemporary fiction, it all depends upon my mood.'

'Tell me.' Lucho squatted down and poked around on a shelf under the bench.

For a second I felt foolish; suddenly back in school and being asked to recite. 'When I was growing up I fancied that I liked the Russians. But I think I was trying to impress people. I still like Turgenev, even though he's no longer fashionable. I read Sartre, Kafka, but I am not sure that I ever understood them. Even our own Joyce I hated until a few years ago.'

Lucho emerged from his search clutching a tin of tomato paste. 'And why was that? Why change your mind. I am impressed that you even hated him. Most people don't understand enough to care one way or another.' He opened the can and set it to one side while he checked the water on the fire. 'Salt in the water and the potatoes can go in. They need to cook so we can mash them.'

'I suddenly got it,' I said as I found the salt and added a couple of pinches to the pot. 'I heard someone reading a piece of *Ulysses* and I understood.'

Lucho nodded and picking up a fat cuy, cuddled it in his arms like a baby, rolling it on its back and stroking its tummy. 'Ah,' he said softly. 'You unlocked the secrets of indirect speech.'

I dropped the potatoes in the pot and turned just in time to catch an onion that Lucho tossed in the air towards me.

'Peel and chop.'

'Where did you learn so much about literature?'

'In another universe I was a professor.' Lucho's voice was tinged with nostalgia. He held the cuy in front of his face and examined it. 'I did my thesis on Nabokov, my dear, sweet, dead Nabokov.' Employing the same skilful twist as he had on the garlic, he broke the cuy's neck. 'You know that he was a—'

'Lepidopterist.' I said, my eyes smarting from cutting the onion. *Cleopatra.* It came to me; the name of my first guinea pig.

'I wrote a thesis on the source of his creative spirit. You see he had always claimed that he had no idea where it sprung from.' He dropped the limp body of the cuy into the second pot of boiling water, wiped his hands on his jeans and crossed over to the bookshelf. He searched for a minute, then, pulling out a book, took it over to the lamp on the table and thumbed through it. 'Here... *Neither in environment nor in heredity can I find the exact instrument that fashioned me, the anonymous roller that pressed upon my life a certain intricate watermark whose unique design becomes visible when the lamp of art is made to shine through life's foolscap.* That's from *Speak, Memory.*'

'I've read the quote somewhere, but not the book.'

'You know Nabokov?' Lucho put down the book and crossed back to the fire.

He took a fork and lifted the cuy from the water, let it drip on the floor for a few seconds then depositing it on the bench, proceeded to scrape the hair from the body. 'Oh and we need a chilli. You know, pips out, cut in strips.'

'I read *Lolita* when my parents told me I mustn't. I read *Pale Fire* because I liked the title and *Invitation to a Beheading* because everyone else was.'

Suddenly Lucho stopped what he was doing. 'Ah, we have a missing ingredient. I'll be right back.' Without further explanation, he plucked a book from the shelf and hurried out the door. 'Excuse me,' he called over his shoulder. 'Can you fry up the onions, garlic and chilli and then toss in the tomato paste?'

Lucho returned ten minutes later with a small quantity of minced beef. 'A donation,' he said as he tossed it into the pan and stirred vigorously. Satisfied it was well on the way he turned from the stove, opened a bottle of scotch and poured two glasses. He handed me a glass and began removing the stones from some black olives. 'We are making progress, I think.'

'And?' Yazami's voice interrupted and I had the disconcerting thought that I had stopped speaking aloud and was merely recalling the events in my mind.

'Maybe it is not interesting,' I mumbled and, as I did, realised the source of my hesitation. I was self-censoring. There was an undertone to what happened next that was disturbing and I was far from certain that Yazami would understand. I was not even sure that I did.

'Richard, please. It is a story and I love stories.'

'Maybe not the next part of this one.'

'Story,' Thami said, and grinned at me. 'Story!'

We were still at the bench, side by side when something changed and I experienced a feeling that is like nothing before or since. At times I felt the older man's thigh against mine; accidental. The first time it had happened I moved away, but subsequently I stood my ground, avoiding eye contact, confused by an unexpected flood of distracting and disturbing thoughts. *This is not me*, I told myself, but at the same time was aware that I was pressing myself forward against the bench, teasing a cramped erection. It seemed incomprehensible that Lucho could not sense my confusion.

'What are we making?' I asked.

'*Mestizo cuy* with *Papas Rellenas*,' Lucho slid the seasoned mashed potato and egg mixture towards me. 'It should be cool enough. Now, make balls from it and pass them here. And tell me about Nabokov the lepidopterist. I only know his writing.'

'But surely you have come across the references to it in his fiction?'

'Salacious, no?' Lucho laughed. 'He has some rather phallic cater-pillars. *Por cierto,* you know that Lolita has a nickname?'

'Yes, I think so...' I had a vague recollection of it, but it didn't spring to mind

'Dolly was the nickname and this is Nabokov's joke. Dolly comes from a play on the Russian word *kukol'ka* which means both "dolly, little doll" and "chrysalis, pupa".'

'You speak Russian?' I asked.

Lucho shrugged, 'At a certain stage of my education it was deemed necessary.' He took the first of the potato balls and after scooping out a hollow, stuffed it with the mixture from the fry pan and, be-fore sealing it popped in a black olive. Over on the fire the cuy, wrapped in tinfoil, was nearly done.

'Nabokov had a devious mind.' I said.

Lucho elbowed me playfully in the ribs and nodded at my hands, covered in mashed potato. 'You seem to like cooking.'

'I do,' I said huskily. Every instinct told me that Lucho was playing with me, but having never experienced feelings for a man before, I forced myself to concentrate on the job at hand, but not before I wondered how those strong hands would feel; imagined that black stubble against my flesh.

'The butterflies...' Lucho said, letting the moment pass.

Thankful for the easing of the tension I took a large sip of scotch. 'Nabokov named butterflies. And some people named butterflies af-ter him, but perhaps the most interesting are those species named for his characters.'

'Tell me.'

'*Madeleinea Lolita;* it's a Peruvian butterfly; quite gorgeous, black-ish brown with iridescent metallic blue basal and medial diffusion.'

'How wonderful.' Lucho turned to me. 'This is true?'

'I swear. The great Zsolt Bálint, the curator of the Hungarian Nat-ural History Museum, named it. And there's *Madeleinea cobaltana,* which is named after Kobalt, the Zemblan mountain resort in *Pale Fire*. Now that is a strange book.'

Lucho's eyes were glowing with pleasure. 'I so love it when art and science melt like that.'

'Meld,' I corrected softly. 'The word is meld, Lucho.' It was the first time I had spoken the man's name. I felt suddenly ridiculous; like a schoolboy with a crush. *'Madeleinea mashenka.'*

'Mashenka; the title of Nabokov's first Russian novel.' Lucho wiped his hands and reaching out stroked the back of my neck. 'Are they from Peru?'

The hand on my neck was like electricity but I managed to nod. 'Metallic; green with a narrow black margin. And best of all, perhaps is *Madeleinea vokoban.'*

'Vokoban?' Lucho's hand dropped away. 'I don't know of anyone by that name in his novels.'

'It's "Nabokov" spelled backwards.'

The delight on Lucho's face was so luminous I found myself laughing.

'We fry the *Papas Rellenas* and then we eat, eh *choche?'*

Finally, we sat on opposite sides of the table and ate. Thankfully I relaxed as the unnerving erotic thoughts gave way to my desire for food. Lucho, seemingly oblivious to what I had been feeling, devoured the meal with relish, all the time chattering away about his beloved Nabokov and how he had some rare condition that meant he saw letters as colours. 'Imagine that!' he exclaimed. 'Opening a book would be like releasing a rainbow!'

Later still, I lay in a hammock as Lucho undressed. The man's muscles rippled like molten gold in the low glow of the turned down lantern. He was smiling; a man at home with his nakedness—assured and unselfconscious.

'Doctor Mariposa,' Lucho murmured with what sounded like a strange sense of longing. 'You have given me some wonderful gifts. In the morning, I will repay you.'

Sleep came easily and the next thing I knew was the touch of Lucho's hands, shaking me awake.

'We must go,' Lucho said 'It is a new day and much needs to be done.'

Still bleary from sleep I struggled free of the hammock and donned my clothes. 'It is early?' It still appeared to be night.

'Dawn and I must set you on the path.'

Without another word Lucho led me from the hut and set out briskly through the forest.

For an hour we travelled in silence; our relationship no longer intimate but professional; the guide and the guided. Finally, we rounded a turn in the path and Lucho embraced me. 'Travel safely, Doctor.' He pointed through the mist. 'Down there is your camp. Maybe we will meet again.'

Disoriented and perplexed, I could think of nothing to say. 'Thank you...' But Lucho was gone. I turned and slowly trudged down the hill, approaching El Paraiso from an unfamiliar direction. It had rained in the night and the path was treacherous and several times I found myself clinging to vines to avoid slipping and falling over.

To my surprise the camp was still quiet. In fact, the whole jungle seemed deathly still and silent as though a command had been given that the birds should not sing. I remember thinking at the time that the students had slept in after staying up late awaiting my return. It was understandable that they would have been concerned. I entered the dormitory hut and peered along the bunks. They were empty. I went to the breakfast tent and found that it too was deserted. It occurred to me that maybe they had decided to take the canoes and look for me along the river, but the five canoes were still up on the bank where I had last seen them.

Returning to the breakfast tent in order to make some coffee while I contemplated what to do I realised that there was something else about the scene that was not as it should be. All the storage boxes were missing. The shelves, where the coffee and tea were normally kept were bare. It was then I saw the note protruding from a book on the fold-out table. I read it once and then, sitting, read it again. It was like a nightmare.

The demand for the return of the students was twelve million dollars. The conditions were not negotiable. The note was signed *Sendero Luminoso*. The Shining Path.

For a while I sat, numbed by shock. I knew that I should get in one of the canoes and go down river to raise the alarm, but still I sat. After a time, I reached out and picked up the book that had contained the note. For a second or two I thought I had gone mad but there was no doubt and I opened it certain of what I would find.

The inscription was in the same handwriting as that on the ransom demand.

Sendero Luminoso is like megalpygid larva, small but urticaceous and should be handled with care — Lucho.

The book was *Nabokov's Butterflies* by Vladimir Nabokov. Over where the sun had just touched the river, there was a flash of colour, a cloud of translucent wings above the water's coruscations. I turned to the first page and started reading.

'And?'

I was unaware that I had stopped speaking out loud and the intrusion of Yazami's voice startled me back to the present.

'There is more,' I took a deep breath and continued.

It must have been no more than a couple of minutes later that I glanced up, aware of an unusual amount of insect activity nearby; not butterflies, but flies. Putting the book down I walked to where a small path lead from the river up the hill in the direction I had taken the previous evening. The two bodies were so badly mutilated, the clothes so blood-soaked and my shock so profound that it took me a long time to identify the two young men. They had not only been shot but also hacked, with cuts so deep that bones were exposed and one looked as if he had been disembowelled. They had not just been killed, they had been butchered, and all because of me.

There was silence for a long time. I avoided looking up, knowing that Yazami's eyes were fixed on me. Finally, he spoke. 'And what happened to the other students?'

'The government stance was that they wouldn't deal with terrorists and so consequently the ransom was never paid. There was an enquiry of course and much was made in the press of the note that Lucho had written me. I was questioned for hours and labelled as uncooperative, but what could I say? How could I say? Of course, I told them the man had sheltered me, but that I drank, joked and cooked with him? How could I say anything about that? Truly Yazami, I have never felt such shame.'

I flinched as he reached out and patted my arm.

'You couldn't say that you found him attractive, of course not. And it would not have saved anyone.'

'There's not much more. Just when I thought things were quietening down, they found the remains of the other students in a shallow grave. The police called me in to show me the photographs. They were unrecognisably decomposed. There was another flurry of stories in the press. You can imagine the kind of thing—*He chased a butterfly while students died*—and it wasn't just the media that blamed me, the parents did as well. I resigned and left the country. I have never been back.'

Yazami held the pipe out for me, but I shook my head. For once I had had enough.

Richard: The gate of peacocks

Several weeks after my recounting of the events in Peru, Yazami asked me about it again. My response was unfortunate to say the least. An irrational anger welled up in me because, as far as I was concerned, the episode in the cloud forest should never have been aired in the first place and was now closed and I intended that it stay that way. But Yazami was insistent and for the first time I swore at him. There was a background to my irritation with him as whenever I wanted information from him on one particular subject he was less than forthcoming. Maybe he didn't understand that so much had changed in the previous weeks and I was hungry for answers. It is true that my questions were at times half-formed, but Yazami failed to see it was important to me. Time and again I asked him about the woman in the aqua dress whom I had danced for at the *lila*, and every time he lapsed into mumbo-jumbo about *djnun* and spirits.

'If she was a spirit, then was her knife real?' I asked.

'I didn't see her. What did she look like?'

'I can't tell you.' How could I? If he knew what I felt when I looked at his sister, Mira, he would have been shocked. It shocked me still, even though she had been working in my house since the beginning of summer. Each day she would arrive, covered from head to foot. Once in the house she had taken to wearing her hair out and removing her *djellaba*, changing into a dress and t-shirt or blouse, while she worked. The sight of her hair or those long tender fingers was enough to send shivers through me. Not once did she look me in the eye but it is only fair to confess that I watched her while she

157

worked. Sometimes, as she scrubbed the floors, she would hitch up her skirt and I would see her legs, her thighs, and glimpse, at times when she wore a loose blouse, the mounds of her breasts. It seems shameful in the telling, but I swear I was unable to look away. Often, after she departed for the day I would lie on my bed and conjure her in my mind.

'Was her knife real?' I repeated, knowing that Yazami would eventually have to answer.

'It is the knife of the *djnun*, it exists elsewhere.'

I let my derision show. 'Elsewhere,' I snorted. 'Then how do you explain the cuts in my head?'

He couldn't. Not now, nor when I had asked him on other occasions, and as usual, he skipped sideways.

'There are different types of these people...'

'These people? What do you mean?'

'*Djnun—afarit, mluk, ghwal* and *shayatin*—these people are not like us, Richard and don't obey our laws. They shun salt and we don't say their names.'

'Ah! But you know them! You know *her* name.'

There was darkness in his eyes and he told me I should get more rest.

'Maybe these people are angels,' I called after him, but he didn't reply and the next thing I heard was the slam of the door to the street.

Getting close to Moroccans had been my intention from the beginning, but it was becoming clear that it was a one-sided closeness. While on the surface I had developed strong feelings for Yazami and in a peculiar way, for Thami, deep down we were worlds apart. In the subterranean world of the subconscious lay a chasm of cultural differences that defied my attempts at bridge building. My endeavours to cross this divide proved futile—each fragment of understanding opening up even bigger differences in our perception. Yazami sensed this as well and yet, to his credit, not once did I feel he was giving up on me. With the patience of a father for a son, he would tell elaborate tales in order to explain this or that point of view and while I enjoyed his storytelling immensely, my comprehension encompassed little more than the thread of the narrative. Nuance and inflection were lost on me. The concepts I grappled with were like a stack of Russian dolls, except in reverse, each one revealing bigger and bigger gaps in my understanding.

'It is a stupid exercise,' I finally snapped after another failed attempt to get to grips with some obscure issue. 'Can't we just like each other?'

He spread his hands in resignation. 'We do, Richard. But you insist on asking questions about things I never think about.'

'It's understandable, surely?'

'Is it? When you lived in your country, did you keep questioning your neighbours about their beliefs? Did you ask your friends if they believed in their Christian saints, or if they had ghosts in their castles?'

That shut me up. But he wasn't finished. Yazami was like that. Sensing a new line of thought he would follow it, teasing it out like a spinner's yarn.

'It is interesting that it is always you who is asking questions whereas I prefer to sit, share a pipe, drink tea and tell stories. I often think if the Americans sat down and had tea and a talk more often there would be less need for their guns and bombs. They would certainly stop acting with such stupidity.'

'Mint tea diplomacy,' I laughed.

'I was being serious,' Yazami sighed. 'We are just as much to blame. It is not a comfortable position being caught between *haqq* and *hshumiyya*—between obligation and shame. As Muslims we are obliged to hold to our beliefs and yet those who commit atrocities in our name shame us. We have an obligation to welcome non-Muslims but shame at the way we have... what is the English word for when you take a position outside of a debate?'

'You mean you marginalised yourselves?'

'Yes, marginalised. We marginalised ourselves.'

I waited for him to continue, but he had taken himself to an uncomfortable space. He slipped one of his slippers off and flexed the sole, fiddling, as he wrestled with his thoughts. Eventually he continued, looking up at me with sad eyes, the fire in them dulled by a deep weariness.

'We moan that our great civilization is falling behind, we complain that we are victims, our image held hostage by fanatics in faraway places, yet when we have a chance to open our eyes or take a step forward, we falter because we do not really trust what the West is wanting to sell us. So, we return to the past.'

'Not everyone,' I protested. 'Look at the young people—'

'*Jrad hbouba!*' he growled. 'They want things, not thoughts. They are seduced by what they see on cable and dream of going to America. Do you see what is happening with their smartphones or in the Internet cafés?'

'I never go into them—'

'They sit there chatting online, on Whatsapp or Skype, and put photographs of themselves on dating sites. Why? Because they want to attract a boy or girl who will agree to marry them so they can go to America; America, fuck it! What future do you think a country has when its young people want nothing more than to leave it? Yes, we need to modernise, but we do not need to forget our heritage on the way.'

The fire was back in his eyes and for a moment I tried to imagine him in a position of power; the Minister for Culture, or maybe Islamic affairs. It was never going to happen. That Yazami aspired to be the voice of the voiceless was admirable, but he wrote his plays in *Darija* and failed to get them staged. Being the voice of the voiceless is a pretty empty calling if nobody is listening.

'Let me tell you what happened yesterday when I was in Seffarine,' he went on, 'A young man, maybe twenty or twenty-one, was leaning against a wall saying obscene things to some French women tourists. He was speaking *Darija* in a sweet voice as though he was being polite but he was explaining what sexual acts he would like to perform on them and calling them... well words not even a pig should hear. Of course, the women didn't understand his degrading insults and so were smiling and laughing with him. It was obvious from his accent that he came from Casa and so I went up to him and told him that he should be ashamed of what he was doing. He spat at me, calling me a *Fissa*—which to a *Fassi* is a great insult—and told me to get stuffed, *aoud lihoum!* Is that what we are to expect in the future?'

His pipe was on the ground, so I picked it up and began to clean it. 'My father said the same things about young people when I was growing up. It is generational...'

'This is worse. This is a sickness that has infected everything. Don't misunderstand me, I am not one of those who thinks we need *shari'a* and *jihad* to clean up the world; that road leads to a Taliban or ISIS wasteland. No, I am not advocating Islamic revolution but Islamic evolution. We need to come into the modern era.'

'Surely there are Muslim intellectuals—'

'A handful,' he waved a hand dismissively, 'they talk to the wind. No, this has to grow from the ground up. We need to reclaim the pulpits, reclaim the printing presses, the television. If we could create an Islamic channel that was showing real life rather than just the latest atrocity in Iraq, Pakistan or Syria.' He paused for a moment then shrugged. 'We need to follow the original example of the society Prophet, peace be upon him, and his companions.'

'Which was?'

'A society of equals. Men and women equal. Respect for the people of the book. Jews, Christians and Muslims. Not the so-called teachings of the scholars centuries later, whose proclamations undermined the values of tolerance and compassion.'

He was starting to sound like Ayatollah Fidel, so I tuned out. Knowing there was no way I could placate him, I did what I always did when he was so worked up, I packed the pipe and handed it to him. Getting close to Moroccans was a rocky road.

The Europeans I discovered were not much better. Sadly, you couldn't "unknow" them or pretend you didn't see them in the street. In that respect Fez was a tiny village in which the expat community was small but highly visible. Of course there were exceptions, but by and large the Medina of the Europeans was a closed system, feeding on itself, fuelled by gossip, envy and red wine. Everyone knew everyone's business, and even in the short time I had been in Fez, I had seen cliques form and then splinter, friendships and affairs blossom then wither. If the conversation wasn't about building, real estate and restoration it concerned who had arrived, who had left and who was sleeping with whom. I found it tedious. The visibility in public was however something I could remedy. Since the revelation that by donning a *djellaba* I could blend into the street, I had purchased a simple black one with a touch of subtle red embroidery around the neck and hood. While I couldn't quite go as far as wearing *babouche* on my wanderings around the Medina, I did have some at home. The result of my purchase was that in the alleys and lanes I simply melded into the crowds and nobody even glanced at me. There was no ridicule, no jeering, simply no reaction. It was only when I stopped walking that the problems started.

'You look like death warmed up.'

The voice was Sandra's and I resented it. I was slightly stoned and so I instructed my head to look up. The instruction was obeyed and I could see her quite clearly silhouetted against the large mulberry tree at the top of the Tala'a Sghira beside Tuhami's small street restaurant. It was becoming more and more obvious that I was going to have to stop coming out in public if I was going to be continually accosted by these people.

'What have you done to yourself?'

She meant my I scalp, I suppose, but it could well have been my hair which I had allowed to grow. Or maybe it was that I had stopped shaving and my beard was progressing at a faster pace than my hair, albeit with a lot more grey. I plumped for my scalp. 'I cut myself.'

I must have mumbled because she sat down with an annoying look of distress on her face.

'Richard, someone attacked you.' As if it was a fact. None of her business, I thought and returned to eating. She will go away. I will make her go away and leave me alone.

She lit a cigarette.

'I was going to ask you what you think about my idea. I have decided to open an agency to help newcomers buy and restore houses. If you think about it, when we first came here we were so naive, clueless really. But now we know how to work the system, we could assist others and save them all the hassles of having to deal directly with the Moroccans. It's a great idea and I just know there would be money in it. I suppose we would have to market it at first, but, hell, this place is wide open, don't you think?'

Thinking was the last thing on my mind. Out of the corner of my eye I saw her signal to Tuhami for some food and knew I would have to leave.

'Richard!' She snapped as I stood up. 'Don't just go. I really want to talk to you.'

Somehow, I managed to keep a lid on a sudden and uncharacteristic surge of anger I was experiencing. I wanted to grab hold of her, shake her and tell her to stop being such a stupid fucking bitch.

'I have to meet Autumn,' I said.

'Who?'

As I marched across to the Tala'a Kebira it dawned on me that I hadn't paid Tuhami. I hesitated and was about to turn around when I saw four people coming up the Tala'a—Malcolm, Bridie, James and, tagging along in the rear, Bridie's Moroccan, Mohammed from Marrakech. They were probably on their way to Tuhami's to go ooh and ah at Sandra's latest bowel movement. The last thing I needed was another facile conversation, an update on restorations and all the usual expat twaddle. As far as Tuhami was concerned, I knew he would understand and know that I would pay him on my next visit. There was no time to waste. Finding myself underneath the ruins of the famous Water Clock outside the Bouanania *Medersa*, I ducked in behind a gaggle of camera-wielding tourists, and kept my head down while I figured out what to do. To my left was the narrow tunnel-like alley, Derb Magana, dark enough to afford some protection and I slipped into its shadows and watched as the trio of expats meandered up the street with their Moroccan, deep in conversation. My heart was beating and a familiar sick feeling was circling my stomach.

After a couple of minutes the nausea passed but I was just about to make my escape when I saw him.

At first I thought the man to be a tardy German left behind by the tour group, someone who had fiddled too long with his camera. He stood, illuminated in a shaft of sunlight at the end of the alley; short, thickset and barrel-chested, the slightly puffy face was gaunter now but I knew it, knew him, the same chin swathed in dark stubble. It was not possible, I told myself as I watched him push his panama hat back on his head revealing the short black hair that I had tried so hard to forget. He removed his sunglasses and began polishing them on the fabric of his t-shirt. This time my heart felt as though it had stopped. I was back in the cloud forest. Lucho was in front of me, his soft hands holding the small guinea pig. Lucho of the Shining Path.

The effect was seismic, the earth beneath me shifted. Dizzy and disoriented, I felt myself toppling forward. Just in time I shot out a hand and steadied myself against the wall, gasping in an atmosphere suddenly stripped of oxygen.

It was a mirage, it had to be, a nightmare in broad daylight. Taking another deep breath, I straightened up and peered down the tunnel. The man held his sunglasses up to the sun, checking they were clean and then, before putting them back on he looked into the shadows, the eyes fixing themselves on me, holding me against the wall. There was a thin smile on his lips, but it was the eyes—dark glowing orbs with a tinge of yellow—that fused me to the spot; the eyes of a jaguar.

Behind me the shrill laughter of a woman, but I could not drag my eyes away. On the Tala'a the flow had stopped, frozen, a street of statues, held in place by my fear.

'Sorry, Michael, I had to wait for my change.' The young woman brushed past me and hurrying up to the man, who seconds before had been another, took his arm. 'I just have to tell Anna and Jilly that we had camel-burger.'

'Let's find this henna souk,' the man smiled. 'I have to get presents for half of Norwich, remember?'

The man who was not Lucho gave her hand a squeeze and the street moved again, much as it had always done. But something had changed, shifted, for now I knew that there were shadows and wraiths that could walk abroad even under a clear blue sky.

Behind me, further down the alley was a café, one of the only restaurants run by an expat. The owner, the flamboyant, George, had arrived from the high-pressure world of the Toronto restaurant scene and fallen in love with the Medina. Few had paid much attention, thinking his dreams of a life in Fez just that, dreams. Like others I had thought that his ardour would cool in the face of the behemoth that is Moroccan bureaucracy, and he would fade away, returning whence he came, like so many before him. None of us had taken into account his tenacity and, the reason I now respected him, his genuine desire to get close to the locals. He was one of the few expats I was happy to spend time with. He could also cook up a storm and was generous with his skills. Needing a drink, I walked the few short steps and entered the café.

Apart from two couples that I took to be French tourists, the café's patrons were Moroccan. With a wordless greeting—a nod and a hand to my heart—I found a table in a corner and tried to still my senses. My head was spinning and the nausea, though abating was still an uncomfortable background to my adrenalin-fuelled system. Of course, it had not been Lucho. However, because (other than my lapse into storytelling) I had assiduously avoided contemplating my past, I had never considered that he might still be alive, and the possibility that, if so, he might come looking for me. I dismissed the thought but not the residue of paranoia that lingered leaving me distinctly uncomfortable.

'What's your poison, Richard?'

I looked up into a friendly face, a smiling face, George's face.

'Nice *djellaba*,' he added without a trace of mockery.

'Thanks, *Nus-nus* and a glass of water.'

'Sidi Ali, alright?'

It was the bottled water I preferred, so I nodded.

'You okay?' A look of concern flitted across George's face.

'Don't ask.'

'Not a problem, comrade,' he grinned. 'One *nus-nus* and a Sidi Ali coming up.'

That was what I liked about George; he is sensitive enough to know when to leave something alone. Mind you, I wish he hadn't used the word "poison" as it immediately evoked the images of dead hands and witchcraft from Yazami's bizarre tales. While I had taken the story with a grain of salt I nevertheless found myself flinching every time someone offered me couscous

'*Nus-nus* and Sidi Ali,' George said, dragging me back to reality. 'I hope you're feeling better soon.'

'I'm fine George,' I said a fraction too sharply.

Later, I went home and arrived without incident. These days I timed it so that the workmen had gone and I could be alone. Unknown to anyone I had been working my own magic; a magic so cunning that nobody suspected. I conjured them and they arrived; the twins—hand in hand—autumn and illness. That I needed to get ill was obvious and as the summer trailed off, I obliged, inventing a cold at first, then a fever, welcoming it like an honoured guest.

The gift the guest brought me was solitude. I could take to my bed and leave the big cedar doors shut all day, avoiding the dust and the workman and the silent Mira, who refused to look at me. I suspect that was because she knew there was now another woman or possibly she didn't care.

Yazami took control of things. He organised the workers, fewer now that we were nearly done, so he told me, but I no longer chose to look. Upstairs, he said, was very fine. *Very fine?* What did that mean? I made a point of not finding out. And the terrace, newly tiled and plastered with something called *medluck* or *medluke*—I never really caught the word he used. Upstairs is not my realm. It is probably "fine" but I have not climbed the stairs in weeks.

What I did do was to come out at night. Late, after the last call to prayer, I went to the courtyard, wrapped in a thick *burnous* that Yazami had purchased for me. Then I would wait until she called me through the peacock gate. If she failed to appear I would lie back on a banquette and watch the stars wheeling overhead as I talked to people. Aisling sometimes, Eric of course because he was a better listener—dear Eric, alone among everyone I had known as the only person I truly missed. I should have written or at least sent him a card of course, but with my nights so full, I had no energy during the daylight hours.

It was only a few days after the *lila* that she made her first appearance and in retrospect the most amazing thing is that I was not surprised. In the middle of the night I heard a noise, the tinkling sound of running water coming from the courtyard, even though I distinctly remember having turned off the fountain before retiring. Slipping a cotton *djellaba* over my head, I opened the door and stepped out into a courtyard bathed in the glow of a full moon that was sailing directly above the house. She was hunched on the edge of the fountain, legs tucked, arms wrapped around them, her attention on the running water splashing into the fountain. Often at night I hear the late-night sounds of the Medina, the lone artisan tapping away, the clip clop of a donkey passing down the alley. But this night there was nothing. Not even a finger of breeze reached out for my face as I stood in a silence and stillness so complete that I thought my breathing to be an intrusion.

The hood of her aqua *djellaba* was up, covering her hair, her face was not towards me, but facing the fountain and yet I knew that if she turned I would see those amber eyes, that cinnamon skin. And turn she would, I was certain, for this was a moment woven deep in the tapestry that lay between us.

You bled for me.

The voice was so deep, inside me, around me, accompanied by a slight shifting of the air and the scent of orange-flower water.

I have never taken a Nazarene.

Despite the warm evening, I was struck with a sudden chill and began to shake uncontrollably, to the point where I feared I would fall to the ground. Small patches of my skin quivered and I twitched in involuntary spasms. Under my flesh my bones were aching and itchy.

She laughed, sharp and cold as razorblades. *You desire to feed my hunger, Nazarene?*

'What do you want?' It was my mouth moving but my voice sounded as if it came from elsewhere. A bubble of fear rose in me, emerging in an involuntary gasp.

Be still! She commanded and my shaking stopped. Then she turned her head towards me and brushed the hood back from her face; that face, the amber eyes, lips the colour of pomegranate juice. She was Mira, but not the Mira I knew.

You will never have her if you have me. The words were flung at me like a dagger and I staggered back, recoiling from her power.

'Who are you,' I whispered, knowing that if I was being tested, I was failing.

Do you want to call me by her name?

I shook my head.

There are many names I am called. Lalla Dghughiyya I am named by some because it was Sidi Ahmed who brought me here centuries ago. Others call me Lalla A'isha Gnawiyya, Lalla A'isha Sudaniyya or Lalla...

'A'isha...'

A'isha Qandisha.

'A'isha Qandisha,' I repeated, knowing even as I spoke it that it was more than just a name. It was promise and threat, pleasure and pain. It was a prison into which I was begging admittance.

You will only have me. Swear it. Swear it now.

'I swear.'

And no other, unless I tell you to do so.

'I understand.'

She stood, or rather was suddenly standing, for I didn't see her move until she was before me; the tallest woman I have ever seen. Running a finger down the front of her *djellaba* she cut the fabric and gathered it with her other hand so she remained covered.

Tell me your true name.

A quiver of fear ran through me but I told her.

Marcus, Marcus... she rolled it around her mouth like a morsel of flesh; the sound of it on her voice, a balm that soothed away the past and glowed a soft burnt orange.

Without another word, she walked past me to what had been the door of my salon. In place of the great cedar panels was a gate of peacock feathers that parted as she went inside. Far away in the recess of my brain a voice told me not to follow, insisting that this was delusion and that I could stop myself if I wanted. The stupid voice had no idea... and neither did I.

Let me try and describe the indescribable.

Stepping through that iridescent gate I entered the shimmering realm of A'isha's wild and untamed magic; a realm so foreign, so removed from my western concepts of magic, as to be incomprehensible. This was not some folklore born from stereotypes handed down from generation to generation, no myth from bygone ages incarnate. I had entered a space that existed without names or form, a space that lived and engulfed me, a space in which thought was alien and yet all that existed was thought.

The space was A'isha in all her forms. I have a vivid recollection of her standing naked in front of me, a beauty so terrifying that I recoiled as if my eyes had been splashed with acid. The moment of transition, of fear and disorientation, passed and I became at one with the space. Enraged by a lust so deep it transcended flesh; I stood my ground and claimed her.

A'isha kissed me and I dissolved into the cavern of her mouth, a chamber of delirium and transcendence. Roots of a giant fig tree curled through the space, through us, her legs ancient and strong, her hair, the matted fibres of wet roots from plants above the grotto. Water or perhaps it was blood, flowed on a stone floor that transformed, becoming soft moist moss, then mud, as we sunk down. In this dank swamp a beast was rutting, its haunches punching air that swirled, thick with smoke, from guttering candles and incense.

This is Ayn Kabir and in this place, you will obey me absolutely.

'Of course.'

Anger welled up in me, a massive anger, at the realisation that, until this moment, I had been denying my true nature and in that moment of revelation, I saw that the rutting beast was me.

Her transformations were endless. One moment it was Aisling, her back arched, her head thrashing from side to side; Rachel too, grim and determined, her cries of passion a thin keening in blackness on the edge of hearing. And Mira. There were others, but always it was A'isha, gorging herself, feeding an insatiable hunger that consumed me time and again, yet left me charged, prepared to indulge her every whim. With my senses scrambled in the warp of chaos she was creating I saw, rather than heard, my own voice woven, a blood red weft on her loom: *Hahiya jat Hahiya jat Hahiya jat Lalla 'A'isha!*

I would not leave you with the impression that she was incapable of tenderness, but those rare moments came later. Sweet glowing moments filled with amber eyes, cinnamon skin slicked salty with sweat and the smile of a quiescent Mira, curled as soft and compliant as a faun, offering me her nipples while nibbling my neck with lips stained with the memory of pomegranate.

Are all the Nazarene like you?

Her mouth was drawn in a cruel smile.

'I can't speak for others.'

A change flowed around us and she stood, dressed again in Mira's body, above where I lay, spent, on the courtyard tiles. In her hand a knife, ivory handle tilted towards me; a challenge rather than a request. Taking it, I slit the flesh on my arm and felt a swelling joy as this now diminutive woman gently cleaned the wound with her tongue. Over her shoulder I saw that the doors of my salon were once again solid cedar.

Finally, she looked me in the eye and spoke with the voice of ice.

You shall have none but me and should you speak of this to anyone I shall kill you. To please me you will wear black and red, grow a beard and not cut your hair. You will only burn black jawi incense and when I demand it you will perform the hadra. Is that understood?

There was no need for me to respond for she knew that in that moment I would agree to everything she asked of me.

Good, then I will come again, inshallah.

Inshallah, I mumbled as I tumbled backwards.

Later, roused by the first call to prayer, I got to my feet and staggered to bed. My memory is not clear but I vaguely remember that the cut on my arm was aching and as my head hit the pillow I could smell a faint odour of turpentine.

Night after night she came and took me into her realm. Yet, it was not always the same place. Sometimes, her grotto at Ayn Kabir, sometimes a garden overgrown with weeds, at others a palace with rooms that we had no need to enter for they formed and dissolved around us. While I have vivid memories of the settings, I have little recall of our conversations, beyond the fact that she often tried to taunt me with lurid tales of her many other lovers, but when her descriptions failed to provoke me into jealousy or anger, she ceased. I may be fooling myself, but I do have a sense that she was surprised by my attention to pleasuring her rather than just myself. I could well be wrong.

Yazami once told me of an old Moroccan saying that he firmly believed in. *Better a handful of dried figs and be content with that, than to own the gate of peacocks and be kicked in the eye by a broody camel.* Yazami was wrong.

Part of me knew that I was going, or had gone, insane. But the visions were too seductive and I let myself go deeper and deeper. In amidst the chaos in my head there were flashes of clarity that seemed real; a glass of tea in my hand, a portion of bread dipped in olive oil and the unexpected arrival one afternoon of Yazami and Mernisi tugging a reluctant sheep.

'*Eid Mubarak Said*,' Yazami said. 'Tomorrow you can cut its throat.'

A'isha: Eid Mubarak

Blood runs across the floors of houses, through the drains, and in the streets before seeping into the ground and streams. Waking in the evening of Eid El Kbir, the blood calls to me. In the pools and grottos the water is the colour of roses. Rising up, I pass the piles of skins and entrails and see the remnants of the fires where sheep and goats heads have been scorched and cooked. The smoke from fires still hangs in the still air. It is my time and it is glorious.

Richard has had blood on his hands. Though I did not witness his slitting of the sheep's throat, I sense the scene; the blood spurting, the last feeble cries of the sacrifice and his friends tugging the skin from the animal. He is becoming familiar with blood.

For now he is content to give himself to me and I content to play with him. Yet there is more to his blood and I will know it before he becomes my sacrifice.

Richard: The gathering of baraka

The weeks after Eid were tiresome. I existed in a state of perpetual exhaustion, with little or no attention to anything but the coming of night. Fortunately, I found it increasingly easy to sleep during the daylight hours and when sleep was not possible I decamped to the café at R'cif where I established myself against the rear wall of the forecourt. Once this had been crazy Thami's haunt but he was now ensconced in my house, no doubt polishing something or other. My liking for the man had grown as I sensed that he was blessed but in a way that eluded me. His English had only marginally improved but his clarity was remarkable. When he grinned and told me to "fuck off" I understood his pride in mastering the phrase and felt the affection in the words.

My relationship with Mernisi, Mustapha and the other workers was still strong but Yazami was concerned that they had slowed down as they neared the completion of the restoration.

'It's understandable,' I told him. 'They'll be out of work soon, won't they?'

He shook his head. 'No, Richard, craftsmen like them will always find work, there are other crazy foreigners buying houses, you know.'

'Then why are they on a go slow?'

'Because they don't want to leave the house, they don't want to leave you.'

'Twaddle,' I scoffed. 'I am just the cash machine—'

He cut me off with a dismissive gesture. 'No, Richard, they genuinely like you. You are different from other bosses. You don't beat them or shout at them...'

'Well, I am hardly likely...'

'And then there is the house.'

'What about the house?'

He leaned over the coffee table and pulled me closer, his voice a low, conspiratorial whisper, 'They sense that *she* is happy here.'

'Who do you mean, Mira?' Silent, sweet, beautiful Mira—oblivious to what passed between us in A'isha's dark realm—a virgin whose body I had enjoyed so many times now. A rush of blood coloured my cheeks, as the shame of what I was doing struck me. But could I have stopped using her, could I have refused A'isha's manifestation? It was pointless to consider because I knew that, faced with a choice, I would do the same again.

After the first few tempestuous weeks A'isha had taken to vanishing for several days at a time. Her infrequency caused me considerable unhappiness and the nights when she did not appear I prowled the courtyard, splashing the tiles with orange-flower water and even cutting myself so that the blood would attract her attention. Yet days would pass without her and then she would appear with lurid tales of trysts with the multiple lovers and "husbands" as she referred to the men who had devoted themselves to her.

'Not Mira,' Yazami hissed, 'You are going crazy, *khoya*. You know *who* I mean. They feel there is *baraka* here.'

He still refused to say *her* name. I found it annoying so I tipped forward on my chair and touched his hand. 'You mean *Lalla* A'isha?'

It was as if I had struck him.

'I have to get back. Mernisi wants a hand to take some scaffolding down.'

His tone was curt to the point of insolence. Oh shit, I thought, now I have really pissed him off. But Yazami was like grass bent by the wind; he always straightened when the storm had passed.

The waiter, Si Mohammed, watched Yazami leave and came over with a croissant and a *nus-nus*. He had taken to looking after me and maybe it was the tips, but I chose to think he actually liked me. How would I ever know? There was in me, I realised, a deep and foolish desire to be not only liked but also acknowledged for the effort I was putting into assimilating. Yet, even as I thought it, I saw the idiocy of my efforts. Assimilation was a path marked "no entry"; a path to hopelessness in a land with no St Jude at fullback. I chuckled out loud at the image of Jude in rugby kit and, ignoring the stares from some of the young men in the café, ripped the croissant to pieces and spent the next few minutes soaking up my entire coffee and thinking about the stranger I had seen that morning.

It had been reasonably early, around the time of the second call to prayer, and having endured a night without visitation, I had stumbled out into the alley to procure a baguette and bottle of Sidi Ali. As I was walking back from the *hanut* I saw a European carrying a tea-towel covered tray. Protruding from the side of the towel I could see the outline of unbaked bread. The man was heading to the bakery. I checked myself; this was a white person, a European and yet he was taking his bread to the bakery just like a Moroccan. The man had not appeared to notice that underneath my *djellaba* I was also European and passed by without a glance in my direction.

What was peculiar was that not only had I never seen the man before, I had never heard of any other European living in my district. I felt cheated. He looked as if he had assimilated rather well. Maybe he had managed to wrangle a tourist visa for St Jude. I never saw him again and when I asked Yazami and Yusuf, they professed to having never heard about him. It is possible I imagined him.

It was after midday when I left the café and made my way home to find the workers all gathered around the fountain while, in the kitchen, Mira was deep in conversation with an older woman dressed in traditional costume, her headscarf supplemented by a hood.

Before I had a chance to go and introduce myself to the stranger, Yazami sidled up to me and taking my arm, guided me to the far side of the courtyard. All traces of his previous animosity or displeasure appeared to have evaporated in the warmth of midday.

'*Lalla* Fatima Fasiyya, she's a *sharifa*—a descendant of the Prophet. An important woman and some say, an '*aguza*.'

'She's a witch?'

Yazami shrugged. 'She's a powerful woman.'

'So, what is she doing here?'

'*Lalla* Fatima is advising Mira about certain matters.' He shot me a dark look. 'Things which are between women stay between women.'

'You mean you don't know?'

He raised his hands in a gesture of surrender. 'Richard...'

'Okay, I know when to stop digging.'

That appeared to cause Yazami some relief and not a little amusement. 'You are in danger of becoming wise,' he laughed. 'Now, before Fatima leaves, it would be appropriate for you to give her a gift.'

'Really, what does she need?' I nearly suggested a new broomstick, but stopped myself in time. Unfortunately, I failed to fool Yazami who immediately picked up on my tone. His brow furrowed as he squinted at me and slowly shook his head. 'Richard, do not joke about these matters. There are rumours about you and *Lalla* Fatima could be an important ally.'

'Rumours, what rumours? And what the hell are "these matters" that are so damned secret women's business that we can't talk of them?'

'This is not the moment. You trust me, don't you?'

'Like a brother,' I replied and meant it.

'Then trust that I will talk more of this when we are alone. For now, I suggest you get some of the *jawi* you asked me to buy for you. You have more than you will ever need and such a present would be very significant.'

Without waiting for my approval or otherwise he let himself into the salon, located my stash of the black aromatic resin and wrapped a generous quantity in a twist of paper.

'Here. I will do the talking and then give you a nod if it is right to present it to her. Don't forget, only use—'

'My right hand. I'm not a complete idiot.'

'Not yet complete.' Yazami sighed.

'What do you mean *if* it is right? I thought you said I *should* give her something.'

'I was being over hasty. It depends on the outcome of my plans.'

'Oh, so this is something you set up?'

'Not directly. And I cannot control the outcome; the camel driver has his plans and the camel has his.'

'Ha! So Yazami can get things wrong?'

Yazami grinned slyly. 'It has happened that I have made mistakes. Only *Allah* is perfect.'

Half an hour later Fatima emerged from the kitchen, called Yazami over and engaged him in a terse conversation. My distinct impression was that she was lecturing him, but not understanding more than one word in a hundred, I could be wrong. For all I know they might have been discussing Barcelona's clash with Arsenal. The local café had been showing reruns for the last few days and even as a football illiterate I could describe Jens Lehmann being sent off after bringing down Samuel Eto'o; by the reaction of café's patrons you would have been excused for thinking Morocco had won the World Cup.

I had to wait until Fatima departed to discover what they had been talking about. However, before that happened, I was invited over for what felt like paying my respects.

'*Lalla* Fatima says it is a pleasure to meet you,' Yazami translated. 'She admires the work you have done in restoring the house.'

'Not actually my work...' I began, but was ignored.

'*Sharifa* Fatima hopes you will have many healthy years of happiness in the house.' Yazami concluded and nodded at me. Following his cue, I produced the small packet of incense, wishing that I had asked Yazami to wrap it in something better than old newspaper.

'Please tell her it is an honour to have her visit my humble house.' I obviously had the tone right for Yazami beamed as he translated. Empowered by my success I added. 'It would please me if *Lalla* Fatima would accept this small token of thanks for the pleasure of making her acquaintance.' I handed the incense over. 'It is *jawi*,' I said, 'but I am not sure what that is.'

'*Luban jawi*,' *Lalla* Fatima said and her face broke into a wide grin that revealed a better set of teeth than most Moroccan women of her age I had encountered. Yazami murmured something and the woman's response was long and, judging by Yazami's frown, complex. A couple of times he nodded and then, when she was done, translated.

'Fatima says it is very important incense and your choice of it as a gift confirms the good things she has heard about you. She also says that although it comes from a far distant place, it has been known in Morocco for centuries.'

'That's interesting—'

He touched my arm. 'There's more.'

'*Luban jawi*,' *Lalla* Fatima repeated almost wistfully.

'It comes from Java and is not only used as incense but to make...
to make...' He switched back to *Darija* and had another conversation, thankfully a shorter one. I was interested in the source of the incense, having spent some time in that part of the world hunting the Sumatran Sunbeam—*Curetis saronis sumatrana*. I had a vague memory of a small local industry producing what they called Javanese frankincense. The villagers would damage the trees and collected the aromatic resin. *Styrax Benzoin*—that was the tree and if I remember correctly, butterflies avoided it. Sometimes I marvel at how my brain has kept such odd facts filed for airing on unlikely occasions.

'Ah! Now I understand, *lait virginal*; the milk of virgins.'

'What?'

'She is saying that if it is dissolved in alcohol—'

'A tincture.'

'Yes, that. Then mixed with rose-flower water it is called "milk of virgins" and women put it on their faces to make their skin glow.'

Yazami's face was glowing but I figured it was more because of the frank conversation with an older woman than any application of virgin's milk.

After a few more pleasantries, Yazami showed *Lalla* Fatima to the door.

'What the hell was all that about?' I asked when he returned.

He perched on the edge of the wall-fountain and tugged at his beard as though seriously considering how to reply, the mischievous look in his eye was a dead giveaway. 'I think it was an exchange of *baraka*.'

'You gain *baraka*—a blessing—by talking about virgin's milk? Give me a break.'

'She was bestowing some of her *baraka* on you and in return she got a small amount of *baraka* from you.'

'Oh sure, we blessed each other.'

Yazami pushed himself off the fountain and came over to the table to pack his *sebsi*. 'She has *baraka* because of who she is and you because of where you live and who you live with.'

'You mean *her*?' I had learned to avoid terminating our conversations by never uttering A'isha's name. 'Is that what the rumours are about?'

Yazami looked me up down and returned his attention to the ball of *kif* he was rolling. 'A foreigner wouldn't add everything up but Moroccans can and do. We are subtle like that.'

'Add what things up? For Christ's sake, Yazami stop talking in bloody riddles.'

Yazami snorted. 'Not for Christ's sake, for *your* sake. How hard do you think it is? Take a look in a mirror. Your hair is all over the place, you have grown a beard and you're not just wearing a *djellaba*, you are wearing black and red. Whose colours do you think those are? And black *jawi*? Everyone knows that's *her* incense. You might as well have a sign above your head.'

There was a force behind his words, a real intensity and yet I sensed it born from frustration rather than anger. 'Is that a bad thing?' I asked.

'Richard, we all have to walk the path that unfolds before us. My only caution is for you to walk, not run. A while ago I joked about you becoming *shahbi*—one of the people, and all I am saying now is take care not to rush. Few westerners ever get to glimpse what I suspect you have seen. Treasure it, but be careful, very careful.'

He was no longer joking, but neither was he finished.

'*Lalla* Fatima was not just here because of you, she came because there was something that needed to be said to Mira, but it does concern all of us.'

'Yes?' I took the pipe and waited while he fished in his pocket for his lighter.

'For the last few years Mira has wanted to take Thami to a very special ceremony in the countryside near Meknes.'

'What kind of ceremony?'

'A week after the Prophet's birthday there is a *mousem*, a pilgrimage to the tomb of the Sufi saint, Sidi Ali ben Hamdush. The climax of the pilgrimage is a *lila* and a performance of the *hadra* and Mira believes that if she makes a sacrifice and takes Thami along to the *hadra* and then there is a chance he will be cured or at least his condition will improve.'

After inhaling a mouthful of smoke, I handed the pipe back. 'Cured by a sacrifice to a saint?'

'No, the sacrifice is to her.'

'Sorry, I'm confused; a sacrifice to Mira?'

Yazami leaned across the table and lowered his voice. 'No. The sacrifice is to *Lalla A'isha*.'

That he said the name out loud was an indication just how serious the discussion had become, so I decided against interrupting and nodded for him to continue.

'Each year I have refused to let her go because it is a dangerous undertaking and there was little chance that Mira would be admitted to the mausoleum where the *hadra* is performed. However, since things have changed I decided on a compromise. You remember the Hamadcha *muqaddim*, Abderrahim?'

'Yes, the leader of the musicians at the *lila*.'

'He and his team will perform the *hadra* inside mausoleum so I talked with him and he has talked with *Lalla* Fatima. What we have arranged is that instead of Mira going, I will take Thami. Abderrahim and Fatima have given me an undertaking that we will all be admitted.'

'All?' I had a sudden premonition of where this was going.

'Not Mira, of course, but we all agree that you must come.'

That was the moment I should have seized. In that instant I should have told him that I was not going anywhere and certainly not somewhere that I might be expected to dance and make a fool of myself again. Assertiveness has never been one of my great strengths and so it proved once again. Instead of standing up for myself and speaking out, I allowed myself to be included in whatever Yazami was hatching without consultation. Instead I retreated, muttering something about discussing it later I went to the salon for a rest, where, despite the amount of coffee I had consumed, I fell asleep almost straight away.

It is rare that I dream of taxonomy and I would hazard a guess that it is rare that anyone does. To go further (*kif* has that effect) I would argue that taxonomy is particularly difficult to dream at all. The rigid divisions of science are not given to the flowing, interweaving and melding that most dreams rely on. Yet, somehow, I managed to produce a dream from seemingly unsuitable subject matter.

It was, I confess, not the sort of taxonomic dream that one taxonomist would willingly share with another, as it was too basic. This was not upper stratosphere high science, rather a guided descent down the taxonomic ladder from the platform built by Linnaeus. Like a child on a playground jungle gym I swung quickly from *Lepidoptera* to my favourite members of the Super-family *Papilionoidea*—the true butterflies—the gossamer winged *Lycaenidae*. A warm welling up of pleasure accompanied the images as I reviewed and explained the features of the *Lycaenidae* to an audience who appeared (as they can do in dreams) to have been there all along. It was good to be on such solid ground, in the familiar territory of the knowable; the names, the classifications; things worth discussing and arguing about. That was what first attracted me to *lepidoptera*—they could be pinned down.

'And this,' I dreamed myself saying, 'is Morocco's *Plebicula atlantica*, the Atlas Blue and here's an interesting fact. The adult males are predominantly blue due to reflected light rather than pigmentation.'

'Have you ever seen one,' a woman's voice asked.

Although I looked around I couldn't see a woman anywhere. 'Of course I have,' I lied. It was then that I woke up.

After dressing and grabbing a warm jacket (just in case), I checked the time. It was only 3.30 in the afternoon; plenty of time. Having checked that Mira was not in the kitchen, I tossed a bottle of Sidi Ali, a round of flat bread and a handful of dates into a plastic bag and made for the door.

'Are you going, Richard?'

Yazami had a sixth sense when it came to keeping an eye on me. He meant well, but I didn't need babysitting.

'Off out,' I said hoping it was sufficiently oblique. It wasn't.

'Shall I come with you?'

'Thanks Yazami, but I would prefer if you would keep an eye on Mernisi and the boys. We don't want them slowing down, do we.' Maybe I shut the door a fraction too quickly because I never heard his response, but I could imagine it.

Yazami might well have plans for me, but I had a plan of my own and that was to keep the left-hand side of my brain fully engaged. In the last few weeks I had been running out of control, too much craziness, I told myself. So, I determined to go hunting for an Atlas Blue. The chances of finding one were minimal given the lateness of the season, but it was good to have a mission and as I strode down the alleys to R'cif, I felt better than I had in weeks. Notwithstanding the pleasure afforded by my nights with A'isha, I had been experiencing disconcertingly regular panic attacks that left me trembling and drained to the point where I felt that a modicum of control over my life was necessary. A butterfly hunt seemed like the perfect antidote.

The souk was in the process of opening again after the long afternoon break. Stallholders were pulling back the tarpaulins and sheets of plastic that had covered their produce, vegetables were being arranged, herbs freshened up with a splash of water and the cats, who also take a siesta, were prowling back and forth in anticipation.

At R'cif my good mood was enhanced by the presence of a vacant taxi without a screaming horde of women fighting for possession. However, a problem arose when I explained where I wanted to go.

'Djebel Zalagh? La Sidi. Non Monsieur.'

I repeated that I wanted to go to Mount Zalagh but because I couldn't command enough *Darija* to explain how important my journey was, that was where the conversation ended.

The next taxi driver was more accommodating, nodding and smiling as I sunk down in a seat unencumbered by the presence of springs or even much upholstery.

'Djebel Zalagh,' I said.

He paused from fiddling with the radio and looked at me.

'Djebel Zalagh? Wakha Sidi.' He continued surfing through the static until he located a station broadcasting Qur'anic chanting. I suspect he was deaf or detested conversation because he turned the volume up to the point where I could feel the metal beneath me vibrating like a sub-woofer. There was no sign of seat belts and the driver's only concession to safety was a hastily yelled *"bismillah"* as we set off.

After executing a U-turn that came close to sideswiping a donkey, we barrelled off around the edge of the Medina towards Batha and beyond.

There is in Morocco an inverse relationship between the power and mechanical condition of the 2600 little red taxis, and the speed at which they are driven. My *petit taxi*, a Fiat Uno, sounded as though it needed a tune up several million kilometres ago and yet the driver, a man in his seventies, drove like Lewis Hamilton on crack. His myopic squinting through Coke-bottle lenses did little to instil confidence, but I took a modicum of comfort in the sheath of stained plastic dangling from the cracked rear vision mirror. It contained a verse from the Qur'an. It was good to have divine insurance.

When the cold air rushing in became bothersome I discovered that the handles to wind up the windows had been removed or stolen. Weaving in and out of traffic, swerving to avoid a bus coming at speed on the wrong side of the road, dodging pedestrians—the old man took it all in his stride. He seemed unflappable, supremely confident of Allah's protection. It was also possible, I realised, that he was acutely blind.

After passing the Palais Jamais Hotel we came to the edge of the city where, instead of continuing to the base of the mountain that loomed above us, my driver stopped abruptly. My wearing a *djellaba* obviously did not fool the man and with the well-developed mime and charade skills necessary to communicate with crazy foreigners he indicated that if he went any further he might be picked up by the police. Not even this setback could dampen my ebullient mood and after paying him a lot more than what the meter would have read had it worked, I found myself enjoying the challenge of hitchhiking for the first time in over thirty years.

To my surprise, it proved remarkably easy. Within a matter of minutes a truck overloaded with hay bales cruised to a stop and a door that had started life on some other vehicle was thrust open. The driver leaned over and with a gnarled hand pulled me into the passenger seat—a metal café chair tied in with number 8 fencing wire. There seemed to be no floor in the cab and the noise was so loud that I had trouble believing he heard me yell my intended destination, nevertheless after some more shouting back and forth there was an agonising crunching of gears and we chugged off at a far more relaxing pace than my previous ride.

My fears about where we were going were soon allayed as we turned off the main road and started a laborious climb up the winding bends at the foot of the mountain. Another kilometre or so brought us to a fork in the road and after a little more yelling and pointing I realised that he was going left and I should continue on to the right, so I thanked him and clambered down.

Ahead of me lay a rutted track that would have tested any four-wheel drive vehicle. *Not a problem*, I told myself, *you need the exercise.* Apart from a chill breeze, the day was perfect, the sky cloudless. Above me a kestrel hung on the wind watching my slow progress. The steepness of the climb tested my diminished fitness and required that I spent a considerable amount of time sitting on boulders searching the dry dusty landscape for butterflies. At this I was not particularly successful, my only sighting being a rather battered male Black Satyr, *Satyrus actaea*. It is a dull looking member of the *Satyridae* but the tell-tale spot on its upper wing—a black eye with a white iris—makes it easy to identify. The hot dusty terrain would have suited it well, though I was surprised to see it so late in the season. I toasted my first Mount Zalagh butterfly with a swig of water. Bringing only one bottle of Sidi Ali had been a mistake, and so from then on I rationed myself to small sips at frequent intervals.

Shortly after my second or third stop I heard a yell from further up the hill. A family at work in their olive grove had caught site of me and were waving a welcome. I waved back and plodded on.

Several minutes later a boy of about ten came down the track on a donkey, I paused to take a sip of water and to greet him but as he came abreast of me he smiled shyly and prodded his animal forward.

My rate of ascent was painfully slow and before I reached the family, the boy and his donkey had returned from down the hill and passed me again. In one hand the boy was clutching a bunch of mint so fresh that I caught a faint trace of its scent on the air as he rode by.

Eventually I approached the grove of olives where the family, having abandoned any pretence at work, were crouched in the dirt watching the unexpected entertainment—a foreigner in a *djellaba*, scrambling up to their barren kingdom. I suppressed a momentary image of eagles watching prey. As I drew level with them I touched my hand to my heart and much to their considerable amusement, collapsed onto the ground in order to catch my breath and let the pain in my calves and thighs abate.

What followed was a very one-sided conversation. My few words of *Darija* allowed me to do little more than introduce myself and although I had reached the point where I could understand fragments of everyday chat, it was of little use. The family were *Imazighen*—*Amazigh*, which used to be called Berber, and conversing in whichever one of the languages they spoke. None of this mattered, for once they had judged me to be fit to continue, they helped me up and indicated that I should follow them along a narrow track beneath the trees.

To my amazement, and relief, we had walked for no more than ten minutes when we circled a rocky outcrop, stepped through a row of prickly pear cactus and found ourselves on top of Mount Zalagh.

The family home, an aerie if ever I saw one, had a view that, if not for the difficulty of access, would have had a developer salivating. The panorama encompassed the entire Saïss plain and reached from Djebel Teghat on the right to the dark brooding massif of Zerhoun far away to the left. Closer at hand, nestled in the folds of Djebel Zalagh, was the Medina, its halo of blue haze penetrated at one point by the oily black smoke of the ceramic factories on the outskirts. Despite the pollution, the minaret and roof of what I suppose was the Qarawiyne shone in the late afternoon sun like green emeralds encircled in citrine.

A young boy's hand tugged at my sleeve and I was dragged away from the view to be offered what I suspect was their only chair now carefully placed in front of the wattle and daub constructions that made up their home. Having established that we couldn't communicate in words, we sat in a comfortable silence as a number of other people came and joined us. It was, I decided, not a family but a tribe.

The *Imazighen* dwellings were not so much single houses as a ring of small buildings, some for humans and others for the wide variety of animals that wandered freely. Lean goats and straggly looking sheep were grazing under the watchful eye of a boy who couldn't have been older than five or six. Several hens, as well as dogs and cats appeared to be quite at home with each other in the small courtyard in front of what I took to be the main house, until a cow emerged, being shooed by an elderly woman carrying a tray of glasses and a huge pot of mint tea. When I produced my piece of bread there was a murmur of appreciation and a young girl was sent scurrying inside to fetch more bread and a bowl of olive oil.

Being unable to follow the conversation, I amused myself by trying to classify the group. A human taxonomy of the *hominidae...* genus *homo*, species *homo sapiens*, subspecies *homo sapiens sapiens*. This tribe were all... I searched in my head for a descriptor—*Amazigh robustus, Berber Zalaghi, Berber Moroccanus?* No, I cautioned myself, stick to areas you know, stick to butterflies. The mind is a bizarre organ for my next tangent had me wondering if there had been a time when early anthropologists collected skulls, skeletons and hair samples to take back to their museums and universities. They had certainly done it with indigenous Australians, Native Americans, Inuit and the New Zealand Maori. Had they thought of them in the same way as exotic butterflies? They were certainly more difficult to pin to a board. It was a ghoulish thought, so I dragged myself out of the mental mire and back to the hospitable families in front of me.

Of the twenty-three adults, fifteen were women. I supposed that there were other men but that they had probably left the mountain to find employment. The children, whom I failed to count, appeared to belong to three younger women, all of whom had the glowing appearance of good health that comes with hard physical labour; the work horses of the mountain. Whereas all the men were as thin as whippets, the older women were plump, with one exception, a striking looking woman with penetrating eyes.

Probably in her early forties her face was gaunt and remarkably unlined. There was something arresting about her appearance for despite her luminescent eyes she had a fragile quality about her as if her soul had been gradually eaten by the mountain and only her skin, stretched over her cheekbones, taut like leather on a drum, held the spirit world at bay. I knew it would probably have been inappropriate, but it was the first time I wished I had a camera so that I could capture her face before she vanished completely.

It was the sugar of course, for by the time I had consumed three glasses of the extremely sweet mint tea I was on a high and knew it was time to make a move.

What followed was an enjoyable but complex series of mime performances in which (if I understood them correctly) I was offered a place to sleep for the night or a ride down the hill on a donkey. When I countered by using my hands and fingers to explain why I was going to keep walking around the top of the mountain there was much laughter and soon the entire community were flapping their hands, thumbs linked, in prefect imitation of the way western children make butterfly shadows on a wall. The unaffected spontaneity of the *Imazighen's* generous offer of transport or accommodation was heart-warming but when a thin sad-faced man came forward with a woman in her late thirties and turned her round for me to inspect, I decided it was time to leave.

Down in the Medina my coffee man, Yusuf, had told me that any number of families would be only too happy for me to take an unmarried or widowed daughter off their hands. It was not a plan on my agenda and my attempt at miming a polite refusal appeared to leave them rather perplexed. However, after a few words from an elderly man, a chorus of 'inshallah' and some awkward handshakes, I was on my way again, tracking up through prickly pear and thorn bushes onto the rocky slopes of the mountain.

Stopping for a moment to get my bearings I heard the sound of footsteps behind me and turned to see the woman who had so captured my imagination carrying a bundle and hurrying up a goat track to my right. Signalling me to follow but not pausing to check that I would do so, she rounded an outcrop of weathered rock and made for a small hillock where a lone tree, bent by years of high winds, leaned over the side of the mountain. There she halted and waited, watching, knowing that curiosity would get the better of me.

Instead of following one of the goat paths, I cut across the intervening terrain to where she stood, the bundle at her feet, her face impassive. I stepped around the exposed roots of the tree and found myself on a natural platform, a small flat area, but unlike the surrounding hillside, surprisingly verdant with a mixture of grass, moss and a few reeds. It was when I turned to try and ascertain the source of water that I saw the cave, a narrow triangle of shadow beneath the tree.

Gesturing me to duck my head, the woman crouched and shuffled forward into the darkness and then, sensing my hesitation, called to me to follow.

'*Aji sidi!*' The voice that issued from the cave had none of the fragility I had imagined in her. It was a command, not a request.

It is strange the way one becomes sensitised to cultural issues without consciously deciding to do so. My concern did not spring from a fear of confined spaces but rather about entering an enclosed space with a woman. Having considered it, I set my qualms aside and followed her.

It took a few seconds for my eyes to adjust to the small amount of light but when they did I saw that what had appeared from outside to be little more than a niche in the rock was a reasonably large cavern, almost circular as if a large round boulder had been rolled away leaving the space of the cave behind. The ceiling, though not high enough to allow me to stand unbent, was round and smooth. My first thought was that the cave was not particularly deep, but then I realised that what I had thought to be the back of the cave was actually a tangled curtain of tree roots, reaching down from the ceiling, through the space of the cave and into the earth on the floor.

Beside me the women struck a match and lit a small candle. As the light flared I heard myself gasp and felt a shiver across my scalp. Attached to the roots of the tree were dozens of pieces of cloth tied to the roots. They were all red and black.

On the cave floor I saw the stubs of old candles and the ashes from small amounts of incense.

'*Luban jawi*,' I said.

'*Iyeh, jawi.*' The woman whispered. She turned her face to mine and then pointed at the red embroidery around the edge of my *djellaba*. '*Lalla Sudaniyya. Lalla...*'

'*Lalla A'isha.*'

It may have been the flickering of the candle but for a moment her eyes appeared to burn with a fierce intensity as suddenly she radiated a power that was palpable.

'Karima,' she said. For a moment I was confused but then I realised that she was telling me her name.

'Ah! Karima,' I said and touched my hand to my heart.

She nodded and then tugging my sleeve, swivelled around to show me something else. It was the source of the water. Issuing from a crack in the rocks a tiny stream of water was trickling down into a small stone basin. From there it flowed over the edge and across the floor of the cave to the outside world. My Berber Karima scooped her cupped hands in the basin and drank, then moving out of the way, gestured for me to do likewise. The water felt very cold and tasted slightly metallic, as though it had been on a long subterranean journey before emerging in this special place.

Without a word, the woman crawled out into the daylight. I followed, blinking in the late afternoon sunlight, to find her unfolding her blanket. She handed me two rounds of fresh bread, a small plastic bag with goat's cheese and then pushed the blanket, two candles and a box of matches at me. When I started to thank her, she shook her head and looked at me for a moment. Her fragility had returned and her eyes were no longer burning, as if in the decision to return to her home she had resigned herself to living a life of unfocused regret.

'*Sidi Hammu Qiyu*,' she said slowly and pointed at me. Then, seeing that I clearly didn't understand she repeated it. '*Sidi Hammu Qiyu*'.

My sadness at not understanding was oddly profound as was the sense of loss when she turned and walked away. Not once did she look back.

When Karima was out of sight I stood for a long time looking out over the landscape below me. The vista was breath-taking, but while my eyes were taking in the view my mind was back in the cave wondering if I dared take up the challenge so obviously laid down by the blanket the woman and left me. The notion of spending a night on the mountain had never been part of my plan and flew in the face of my reason for coming in the first place. It had been my intention to put some distance between the Medina and myself; between me and what felt like the onset of a madness hovering around me.

As I turned back to contemplate the cave, a fluttering movement in the grasses to the side of the platform gave me a sudden thrill. It was the kind of movement every lepidopterist recognises instantly. This wasn't the butterfly of my dream—not the Atlas Blue—but *Lysandra punctifera* the Spotted Adonis Blue. For the second time in the last couple of hours I regretted not having a camera because the butterfly alighted on a rock no more than an arm's length from me. It was in perfect condition and judging by the blue colour it was a male, similar but larger and brighter than its European relative the Adonis Blue, *Lysandra bellargus*. Its most distinctive feature, the row of sub-marginal spots on the upper side, was clearly visible. It is true that I've seen a single male *bellargus* in Europe with the same spots, at least on the hind wing, but there was no doubting this was *punctifera*.

Then it took to the air, a magnificent sight, blue flashes in the sunlight alternating with the relatively inconspicuous underside until it vanished into the lengthening shadows on the hillside.

My feeling of contentment was such that I took the blanket, folded it into a cushion and sat, back against the smooth rock beside the cave entrance, and watched the sky turn golden. Away in the distance two birds were chasing each other, swooping and rising, carving great elliptical paths through the air. It was a perfect moment.

It is difficult to recall how much time was swallowed up by that moment, but my next conscious memory was that the moon was sailing up to my right and beside me the air shimmering and flickering, then *She* was there, a soft aqua shadow at my side.

Below us the smoke haze had cleared and the lights of Fez sparkled; a scattering of gold and gems, set against the dark velvet of that vast plain. Close at hand a night bird scolded and I caught the sudden movement of a small bat flitting around us. For a time she didn't speak and simply sat next to me, hugging her legs to her chest. When she did speak it was not a voice of command, but rather of one who has surrendered and is content to reside in the moment. Her voice was low but its resonance reached me not just through the air but also through her body, pressed so warm against my side.

Did you know that the Imazighen, the Berber, believe that the sky is illuminated by a female spark that has escaped from hell?

'A female spark, you mean the sun?'

Yes, a spark from hell. She escapes every morning and is condemned to return every night to lie down and sleep. And when the Maker of Worlds is displeased with men he summons a huge winged Afrit, a giant djinn from deep underground and commands that he swallows the spark; swallows the sun. When men see the sun vanish at midday they become afraid and follow Allah's will. Then the Afrit vomits up the spark and it is allowed to shine again.

'What about the moon?'

The Imazighen tales tell that the moon is a young virgin who has strayed from paradise. At the beginning of every month she is born and begins her search to find her way home. For a while she grows in confidence and then she realises she is still lost and her pale fire begins to fade. At the end of each month she dies.

'That's sad.'

It's just a story.

There she fell silent and for a while all I could feel was weight against my arm and the soft rise and fall of her breath. A slight breeze had sprung up and was tracing my face with cool fingers. High above us a few small clouds were drifting while below; over the plain to the left there were pockets of mist. Fez still glowed but now the entire plain was dotted with pinpricks of light scattered like stars in the black, a mirror image of the sky.

A'isha's attention seemed far away, her head turned towards the deepest shadow that was Zerhoun.

'What is it you believe?' I asked.

She didn't reply immediately, but when she did she dragged her attention from down in the southwest and ignored my question.

Do you know what the Imazighen say about this mountain, about Djebel Zalagh?

She didn't wait for me to respond.

A long time ago the tailors of Fez were renowned throughout the world for their fine clothes. Rumours of their skill reached the ears of a giant named Idris. He too was a master tailor and could not abide the thought that maybe there existed mere men whose craft skills matched his.

'Ah, he was jealous!'

So, Idris set out for Fez and when he arrived was far too big to get inside the city gates so he called the tailors of Fez to him and demanded that they make him some clothes. The tailors agreed and a week went by. Then the tailors returned and presented Idris with the best work they had ever done. However, as not one of the tailors had been brave enough to measure the giant, none of the garments fitted him. Idris was so incensed that he squatted before the gates and defecated. Thus was the creation of Djebel Zalagh.

Almost three thousand feet high... it was a bizarre image. Beside me A'isha had turned her attention back to the distant Djebel Zerhoun.

That place has a very different story.

'Tell me.'

No, you will visit me there. For now, let us go in the cave.

She began to rise, but I reached out and caught hold of her *djellaba*. 'I asked what you believed and you ignored me.'

As she stood and looked down at me I expected those amber eyes to burn with anger at my impertinence, but to my relief she squatted down and holding my face in her hands kissed me on the forehead.

Far exalted is our Lord, Lord of Power, above what they describe; and peace be upon the Messengers; and all praise be to God, Lord of the Worlds. That is what I believe. Now, come lie with me, I am in need of your body.

I took the blanket into the cave and with a soft magic it was no longer a cave, but a garden and we made love amidst the scent of flowers and to the sound of the gently tinkling water from a fountain close at hand. Unlike previous occasions our lovemaking was melding, not maelstrom, her tenderness beyond words to describe, her longing sweet and aching and her face, glowing in the candle light, so beautiful I was unable to speak for a very long time.

Later, just before I fell asleep, I asked her what *Sidi Hammu Qiyu* was.

Not what but who.

Her laughter was soft and fresh, falling over me like large splotches of rain. She reached out and ran a finger over my chest.

Sidi Hammu Qiyu is a king among the djnun and he is my husband. I have many, many husbands, but he is chief among them.

'I didn't know you were married...'

This is no time to talk of marriage. Yet, one day we may. Sleep now, my Nazarene, sleep now, my Marcus.

So it was that I feel asleep in a beautiful moist garden, curled around my beautiful A'isha Qandisha and awoke in the morning lying alone on a blanket in a cave where the air carried the sweet scent of orange-flower water and a faint trace of turpentine.

A'isha: The curse of tranquillity

Richard is a disease. He has infected me. I, who have never felt panic, feel panic. I, who have never been threatened feel a danger that causes me to tremble.

Never in the centuries have I suffered like this. He has no power over me and though I crave to cast him aside, I hesitate. His mystery is a narcotic and so I delay ending him. He has crossed the threshold into insanity but still holds me in his head. Is it he or is it I who have shut down my normal response?

His flesh could feed me, his blood sustain me, yet it is that blood that harbours the source of my dis-ease.

Richard has infected me with terminal tranquillity.

Richard: Subspecies—troglodyte

There is an old and oft misquoted line from the materialist philosopher Thomas Hobbes about life without government being solitary, poor, nasty, brutish and short—I have never understood why he omitted the other epithet "smelly". After a few days in the cave, bereft of even the government of common sense, I realised that was a prime example of the veracity of a Hobbesian point of view. I was lacking the brutality but the other descriptors vied with each other for pride of place at the top of my list of discomforts.

It had not been my intention to linger on the mountain, but fate, or maybe A'isha Qandisha, intervened. Shortly after sunrise on the second day, awoken by the impudent, persistent virulence of a bird that didn't have the good grace to remain around long enough for me to identify it, I draped the blanket around my shoulders and sat watching the day breaking over the Saïss plain. During the night, a low fog had descended on the landscape so until the sun burnt it off I felt as though I was aboard a high-altitude aircraft looking down on a layer of clouds.

My mind was full of nothingness—not in a nihilistic sense, but rather abiding in a stillness that... I was going to say "comes with perfect contentment", but as I have never experienced such a state it is probably inaccurate and certainly not a logical analysis. Nevertheless, there was a feeling of wellbeing and a lack of madly competing thoughts. I was on the mountain and there was the view. It was pleasant, dispassionate—end of story. Any attempt to imbue the moment with more would be unnecessary embroidery.

Shortly after emerging I splashed a little water over myself, and musing on the tale of Idris the Giant, I added to his legacy, albeit at a considerable distance from my temporary dwelling.

It was as I stumbled back over the broken ground that the first intervention took place. There was no doubt in my mind that what I observed was unnatural. For starters, the *Melanargia lucasi* should not have appeared so late in the season. Yes, the altitude was within its range, but this elusive member of the *Nymphalidae* known popularly as the Moroccan Marbled White is (according to my memory of the literature) usually found in the High Atlas. I should stress that the identification was not a wild guess as I had several seconds in which to study the heart-shaped marks, surrounded by solid black lines that appear to be the consistent characteristic of the subspecies *lucasi* as distinct from the more common forms of the Marbled White.

My brain flipped through the possibilities. Climate change had resulted in a variation of both season and habitat—improbable. This specimen was simply an individual blown off course by unusually strong winds—unlikely. A'isha had discovered my vulnerability and was pandering to it—absurd. Yet, how to explain the two butterflies of the previous day, coincidence? Hardly.

There are moments when, despite my background in science, I have learned it is better to abandon attempts at rational explanation and surrender to the awe of the moment. The arrival almost immediately of a large, fast flying member of the *Satyridae*, a perfect *Berberia abdelkader* was simply too improbable. The Giant grayling not only alighted on the reeds outside the cave, but then circled me once before speeding off into the void between Zalagh and Zerhoun.

> *As at times in hot sunny weather*
> *a guileless butterfly accustomed to the light,*
> *flies in its wanderings into someone's face,*
> *causing it to die, and the other to weep.*

Petrarch's extraordinary image of a butterfly crashing into a person's face captured my feelings at that moment and yet (as always) I zipped off to a third Z—Zalagh, Zerhoun, Zembla. The image that propelled me along this tangent to the outer reaches of the alphabet was that of the hapless bird in the first lines of Nabokov's *Pale Fire*.

> *I was the shadow of the waxwing slain*
> *By the false azure in the windowpane;*
> *I was the smudge of ashen fluff--and I*
> *Lived on, flew on, in the reflected sky*

The twin images fascinated and disturbed me. That Nabokov wrote about a bird rather than a butterfly seemed strange. Maybe he had been too aware of the lines from Petrarch. I found myself pacing around the small verdant platform trying my hand at rewriting Nabokov.

> *I was the shadow of the Satyridae slain*
> *By the false amber eyes with which I'd lain;*
> *A sad echo of Petrarch's butterfly*
> *That flew too close to love and there to die.*

In honesty, I must confess that this mangled work was not a flash of inspiration, had it been so I might beg forgiveness. It was the result of hours of mulling over individual words. I shouted, laughed and cursed but in the end I had it pinned down like a specimen in a drawer. At the time I thought it brilliant. If this was going crazy, I was happy to go along for the ride and stay for a little longer.

In those first days my only visitor was the *Amazigh* woman, Karima, who had first led me to the cave. Each day she would arrive with bread, cheese, milk, olives and fruit. On a couple of occasions she even brought coffee, hot and sweet, along with a small supply of *kif* and a rather battered brass pipe which she handed to me with a look of resigned disapproval. We never spoke, but Karima would inspect the cave, shake out my blanket and tidy up and replenish the candles. The natural spring water provided more than enough to drink, but I needed a container in order to wash outside the cave. My mime skills, improved with so much practice, were effective and the next morning, along with the regular supplies, Karima brought a two-litre plastic bottle. Several times I tried to press money into her hand, but each time I was unsuccessful.

And so it went. Every morning I would await the arrival of Karima with the day's provisions and each night my beloved A'isha would appear. For a little while I can say that it was a perfect situation, however, it was not to last.

What astounded me about the life of a hermit in modern times was that even on the side of Djebel Zalagh my biggest danger was not from flees, rats or stray dogs but rather from fame or, perhaps in my case, notoriety. Within days, word had spread across the hills and down the mountain that there was some kind of madman emulating the life of the saints. Of course, nothing could have been further from the truth. Notoriety was a mixed blessing. My diet improved but my tolerance of strangers was sorely tested.

My first uninvited visitors were a couple of elderly Moroccan women whose escort, a younger man, remained at a disdainful distance, squatting on the hillside, observing, but not intervening as they made their way over the uneven hillside. They did so with some difficulty, one of the women, walking with the aid of a stout stick and so unsteady on her feet that I was moved to offer assistance. My attempted gallantry was rebuffed. Her companion hissed at me, shooing me away like some bothersome dog. They made no attempt to converse, preferring to make their way directly to the cave and, as I discovered later, burn some incense and tie ribbons on the tree roots. They left without uttering a word and I sat for a long time visualising them struggling down the long rocky path to the main road. Perhaps they had donkeys.

Subsequent arrivals were more willing to engage; shaking my hand and speaking to me, even though I didn't understand a word. I also became the recipient of a variety of gifts from basic food, small amounts of money (which I declined), to clothing. The gift of a rock solid, eighteen-inch-high, cone of sugar, while intriguing was useless and I would have needed a hammer to break it. In the end I gave it to Karima who, if the string of *"shukrans"* and *"Barakallahu fiks"* was any indication, was delighted to accept it. I particularly appreciated the red *tarbouche* and took to wearing the traditional hat at all times other than when I slept.

Later, when a steady stream of visitors began to arrive, I noticed that Karima was charging them a few dirhams to bring them along the goat path to the cave and on the increasingly frequent occasions that people brought chickens, and once, a sheep to sacrifice I (and I daresay the *Imazighen* families) ate well. What they thought of me is anyone's guess, but one thing was not in dispute, I had in a very short space of time become a steady source of income. I suspect that Karima and her extended family group were actively promulgating the myth of the madman in the cave for their care of me soon extended to several visits a day.

After the first few weeks it became clear to me that those who made the arduous trip up the mountain were doing so because they had problems, psychological, physical or financial and with each visit I became increasingly depressed at the hopelessness of their quest for healing. The expectation of every one of the arrivals was that they would be cured of what ailed them. It was not going to happen, but I had neither the command of language nor the heart to disabuse them of their faith, no matter how ill-founded. The exact part I was supposed to play in their expectations was never clear, but that an expectation was present was as incontrovertible as it was pathetic. I was acutely uncomfortable at being cast in a role I had not chosen and certainly not morally or spiritually equipped to fulfil, so I resolved to leave the mountain as soon as possible.

It would be dishonest to say that it was only my moral scruples about being a fake that forced my decision to abandon the cave. It was not. The truth is that since the day the first visitor arrived, *Lalla* A'isha had vanished and all the incense, candles and sacrifices did nothing to bring her back. My placid mental state in the first few days had been some relief, but with A'isha's disappearance I came to see that it was not calm that I craved. That I missed her goes without saying, but it was not the aching feeling of loss that I often read is associated with love, but more the lack of adrenalin and the indefinable frisson of danger our relationship had provided.

At first the cave had felt like a doorway to her world and to a connection with an excitement that had become addictive. Now it felt like a hollow tourist attraction.

The faint hope that she might choose to return caused me to vacillate and so I remained a little longer, but in a very agitated state. My mind filled with competing thoughts and a rising sense of despair, not just at my present position, but at the course of my entire life.

Introspection has never been my strong point and when it came to my reinvention of myself it had always been a non-event. But now, half a planet and half a lifetime away it became a niggling discomfort, an undertow of melancholy that I couldn't escape. Changing my name had been the beginning and that and my relocation to Australia convinced me that I had achieved the goal of obliterating the past. Yet, I realise now, I was fooling myself. Suppressed but not destroyed would be a more accurate reading. Now I wonder if it is ever possible to have buried the past, to reach what the Americans nauseatingly call "closure".

Pondering the phrase "buried the past", I imagined my old self, cramped in a coffin, living a wraith-like existence but knowing with great certainty that the day would come when it would emerge to claim its rightful place and to expose the present me as a fiction of no substance.

Being a fraud, a charlatan, takes a certain mindset and it was not one I possessed, or so I told myself. In those dark moments I wondered if that was entirely true and that having changed my name so many years before was I now an imposter in my own life, an actor playing the part? It was a strange and uncomfortable thought, so I did as I always do when confronted by my own black spots, I voted for denial. But there, on the mountain with nothing to distract me but the suffering of my visitors, I was outvoted and I eventually returned to the subject, albeit in a circumspect manner.

Marcus Brennan becoming Richard Duane had been a metamorphosis of need; a strategy intended to distance me from the guilt and nightmares of the past. If it had been successful, then why was I feeling more and more like Kafka's Gregor Samsa; a bug crawling around in the damp confines of a cave in an isolated mountain in a foreign country? Was I, to paraphrase Petrarch, so dazzled by love that my soul was blindly consenting to its death?

Metamorphosis has fascinated me since my student days when it was the subject of a friend's PhD. In the insect world it is a way of exploiting different ecological niches. The larvae are simply eating machines that turn plant matter into insects. The flying stage is all about sex and delivering eggs to new sources of food. On pupation, that is becoming a chrysalis, almost all the cells in the body are destroyed by the process of *apoptosis*—programmed cell death. This is similar to the processes that stop normal cells in humans becoming immortal—and cancerous. A butterfly is built anew from groups of undifferentiated groups of stem cells called "imaginal discs". This allows them to completely transform their bodies from a caterpillar to a beautiful winged adult, but metamorphosis also gives the *Lepidoptera* the opportunity to kill off infections. When all the cells die at pupation, all the infections in those cells are killed off with them, and the insect can rebuild, clean and new, and they emerge as a beautiful butterfly, flying away to find a mate, live on nectar and find a good place for the next generation.

For a few minutes I struggled with the notion of transposing the metaphor to the human realm, to be precise, to my own case but then another synaptic storm broke out and I had a flash of my heart being transplanted... more than merely a heart, my whole being. Becoming Richard Duane had been not a metamorphosis at all, for that would have killed off all of Marcus Brennan's toxic cells. No, it had been a transplant and because of the residual toxicity it was rejected; tissue rejection, life rejection. I was spiralling out of control.

An internal battle between metamorphosis and transplantation raged away with images of my cave, first as a cocoon and then a grave competing with a vision of my heart, diseased and eaten by cancerous guilt, being sliced out and tossed from masked surgeon to masked surgeon before being abandoned on an operating theatre at which point the lights went out.

I must have fallen for when I came around there was blood in my scalp—blood and no *Lalla* A'isha. Gripped by a sudden terror I lay, wrapped in my blankets but unable to still a trembling that felt like the onset of a serious illness. Yet, even as I thought it, I was swept away by fear of where my journey was taking me and a deep sense that this was not a physical illness, but madness and that accepting it was the safest course. Lost in the arms of A'isha seemed preferable to what the so-called real world had to offer. If I was indeed turning into some kind of holy fool then remaining in the cave was no longer a necessity. My headspace—my insanity—if you will, was transportable and so, return to the Medina, I told myself, for at least there I had a cocoon where I could stand upright without smashing my head against rocks.

Between resolve and resolution lay a few hurdles. The first was the weather. For three days the mountain was beset by storms and then on the fourth day, with still no sign of A'isha, I rolled up my blanket, donned my *tarbouche* and prepared to leave as soon as I had received the usual breakfast of coffee, bread and olive oil. My energy seemed drained and despite the constant supply of food I realised I had lost weight and was acutely aware of the filthy state of my entire body. Somewhere in the last days I had stopped washing altogether. Yet, my mental state seemed fine and since my fall there had been no reoccurrence of the brainstorm that had literally rocked my head. My father's voice: *you need some sense knocked into you, not out.*

Much to my dismay, when Karima appeared on the now well-worn goat path between the prickly pear cactus and the cave, she was not alone. The man with her was wearing a baseball cap, smart hiking clothes, sporting a camera around his neck and over his shoulder one of those ridiculous little sacks the tourists call day-packs. Reaching into the cave mouth I retrieved my *tarbouche* shoved it firmly on my head and returned to watch them making their way towards me. The bad weather had departed to the north and apart from a few scattered clouds and a chill breeze gusting around the hillside there was no sign of the previously inclement weather. High above me a kite was being buffeted by stronger winds.

'*Salaam aleikum, labas?*' Karima greeted me and laying down a small square of carpet began unpacking her basket.

'*W'aleikum salaam, lalla, labas, humdullilah,*' I responded and turned to meet my male visitor.

'I'm Jonathan Shade. It's a pleasure to meet you sir,' the man said. He made no attempt to shake my hand but squatted down beside Karima and, producing a can of Coca Cola from his day-pack, added it to the provisions she had laid out. Then he got up and without asking permission wandered over to *my* cave and stuck his head in. It felt like an unforgivable intrusion.

His accent was American; not harshly so, but rather soft and slow, like a newscaster on Diazepam. Nevertheless, his presence was grating. Why is it, I wondered, that some Americans have the annoying habit of referring to people as "sir" and what possessed him to imagine I would be thankful for a can of Coke?

Karima, perhaps sensing the hostile atmosphere, gave me a curt nod, brushed down her skirts and left us.

'Some set up,' Shade observed dryly. 'Mind you the view makes up for the lack of home comforts, huh?'

'I'm Richard,' I said as evenly as possible and extended my hand. For a second he looked at the ingrained dirt under my nails, glanced up at my face and back to my hand. To give him credit he didn't even flinch as he shook it.

'Call me Jonathan, sir.'

'Jonathan.'

'That's it. Now, do you mind if I ask a few questions? I'm kind of interested in how you came to be here and what exactly it is you are doing...' He glanced at my meagre breakfast spread and checked himself. 'I'm sorry. Would you rather I came back after you have eaten?'

The notion of him coming back was as unpalatable as his being there in the first place so I shook my head and offered him some bread. 'You're welcome to join me.'

'No thank you. Stomach, you know. Not quite acclimatised to the local food sir.' He patted his stomach to make sure I understood. Up close he looked to be no older than twenty-four or five, boyish faced, generous mouth, slightly puffy cheeks showing the glow of his hill climbing exertion. The hair protruding from his cap was blond and as pale as his complexion.

I tore off some bread, dipped it in the olive oil and let him wait while I chewed it a little slower than normal. After a couple of pieces, I picked up the glass of milky coffee and moved to out of the wind with my back up against the rock face by the cave entrance.

'So, Jonathan, what exactly is it you want to know?'

'Well, sir, I'm doing—'

'Let's drop the "sir" business.'

'Yes, sir, I mean, Richard.'

'You were saying?'

'I'm a post-grad student at a University in America—'

'Fuller Theological Seminary.'

His jaw dropped and a look of shock crossed his face like that of a sceptic suddenly faced with incontrovertible proof of mind reading. 'How did you...'

'It's on your cap, Jonathan.' His black mesh baseball cap read: *School of Intercultural Studies—Fuller Theological Seminary.*

He blushed, adding more colour to his already pink cheeks, then covered his embarrassment with a nervous laugh and looking around selected the driest boulder on the edge of the platform, sat down and began again. 'I'm studying medical anthropology.'

'Really, it's not a field I am familiar with.'

'My particular interest is in the so-called curative practises of traditional and primitive societies.'

'I'm sure that's fascinating,' I said encouragingly, my gaze far out down the valley to where Zerhoun was an anonymous dark mass under the last of the retreating storm. I wondered what butterflies lived there and if maybe one day I would travel there and find out.

'They have curative practices, these primitives?' I asked as innocently as I could.

'Well, I understand that a lot of people have been coming to you in recent times.'

'There have been a few visitors.' I agreed, 'but I never understood why they bothered.'

'I interviewed a woman who claims her son's condition improved,' he said tentatively.

'And what was his condition?'

'Possibly a temporary psychotic disturbance...'

'She told you this?'

'Not directly, you see I find it best to work through a translator who simply gives me the language. To have a translator who is also an anthropologist has drawbacks, especially if he is from the same background as the subjects. His degree of objectivity is hard to gauge and there is the danger that he will omit certain aspects that he takes for granted. His assumption that they are basic beliefs and do not need exploration can be a great hindrance.'

'So, what did your objective translator tell you the woman said?'

He was obviously in his element, his voice gentle and coaxing as though he had spent his life conversing with children, kittens or maybe exotic foreigners. He leaned over and confided in me. 'She said he was being controlled by a spirit. You see, an uneducated person would draw on the folklore of their tribe to define an illness, but it is not the condition that is as important as the way the tribe deals with it and in that respect I understand the Sufi brotherhoods have esoteric methods of resocialising those exhibiting deviant behaviour back into the objective reality that prevails in the group.'

It took a lot of control, but I maintained a straight face. 'The prevailing objective reality?'

Jonathan nodded enthusiastically. 'Exactly! The symbolic universe of the society is exactly it.'

'And you want to study this?'

'Yes, sir, yes I do.'

I turned my attention back from the distant hills and looked at him for a moment. It was too easy to be cruel so I took a deep breath and decided to be straight with him. 'Then you should make contact with these brotherhoods and ask if you can observe their work.'

'Ah, but don't you see, if I do that they may well stage something for my benefit. No, that's why I came to see you. I am really interested in what you have learned and how you practice.'

For a moment I felt as if I had been transported to another planet. But judging by the look on his face he was serious.

'Jonathan, let me tell you something. I don't do anything esoteric, nothing exotic. I have never cured anything or anyone in my life.' If I expected him to be crestfallen I was disappointed. A look of joy flashed across his face.

'So you do nothing?'

'Nothing,'

To my surprise, he clapped his hands together in pleasure. 'Oh, that is so Sufi! I knew that this was going to be special. When you ask a true Sufi about the way, about the path...'

'I am not a Sufi,' I protested.

'... they always claim not to be one.' He beamed with joy. 'Sir, I cannot tell you how honoured I feel. If I can just spend a few days observing how you practice and maybe talk to some of those who you work to cure, I am sure it would reveal some very interesting things.'

Standing on a steep shingle slide, with every step up causing me to slither further and further down, was the way it felt. It was then I remembered an expression about a glass arrow that Yusuf, or maybe it was Yazami, had used. All it needed was a dash of sincerity and a hint of a long remembered Holy Ghost Father, whose outstanding ability was to make the Gospel according to Mark sound as if it was a newly released paperback.

'Listen, Jonathan, your work sounds really important, but one should never shoot a glass arrow at a painted deer. Skilful means must be employed. I will give you a name of a man who can answer all your questions. Now, you must keep it to yourself and never reveal that I told you.'

He dived into his backpack and produced a notepad and pen. '*A glass arrow at a painted deer.* Awesome.' He scribbled it down and looked up with wide puppy-eyes. 'Right, ready.'

'The man's name is Muqaddim Abderrahim. Have you heard of the Hamadcha?'

He glanced up, a dubious expression on his face. 'One of the smaller Sufi brotherhoods, I was hoping for one of the more important...'

'Jonathan, don't make the same mistake as previous scholars. Do not underestimate the Hamadcha, they are the holders of a pure lineage.'

'Okay, I hear you.'

'You find Abderrahim and tell him that you spoke with a man named Mernisi and he told you that Abderrahim would show you a *lila*.'

'A *lila*, a night ceremony I've been reading up on them. Cool.'

'I promise you will see some... er... resocialising practices of great interest. Just never mention my name. Don't even hint at it, otherwise the path will come to an abrupt halt.'

There was more like that, much more, with Jonathan talking while I kept an eye out for butterflies that never appeared. Then he took the obligatory photographs and departed with one final breathless observation.

'You should keep a journal of your spiritual journey, people would find it inspirational.'

I shook my head. 'Sadly, you cannot understand a carpet by taking the threads apart and examining them. From threads alone a carpet is unknowable.' Sometimes I surprise myself.

'Valuable stuff,' he responded sagely.

I assured him that if I ever embarked on a spiritual expedition I would take his advice. Despite my tone he appeared to find my answer encouraging.

Reading back on what I have written about Jonathan I was tempted to edit him more sympathetically, but to do so would be to alter the truth. I sincerely hope he found what he was looking for and that he completed his thesis, albeit without an accompanying photograph of the "Sufi" he was so thrilled to discover living in a mountain cave in Morocco.

Later that day I had a final glass of tea with the *Imazighen* community and said farewell. Karima was genuinely sorry to see me go, and I like to think, not simply because of the loss of income that my departure would mean.

I was a third of the way down the mountain when she caught up to me and presented me with an orange plastic container. It was full of their beautiful homemade olive oil.

A'isha: The strength of absence

I am withholding from Richard. Punishing him with absence. Let him play with his butterflies or dance for the little spirits, the mluk. His craving for me will not be assuaged by their pathetic music. He will never be satisfied, no matter what they offer him.

Better still, he will sink into depression and be unable to sleep. He will pass his food aside and wither. His body will ache for me, but have no relief. His anxiety will tip him further into madness and leave him drained in a pool of his own sweat. Maybe I should leave him like that. And yet... and yet...

Richard: The winter chrysalis

There is a chasm between self-image and the way others perceive us. There is also a yawning gap between our self-image and that which we see reflected in a mirror, in my case, to be more precise, my reflection in a shop window. Si Mohammed's antique shop had been one of my favourite places to shop for knick-knacks with which to complete the decoration of my house. Over the previous few months I had bought several *Amazigh* rugs known as *handira*, a brass menorah that had once been owned by a wealthy family in the Jewish quarter, the Mellah, and a superb Syrian water jug fashioned from silver. It goes without saying that I paid more than they were worth, but as Si Mohammed said so affably on each occasion, "when the seller and the buyer are happy, everyone has a bargain, *humdullilah*".

The trip back from the mountain had been accomplished thanks to a driver who allowed me to share the back of his small van with two incontinent goats and had the decency to drop me off outside the Bab Bou Jeloud. It was on the walk down the Tala'a Sghira that I paused to look in Si Mohammed's window, normally a showcase for exquisite *Amazigh* jewellery and fine old ceramics. If he was displaying such things, I have no recollection, because the sight of a bearded madman looking straight back at me arrested my attention. It was not so much the stained *djellaba* and grubby *tarbouche* that I found so disturbing. It was the hollow cheeks, the haunted eyes and matted hair escaping from under the hat. Even in the reflected light I could see that the beard and hair were grey. Presented with the evidence of my appearance, I refused to believe it and glanced to either side to see who this fellow was. He looked like a vagrant, a *clochard,* as the French say.

That I was horrified, would be an understatement; however, what happened next was even more troubling. Si Mohammed's assistant, Lahcen, who minds the shop whenever his boss is away came out into the street, failed to recognise me and after pressing some coins into my hand nudged me firmly away from the window and on down the Tala'a.

'You have come back to us,' Yazami said as he held the door open for me. There was no look of disdain on his face, no disgust at my dishevelled appearance, but there was something in his voice that was reminiscent of the Holy Ghost Fathers at school whenever I stepped out of line. Out of the corner of my eye I saw Mira standing beside the steps down to the kitchen, her hand to her mouth failing to hide an expression of horror.

'I spent a few days up on—'

'Djebel Zalagh. I know. And it was weeks not days.' Yazami waved his hands in a dismissive manner as if my vanishing and reappearance was quite within the bounds of acceptable behaviour. He regarded me for a moment, stroking his beard and sucking his moustache. 'The point is what you are going to do now.'

'First, I want a shower, then some tea and we can have a chat,' I replied and wrenched my eyes away from Mira who hadn't stopped staring at me as if I was a total stranger.

When I explained that for the next little while, a few weeks at least, that I wanted to be alone, there was some initial resistance. Yazami argued for about half an hour but in the end I prevailed. As the house was essentially completed, I ordered the remainder of the work to be put on hold.

'But what about Mernisi, Mustapha and the others, what are they to do? They were relying on having work right through the winter?'

'We can give them a bonus, call it holiday pay,' I said. By the look on his face the concept was totally alien. Then he laughed and agreed.

'And Mira?' he asked.

'She can still come three times a week and cook and clean. But she's not to disturb me.'

'Disturb you doing what?'

It was my turn to laugh. 'Yazami, I am going to write a book.' I saw the familiar sceptical frown beginning to creep across his face as his hand moved in its reflex way to his beard. 'No, my friend, not a play, I'll leave that to the master playwright.'

'What sort of book?'

'A journal of sorts, I suppose. The story of what has happened to me.'

'And what has happened?' he asked.

It was a fair enough question, given the circumstances. Although I had showered and brushed my hair, I still looked like an escapee from an asylum or some 1970s commune. 'That is why I am going to write it, so I can find out,' I said, feeling rather proud of my clever evasion.

'And what should I do?'

'You mean for money, if I don't need you anymore?'

He looked genuinely hurt.

'How can you say that? This has never been about money, has it? Did you think that I have spent all these months with you, for money?'

'I didn't mean it that way.' He looked so upset I hastily added, 'I really am sorry.'

'No, Richard, from now on I won't accept a dirham from you.' He got to his feet and holding himself stiffly erect addressed me formally. 'I will inform the workers they are no longer required.'

'Oh for fuck's sake Yazami, you know what I mean.'

'No, Richard, I don't think I do. You sound just like the others, the foreigners, who think Moroccans are an exotic species to be bought and sold to amuse you. I had thought you different.'

There was nothing I could say to that.

'Let me tell you something.' His voice was as cold as a mortician's slab. 'Your street, *Aqbet el Firane*—do you know what that name means?'

I shook my head.

'The Hill of Mice,' he said as he turned and walked towards the stairs up to where the Mernisi and the others were working on the terrace balustrade. Maybe I should have called him back, but I didn't.

After that life became rather strange. Yazami vanished and it was left to me to pay off the workers. That was not a happy day and despite the language barrier it was clear that Mustapha and Mernisi were upset, not with the cessation of the renovation or termination of regular cash, but with having to leave the house and the work, which Mustapha proclaimed with a tear in his eye and hand to his heart was "*travail du cœur*". I believed him.

Of Mira there was no sign and so instead of my normal practice of sending her to shop, I spent three days stocking the house with everything I would need for the winter. In the local souk I purchased a large quantity of bottled water, long-life milk and dried fruit. At the supermarket in the *Ville Nouvelle* I bought toothpaste, a pile of notebooks, chocolate, canned food, pasta and pasta sauces.

In the liquor department I selected spirits and wine, more than I could carry and so had to make two trips. On the second I ran into an unexpected hurdle; the clink of wine bottles in my shoulder bag was enough to cause the first three taxi drivers to refuse to take me. Eventually I found a less devout driver, an out of work *zellij* specialist, who insisted on showing me his photo album full of jobs he had done in the past. The work was impressive and I was sorry to have to tell him that all my *zellij* was now repaired.

Back in my house, I packed my supplies away and then carried my courtyard table indoors where I set it up as a writing desk. For a few minutes I felt as though I was back at university about to begin a major assignment, certainly my method was the same in that I spent an inordinate amount of time arranging and rearranging pens, pencils and of course all the old notebooks. Everyone who writes has their own little rituals and I am no different. An outsider would possibly mistake the process for a form of procrastination and while it does contain some elements of that, it is more a psyching-up and demonstration of how seriously the task ahead is taken.

Finally, my new environment was ready and as is usually the case, I was not. However, determined not to be intimidated by a blank page, I took my finely sharpened pencil and wrote: *This is where Australia ends...*

It was a beginning and certainly deserving of a cup of tea.

Having had no previous experience of a winter in Fez, I was unprepared for how rapidly the season changed from that soft golden autumn to the cold edge of winter. Locals had told me that the climate had been changing in recent years and that twice there had even been snow falling in the medina. I had listened but couldn't really conceive of cold weather in Africa, the concept being at odds with a lifetime of images that revolved around arid landscapes bleached by a venomous sun. Suffice to say the sudden plunge in the night time temperature to around minus one or two had me making another journey to the *Ville Nouvelle* in order to buy a heater and two more blankets. During the day my courtyard thermometer showed temperatures hovering around fourteen or fifteen Celsius and so I took to keeping my heater on twenty-four hours a day.

Much to my relief, the writing went well. It was the perfect defence against the demons that plagued my sleep. During the day it was an easy task to avoid anything but the words on the page, words that flowed from my pen with more ease than I had experienced in the past. Previously my writing had been academic and involved a great deal of research and arduous teasing out of arguments that would pass muster with my peers. Now, free of those restraints, my pencil flew. Whenever I had even the slightest hesitation I went back to my notebooks and it normally only required the reading of a couple of pages to get me fired up again. I did need to be careful not to get engrossed in the notebooks—that was too seductive—but I became adept at dipping in and then moving back to my task.

The only flaw, and I must admit to myself it was a large one, was that I had no clear of idea of what I was writing or for whom. No, I am being too harsh on myself. I did set out with the idea of taking my notebook entries from the time I left Australia until the present and rewriting them in a coherent fashion. However, the actual writing was delivering more than simple recordings of my day-to-day activities and I found I was embroidering the facts with reflections and commentary, albeit on my own life. Yet, though I seemed to have strayed from condensing a journal into something more autobiographical, it was all so pleasurable I gave the direction it was taking little thought. Enjoy the ride, I told myself, and I did, writing far more each day than I had ever done in my life. It was only the necessities of fuelling the machine that caused me to pause. Even in this I became disciplined, synchronising my schedule around the calls to prayer.

At dawn I would make coffee, a bowl of porridge laced with cinnamon and then work through to midday editing and revising the previous evening's writing. As soon as the muezzin's call echoed around the house I would stop for lunch, usually a tin of beans and another coffee, before returning to writing new material. The afternoon was the easiest time, with just a short stint of work until the mid-afternoon call from the mosque—the signal for a cup of tea and a biscuit or two. At sunset I would pour myself a glass of red and, if the weather permitted, sit in the courtyard for half an hour as I read back through my notebooks. This change of venue was important, as by this stage of the day I needed a break from the confines of the salon I had begun to refer to as "my studio". As soon as the sound of the call to prayer reached me, I would stand, stretch and tell myself out loud that I should get out more. I never failed to find this amusing.

The final call to prayer, some two hours after sunset, was the signal for dinner and often a second or third glass of wine; never more than three. As none of the pasta sauces I had stocked up with were particularly inspiring, I often experimented by adding olives, capers or anchovies. Apart from a spectacular failure involving preserved lemons, it was usually a success.

The wines on the other hand were all superb. The French legacy was obvious in almost every bottle and I enjoyed a geographical tour of the country's wine regions from the comfort of my house.

About three weeks into my winter hibernation there was a knock on the door and I opened it to find Mira standing there, her eyes carefully avoiding mine. I knew it was Mira and not A'isha for A'isha had no use for doors and in any case, she had ceased coming at all. Without a word Mira entered, followed me down the stairs and then peeled off towards the kitchen. Having no words to say to her I returned to my studio and tried to continue work.

Twice in the next hour I poked my head out to convince myself that she wasn't a mirage. Each time I saw her following her normal routine of washing the floors then mopping them with a large cloth which she pushed back and forth with a broom. Not once did she look at me, and there was no word of farewell when she left. She was there and then she was gone as if she had never been, or so I thought at the time, but that evening I discovered a pot of lentil soup on the stove. Sitting on the bench were two rounds of fresh bread and a plastic bag containing a knob of butter.

The routine suited me well and after the first month of winter I was content with the progress on my writing. On two occasions I made major shopping excursions to the supermarket, but as Mira had taken to purchasing the basic necessities I only needed to stock up on the luxuries, coconut milk, red wine and chocolate. I am tempted to say I was contented, but an eerie illusion of calm is probably a better description.

That A'isha had not returned was both reassuring and troubling. Once visitors had arrived on the mountain I had become the focus of attention and A'isha had reacted by abandoning me. She had been, I attempted to convince myself, a temporary aberration, a visitation brought on by my unbalanced state due to *kif, majoun* and my inability to cope with my changed circumstances. Had she been real? No. And yet... and yet there were still moments when the memory of her presence felt like a loss and I had to admit that the times when she had infected my brain had seemed coherent, solid and irrefutably real. Like a drug she had taken me over and brought with her the gift of forgetting. Not once in her company had I been plagued with the terrors of the past, the phantoms of the cloud forest. When I thought of her, my pulse would quicken and the hunger of the nympholept rose up in me; a craving that took time to abate. Maybe, I conjectured, she had existed only because I willed it so. She was my creation, a dream that I had manifested from a deep longing and a suspension of disbelief. But if that were true, I found it hard to comprehend why, if she was the product of my subconscious, she had escaped me. In my notebook I saw I had crossed out the word "escaped", as it implied a sentience that I was unwilling to accord her. Despite this debate in my head, I still found myself acting like a junkie in search of a hit; going to the courtyard at night, sprinkling water on the tiles, whispering her name and peering into the gloom with a strange melange of fear and hope that she might appear and infect me once again.

You desire to feed my hunger, Nazarene?

The voice is in my head.

When I demand it you will perform the hadra. Is that understood?

Yes. Yes, I say out loud.

Marcus, Marcus...

It is not her voice, but the voice of memory.

Then, one night, as I hunched over my work, blowing on my fingers to warm them from the numbing chill, there came a knock on the door. My first thought was that Yazami had forgiven me and was coming to build bridges. It was a thought I welcomed. His absence from my life had left me bereft of the only real companionship I had ever had. There had been Eric of course, but he had not offered the same level of intellectual stimulation that Yazami provided. Friendships with men had never come easily and, if asked, I would have referred to "acquaintances" rather than friends. With women my history was straightforward—I had ruined almost every friendship with intimacy and dependency that eventually ran their seemingly inevitable course towards separation, after which the retrieval of friendship was impossible.

The thought of Yazami had me striding across the courtyard and up the stairs to the door. However, when I opened it, I was confronted not by my Moroccan friend but by Sandra's pale face creased by a wan smile.

'I hope you don't mind,' she said and tugging her coat tightly around herself, stepped inside.

In the kitchen I made a cup of herbal tea: *Louisa*, the locals call it. I have never asked but I suspect it is verveine or some such—green leaves, golden liquid, a dash of fig honey—perfect for whatever ails her. And something obviously did because Sandra hovered by my shoulder, even though I had offered her a seat. Her neediness was palpable. There was some chit-chat I don't recall and then we went across to the salon where she took off her coat and huddled by the heater as I self-consciously tidied up my notebooks and put away my writing.

'You've been working, I see,' she said

'Just scribbling down a few thoughts,' I conceded, reluctant to talk about myself.

She eyed the pile of notebooks. 'That looks like a lot of scribbling. You must have been having a lot of thoughts. Is it fact or fiction?'

'What I'm writing? Fiction, I suppose. My life as I would like it to be.'

She sipped her tea and then after a pause said, 'You're lucky Richard.'

'I am? That's news to me.'

'Oh, don't be flippant.' Her voice carried a hint of bitterness. She pointed to the notebooks. 'At least you have something to occupy yourself with.'

'Doesn't everyone?' I asked her.

She looked at me for a long time, frowning.

'How long since you went out?' she eventually asked.

I shrugged, 'I don't know, several weeks. Why?'

'Richard, the place is deserted. There's nobody here.'

'I seem to recall several hundred thousand Moroccans...'

'Oh Jesus, stop being so fucking holier than thou, of course I don't mean the Moroccans.'

'Well, if you're talking about expats, I wouldn't know. I don't tend to have much to do with them.' It was not my intention to be rude to her, but I resented her intrusion and saw no point in playing out whatever role she had in mind for me.

'No you don't, do you.'

'I didn't come to Morocco to hang out with the foreigners,' I said. Sandra placed her tea glass on the table.

'What did you come to Morocco for, Richard?'

It's funny how an apparently simple question can stop you in your tracks. Why did I come? That was why I was writing the book, or at least that was part of it, to discover the answer. So far I wasn't anywhere near discovering the answer.

'Does anyone know that when they arrive? Isn't it that we are intrigued and once we get here we are ensnared.'

'Ensnared?'

'Beguiled, maybe.'

'Yes, the enchanted city.' She spoke so softly she might well have been speaking to herself. 'Yes, and then it is too late.'

'Too late for what?' I asked, feeling I was intruding on her thoughts.

She hesitated, and for a second I thought she was going to cry. Her lower lip trembled until she sucked it in and bit on it. Clamping down, I thought, but on what?

'Too late for happiness. It's not enough, Richard, the Medina is not enough. We think it is, we buy a house and go through all the hassle of renovation and for a while we are just too exhausted to realise that we have never answered the question, "what happens next". What are we going to do now the house is finished? It's then we have to face the Medina, no, face ourselves and answer the question about why we came here in the first place.'

'But there's a whole world outside your house. It's big enough that you could spend several lifetimes exploring it. Music, culture, religion, the whole box and dice is just waiting to be delved into.'

Sandra shook her head. 'But most of us don't do that, do we. We wrap ourselves up in the little cocoon that is the expat community, gin and tonic, gossip and parties.'

There was nothing I could say to that, so I sipped my tea and waited for her to continue.

'You want to know what is really getting to me, Richard?'

Despite my annoyance at having been disturbed I found myself feeling sorry for her and so I nodded. 'Tell me.'

'I'm lonely. I am terribly, deeply lonely.' Her voice choked up and a tear ran down her cheek. 'When winter came so many of my friends went away and now there's nobody I can talk to.'

'Some people must still be here...'

'Sure. Mark no longer talks to me because I wouldn't go to bed with him. Bridie thinks I am after her friend Mohammed, which is just plain stupid. James has left Angela and all he wants to talk about is what a bitch she was.'

'That can't be very pleasant...'

'It's ugly, Richard, fucking ugly. At least I know why I came here. I studied Islamic architecture and wanted to experience it from the inside. To live in it; you know, the full Medina experience. But I've become stuck. Yes, I love the city and have learned how to get by in *Darija*, but that's not enough. Not by a long way.'

'What about Moroccans? You must have a lot of Moroccan friends now.'

'Not really. A few that I would call friends, but mostly just the staff in my *riad* and I have to keep a certain professional distance from them.'

'But your guests?' I asked, flailing for an emotional rope to throw her.

'Guests,' she snorted. 'God help me it is all I can do sometimes to stop myself strangling them. If I hear another rich tourist bragging about how they bargained "like a Berber" and got some stupid carpet for next to nothing, I will kill them. Or the whining, complaining idiots who go on about rubbish in the streets, or donkey shit or faux guides. They drive me nuts. I see them arrive and I can tell straight away that whether they are going to like or hate the Medina. And to tell you the truth, I no longer care. You know I had a freaking Southern Baptist the other day who wanted me to do something about the racket outside his bedroom. You know what it was? The call to prayer.'

Her anger and frustration was easier to deal with than her emotional neediness, so I attempted to steer her in that direction.

'So, what did you do?'

A smile crept over her face. 'I suggested that next time he went on holiday he should visit a non-Muslim country. What an idiot.'

'I rather like the call to prayer,' I said. 'And the singing between three and four in the morning.'

'I sleep through it these days.'

'It's so beautiful I sometimes set my alarm so I don't miss it. When the wind is in the right direction you get the strangest phasing of sound as the different mosques join in. It sounds like an angel choir.'

It was true. One of the greatest pleasures for me in Fez occurred on the nights when I awoke at around 4.15 am in time to hear the entire performance. Wrapping something warm around me I would go up to the terrace, huddle against a wall and listen to the nearest thing on earth to celestial music. For forty minutes or so I would gaze out over a Medina glowing in moonlight or starlight, the illuminated minarets like fingers point to heaven, and I would feel myself bathed in the music.

'Maybe that's the difference between us Richard, you are an incurable romantic, whereas I'm a realist.' Sandra picked up her glass, wrapping her fingers around it as if to warm them up. She took a deep breath, a shudder running through her. 'And I have made some big mistakes. You are probably the only person in the Medina who doesn't know.'

Leaning forward, I touched her hand in what I hopped was a reassuring gesture. 'Sandra, we all make mistakes—'

'No! I want to tell you.'

'I don't need to know...'

She held her hand up to stop me. 'Richard, I had an affair. Not just one of my flings and God knows, I have had enough of those.'

'Sandra—'

'It was almost three years ago. I fell in love with a young Moroccan called Haroun and for a few weeks everything was fine. Then his family started putting pressure on him to get married. You talk about having Moroccan friends; well let me tell you, his family were so friendly I nearly choked. His sisters and mother were always on my door wanting to have tea or to take me to the *hammam* or shopping and his older brother began to spy on me to make sure I was behaving. At first I didn't mind, after all I was in love and everything was exciting, but the marriage thing? Stupidly I agreed and the next thing I know they are insisting that I had to buy another house. Haroun and I argued about it and what became clear was that he had different plans for us. His idea was that we would move to the States.'

The tears were now streaming down her face and she sniffed a couple of times before continuing.

'Eventually we came to a compromise. I purchased a small *dar* in Batha so at least we had some privacy away from my *riad*. You might have heard of it, *Dar Limun*? It was owned by a Swedish woman who restored it and then decided she preferred Marrakech.'

I shook my head.

'Anyway, after that things quietened down for a while until Haroun became ill and his family accused me of trying to poison him. I mean, really! Can you imagine?'

'Why would you do that?'

'God knows. They probably thought I was trying to get out of the marriage.'

'And were you?' I asked as I topped up her glass.

'Up to that point, no. Somehow things had drifted along to the point where I felt that being married might be a good idea, as obviously they disapproved of Haroun living with me and marriage might smooth things over.'

'Hardly a reason to get married.'

'No, and what really annoyed me was that even after Haroun re-covered they didn't once criticise him for living with me. It was always me that was the problem. In their eyes I was some sort of slut. Things got even frostier with his family, and whenever I complained to Haroun about it he would just say not to worry. He just didn't see the double standards. We ended up having such a fight about it and he told me just to get used to it and what men did was fine. What was the expression he used—*arajal bhal anahla ala alward wzhar*: the man is like the bee flying around roses and flowers—he can taste wherever he pleases. Or as his other gem; *Mashrish l hout fl bahr*—you don't buy the fish in the sea. At that point I stormed out.'

'Better off out of it, I would say,' was all I could offer. But that wasn't the end of her story.

'But that's the problem. I'm not out of it.'

'I thought you said this was couple of years ago? You're not still in love with him, surely?'

Sandra wiped the tears away with the back of her hand and shook her head. 'Christ no, but I can't get him out of the house.'

'Oh Jesus.'

'The whole fucking family is there and so I can't sell the place or even get inside.'

'But what about the police?'

'Hah!' she snorted derisively. 'They say I will have to go to court and get an eviction order.'

'And?'

'Have you any idea how many years that will take?'

'Unless you pay someone.'

'Unless I pay someone, and I have never done that. Not once.'

'Is he paying you rent?' But I knew the answer even as I asked it. 'Of course not.'

We finished our tea in silence and Sandra moved to sit beside me on the banquette. Then it was a hand on my arm and the murmured request to stay with me.

'Just for the night?' she hastened to add as she felt me tense up beneath her hand.

To give her her due, she took my polite refusal in good grace, albeit with a touch of sadness.

'You are different from the others,' she said. 'I like that about you.'

Then, to my surprise, I found myself confessing that I liked her too. In that moment it was true but it was, I like to think, a compassionate affection rather than anything else.

You will only have me. Swear it. Swear it now.

I conjure A'isha's voice. It is no difficult task. She is so close.

I have heard that the first step to recovery is to admit that you have a problem. So, I will say it. I am crazy. However, owning my insanity did nothing to abate my hunger for her. Sharing the problem with Sandra was not my intention but I did so anyway, although only in a partial way.

'And anyway, I am actually having a relationship with someone.' It was a thought not intended to be spoken aloud. Thankfully Sandra's expression was not one of incredulity, but tenderness as her dim frown waned.

'Oh Richard, that is wonderful. Who is she?'

My brain went into a spin, attempting to recover from my unintended revelation. 'I'm not sure.' It was all I could come up with and, to her credit, Sandra pretended she understood.

After she left I wrote in my notebook that I rather liked her. Then I crossed out the "rather". The self-admission about my feelings for A'isha remained unwritten, for I was as unsure as Swinburne's nympholept as to its true nature.

> *Is it rapture or terror that circles me round, and invades*
> *Each vein of my life with hope—if it be not fear?*

The recipient of my hesitant love was, after all, a shape-shifting mirage; was it Mira or A'isha? Were they interchangeable, I wondered and hated myself for the random thought that suggested either would do. No, I told myself firmly, A'isha is done with, consigned to wherever one sends figments of one's imagination. If only it were that easy.

One evening, a week after Sandra's visit, suffering from hunger and a low-level bout of claustrophobia, I wrapped myself in the warmest clothes I could find and trudged up the Hill of Mice to Batha. For some unknown reason Mira had not turned up for several days and I was running out of food to the point where, the previous night, I had been reduced to a trick from my impoverished student days of cooking a quantity of rice and adding soy sauce to half and coconut cream and honey to the remainder; a spicy main course and sweet pudding. One night of such fare was enough and so I made my way to Tuhami's hole-in-the-wall street café where I was greeted like a long-lost brother with kisses and heart touching. If the warmth of his welcome was disarming, his offering of food was alarming. Before I could order something nourishing he presented me with an outrageously sickly-sweet cake, a glass of almond flavoured yogurt and some potato cakes in hot chilli sauce—in that order.

Although it was bitterly cold I spent a pleasant enough hour nibbling at the strange combination of foods. Then Tuhami shed his grubby white jacket and, after calling someone to mind the shop, tapped me on the shoulder.

'Yalla, khoya!' he commanded and strode off down the hill, pausing only to check that I was still in his wake. Turning left towards the Post Office in Batha he continued to where a taxi was waiting. Without explanation, he opened the rear door and shoved me in before getting in the front seat and rattling off a destination that I was unable to understand. Mutual understanding is not usually an issue with Tuhami, his affection for me is undeniable and, as he once explained through a bi-lingual acquaintance, "friendship is the best language". I have often suspected that there is a poet deep inside Tuhami. On this occasion, however, my understanding was zero.

Within minutes it became obvious that our destination was the *Ville Nouvelle* and for a moment as we careered in and out of traffic like a drunken figure-skater, I wondered if I had been kidnapped. The frisson of excitement was wonderful. Was I accompanying him on an errand or to join him in some forbidden pleasure? An image of nymphs, of *mluk* or other beings, flashed before me and for the first time in weeks I had a craving for the taste of *majoun*. It would have been simple enough to have procured some, but I preferred the more balanced mental state that had come with the banishing of A'isha. *Majoun* would have been too easy a doorway for her to return through and having won my tussle with her I decided to let sleeping *djnun* lie.

Our destination, it transpired, was a smoke-filled bar filled with Moroccan men. Inside, Tuhami, grinning from ear to ear, pushed me through the crowd to where some of his friends were hunched over a small table covered in beer bottles.

'Heineken or Flag?' he asked and without waiting for my reply yelled out an order to the waiter.

Somehow my foreign status or maybe my age worked in my favour and a chair was produced. For his part Tuhami ordered a younger man to sit elsewhere. Once seated, the introductions began. Opposite me, drunk, mumbling and incoherent was Moulay the Barber—the world's slowest hairdresser—whose hour and a half long haircuts were like a meditation and the end result was superb. Seeing him drinking was a shock because I had grown accustomed to the abstemious habits of the Medina folk. Abstemious on the surface only, it appeared.

To my right, dressed in an extraordinarily bright and snappy yellow jacket, was a man in his eighties. We nodded, shook hands and touched our hearts. Then the beer arrived, not single bottles, but four each.

'Tuhami—' I began to protest.

'*Skout!*' he snapped, emphasising the order to keep quiet with a slap on my back.

The Moroccans consumed the beer with extraordinary speed and I struggled to keep up. The old man grabbed my hand and held it as he began a long and convoluted story in a mixture of French, *Darija* and German. The detail of his tale, delivered with coughs, splutters and a good deal of passion, was impossible to follow but my nodding and smiling worked the trick. The gist seemed to be a recounting of his time in French army during World War Two. Several times he mentioned Rome. I caught the words Italy and the easily recognisable Charles de Gaul. With each mention of de Gaul, the old fellow saluted and exclaimed '*Un grand homme!*'

By the time I reached for my third beer I was being shown his French army pension card which he proudly informed me gave him more than two thousand dirhams a month. I think he also invited me for couscous, but I can't be sure.

On the other side of me I sensed that Tuhami was impatient to move on so, as he got to his feet, I slid my last bottle of beer across the table to the old soldier. His beaming face was a treat.

There had been a transaction that I totally missed, for as we rose, Tuhami reached under his chair and produced a large plastic bag, which he nestled in his arms like a baby.

Moulay the Barber insisted on joining us and the three of us lurched into a taxi and sped back to the Medina where, after paying for the taxi, Tuhami handed me the plastic bag and pointed in the direction of his restaurant. Now I got it. The bag was heavy because it was packed with bottles and I was, so to speak, a drug-mule. If I had any uncertainty, it was put to rest by the way Tuhami ambled a fair distance behind me, with an affectation of nonchalance that could have won a ham-acting award. A few months earlier he had been arrested for drunkenness and it was natural that he should be paranoid about being caught taking alcohol into the Medina.

Having delivered the booze, I extricated myself from Tuhami's embrace and headed home, refreshed by my adventure, if not by what I had consumed.

There was one more incident on the way home; an occurrence which I had never seen before or since. Standing under a corner light, deep in the Medina, was an old man, a melancholy magician performing magic tricks. It must have been well after 11pm and, other than the two of us, the streets were deserted. Why he had chosen this street, this corner, was just as much a mystery as the reason he was performing at all. In total silence, and seemingly for his own benefit, he conjured an endless array of objects, plucking coins, cards and plastic flowers from thin air. Not once did he look at me, or speak or even hold out a hat for a few coins. It was simply a performance. For a good five minutes I paused, held, not by the performance, but the incredible sadness of the man. He was good but lost in his art and, as I turned to move away, I was struck by the thought of what a magician has forgone in order to perform. The awe and wonder that first attracted him as a child has become banal, the magic nothing now but trickery. The magician sacrifices magic in order to perform it.

Richard: A burning moth without a flame

My memory of the next few weeks is a hazy blur. Whereas a couple of months earlier I had feigned illness in order to escape the chaos of the renovations, now I was struck down by the real thing. I suspect that it was A'isha's doing; an attack in retaliation for my attempts to rationalise her away.

It began with lethargy and progressed from there to a somewhat more serious condition that included night-sweats and fits of coughing that had me wishing I could just die and be done with it. Most of each day was spent in bed or wrapped in a blanket on a *banquette*, wracked by shivers and the beginnings of fever. If it occurred to me that I was really ill, I can't recall, but even if I had, there is little I could have done for I was soon incapable of more than a few steps before I needed to sit. Strangely, I was not concerned but convinced that I would be fine if I just rested and slept a little more.

By the time the fever was full-blown I was dipping in and out of delirium, retaining only fragmentary memory of the passing of days. A few moments here, some images there, are all that I retain. Yazami's face floated in front of me once, but whether it was real or imagined I can't tell. Often, I saw, or sensed the presence of A'isha, standing over me, gloating at my inability to move or speak her name. Had I been able I would have cursed her, for whatever remained of rational thought was urging me to purge her completely from my system. Not once did she speak to me but her laughter pierced me, causing me to shake uncontrollably.

That I ate something from time to time is possible and most certainly I must have drunk soup or water, although who brought it to me is a mystery. I would like to think that it was Mira, but I can honestly say I don't know.

The clearest moment was also the worst. My body was so hot I felt that my flesh would blister, bubble and melt. A horrible vision of spontaneous combustion, of self-immolation, fixed itself in brain and I knew that if I didn't reduce my temperature I would die. Somehow I rolled from the bed and shed my clothes. Crawling to the door and pushing it open, I collapsed into the courtyard. Everything went black, and for a blessed moment, I was struck by the thought that I had died; that my torment was over.

After I regained consciousness it was late, for when I dragged myself across the courtyard, it was into a pool of moonlight. The night-time temperature was probably as low as two or three degrees Celsius. It was cold. Yet I was burning and in order to cool down I lay on the tiles in front of the fountain and begged someone to pour cold water on me.

There was no one to do so and I lay still, gathering my strength, knowing what I must do. Eventually I was ready, and with a final effort, clawed my way up the side of the fountain. After two failed attempts, I got to my knees and leaned over, allowing my face to flop forward into the water. The sensation was not the cooling I so desperately felt I needed, but the opposite. My head descended into a cauldron of molten metal, lead, silver, it didn't matter and I felt no pain even as my skin flared and burned. The last vision I have is of my skull, stripped of the flesh, smouldering and smoking amidst the reek of burnt flesh; the stench of witches at the stake, the acrid smoke of martyrs, the bitter ashes of St Joan. The sound of my voice screaming at—or for—A'isha, for Mira, for anyone, rose with the smoke and vanished into silence and moonlight. Then the darkness came and I welcomed it like a lover.

My physical recovery was slow. Yazami, no longer a phantom, sat at my bedside day after day, with the perpetual frown of a concerned relative. Once, when I mustered the energy to tell him to cheer up, he snapped at me to save my strength. After a couple of weeks, he took to telling me stories. They may well have been simple but to me they were long and involved tales that I drifted in and out of as my concentration waxed and waned. Sometimes my mind picked up a thread and would stay with it, only to find that I had drifted off and was weaving a completely different story. Or possibly I was embroidering as it went along, going down paths of my own making so that by the time I registered his words they no longer made sense. Occasionally I fell asleep, lulled by the soporific sound of his voice, and when that happened I dreamed new stories woven from the yarn Yazami had spun. Despite the inconstancy of my attention, he persisted, as did his sister.

Every afternoon Mira prepared soup and brought it to me, holding the bowl, feeding me like baby. As I improved she added bread to the menu. Breaking it with those long slender fingers, she would dip it in the soup and hand it to me. Inevitably our hands touched, but if she felt anything, she gave no indication. When, once or twice, those amber eyes flicked up and held mine, it mattered not if the smile in them was real or imagined, for it was as sustaining and healing as the soup.

It was only as my health began to return that it really sunk in how ill I had been. Walking short distances, even around my house was tiring, but with each passing day I managed to stay out of bed for a little longer. With my returning strength came a desire to get out of the house. The feeling I had was not claustrophobia, but simply a longing to reconnect with the world beyond my walls. Spring had arrived; days were getting warmer and longer and the scents and sounds carried on the breeze were an invitation I longed to accept. When I did need to rest, I took to wrapping myself in a blanket on a banquette in the courtyard where I could watch the Atlantic Swifts swooping in the square of blue above my head. Later in the year, with the onset of summer, the colour would fade, but in these days it was a delicious, impossible blue.

As each day came to an end, Mira would fuss around making soup and shooing me back to my room where she insisted I have the heater on and, for some reason, all the lights. She never spoke as such, but made odd clucking and tutting noises with her tongue. It was only in my head that we had long conversations.

Finally, I felt strong enough to venture out and I will never forget that day. It was as if I was seeing the Medina for the first time. To others I must have appeared a madman. My beard and hair were long and untamed, my beloved black *djellaba* more than a little frayed, yet I couldn't have cared less. Walking with the stumbling, shuffling gait of the well-practised insomniac—a dreamer half woken, the woken half sleeping—I traced a path through the streets to the Sagha *funduq*. Here I was forced to stop, my senses assaulted by familiar wild magic. There was no time for me to resist, even if such resistance had been possible. *She* was showing me her power. *She* was saying, *look what I can do, even in broad daylight.*

History swirled around me, dizzying, disorienting, until the kaleidoscope slowed and the caravanserai doors swung open, allowing its ghosts to roam the present. The sounds of the past revived; the coughing of long dead camels, the braying of a donkey protesting the weight of sheepskins, a rooster calling from high on terrace wall and the shouted greetings of travellers reunited after the long journeys from Marrakech, Timbuktu or beyond. Goods came and went on camel or donkey train, on mules, or carried by black slaves; men from Africa, huge beasts of burden, whose scarred bodies bent beneath the weight of merchandise or the live animals slung around their necks.

Rough, cloth-wrapped bundles, wooden packing cases, rolled carpets; all were being unpacked, repacked, inspected, bought, sold or haggled over. In front of giant scales, big enough to weigh a man, a queue was formed, sellers and buyers anxious to check the weights and close the deals. Three Jews from Lihoudi sat huddled in discussion, ignoring the sea of hands offering baubles, beads, cakes, pastries, herbs or *kif*, for their minds were on more precious cargo; spices from India, fine silks from Persia, Syrian silver, Iraqi glass. Their skin and even their eyes were the colour of gold, for these men were goldsmiths, whose days and nights were filled with the glow and dust of their trade. Their sweat was an amalgam and even as they slept the metal seeped through their pores, which is why, it was said they never went to the *hammam* or gave their washing out, but kept it at home where their wives could retrieve the valuable deposit of their perspiration and their dreams.

Glasses of tea, of coffee, of camel's milk were trotted back and forth by boys, their simple *djellabas* stained with the badges of their trade. The noise was intense, a babble of languages, of accents, dialects, of grunts and groans, of coughing, spitting and curses.

Laughter too, a woman's, issuing from behind a window grille, high up. The notes wafting like feathers into the square below.

A cry went up and people turned to stare as a wealthy merchant came from l'Marqtane in Achebine, with three newly purchased slaves roped together. All were young attractive women, two with the blue-black skin of the Nubians, the third as pale as longing, her red hair tossed over her shoulder, the remnants of her Irish skirt protruding beneath the hem of a cheap shift thrown on for decency. Unbowed like her African sisters, she held her head high and met my gaze; insouciance her only defence.

That these were ghosts mattered little, for the doors between the worlds was now wide open and I allowed myself to flow with the history until it took me up some stairs to the present, to a tea shop where I sat with old men on dusty carpets and drank mint tea and shared a pipe.

See what you will lose if you abandon me.

Her voice in my head was accompanied by a quivering ache that had me holding my head in my hands.

'I will never abandon you,' I said out loud.

The old man beside me on the rug, lifted his pipe in salute. '*Ma'fe-hmt,*' he cackled, his liquid laugh emerging from between toothless gums.

'I don't understand either,' I replied. And it was true. Why would I abandon her, even if such a thing were possible?

For the next two days I returned to my bed and there I would have stayed for a good while longer if Yazami and Thami had not intervened.

'Come, it is time to make a journey to the Festival of Sidi Ali.'

Yazami handed me my shoes, leaving me in no doubt that I was included. It was still very early in the morning and I had no intention of going anywhere.

'Sidi Ali,' Thami beamed.

I am not certain Thami really understood where Yazami intended going, but his excitement was obvious.

'Enjoy yourselves,' I said with as much finality as I could muster.

'Sidi Ali,' Thami repeated and grabbing my hand shook it as if concluding a deal.

'Don't argue! You are coming. We are going to get you cured once and for all,' Yazami said and without asking began gathering whatever he thought I might need for the trip, shoving blankets and clothes into a heavy-duty plastic bag.

'I don't feel like it,' I protested. 'Anyway, cured of what?'

'*Her,*' Yazami frowned, then his face relaxed into a grin, 'or maybe of yourself.'

My protestations were in vain and, after a glass of tea, the three of us walked down to R'cif, where a badly battered Renault Elf delivery van was waiting. The man who climbed out to greet us was introduced as Larbi. There was something familiar about him but it took Yazami to prod my memory; he had been one of the musicians at the *lila* I had witnessed. He was an extremely tall individual with a very good command of English which Yazami confided in me was the result of having spent several years as a teacher in Rabat before returning to Fez to follow in his father's footsteps as a musician.

For Larbi, driving involved a certain amount of physical origami; the first fold at his waist in order to fit behind the wheel, the second at the neck so his head bent far enough forward to avoid the roof and finally his arms folded and locked into his sides, held in place by the door on one side and my body on the other. My status as resident madman gained me the passenger seat, a dubious position as it exposed me to a very direct view and possible involvement in the consequences of Larbi's kamikaze approach to driving. By the time we had gone less than a dozen or so miles I had descended into fatalism and no longer counted the number of times he overtook on blind corners. Crouched uncomfortably in the back, Yazami and Thami seemed either unaware or unconcerned about the high probability of being wiped out by a speeding *grand taxi* or overcrowded regional bus. There were no seats in the rear of the van so Yazami and Thami were squatting on our luggage while holding on to whatever they could each time we careered around a corner. It can't have been pleasant.

Normally I would have enjoyed the break from the closed confines of the Medina and revelled in the wide sweep of landscape but as each kilometre sped past, I felt an increasing sense of unease.

At some point, I remember we stopped beside a spring that gushed out of the side of the hill.

'Very pure water,' Larbi explained to me after he had filled several large bottles. 'Some say it's...'

'I'm sure they do,' I said, cutting him short. Springs and water did not seem sensible places to hang around and the sooner we stopped talking the sooner we would be on our way. Yazami wandering off along the road with Thami and striking up a conversation with a local farmer exacerbated my irritation.

The landscape appeared dry, the fields stony and what soil there was poor, yet it was probably perfect for the small olive and citrus groves that chequered the landscape, their boundaries delineated by rows of prickly pear. Away to my left in the haze of the morning lay a lake, its milk-blue surface reflecting the pure white puffs of cloud above the surrounding hills. It was then I realised where I was and for a moment my spirits lifted. This was the landscape I had gazed upon from my temporary home in the cave on Djebel Zalagh; this was the area around Zerhoun.

My improved state of mind lasted only as far as the outskirts of the city of Meknes where a feeling of dread rose in me, a physical feeling that manifested as nausea and trembling and once again I wished that I had never set out on this road. Ahead of us, somewhere in the mountains was A'isha's grotto, a place I had seen only in delirium or ecstasy and yet, even as I shivered with fear, I felt a tug of desire to sink down in its depths, to be consumed and possible set free by her deadly affection. I could see the knife, feel the incision and the warm sticky flow of blood. I choked back the desire to vomit.

'Are you okay?' Yazami asked.

No. No I am not okay. No, I am feeling really ill.

'Yes,' I lied. 'I'm fine."

In the central square, Larbi paused while three more musicians clambered into the back of the van. The men alone would have been enough to cause problems for the aged van, but the addition of their instruments, bedding and various food parcels, proved to be insanity. Then, just as we were about to set off again there was a cry from the street and the head man, the Hamadcha *muqaddim,* Abderrahim, appeared. He opened my door and stood smiling patiently for me to vacate the seat. As I got out, he embraced me warmly, kissing me twice on each cheek. Then he stood back and stroking his moustache, looked me up and down.

'I hear you have been unwell.'

'Some bug...' I began.

'Sidi Ali and the Lady will take care of you, *inshallah,*' he said as he stepped around me.

The Lady? *Others call me Lalla A'isha Gnawiyya, Lalla A'isha Sudani-yya or Lalla...*

Apparently, my illness was not considered bad enough to place me above him on the seating order. Dutifully I made my way to the back and squeezed in between a set of hand drums and one of the musicians who squinted at me with fierce eyes then, giving way to the inevitable, moved a couple of inches and smiled with a face full of nicotine-stained teeth.

Getting underway was a problem; the engine coughed, whined, slipped out of gear and then stalled. Larbi seemed completely unconcerned and after muttering a prayer, turned the key, causing us to lurch forward. He ground the gear lever backwards a notch and tried again. This time the engine started and we gathered momentum. Zero to forty in half an hour, I thought, as a chorused '*humdull-ilah*' came from the cramped occupants in the back of the van.

The suspension was not up the task and for the remainder of the journey the car, swerving back and forth across the road, bottomed out with bone shaking regularity. Feeling ill, I tried to keep my attention on the increasingly beautiful scenery out of the rear windows, however my sense of insecurity soon had me craning my neck to catching a glimpse of whatever was about to wipe us out. Cars, trucks and buses rushed towards us and, as if aware that we were a vehicle out of control, always managed to avoid us at the last minute. That we survived that wobbling, bone-crunching ride seems little short of a miracle.

'Beni Rachid is just up the hill,' Yazami shouted, startling me, his voice coming from just behind my head.

'Beni Rachid,' Thami echoed and laughed.

'Who is Beni Rachid?' I asked without taking my eyes off the *grand taxis* hurtling towards us. Suddenly one of the approaching vehicles, seemingly oblivious to our existence on the road, pulled out to overtake. In the moments before death, nothing flashed before my eyes—no past, no present, no future. No scrolling the credits of my life—just an ancient Mercedes intent on committing suicide. At the last instant we both swerved, and Larbi, for the first time revealing he had an inkling that life on the roads might be dangerous, laughed dryly. Abderrahim appeared unfazed.

'Beni Rachid is the saint's village,' Yazami said.

'Good,' I said. I couldn't have cared less.

The climb through olive groves to the village was accomplished in first gear and it occurred to me that we could have walked faster. It was a prophetic thought, for as the outlying buildings came in sight, so did a traffic jam. Trucks, cars, *grand taxis*, mules, donkeys, pedestrians and even a number of camels were grid-locked at a narrow crossroad; peak hour in Beni Rachid. A more bizarre place for traffic congestion was difficult to conceive.

We ground to a halt and suffered the ignominy of being overtaken by several donkeys and pedestrians. I wriggled my back against the wall of the van, laid my head against the window, closed my eyes and tried to think of anything else other than car wrecks, traffic and Morocco's horrific road toll. Anything but... I was startled upright by an engine backfiring beside us as an ancient motorbike wobbled past, its tyres spinning in the gravel. Then I laughed. Two wild looking characters in *djellabas* and gold turbans were riding a 1951 Norton Big Four—the same model that I had first watched Eric restore, what seemed like a lifetime ago. For a moment I wished he could be here to see the bike, the camels and crowds streaming up the hill. But I knew, even as I thought it, that he would have had eyes for nothing but the motorbike. It was another time when I wished I had a camera to record the scene for him, but had to content myself with a mental note to write him a letter when I came down off the mountain.

Beside me Larbi swore and I turned my attention to the direction of his anger. Steam was hissing out from under the bonnet; the radiator was boiling.

We all piled out into the chaos on the road. Abderrahim, unencumbered by any luggage, strode off, leaving us to cause our own small traffic jam as we unpacked to continue by foot. Walking would be a relief, I thought as I stood gazing over the spectacular view of the wheat and barley fields far below us. The air was still, with no hint of a breeze, so that each little village below us was wreathed in a soft blue haze from cooking fires; the smoke wrapped around them—transparent blankets through which the spires of mosques protruded, their tile work glinting in the late morning sun.

Having promised Larbi we would send some bottles of water and a donkey to carry the remainder of the luggage and food, we set off up the track, an enthusiastic Thami in the lead; the musicians trudging along with their precious drums and Yazami at the rear. As we came to the crossroads we discovered the cause of the traffic jam. An enormous load of hay had dislodged itself from the back of a camel and, had the roads been wider, might well have provided a suitable roundabout. However, the entire road was blocked and a heated argument was going on between (on one side) several police and a couple of soldiers and (on the other) the stalled pedestrians. In the middle, was the camel driver, who was using a stick to ward off donkeys and mules intent on a free lunch. The police were press-ganging reluctant pilgrims into setting their loads down and assisting in packing the loose hay back into the huge net on the disgruntled camel. We skirted around the outside and, leaving the shouting behind us, climbed higher into the cool mountain air.

At the top of the road we came upon a market square, ringed with flagpoles and covered by hundreds of small tents and stalls selling everything from clothing and food to live chickens, sheep and goats.

'For offerings,' Yazami explained in an off-hand manner, his attention elsewhere. Thami had vanished into the throng and Yazami's concern was obvious.

'Over there,' I said, seeing the familiar rounded head and gap-toothed grin. He was squatting down on the ground, entranced by one of several elderly women who had erected sun umbrellas and were offering henna designs. The more enterprising had small displays of faded photographs mounted on cardboard; others had simple books with black and white illustrations. Judging by the huddle of younger women around each umbrella, the women were doing good business. Thami was talking to himself but neither the henna artist nor her client appeared to be disturbed by his presence. Then the old woman grasped Thami's hand and with a few deft strokes painted a design on the back of it. She blew on it a couple of times and indicated that Thami should continue to do so until it was dry. Grinning, he got to his feet and still blowing on the thick lines of henna, shambled back to us.

'Golden,' he mumbled.

'*Iyeh*,' Yazami sighed and herded us on, following the direction the musicians had taken through the crowd.

Leaving the square, we plunged down a steep goat track between low mud-walled houses and around a series of ever-narrowing twists and turns. We walked the length of the village souk and entered a square with a small public wall fountain where a man in a trance was drinking boiling water from the spout of a kettle. A companion was holding the audience's attention with descriptions of medical cures that appeared to involve dead lizards, a bat's wing and gnarled lumps of root. The cures looked deadlier than any disease I could envisage. Then it was on and up again, and here, even so far from the main square, there were people everywhere and we were forced to jostle our way through. Thami, protective of the wet henna on his hand was walking slowly, the hand raised in the air and lowered each time he remembered to blow on it. A young woman, wearing traditional *djellaba*, headscarf and modern diamante-spangled sunglasses, walked by with two hennaed hands aloft, causing Thami to stop and stare in wonder.

'Golden, golden,' he repeated softly, his face glowing with pleasure.

'*Yalla*, Thami,' Yazami growled. He appeared to be in a hurry and was irritated by Thami's constant distraction. I thought of reminding him that it was because of Thami we had undertaken this trip in the first place, but I kept my mouth shut.

Our destination, it transpired, was a disused *hammam*. We were welcomed by a fat, smiling, bundle of a woman; a Berber with the characteristic tattoo on her chin. She shooed us before her like chickens, flapping her hands, clucking and laughing dismissively when Yazami pointed out the lack of any seating or even a table for food. Then, with some pride, she pointed to a single faucet that, after a thump with a piece of fallen brick, was coaxed into dribbling on the floor, where, there being no drain, the water simply puddled on uneven and cracked *zellij*. The lump of brick was also employed to turn it off. The toilet was a hole in the floor in an open cubicle. A length of hose was produced and our hostess demonstrated how it could be jammed onto the tap from where it aspired to provide enough water for simple sanitation.

By comparison, the sleeping quarters were luxurious.

'Welcome to the Sultan's Palace,' Yazami muttered with a wink as we ducked beneath an arch and entered the deepest recess of the *hammam*. Although little more than a shell, the room was spacious and relatively clean. The high vaulted ceilings were in disrepair, but the various layers of plaster and coats of paint had deteriorated into a pleasing pastiche of colours, remnants of some giant artist's palette. The only source of illumination in the cavernous space was high up in the gloom; a pair of circular air vents, which, at this hour of the day, cast circles of sunlight that hit the floor at either end of the chamber. Thami made a beeline for the nearest pool of sunlight and for a few seconds stood, face up bathed in sunshine, glowing and making little cooing sounds of pleasure.

Straw matting and a couple of spare cushions were produced and within a few minutes the pecking order for sleeping was decided. The musicians took the back corners, leaving Yazami, Thami and I to roll out our blankets near the door where a chill draft was a permanent feature. There was no sign of Abderrahim. As *muqaddim,* he obviously had more upmarket sleeping arrangements.

The musicians wrapped themselves in their blankets and were soon either resting or smoking. Thami placed his blanket in one of the pools of sunlight and was alternately holding his hennaed hand up or blowing on it. Yazami was flat on his back, eyes closed.

'What about Larbi?' I asked.

'Oh shit.' Yazami sat up and throwing a jacket over his shoulder headed for the door. 'Keep an eye on Thami.'

Lying down seemed a good idea and, despite the hardness of the floor, I must have gone to sleep, for when I awoke it was two hours later and the musicians had vanished. To my right Yazami was snoring. I peered through the gloom looking for Thami, only to discover he was curled up on the end of my mat like a cat at the foot of a bed.

It was late in the afternoon when I was taken to where the musicians had gathered at the top of the village souk. Twenty minutes later, Abderrahim appeared, looking suitably rested, and the preparations began in earnest. From somewhere, a red *djellaba* was produced and slipped over my head. A red *tarbouche* came next, followed by a pair of brand new yellow *babouche.* I was beginning to feel I was part of some bizarre initiation into the Hamadcha, and I wasn't entirely comfortable with it. Abderrahim put an arm around my shoulder and squeezed me affectionately.

'You're looking better already,' he said.

Looking maybe, but I felt as though I was in the middle of some strange fantasy. The Medina of Fez I had grown accustomed to, but here, in Beni Rachid, I was a total outsider and for the first time in months I felt a touch of paranoia and the disturbing sense of disassociation that comes with culture shock. There were no reference points, no social markers, nothing that felt familiar. Catching sight of a Moroccan army captain in modern dress was oddly comforting. But everywhere else I turned I was confronted by the weird;

turbaned heads, *Gnaoua* musicians with shells sewn into their hats, women with facial tattoos, a man—naked from the waist up—beating himself with a spiky cactus and everywhere hands; hennaed hands, hands carrying live chickens, hands offering herbs, bangles, shell necklaces, fake designer wristwatches, gnarled and misshapen hands of beggars. On the cobbles between us and a low wall, a blind man in a yellow tunic had set down an orange and white-striped plastic tablecloth on which waddled half a dozen tortoises, each with its price written in Day-Glo-pink directly on their shells.

The other twelve members of the troop were assisting each other tying bands of white cloth around their foreheads. I guessed that it had some religious symbolism and wondered why I wasn't offered one. It also occurred to me that perhaps they were only intended to keep their hats in place when they danced.

Once they were dressed, several of the men gathered twigs and scraps of cardboard and paper, lit a small fire in the middle of the street and proceeded to warm the skins on the small hourglass shaped drums. From a distance they had looked very traditional, but up close I saw that the bright green, blue and red colour around the drums was, in fact, plastic tape. After my first experience of a *lila* I had asked Yazami about these drums and become totally confused by the apparently different names he employed; *gwal, tarija* and *harazi.*

'Do you mind, er, upholding one of the flags?' Abderrahim asked.

'Flags?'

'Is that improper words?'

I shook my head. 'Flag is good. If you have a flag then I don't mind *carrying* it.' It would be a relief to have something useful to do. The preparations had been going on for over an hour and I still had not the slightest notion about what was going to take place. The nausea I had experienced in the van had gone, but I was still feeling tense and apprehensive.

'You will *carrying* the flag green,' Abderrahim said, proudly incorporating his latest English verb.

There was no sign of any flag, so I perched on top of the wall beside the tortoises and watched the crowd. With every minute it was growing in size. There appeared to be thousands of people lining the pathway, waiting, I suspected, for us to do something. Around us latecomers were streaming down the narrow street; much to the annoyance of a group of soldiers who were attempting but failing to take control and keep people behind barriers.

'Herding cats,' I said to no one in particular.

'There are cats?' Abderrahim frowned. 'There are always cats, but I think they have gone because the bull is coming, *inshallah.*'

I wondered if it was a joke. In front of us the crowd parted to allow a young man in a yellow t-shirt to pass. For some strange reason he was tossing an enormous terracotta pot in the air and catching it.

'Ah,' Abderrahim exclaimed, 'watch.'

The man stopped directly in front of us. He was clean-shaven and had his hair cut short and neat. But it was his drooping eyelids that concerned me. He appeared unable to focus; his eyes glazed over like a sleepwalker. Too many drugs, I thought as he held the pot with trembling hands. Sensing that something was about to happen the crowd stepped back and fell silent. Suddenly it was so quiet that I could hear birds in the trees and from far away a rooster crowing. A couple of soldiers with batons marched towards us and then seeing the young man stopped, extending their batons across the road as a temporary barricade to the gathering crowd of onlookers.

For several seconds the young man stood still, his eyes rolling in his head. Then with a huge effort he tossed the pot high in the air and to my horror and amazement, stood still, intentionally letting it fall and shatter on the top of his skull. As the shards of terracotta clattered to the ground there was an audible sigh from the crowd and the man who, in my estimation, should have been killed or at the very least, knocked unconscious, wavered a little but remained standing as the blood began to flow from his scalp and down the sides of his face. One of the soldiers applauded.

'Very good,' Abderrahim said and turned back to the job of marshalling his troops as the bleeding man wandered off, a few people collected souvenir scraps of terracotta and the bustle and noise in the street resumed.

'What on earth was that all about?'

'He was tranced,' Abderrahim grinned and then said quietly, 'He does this thing for *her*.'

Yes, I thought, I suppose he does. So, this was another of *her* lovers, another of her many husbands. She would be happy with the blood.

Would I do that for her, I wondered.

There came a cheer from behind us and four soldiers and two security men in business suits came running down the road, screaming and waving at us to get to one side. From behind them came a black and white monster of a bull. Its horns must have spanned a metre and were tied with a blue rope connected to just above the hoof on its left leg. The partial hobbling did little to impede its progress and several pairs of hands grabbed me, pulling me out of the way as the creature lunged forward.

'Ah, the King's bull is arrived,' Abderrahim grinned from the safety of a wall. He extended his arm and yanked me up beside him.

Soldiers and officials were supposedly restraining the bull, but it was an unequal contest, until an elderly man in a stained *djellaba* stepped into the bull's path and spoke to it, softly muttering what sounded like a prayer. The bull stopped and the crowd roared their approval.

'Flags!' Abderrahim shouted, struggling to make himself heard above the din in the street.

Two flags, one green, one red, were pulled from a sack, attached to poles and as promised, I was handed the green one.

'We march to the saint's mausoleum. You walk behind King's bull.'

'Sure... and if it decides to turn around?'

But our *muqaddim* was the one who had turned and was urging the musicians into some semblance of order; *ghita* players at the front, drummers at the rear. I eyed the bull. It eyed me back and bellowed and pawed the ground. I was obviously not blessed with the art of bull whispering like the old man who had brought its initial rampage to a halt.

'*Yalla!*' Abderrahim yelled and as the *ghiyyata* blasted out a long wailing series of notes, we moved slowly forward.

A'isha: There is a river

There is a river that runs through my realm this day. It is dark red. I can smell it as it seeps in between the roots of my grotto. Around it there are thousands who want things of me; thousands who have sacrificed their fowl, sheep and goats. And yet my attention is elsewhere. To feed my hunger it is the one who fears me most that I will have. He is here. I can feel him, here in my heartland. Tonight is my night. Tonight I shall be rewarded for my patience. He shall perform the hadra for me and then this Nazarene will confess to me with his blood.

Richard: Hot hadra

Progress down the winding path through the souk was painfully slow. Earlier in the day it had taken us little more than nine or ten minutes to walk its entire length, now with a seething mass of pilgrims cramming the street we were reduced to a shuffle and frequent stops. Judging by the number of houses I had seen, Beni Rachid was home to no more than between five hundred to a thousand people. Now there were tens of thousands. I remembered Yazami saying that some people walked for weeks in order to attend. For what, I wondered, to see a group of musicians in red *djellabas* follow a bull down a street? Hardly.

The sides of the street were lined with shops and stalls, totally blocked from trading by the pilgrims who had taken up every possible vantage point, including the counters of the more obliging shop owners. The weather was clear and even though we were protected from the sun by a green canvas awning that stretched across the street, it was hot and airless. Not enough oxygen for so many people.

I shrugged the thought away and concentrated on keeping my flag aloft. It was heavy, deep green velvet with a Qur'anic inscription embroidered in gold thread. The top of the two-metre pole on which it hung sported an ornate brass ball that unbalanced the entire affair, added to the weight and wobbled dangerously every time I took a step forward.

The noise in such a confined space was deafening. Not only did I have the *ghita* and drum players directly behind me, but also the crowd itself was increasingly vocal. Worked up by the music, they chanted, clapped, sang and ululated from all sides and every time the bull attempted a charge, or baulked at something, a roar of excitement rang out.

Then it began to rain. Or so I thought. As the drops hit my face I looked up to discover that many of the pilgrims had small green bottles of orange-flower water and were taking great delight in spraying us with it. I'll smell like a perfumed whore, I thought, even while enjoying the cooling sensation.

Being surrounded by the music—totally immersed in it—I found myself at first nodding my head and soon swaying in time. I glanced over my shoulder and saw that several of the drummers, their instruments tucked against their necks, had come to a complete stop, their eyes closed as they moved as I did. To my surprise, the spectators were also beginning to bend from side to side in time to the music. Our tortoise-like advance exposed each section of the crowd to many minutes of the hypnotic rhythm and, as the tempo increased, the impact was extraordinary; onlookers were going into trance.

A scuffle broke out to one side as a large woman, swaying out of control, broke through the cordon of soldiers shuffling along beside us. Two soldiers moved to restrain her but Abderrahim, a glint of satisfaction in his eyes, gestured for them to leave her and she continued dancing beside me. More orange-flower water showered down on us and the crowd clapped and cheered her on.

At first the woman was able to match the rhythm, but then as her trance deepened her movements became increasingly chaotic and there was a gasp from the onlookers as she pulled her headscarf from her hair and, with a flick of her head, released her long black tresses. The swaying of her head side to side became frenetic. A'isha was in her. I felt it like a magnet and it took all my willpower to drag my attention away. But even as I did, I knew I couldn't hold out against the energy that seeped from her, reaching out, infecting me.

We continued, inch by inch down the cobbled street, surrounded by the music, the chanting and general chaos; while beside me the woman had become totally (and a little frighteningly) robotic. Her head was tilted back at an odd angle and her eyes had taken on the same glazed look I had seen in the head-smasher an hour earlier. Now, instead of side to side, she was whipping her hair back and forth with a scary intensity.

I glanced at my watch. Getting this far along the road had taken an hour. At this rate we would take several more just to get through the souk, let alone to the saint's mausoleum.

Despite our slow pace, my own feeling of illness and anxiety about A'isha lifted completely, replaced with a mild elation. The music was in my head, my veins and in my bones. Around me the bizarre now seemed normal and while the drummers handed their drums up to a shopkeeper to warm them up again, I stood, still swaying, drinking in my surroundings.

We had moved deeper into the souk. To the left a butcher sat on one end of his counter happily spraying orange-flower water on everyone within reach; the number of empty bottles at his side a testament to his enthusiasm for the proceedings. Solid metal frames with large hooks protruded beyond him into the street and hanging from them were the freshly butchered carcasses of several sheep and goats. The butcher's assistant, in bloodstained apron and red bandana, was in a light trance, his only grip on reality being the hand with which he grasped one of the hooks between the carcasses. His eyes were closed shut; his face lit by a beatific smile. It was a lovely moment.

There was a crash beside me as the woman who had joined our procession tumbled to the ground, unconscious. Abderrahim and the musicians managed to step around her without tripping. Two soldiers carried her away while an old lady fussed, attempting to fasten the entranced woman's headscarf back in place.

Eventually we arrived at the end of the souk, but even here, where a small square marked the intersection of a crossroad, the crowd was immense. Packing the square thirty or forty deep, people hung from windows and lampposts, jammed onto the lip of a fountain, peered from atop walls and balconies. It was a sea of nodding heads, smiling faces, headscarves, *hijabs*, turbans, *tarbouche* and a scattering of people wearing a black or red fez.

As we rounded the corner a roar erupted and the bull, spooked either by the noise or a sudden realisation of the fate that awaited it, chose this moment to make a break for it and in a move straight out of the rodeo rider's handbook, it bucked and spun around so fast that its minders were flung into the crowd. Now facing me, it bellowed and shook its head as if checking that the irritating people on the ends of the rope were gone. Panicked, I turned to run, but came face to face with a wall of musicians, who, eyes shut, happily entranced by their own music, were blissfully ignorant of the danger that confronted them. The bull, sensing that uphill was not a good option, turned away and with another impressive buck, ran straight into a side alley. This time the crowd's reaction was so loud that the musicians stopped and for a few seconds there was pandemonium; Abderrahim yelling for the musicians to resume playing, soldiers charging after the bull and the spectators behaving as though they were at a football final and the home team had just scored a goal. My knees were shaking and I came close to dropping the flag. The alley into which the bull had charged was a dead end and in a matter of minutes three young men emerged with the animal once more under control. A huge cheer from the crowd greeted them as they handed the ropes over to the soldiers.

As I steadied my nerves, I saw *her*. Leaning against a wall, illuminated by a shaft of late afternoon sunlight, was Mira. Yet, it could not be because she had not accompanied us. The familiar sick feeling rose in my throat as I realised that A'isha was once again mocking me by taking on Mira's appearance. Between us, clothed in shadow, were a mass of people and yet, for a moment it was as if we were alone. Her face wreathed in a smile, her eyes flashing, she gave me an almost imperceptible nod before stepping down and melting into the crowd.

'No,' I said aloud.

'*Yalla!*' Abderrahim bellowed and we moved forward again.

I glanced over my shoulder, but she was gone. I hoisted the flag as high as my aching arms would permit and followed the bull. It no longer frightened me. Compared to A'isha it was easily controlled and I had more faith in those restraining it than I did in my own ability to rein in the bizarre creations of my imagination.

Within a few minutes we were out of the souk and the mausoleum was in sight; the white walls and yellow detailing glowing in the sunlight. It was a much larger building than I had anticipated, some 150 feet in length and topped not by the traditional domed roof but an unusual hexagonal one of glazed emerald-green tiles. The steps to the entrance were hidden beneath a mass of people who had rushed ahead to greet us.

The procession had been going for several hours and now I wanted it to be over. Not only was I tired, but also the pleasure I had experienced at being included in the ceremony had evaporated, leaving me feeling chilled and vaguely numb. The sighting of A'isha had disturbed me and my only desire was to be as far from the mountain village of Beni Rachid as possible.

Finally, the bull was led away and Abderrahim dismissed us with a wave then turned to greet a strikingly handsome man in a white and gold *djellaba*. They strode off together, the crowd parting to let them through.

'Who was that?' I asked Larbi as we headed back to the *hammam* for a rest.

'Sidi Hajj Qasim, the head of the king's Palace Guards,' he whispered in a deferential tone, 'A very big man.'

The plan was that we would assemble at around nine and make our entrance into the mausoleum at ten when the *lila* and *hadra* was scheduled to start. However, at about half past eight we were summoned to a house belonging to Sidi Mohammed Taik, a *wulad*, a descendent, so I was told, of Sidi Ali ben Hamdush, the Hamadcha saint.

Seated on sumptuous carpets and cushions we were served dish after dish of food by a swarm of young men in pure white tunics and baggy pants. The musicians and I were seated along one wall with Abderrahim, Sidi Hajj Qasim and Sidi Mohammed Taik, which, I assumed, was a great honour.

'Hajj Qasim has paid for the meal and for tonight's *hadra*,' Larbi said. 'And in return he will sit with us in the mausoleum.'

'There is no problem with my being there?'

He looked at me, perplexed. 'No, Sidi, you are one of us.'

It worried me that as a non-Muslim I might be ejected.

'Do just as we do. There will be no problem.' He dug his fingers into the couscous in front of us and fished out a chicken drumstick, which he placed in front of me. Despite the fact I had eaten little during the day I was not hungry. However, knowing that a long night lay ahead, I forced myself to eat.

'*Shukran*,' I mumbled. 'All those people outside?'

'The people?'

'The pilgrims, it can't be easy for them, so why do they come?'

Larbi nodded as he swallowed his food, wiped his fingers across his mouth and reached for a glass of water. 'They are here for a cure and for *baraka*.'

'For a blessing from Sidi Ali?'

'And from *her*, from the Lady. Many are women who have problems that she can cure, or else they are possessed by one of the *djnun*. Many people; many reasons.'

'But what if they are possessed by *her*?' I asked as evenly as I could. Larbi looked at me, then down to the carpet beneath him.

'That is a different story,' he said and, obviously not willing to expand on the subject, reached for more food.

The time dragged way beyond the supposed starting time for the ceremony and I was overcome by tiredness to the point where began to think that I would be unable to attend the *lila*. The notion of returning to the *hammam*, wrapping myself in a blanket and sleeping, seemed both practical and inviting. Yet, when we eventually trooped outside it was into a very different atmosphere. The crowds around the mausoleum had doubled and the warm night was electric with expectation under a glorious full moon. The feeling was infectious. From every part of the village I could hear drumming and the wail of the *ghita*. Rhythms competed with each other and from time to time the night air was pierced by high-pitched ululation that rippled down the narrow streets. The frisson of excitement caused me to shiver and after jamming my *tarbouche* firmly in place, I followed Larbi and the others to just below the entrance steps where we waited for Abderrahim, who was strolling behind us at an unusually leisurely pace. He was taking his time, enjoying the salutations of the crowd and the knowledge that nothing would happen until he gave the word. In this moment he was all-powerful.

'How is the baby Hamadcha?' asked a familiar voice behind me and I turned to face a grinning Yazami. Thami, overawed by the press of people, was clinging tightly to Yazami's arm, his face pale and eyes wide.

'Richard, Richard,' he mouthed with a half-smile.

'*Labas*, Thami?'

'*La..la..Labas*,' he stuttered unconvincingly.

I patted his arm.

'Let's hope we can get in,' Yazami said as he eyed the crowd milling around the entrance. Seven or eight soldiers and three police were barely holding their own against those insisting that they be admitted. Up the steps an official in a gold striped *djellaba* was inspecting invitations and showing little compassion for those he turned away, despite their shouted protests.

'Follow me.' Abderrahim stepped up beside us. 'Bring the boy.'

'Not a boy,' Thami hissed. He was the only person present who showed no respect to the *muqaddim*.

'*Skout*, Thami!' Yazami snapped, grabbing his hand and tugging him along in Abderrahim's wake.

At the top of the steps the official stepped deferentially to one side to allow them passage. Then, having delivered Thami and Yazami safely inside the mausoleum, Abderrahim reappeared and for a second stood, regally surveying the crowd. It was clear that he thought of it as *his* crowd as much as that of the entombed saint who lay awaiting us within.

Hajj Qasim arrived escorted by two solidly built soldiers and gave the *muqaddim* the nod to commence proceedings.

Having assured themselves of entry, Yazami and Thami re-emerged and together we stood and watched as the ceremony began in the street. Incense was lit, prayers recited and then, after the drummers had huddled around a charcoal brazier warming their instruments, we finally climbed the steps. The thought flashed through my head that at any moment I would be unmasked and my imagination rioted with images of being torn apart by a crowd angry with an impostor being allowed in while they were excluded. But the people packed in the area in front of the mausoleum seemed content to gather around the groups of musicians who had claimed enough space to set up in and were beginning to drum out the familiar rhythms of the *hadra*. Already people were swaying, dancing and working themselves towards the moment when the ecstasy took over.

It was after 11pm when we eventually entered the mausoleum. Those already inside greeted us warmly, their faces bright and alert, despite the lateness of hour. The interior of the building was not as imposing as one might have expected from the outside. Here there was no ornate carved plaster, no fancy decoration and certainly no soft lighting. Concrete walls and neon strip lights gave the space a utilitarian appearance, more in common with a school than a shrine. The pillared main hall looked as if it had once been a simple open courtyard. Running east west, a high roof now enclosed it and tiered seating had been constructed on its northern side.

Women filled this area, while along the floor of the hall a series of carpets were laid out with a scattering of cushions. This area was the preserve of the men.

Our designated spot was a raised area at the western end of the hall, just in front of what Larbi described as "the place the saint lives". Between us and where the men sat there was an expanse of tiles surrounded by candles. The only other ornament was a large silver incense burner, with a filigreed dome cover through which I could see the glow of hot charcoal.

You will only burn black jawi incense and when I demand it you will perform the hadra. Is that understood?

Even just the memory of her voice was enough to throw me off balance. Larbi interrupted and brought me back to the present.

'Go while you have a chance,' he whispered, nodding towards the room containing the tomb. For a moment, my paranoia took it as an instruction to escape before I was unmasked as an infidel impostor.

'Take your shoes off,' he added, as he nudged me towards the tomb's entrance where the two security guards took one look at my red Hamadcha *djellaba* and held back the waiting pilgrims so that I could enter.

Having stepped through the door I stopped to watch the dozen or so people in front of me. Once they had kissed the doorjambs, the men turned to the right, the women to the left. The saint, Sidi Ali, lay parallel to the western wall so that he could face Mecca. The catafalque was a simple wooden-framed structure covered with layers of red, yellow and white cloth.

There was a slow circumambulation of the catafalque as the pilgrims kissed each side. I followed suit, but when the man in front of me lifted up the cloth and kissed the tomb itself it was a step too far and I stuck to kissing the cloth. I experienced an out-of-body sensation, as though I was observing another person perform an arcane ritual; someone that was not me.

Beside the door I noticed an alms box and fumbled under my *djellaba,* only to find I had no small change. I produced a two hundred dirham note. As I deposited the money the eagle-eyed security guard rewarded me with a huge smile and, as I straightened up, he inclined his head towards mine.

'Thank you, *Sidi,*' he whispered in perfect English and bending down, deftly scooped up some earth from a small pile beside the door. He pressed a small quantity into my palm and then slipped his hand in the top of my *djellaba* and is a surprisingly intimate gesture rubbed the remainder into my chest.

'*Allah o Akbar!*' he intoned, as he guided me out the door.

'Now you have *baraka!*' Larbi exclaimed when he saw the dirt on my hands and *djellaba,* '*Humdullilah!*'

'*Humdullilah,*' I mumbled, and uncertain what to do with the remaining earth, I slipped it into my pocket.

It is difficult to recall how much time passed before the ceremony got underway, or even when it actually started. There had been prayers outside and now there were more. At one point I recall we were offered milk and dates. I do remember thinking how little pomp there was compared to a Catholic mass. What was missing,

RICHARD: HOT HADRA

under the bright neon lights, was a sense of mystery. Abderrahim and the other Hamadcha members recited prayers, but during most of them the women in our audience appeared to be more interested in gossip and greeting latecomers. A few men stood in front of what I thought of as "our stage" and recited a few responses.

Yet, in the same manner as the first *lila* I had attended, the atmosphere built imperceptibly and soon the prayers had taken on a rhythmic quality and first one drummer then another joined in. When Abderrahim picked up his *gembri* and began playing, a few men edged towards the front of the stage and commenced their swaying dance. Around me, still seated, the musicians were rocking in unison. The *hadra* had begun.

The chanted phrases were repeated faster and faster until those around me were hyperventilating, their eyes glazed and, as a strange wave of hot air flowed over us, the women began to ululate. One over excited woman made her way down to the courtyard and began to dance directly in front of us. She didn't remain there long as several men descended on her and bundled her back to the seats. This part of the *hadra* was obviously for men only.

In front of us the dancing men had formed a circle, shoulder to shoulder, and as the noise intensified, I felt a surge of joy as I caught a glimpse of Thami. He was dancing in the middle of the circle, in perfect time to the music, his head lolling to one side, the only sign of his mental problems. What moved me was the respect those men showed him as they formed a ring of protection and assisted Thami in whatever it was he striving for. Yazami was also in the line of men, his eyes shut, his head bobbing left and right in unison with the others.

Out of the corner of my eye I saw Abderrahim lay the *gembri* down and, as he picked up a small silver drum, he signalled us to get to our feet and form a line. Then he danced in front of us, conducting as the drummers increased the tempo and the *ghiyyata* blared out. The chanting of verses had ceased, replaced by a peculiarly aspirated hissing out of the name of God. Shortened to simply '*llah, 'llah, 'llah, 'llah...* over and over, the effect was electric. The entire space felt as though it was pulsating with energy and as the music continued its crescendo, the ululating became higher and more frantic. Thami and Yazami and a dozen other men broke from their circle and formed a line in front of us—'*llah 'llah 'llah!*

As a dance, the *hadra* is deceptively simple. The swaying from the waist to left, centre and then right, seems incapable of producing an altered state and yet slowly the movement incorporates a "bounce" with each beat, a pounding down on the heels, the effect of which is to knock any breath you have left from chanting, right out of your body and causing the dancer to hyperventilate.

In what felt like a heavy, liquid atmosphere, I began to dance. No longer hesitant, I abandoned myself to the moment and became one with music that flowed around me, through me and on which I seemed to float.

A woman dashed into the vacant space between us and the line of men and this time there was no one capable of intervening. Ripping off her headscarf, she became a blur of movement; head thrashing first left and right and then backwards and forwards far faster than seemed humanly possible. Two older women attempted to replace her scarf, but, beaten back by the violence of the entranced woman's movements, they contented themselves with standing either side, supporting her, gripping her elbows so that she wouldn't hurt herself.

For his part, Abderrahim seemed a man possessed, leaping and waving his arms, stabbing his chest with his fists, urging us on with leaps and bounds and all the time hissing '*llah, 'llah, 'llah.*

In front of me, Thami and Yazami appeared to be in a state of bliss. Bathed in sweat, they danced side by side and in that moment I loved Yazami for his devotion to his brother. Whether the *lila* had any beneficial effects no longer mattered. That Thami was so loved was enough.

As the *ghiyyata* wailed, a wave of dizziness hit me, a sudden fever, and, just as I was convinced I would pass out, it changed to a fizzy, tingling feeling of ecstasy and I surrendered to everything—the place, the people, the music, to *Allah,* with the realisation that I was on the brink of experiencing the state the Hamadcha called *hal.*

A fresh burst of ululation dragged my attention back as the woman in front of us collapsed to the ground. For a moment she lay, grunting, her chest heaving and then she fainted completely, lying still as though dead. Surprisingly, there was no concern. The two women who had been attending her covered her face with her headscarf and a couple of men came and carried her away to recover.

Then, as though a switch had been flipped, it all stopped.

We sat, and from somewhere a tribe of men in white tunics and gold baggy pantaloons appeared and served mint tea. It was like half time at the rugby and I half expected someone to run out with slices of orange. For no apparent reason, I started laughing. As a sense of normalcy returned I noticed that I had not been the only one slow to recover. Out in the hall a couple of women were standing as if frozen and a lone man was still rocking back and forth on his heels, his head dropped to his chest. Beside me one of the *ghita* players was lying back on the carpet his eyes open, staring God knows where. He looked content.

'You do good, I think?' Abderrahim, flushed, his forehead glistening with sweat, hunkered down beside me.

'Good,' I nodded. 'And Thami...'

He waved a hand, summoning some tea. 'What we say... Oh my brothers, pray for me. I shall be cured thanks to chanting, Shelter me under your wings, oh children of Mustapha, the chosen, the elected. There is no God but *Allah*. Oh Prophet, cure me. That was what we sung at the beginning.'

'Well, it seems to be working for...' I pointed to the woman who had collapsed. She was sitting up now, a dazed expression on her face as she rearranged her headscarf. Beside her another woman was offering her a glass of water.

'That woman always does same thing. Everywhere we go she is first up. Most people wait for next part of the *hadra*...' He sighed and shrugged.

'First up and first down,' I joked, regretting it immediately.

The tea arrived and he took two glasses, passing one to me. 'It is what she comes for. It is what she needs.'

'There is a lot more to come, though?'

'The first part called "hot *hadra*", the second part "cold *hadra*", but, *khoya*, *shuf*, I think you would be wise to save your energy for the third part, the moment when the lights go out.'

'What is that called?'

'*A'isha's hadra*.'

And what happens...' I began, but he was already on his feet, heading towards where Hajj Qasim was lolling back against the wall of the tomb.

After drinking his tea, Abderrahim stood at the front of the performer's area and called out to the crowd. A queue formed and one by one people came forward, pressed money into his hands and received a chanted blessing from the brotherhood, most of whom were reclining on the cushions. It all seemed rather casual, as those not being blessed wandered around, talking, smoking and sipping mint tea.

'*Sidi!*' a soldier I had seen earlier in the evening escorting Hajj Qasim, hissed. He beckoned for me to come over to where he stood between the pillars that marked the entrance.

As I reached him, he turned and without a word preceded me to the door.

When I first saw the woman in the pale blue *djellaba*, I was struck with horror, then I realised I had, once again, made a mistake. This was Mira, the real Mira, eyes downcast, her hennaed hands clasped tightly together. The guard said something I didn't understand, but guessing he was asking if it was true I wanted her to come inside, I nodded, took Mira's arm firmly and led her inside before my confusion became apparent.

'*Shukran*,' she said quietly and, releasing herself from my arm, moved through the crowd in the direction of the women seated on the steps. Not once did she look at me directly. I searched the sea of faces until I located Yazami. Thankfully, he was seated on a carpet with Thami and hadn't seen Mira's arrival or my part in it. As long as she remained seated with the women she would probably stay unnoticed, I thought as I returned to my place next to Larbi.

'*Mashi mushkil?*' he enquired.

'No problems,' I laughed, suddenly elated. Mira was here and A'isha had not struck me down. The thought seemed fanciful and I reprimanded myself. I was an adult, a rational westerner and should know better than to indulge in superstitious nonsense. The night would continue to be simply a fascinating cultural experience and I would emerge from the other end, tired but enriched.

*

A'isha: The true nature of blood

There is blood that is true and blood that lies. This gawri, the foreigner, has no true blood. His blood deceives and for this I shall extract revenge.

Richard: Too hurried in the head

The cold *hadra* began softly and, in contrast to the hot *hadra*, the dancers drifted down in front of us to dance alone, rather than in lines as previously, and yet, despite the gentleness of the music, the effect was dramatic. For a long while I watched individual dancers, almost patiently, in the *hal* state—the light trance. Then abruptly something would change. Often it was a shift to a new musical phrase or the introduction of a different rhythm, at which point the dancer appeared to lose all sense of physical coordination. They would lurch from foot to foot, sway alarmingly, cry out, and in a couple of instances, produce a small knife and slash their head until blood appeared. Nobody seemed to think this extraordinary. Others, particularly women, would fall to their knees and start smashing their heads against the tiles until they collapsed and were gently carried away to recover.

'*Jidba!* Deep trance,' Larbi whispered to me. 'See...'

The dancer he pointed at, a young woman, was moving to some inner music while a companion tried valiantly to steady her against falling. With a single violent movement, the woman ripped off her *hijab* and released her hair, her head thrashing, alternating between back and forth and sideways in no discernible order. It was riveting to watch because I had an overwhelming conviction that she was in the control of some force so strong that at any moment she might explode. Either the energy emanating from her was too intense, or the music captured her, but whatever the cause, within minutes her companion's head was moving in the familiar manner and as we all watched, she too tore off her headscarf and, releasing the friend's arm, gave herself over to *jidba*—to deep and total trance.

I have no conscious recollection of getting to my feet. Neither do I recall the moment I slipped off my *babouche*, nor the first feeling of cold tiles beneath my feet. Yet I remember being barefoot and remember the wetness of the floor; green *zellij* drenched in orange-flower water. Knowing that I would meet *her* caused me no fear. The music was simply too beautiful to resist and my body was no longer under my conscious control. It had been taken over by the air around it and I was wafted up, drifting this way and that, through sweet clouds of incense smoke. Here, in the warm embrace of subtle currents, a joy welled up in me as I recognised the sensation. This is what a butterfly feels, I thought.

An angelic light surrounded me and I knew I was finally in the safest place in the universe. The relief was so great that I felt no surprise when the tears coursed down my cheeks. It is possible that the *jidba* was only partial at this point for there was a brief moment when I registered that Yazami was by my side, holding my hand. He was golden too; glowing, molten, soft as warm beeswax. I am so stoned, I thought, and then remembered that I had smoked nothing.

In this space my knowledge of the ritual became intimate. I understood why a woman who had first appeared to float through the crowd, flowing, graceful, effortless, was now on her knees like a pig, emitting rasping grunts while crashing her head against the floor, or the man to my left, stiff legged, walking camel-like around the floor, oblivious to all those around him.

Strangely, while the rhythms remained, the beat of the drums had fallen silent, or did not reach the space I had entered. The only music I could hear was a *ghita* in my head, sweet as honey, soft as warm milk it felt. It nurtured me, filling me with forgiveness; forgiveness of all I had done, healing, mending, stitching together the broken, straightening the bent. A spirit entered me, cleaning every molecule, every atom of my being, until I shone in sweet amalgam with the golden light. In this moment, I again rose like a butterfly in an updraft; rose above the cloud forest, above the bodies of the dead, the blood and slashed faces, the hate and remorse, the self-pity and knew that it was not my doing. It was a moment of crystalline purity that I shall never forget.

Hahiya jat! Hahiya jat! Hahiya Jat! Lalla 'A'isha. Hahiya jat! Hahiya jat! Hahiya jat! Lalla 'A'isha.

The reality shifted and once again I was inside the mausoleum. Through the haze of incense smoke I saw the hundreds of pilgrims beseeching *her* to appear. Around me the faces of the brotherhood shimmered into view. They danced, each now isolated by his bliss, eyes shut, mouths drooped open, whispering the call. Then the deep base voice of Abderrahim reverberated inside my skull as he called her—called *Lalla Sudaniyya.*

'Oh, A'isha, rise and place yourself in the service of *Allah* and the Prophet.'

Like a waterfall, more orange-flower water splashed on the tiles.

Hahiya jat! Hahiya jat! Hahiya jat! Lalla 'A'isha. Hahiya jat! Hahiya jat Hahiya jat! Lalla 'A'isha.

The electric lights were extinguished and the universe shrunk to the world illuminated by flickering candles.

Hahiya jat! Lalla 'A'isha...

The candle flames—rings of rainbow halos amidst the blue-white smoke of incense—scintillating. The intensity of the beauty was painful and my universe trembled. Black *jawi* incense, *her* incense, washed over me.

My incense.

'Truly,' I said, as she floated up through the floor to stand in the air above me. Naked, her hair out, tumbling over her breasts, she danced the *hadra* in front of me. I was no longer afraid.

You are dancing for me.

'Yes, for you.'

Follow me.

Without awaiting my response, she sank down, through the floor and I followed, stepping into the soft centre of the floor to where I knew the depths would take me.

Spiralling downward for a moment, I emerged in a place I knew intimately. It was her *hufra*, her grotto beneath the roots of the giant fig tree at Ayn Kabir. Here the stream that ran across my feet was warm and red, the blood of sacrifice. A'isha danced before me now, a knife of raw iron in her hand. Staring deep into my eyes, she slashed her head and stood still for a moment, frozen in a state of ecstasy, as the blood trickled down her forehead, down her cheeks. With a slow deliberate gesture she wiped the blood with her fingers and licked them slowly. Not once did her eyes leave mine. Not then, nor when she handed the knife to me.

For me.

'For you,' I said and such was her hunger that as I cut, she pulled me to her and held her mouth to the wound, her tongue flicking lightly. Then, she pushed me away and took the knife from me, inspecting the blade.

Tell me why a gawri, a non-believer, does this.

Her tone was suddenly harsh and I sensed that something had changed.

'Because you exist in a place I did not believe existed and because you can be as beautiful as the woman I love while being so filled by hate and all this I need to understand.'

Hate? How dare you talk of hate, you who are consumed by it?

And I knew what she meant. Deep down I hated myself, had done for years and yet, in that moment, I saw it did not have to be that way. She too was held together by either love or hate, and I did not sense that it was love.

'I can talk of it because I know that you are right. But I suspect I am stronger than you imagine.'

Fool!

She spat at me.

I can destroy you in an instant.

'That is true, but you can't love me and I suspect if you were going to kill me you would have done it by now.'

I still may.

'That's possible. First, I would like to ask you something.'

There was silence and for an instant I saw her as an old woman. The grotto no longer seemed anything but a hole in the earth with some tree roots, strips of cloth tied to them and blood flowing over the mud on the floor.

Ask.

'The old stories say you came from Sudan.'

It's true.

'Why did you leave Sudan?'

You are too hurried in the head, she said and turning took up the knife and held it out to me.

'No. Not again.'

You cannot deny me.

'I will not cut myself again.'

You would rather die?

'I would rather die than be like you.'

Like me?

'You are unable to feel love, even if I gave it.'

I do not need your love. I demand your body for my pleasure.

'You could have so easily been different. It is not I that am cursed, but you.'

A'isha raised the knife above my chest. Yet something held her hand.

You will make love to me now.

'I will not make love with you again.'

The air between us shimmered, light glinted from the knife blade and, as if a shadow had passed across the moon, the twisted light of pleasure in those amber eyes dimmed.

'They are not your eyes,' I said.

As pure as spring water, a thought surfaced; *the poison contains the cure, the venom contains the antidote.* The thought glowed with an inner radiance and for a moment I savoured it, knowing that it was true. Then, as I waited to die, from far away I heard the sound of my own voice; a whisper, soft as a hint of sunlight.

'At least I have known what it is like to love truly.'

A silence crystallised between us and then in the next instant was shattered, its deadly splinters ripping the air asunder. The effect of the momentary shifting in the balance of power was devastating. A'isha's arms flailed, her head thrashed backwards and forwards and from deep in her being she howled like a wounded animal then screamed as though I had stabbed her.

The dance stopped. For an instant I was in the mausoleum again, Yazami on one side, Mira on the other were supporting my arms. I am certain it was Mira. For the first time she was looking into my eyes and then, just as I tried to speak to tell her... She faded and I spun downward as the narcotic effect of the *jidba* shuddered through me, reclaimed me.

Around me the wild cohort of *djnun* and *afrit*, of demons and angels, spun a web that held me as I danced. The sound of the *ghita* ripped up my spine—white-hot, electricity arcing brightly and I felt my body dissolve. Instead of fear or ecstasy, I experienced a vision of shattering clarity. A'isha and I—mirages, shifting, merging, melding with the past, with comprehension until, like all mirages, it flickered, faded and dispersed into the mist, leaving us with nothing but fragments of understanding. A'isha and I looked at each other as if for the first time. The shock of what we had seen hit both of us and yet I was able to hold to a stillness that excluded interpretation and analysis as much as it excluded emotional reaction. Not so for *Lalla* A'isha. She wailed, a high skirling, the sound intended to rip me apart, but I stood my ground as her amber eyes flared, molten and searing on my face. She dived inside me. I felt her in my veins, my nerves and in every cell of my body. This is what death feels like, I thought, but then she emerged, manifested in her true shape and, shaking with an incandescent rage, screamed at me.

You are a liar, a sham, there is no blood in you other than your own.

I understood and knew she was right, that my vision had been right. The bodies in the grave were struck down by ill chance, misfortune and not by me. I had killed nobody. The blood had been in my mind and not on my hands.

See!

She screamed again, and I watched as the fabric of the tapestry shifted—another view, another reality. I saw the Shining Path come down amongst the students as they slept, saw Lucho's men prod them, take their frightened bodies and beside the grave, shoot each of them in the back of the head; heard the shots, could smell the smoke, blood and felt the percussive impact jolting me through time. I saw too, in the swirling fall into the shallow grave, the way it could have been. Saw the startled birds swoop out and away and the butterflies—oblivious to the import of it all, rising, a small flock of glittering wings against the green.

This was not your blood to give.

Ice-cold now, she rose above me, the silver knife in her hands.

You know nothing of blood. Let me show you blood. This is blood...

A'isha Qandisha, became *Lalla Sudaniyya*, became the young woman she had once been. Unable to avert my gaze, the horror unfolded in and around me.

What she had experienced, I experienced, what she had seen and felt all those centuries ago, I saw and felt as she forced me to witness her moment of destiny—the mutiny and betrayal—the king's own soldiers, breaking into the sacred space at the centre of the temple and taking her; taking her, taking her there, in the blood on the floor, in the blood of the older women, the blood of the priestesses—and one by one raping her. Soldiers, smeared with the blood of her sisters, the blood of her mother, raping her and even as they violated her, cutting, slicing; their knives on her scalp, her breasts, ripping down her legs.

It was then, in the moment of her greatest fear, a moment of holy insanity, she fled into another place, a space where Sidi Ahmed, searching for the music of the holy trance, reached out to her, saying, 'Come with me. I will give you sanctuary and wash away the blood, if you bring the secrets of the *hal* to my master Sidi Ali ben Hamdush.'

And she went, bearing the knowledge of the precious *hal* and *jidba*, but also knowing, with a wisdom born of horror, that she could never wash the blood away, no more than she could—or would—ever serve a man again, no matter how high, no matter how holy.

I suspect that A'isha had not intended I should survive her revelation, but seeing me get to my feet, she drew herself up and pulled away. In a moment of immense stillness, she did that which I least expected, she smiled.

Go, for you have my blood now. I want no more of yours, no sacrifice, no offering, just your absence.

Unsteady on my feet, I watched her shrink—her old manifestation revealed—her ancient frame held together with little more than hate and the memory of blood that once flowed in her veins; blood that she loathed, for it was the blood of one who survived while others perished. She stood before me and I thought her beautiful still, despite her drooping breasts, her hair matted legs, her cloven hooves all chipped and cracked and for an instant I wanted to go to her and wrap a shawl around those frail shoulders. But it was she who went, leaving nothing but the familiar smell of turpentine.

'Your madness has departed,' Yazami said, his face the palest a dark-skinned face can be.

'I felt what it was like to be a butterfly,' I said.

'Shh, she has gone.'

'Gone,' said another voice and I turned to my right to see Thami, smiling and glowing, a picture of contentment.

After a time, a hand reached out for me and I flinched, thinking for a moment that I had failed to banish her. But the fingers that held the damp cloth on my brow belonged to a different woman. It was soothing. Even more comforting was the touch of Mira's other hand, away from the sight of her brother, clasping mine, just for a moment. It was enough.

GLOSSARY

afarit: a type of *djinn* or spirit

aji: come!

'aguza: an old woman and sometimes a "witch"

al-Maghreb al Aqsa: Arabic name for Morocco. Literally, "the land of the furthest west"

amira saqati: literally "a piece of a thing" Slang. Used as a substitute for a swear word

Amazigh: Berber *(plural: Imazighen)*

andek!: Beware! The cry made to warn people of an approaching donkey or carossa

assbar/essbaa: wait

as-salaamu 'aleikum: traditional greeting

barakallahu fik : may Allah bless you

besara: spicy lentil soup

b'ghrir: a crumpet-like bread

bismillah: a blessing (literally in the name of God) used before eating or starting a journey.

bismillah r-rahman r-rahim: In the name of God, Most Gracious, Most Merciful. The opening lines of almost every chapter of the Qur'an

burnous: a heavy cape with a hood

dar: a small house

Darija: The Moroccan Arabic dialect

djellaba: a loose-fitting hooded gown or robe

djinn: a spirit being

djinniya: a female *djinn*

djnun: the plural form of *djinn*

Fassi: a native of Fez

Fissa: a derogatory term used by people in Casablanca for natives of Fez

funduq: a caravanserai or travellers' hotel

gawri: a foreigner

ghita: a traditional oboe like instrument

ghiyyata: the musicians who play the *ghita*

hadra: the ecstatic dance in a *Hamadcha* ceremony

haha: *Amazigh* witches

hal: a light trance experienced during the *hadra*

Hamadcha: a Sufi brotherhood

hanut: a small local shop

haqq: obligation or truth

hshumiyya (hshuma): shame

iyeh: yeah or yes

Imazighen: Plural of *Amazigh*

hufra: grotto

jawi: an incense

jidba: the deep trance that follows *hal* in the *hadra*

jrad hboubal: Insects, pimples! An expression of supreme distaste

kafireen: heathens (singular *kafir*)

khoya: brother

kif: cannabis

labas: "fine" or "okay" both as a question and answer

lila: a Sufi ceremony held at night

majoun: an intoxicating delicacy made from (among other things) hashish, nuts, raisins, honey, ginger, butter and nutmeg

mashi mushkil: no problem

massreiya: an apartment within a *riad*, usually saved for honoured guests or the eldest son

medersa: a Qur'anic school.

m'kench mushkil: It's not a problem; no problem

mlawi: a type of fried onion flavoured bread

mluk: Small spirits usually invoked by the music of the Gnaoua

Nazarene: A Christian or foreigner

nus nus: "half half" hence coffee made from half hot milk, half coffee

riad: a large house with central courtyard and (usually) a fountain and several trees

roqsa: a document giving official permission for building or other   activity

safi: enough, sufficient

sebsi: a small ceramic or brass pipe for smoking *kif*

shahbi: one of the people, also "popular"

shari'a: Islamic law

sharif (sharifa fem):   A recognised descendent of the Prophet

shuf!:   Look! (also used as "listen" as in English)

shwiya: a little

shwiya b' shwiya: little by little

skout!:   Quiet!

souk: marketplace

taifor: a very low round table of *Amazigh* design

tarbouche: a soft felt hat usually in the shape of the more rigid Fez

w'aleikum salaam: the response to *as-salaamu 'aleikum*

zellij: small ceramic tiles